Dykes's pen is fused with magic and poetry. Every word is a gentle wave building into the splendor that is *All the Lost Places*, where struggles for identity and a place to belong find hope between the pages of a timeless story.

— J'nell Ciesielski, bestselling author of *The Socialite*

In *All the Lost Places*, deep truths meet the longings of humanity, whispering of hope, forgiveness, and a love so scandalous it can only be explained by grace. Luscious writing, authentic characters, and an ending that satisfies to the core of the spirit, this novel is another winner from Amanda Dykes.

—Heidi Chiavaroli, Carol Award–winning author
of *Freedom's Ring* and *Hope Beyond the Waves*

Stunning. Immersive. Romantic. With her trademark depth and lyricism, Amanda Dykes delivers an epic tale that will leave readers awestruck. Through the interplay of light and shadows, an unlikely hero discovers the true meaning of his story—and redemption against all odds. Readers, in turn, will learn much about their own stories alongside him, as Dykes so bravely explores the shadows that cloud our lives and the light that remains despite them. Lost places, found anew. A can't-miss novel!

—Ashley Clark, author of *Where the Last Rose Blooms*

Amanda Dykes spins another stunning poetic gift straight from the heart. In a lustrous convergence of two centuries, *All the Lost Places* leads us with courage to the healing and purpose prepared for us. A winner for fans of historical fiction and time-slip stories.

—Olivia Newport, author of TREE OF LIFE series

Books by Amanda Dykes

ALL THE LOST PLACES

AMANDA DYKES

BETHANYHOUSE
a division of Baker Publishing Group
Minneapolis, Minnesota

© 2022 by Amanda J. Dykes

Published by Bethany House Publishers
11400 Hampshire Avenue South
Minneapolis, Minnesota 55438
www.bethanyhouse.com

Bethany House Publishers is a division of
Baker Publishing Group, Grand Rapids, Michigan

Library of Congress Cataloging-in-Publication Data
Names: Dykes, Amanda, author.
Title: All the lost places / Amanda Dykes.
Description: Minneapolis, Minnesota : Bethany House, a division of Baker
    Publishing Group, [2022]
Identifiers: LCCN 2022029125 | ISBN 9780764239502 (paperback) | ISBN
    9780764240829 (casebound) | ISBN 9781493439041 (ebook)
Subjects: LCGFT: Novels.
Classification: LCC PS3604.Y495 A79 2022 | DDC 813/.6—dc23/eng/20220623
LC record available at https://lccn.loc.gov/2022029125

Scripture quotations are from the King James Version of the Bible.

This is a work of fiction. Names, characters, incidents, and dialogues are products of the author's imagination and are not to be construed as real. Any resemblance to actual events or persons, living or dead, is entirely coincidental.

Cover design by Kathleen Lynch/Black Kat Design
Cover image by Angela Fanton/Arcangel
Map by Najla Kay

Author is represented by Books & Such Literary Agency.

Baker Publishing Group publications use paper produced from sustainable forestry practices and post-consumer waste whenever possible.

22 23 24 25 26 27 28   7 6 5 4 3 2 1

To all who have felt lost,
or faced the question that echoes
within these pages:
"Who am I?"

This tale is for you.

Trovato.

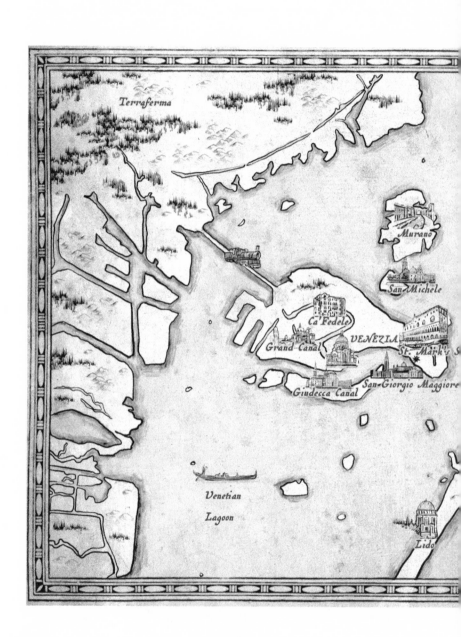

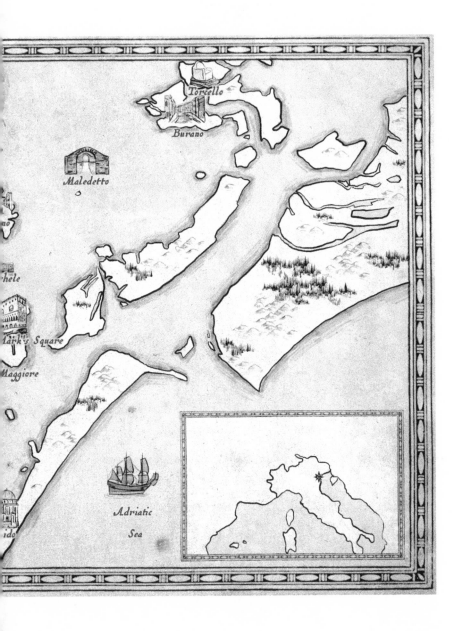

Torcello

Burano

Maledetto

hele

Mark's Square

Maggiore

ido

Adriatic

Sea

". . . phantom city, whose untrodden streets
Are rivers, and whose pavements are the shifting
Shadows of the palaces and strips of sky."

—From "Venice,"
by Henry Wadsworth Longfellow

"The way to love anything is to realize that it may be lost."
—G. K. Chesterton

"Courage keep, and hope beget;
The story is not finished yet . . ."

—Dante Cavellini
(as recorded by S. T.)

PROLOGUE

Once upon the dawn of time, there was water.

Before there were stars, before the Maker set life into earth, breath into lungs, beast or man to roam . . . there was water. Dark and reaching, stirred not by wind but by the spirit of the Almighty himself.

Once upon the dawn of time, water discovered its eternal dance partners: shadow and light. The trio waltzed, webbing diamonds into depths, scattering stardust over peaked waves, spinning gold over ripples.

These ancient waters have never left. They travel around and around, over and over, time without end. From sea to sky, raining back down into the hands of man.

In the centuries since, these eternity-touched waters bore up tempest-tossed ships. Retreated in shivering obedience to the command *Be still.* Furled and stacked themselves into shimmering walls of parted sea to make way for an impossible escape. Have been struck from rock, sprung from geysers, coursed through rivers, tumbled with abandon over falls . . . carried the fleet of the great explorer Marco Polo to the great beyond and back again to Venezia.

And then, in a time of quiet obscurity, whispered a lullaby in those Venetian canals one night as a babe slumbered, tucked safe inside a tight-woven basket. A tiny boat for a tiny boy, currents

9

delivering him toward an orphanage beneath the midnight lament of the bells of San Marco.

But just as the basket breached the building's reflection, a north wind tumbled through, pushing him into lantern-glow . . . where a strong pair of hands pulled him, basket and all, into another life.

The waters flowed on as the babe grew into a man who would look out over the lagoon that had delivered him, once upon his dawn of time, into a life that would change the shape of a world. A story covered over until it was all but lost.

Years passed—a century, nearly. A great rumbling skipped over the canals and into every crevice of the aged floating city when that bell tower fell one day. Crumbling, tumbling, crashing to the ground of St. Mark's Square. Pigeons fled, dust billowed, the bells of San Marco fell silent—and along with them, the last vestige of the basket's tale.

Until one night, in that curious marvel of their eternal cycle, those waters descended again. Across the world, on another square, on another man, in another time. Ushering him into the lost tale with every falling drop of rain . . .

DANIEL

San Francisco
1904

I only ventured out at night, and all the better if it rained.
San Francisco was a place alive—always moving, cable
cars clanging, tugboats trumpeting low. Hoofbeats trotted
while the occasional motor car chugged through a river of voices
tumbling down the city's rises.

But when it rained at night . . . everyone retreated home, and
the city became another place entirely. Alive not with the pulse of
a crowd but with the plash of water that had been around since
nobody-knew-when.

City noises lifted away as droplets descended. I wondered if
they exchanged greetings in passing, the noise and water. Perhaps
exchanged notes like hospital doctors discussing patients. I wondered, too, if I was descending into madness, imagining such. But
imagination came so strange and seldom now, I indulged it.

Excellent ditch made on Lombard Street today, the ascending
din might say to the descending rain. *Prime locale for a puddle.
Best of luck.* To which the droplets would oblige, colliding into
pavement, leaping into rivulets and sliding, unstoppable, into their
new home.

A puddle I now stood beside on the corner of Hyde and Lombard, the rain coming in a wonderful hush. A puddle that now reached up about my feet in small splashes as I took shelter beneath the awning of—ironically—a hat store.

I pulled out my sketchbook, its pages rumpled, vanished droplets leaving puckered paper. My pencil skidded in quick work. This was a good day—two houses in one night.

The first, one of the tall, narrow Victorian row houses up at Alamo Square, had taken longer than expected, requiring extra notes on colors. Thankfully, the brownstone across the street was much simpler.

The ache of my hands from factory work eased as lines joined to climb from the page into a dimensional home. One I would not, this time, forget.

The city knew me best beneath the guise of dark. It was a cosmic joke: the same darkness that once cloaked me in my youth now sheltered me as a grown man . . . but for entirely different reasons. Even so, with each drop of cold rain, my shame eased just a little. As if it were being washed away with the reminder that—though it might take my entire life—I would put things right.

I narrowed my eyes to see better as my pencil scratched away. Square lines here, bay window there—doing their job and facing the bay down below, where Alcatraz stood in dark silhouette. I turned from the isle but felt its presence. Always it was there, always at my back.

"What's this?" a gruff voice said, and a light blazed straight into my eyes. I held up my hand, trying to see.

Memory clawed—phantom grip of wrists apprehended, head pounding, throat closing.

The light zigged and zagged, pulling me fast out of the memory. No one was apprehending me. I slowed my breath and reached for control.

"Hand it over," the man said. My hand mechanically extended, offering the sketchbook to the officer, with his rounded helmet and the glint of brass jacket buttons.

"The *bag*," the voice said, and the flashlight sliced to illuminate my knapsack. I blinked until the man's figure came into silhouette, bright spots dancing as he bent to retrieve it. The dull grey bag jangled, the sound of coins unmistakable.

Coins I could not afford to lose.

Please, God . . . the prayer sneaking past the grate I'd long ago erected to keep my words from approaching heaven. I'd forfeited any right to that long ago.

He pulled out the few contents one by one, holding them up as silent questions.

First, a dented tin can with no label.

"Dinner," I said.

Second, a paper, torn at the corner.

"Time card," I said. The man held it longer, skeptically. Why, indeed, would I have it with me? "I—was supposed to leave it at the cannery," I said. "Made a mistake." My sentences clipped short when I got nervous. Swallowing, I tried again. "I'll return it at—the first opportunity." A phrase that had become the anthem of my life.

Third, a book. Worn on the blue cover from being so often held and nearly pristine within, for being so little read.

This, he did not inquire after, and I gave silent thanks. I didn't know that I could put words to it.

I swallowed hard, for the final item would determine what became of me.

He pulled it out, turning it in his palm. The blue glass jar, chipped at the rim but screwed shut all the same, caught a drop of rain, then another. As he turned it, its contents rolled richly. A deceptive richness.

"And this?" His voice, all suspicion.

"My wages," I said. There was more to the story—why in a jar, why here now—but this he didn't need to know.

He opened the jar and deposited its contents into his gloved hand, counting. "Three . . . and sixty-five," he said. He studied the three dollar bills and the handful of dull-shining change.

He eyed the brownstone across the street, then my drawing, then the money. "You take this, son?"

"No." This word quick and sure. Finally, something I could speak with confidence. "Y-you can check the time card."

He did, and asked how much I was paid by the hour. "By the can," I said, and told him the amount. "Sardine factory on the other side of the bay."

"How many did you can this week?"

Sentences grew shorter in my head, and I pressed my eyes closed and concentrated. *Speak normally.* "I . . . soldered three hundred seventy-five," I said. "A—a penny a can."

He scratched his head beneath his now-crooked helmet, and the gesture made him seem a bit more friend than foe. "That doesn't add up," he said, but he drew back into a curious posture.

"The dinner can," I said, nodding toward where it lay atop my sack. "They sell the banged-up cans to us cheap."

"Cheap . . ." I could see him clearly now, the spots having vanished from my rendezvous with the flashlight. His brows pinched, the crease between his eyes like an arrow pointing at the can. "Ten cents?"

"That's right."

"For something they paid you one cent to can."

I shrugged, long ago having come to terms with that particular irony. "They sell them for fifteen cents at the store, sir. It's still a bargain when you look at it that way."

He assessed my ragtag possessions and my ragtag self—worn trousers and shirtsleeves rolled up. One suspender had slipped down to my elbow in the flurry of sketching. I hooked my thumb and slid it up slowly.

"And you're out here to . . . ?" He let the question trail, waiting.

That answer was too long. Too hard. I looked at my sketchbook and just held it up.

"Draw," the man said.

I nodded.

"In the rain. At night. Fancy yourself an artist?"

"No," I said, and saw he'd need more of an answer than that. "I just . . . needed to get the lines right." That was one way of putting it. The full answer wouldn't make any sense to the man, for so many reasons.

He looked around and puffed out his cheeks, exhaling and shaking his head. "Sorry, son," he said. "A man out in the shadows, studying a house—well, you can understand why I have to check in."

I nodded, words not coming fast enough. I was long out of practice of speaking to people. "Of—of course. I'd have thought the same."

The officer narrowed his eyes, head tilting. "You all right, son?"

Again, a nod. Someday, maybe. Tonight, one step closer.

"Well, don't stay out too long," he said, his voice more paternal and less policeman. "Bound to get cold. January nights aren't too easy on the bones around here. Move along home quick."

"Yes, sir."

He left, the rain easing off a bit as he strode down the hill and disappeared along with his fading whistle.

I set the jar on the ground and retrieved a clutch of various stacked bills from my pocket.

Forty-seven dollars. A fortune. How many months of smelly fish work and numb fingers this represented . . . but it was worth it. I added it to the three in the jar, then counted out the coins again. Carefully creased a corner of my sketchbook paper until it tore easily into a neat square, and etched two familiar words upon it in simple, straight letters.

I'm sorry.

I twisted the jar's lid on, relishing the way the scrape of metal against glass reverberated through my grip. My apology, carved into the night.

I dashed a glance over my shoulder, ensuring I was alone. Slipped across the street, up the front steps—*one, two, three, four, five*—my life was one of counting, always counting—and set the jar carefully on the ground. I lingered only a moment, staring hard, hammering the image of it into my memory, and gave a quick knock before I dashed back into my hiding place across the street.

A man stepped out, his presence and his suit creased into a trifecta of pinstripes, proper things, and perfection. "Hello?"

I clenched my jaw, winced against a rogue stream of water that sneaked down the back of the awning and down my neck. "Look down," I pleaded, much too low to be heard.

He began to close the door, the golden triangle of light becoming a sliver until it barely grazed the top of the jar—and the man stopped. Paused, and picked it up.

Hot shame constricted my chest. What was I thinking? That an old, chipped jar full of what would be rag money to a man like this would somehow wash me clean? Mean something to him?

"Papa?" A voice came from within, and a little girl appeared, dark hair in long ringlets.

My breath caught. I counted, numbers coming at me quick. Eight years back . . .

It was her. She, a sleeping infant, and me, jumping into the window of what I'd thought was an empty house. Hissing through the dark for my cousin Emilio to go back—but not before he'd gripped golden candlesticks and a porcelain figurine of a hunting dog. For the life of me I couldn't remember what its color was, only that it had seemed friendly, with its head tilting one way or the other.

"Put it back," I'd whispered. *"It's a kid's toy—"* and I remembered the sleepy, shuddering sigh of the babe, how it had shut us up and sent us clambering back out through the window.

We hadn't been caught. Not that night, anyway. But years later I'd entered the police station after a served sentence and a few weeks on the job at the factory and asked after police reports. I'd learned that the candlesticks—valued at approximately fifty dollars—had indeed been missed . . . as had a toy-sized dog figurine of unknown value, which had been purchased by the baby's father when he was a boy. For sixty-three cents.

I watched as the man counted the jar's contents. Fifty dollars and sixty-three cents.

He paused. Studied the money. And grew stiff. "Come inside," he said to his daughter, gently nudging her shoulder so that she was behind him.

"What's that, Papa? Can I see?" Her small hand was in the jar before he could stop her, taking out its final object.

"What a sweet puppy!" She clasped her hands around the rough-carved wooden thing, pulling it to her heart and swaying back and forth like it was her own babe.

The man opened his daughter's palm gently, taking the object up.

He turned it, shook his head, and—to my shock—laughed. A single chuckle, with the bounce of a boy and the depth of time, as if it had vaulted from the shadows of his childhood to revel in the gift of a lost thing found.

"Is it for me?" the girl asked, hope buoyant.

"It is," he said. "If it is what I think this is . . . then yes. It's yours." He looked out into the dark, wary once more, and gently ushered the girl inside before closing the door with creaking finality.

Something eased over me, and I squared the house in my vision for one final look, trying hard to fix it in my mind. The image would not stay, I knew, but I had the sketch, and I could check this one off the list and move on to the next. It would take some time to fill the next jar . . . but time was the one thing I had.

ove along home quick," the policeman had said.

I moved quickly, but as for "home" . . . well, it still took some time to reach, and even then—was it home? Did that matter, except that it was the only place fit for the likes of me? The Great Sand Waste, some called it. Others called it the Outside Lands. For a long time, it was the dwelling place only of the dead, with four cemeteries and stretches of sand forever. When the city began to switch from railcars to cable cars, it became a graveyard of railcars too.

It seemed fitting that I take up residence in this land of the obsolete. Not to mention, the rent was low—or free, rather. As good as a palace, and I wasn't the only one to think so. Others had moved into the old railcars too. An odd grid of makeshift streets formed; paint and curtains went up as windows glowed, vanquishing the air of abandonment. "The Sunset," they started to call the neighborhood, and even in that there was truth. For we, the ragtag band of outcasts that had landed here, were gripping the tailcoats of fast-fleeing life.

And like the sunset, sometimes it glowed all the brighter for the sheer uncertainty of what we had and how long it would last. The ocean to the west bound us in, tides climbing as if to ensure I didn't escape. Where those waters carried ships out to adventure at sea, they were to me a wall. With the rain gone and the moon high, the only sounds were waves tumbling and wind keening through our sand-sifted streets. Nothing of the garlic-spiced, music-laced city breezes I'd grown up with. In fact, it was entirely across the peninsula from my boyhood home. As far as I could get, without disappearing into the ocean.

My railcar house silhouetted squat and square, and my tired legs took me over the threshold. Strange, usually the neighborhood mongrel of a dog was waiting for me here, rising like a scruffy apparition to greet me. We understood each other. Street roamers, belonging nowhere, not fit for real society. He devoured anything and everything, edible or not. I wouldn't be surprised if he had rocks rolling around somewhere in his stomach, and had christened him *Ballast* accordingly.

But no Ballast beside the steps. He could be bedding down somewhere else; he was a sort of collectively owned and loved pet among us all, though mine was the home he frequented most.

I lit my solitary kerosene lamp, keeping the flame low. The room was a simple box, not unlike my cell had been, but opposite in one distinct way: It held freedom. Or the promise of it.

Each of its four walls served a clear purpose: Gateway, Galley, Gallery, or Gale. The Galley was the wall opposite the door, where a dresser with a missing drawer stood in as kitchen. On it were two stacks of banged-up tins, my rations.

And beside them, lined up like soldiers, their faded linen spines providing the singular splash of color, the *Piccole Storie de Venezia*. Little histories written for children in a place far across the world, whose tales and descriptions filled my daydreams as a child. They were of little use now. For daydreaming was a thing long ceased, and it wasn't likely I would ever have anyone to pass them on to. But still I kept them, a vestige of a better life.

The Gale was the name I'd given my "bedchamber" in jest, where my hammock was strung next to the west wall and the sea wind blew fierce through cracks and holes, which I filled on continual rotation with a mixture of tar and clay. Perhaps it was foolish to place it in the path of the most wind . . . but the wind reminded me I was alive. It rocked my hammock. Whistled music through the cracks. It filled the place with morning air and told me that my heart beat for a reason. I wasn't entirely certain what that reason was, but . . . the wind swirled in every day, regardless, like a secret from afar.

And the Gallery . . . I crossed to it now, a simple planked wall to the right with a row of sketches. Each of them a house—some large, some small. I pulled out tonight's sketch of the brownstone. Closed my eyes before looking at it and willed the form of the building to appear in my mind.

But no. No image appeared. *Blank canvas.* Like always. My mind . . . felt broken, somehow.

Once upon a time, I had been able to lie in my bed and imagine entire worlds, sketch them in a flurry, fill lines with hues and shadows of paint, bring something a little good to the world. Now, unless the subject stood before me, I could not sketch a thing. Even the pen of my boyhood, brought over from Italy by my own mother as a young woman, lay dormant in this keeping place. Blown of Murano glass and twisted into color, it seemed too fine and full of life to use on my precise and lifeless creations—which were not creations at all, but mere copies.

I speared the edges of the two papers onto a nail protruding from the wall. They swung to a standstill and a wash of relief settled over me. Six houses down, one more to go.

The last one would be the hardest. It was the only one I had a sketch of before having made restitution. Etched in ink. It stood before me in its funny form, a bakery on a triangular slice of city, streets running its boundaries, life within. And a rotting roof atop, which I had resolved to save enough to fix. The drawing was accurate and technical and absolutely lifeless. Someday, I hoped, I would be able to draw it with some semblance of the warmth it held.

I pulled out my remaining coins—a nickel and a penny—and deposited them in a jar under the floorboards. It wasn't much. But it was a start.

A rustling sounded behind me and I froze, old instincts signaling me to hold my breath and make myself invisible. Instead, I turned slowly, and relaxed when I spotted a familiar scruffy figure, trotting my way on four paws.

"Hello, Ballast," I said, lifting a hand to pet him. Lopsided face with a canine tooth snagging one of his jowls and propping it up like a half-grin. "How'd you get in here? You been here the whole time?"

Ballast circled, lay down, and curled up with an off-key grunt. "You and me both," I said. I replaced the floorboard with a satisfying click and turned to put out the lamp. Darkness was an odd sort of homecoming. When the physical lights faded, it made that blank canvas of my mindless stark. I breathed deep for the first time in a long time, weary to the bone.

Rubbing my eyes, I turned and began my descent into the hammock, eyes already closing.

"Let a fella breathe, will you?"

My eyes flew open. I staggered back.

The hammock swung crooked and heavy, and I could barely make out something else crooked, too: a grin.

I grabbed for something and found only my wet umbrella, hanging on the hook. I pointed it at the man.

"Wh-who are you?" *Sound fiercer.* "What do you want." I extended the umbrella, sword-like.

"Look like you've seen a ghost, Danny Boy," the voice said. "Aren't you going to offer your old pal a drink? Cake? Cut of your shares like old times? Perchance?" This final word shaped with pluck and punctuation.

My throat thick, I narrowed my eyes. "Emilio?"

"Nah. Had to get rid of that name a while ago. Got into a scrape, you know how it is." He laughed, and it was definitely Emilio. "'Course you know how it is."

"How did you find me?"

He swung his legs over the hammock like he was on holiday on a beach somewhere sunny. "*Find* you," he said. "You lost your edge a long time ago, Danny Boy. You're like a lost dog, wandering the streets like you do. Drawing houses and . . . buying umbrellas?

What do you mean by all the umbrellas, Danny Boy? That one you've got there isn't looking too good, and I've seen you get three new ones at least in the last . . ." He blew out his cheeks and then threw up his hands as if the calculations were impossible.

What's it matter to you?

I wanted to ask it. Truth be told, part of me wanted to toss him out and maybe even slug him for his part in why I was even here. But part of me also wanted to pull him in, slap him on the back in an embrace, and ask him to tell me about every last cousin, *zio, zia,* neighbor, friend, and foe. The last two of which—in our circle—were often the same people.

He opened his eyes wide, shaking his head and awaiting my answer. "The umbrellas aren't for me," I said. That was all he needed to know.

"You always were an odd one," he said. And made it sound both insult and compliment. "Anyway. The boys all know about you."

"They know I'm here?" I'd worked hard to make my life obscure. Invisible.

"Relax," he said. "Only I know. Listen," Emilio hopped up, a head shorter than me. He'd always been the wiry one, darting up fire escapes and into small windows when the rest of us couldn't. "I came here as a favor to your ma."

I planted the umbrella's tip on the floorboards and leaned in. "Is she all right?"

He tipped his head back and forth, weighing the answer, letting out a sound of uncertainty. "Bank trouble," he said.

I went cold. "What do you mean?"

"Giordano's. She asked them for a loan, they wouldn't give it to her. You know how they are."

Fire lit in my gut. The thought of anyone refusing anything to Mary Goodman, possibly the most upstanding citizen this whole bay city had ever known . . . but I did know "how they were," as Emilio said. They ran largely on reputation. And in the matter of money, if one's own son was a thief . . .

"What's she need a loan for?" I hated that I didn't already know.

Emilio shrugged one shoulder and sauntered the two steps to

the Galley, rummaging in the drawer, pulling out a can, rummaging again for the opener and a fork. Helping himself, then pulling a face at the fishy smell.

"House. Something about trying to increase a bank note when they wanted it decreased. Repairs, upkeep, all that."

My mind raced. I thought to the jar in the ground. *Six cents.* Six cents was what I had to my name. I thought to that jar I'd delivered tonight and groaned. I could have used that for her. Paid the brownstone house back later.

"If I'd known . . ."

Emilio whacked my chest with the back of his hand. "Whose fault is that?" he asked, then made for the door. "Anyway. Thought you should know." He paused, one hand on the weathered door-frame. Turned, slapped his wrist and opened his palm, launching a gleaming disc into a tumbling arc. I reached out and caught the quarter. "For your collection," he said, lifting his chin at my floorboard-bank.

Emilio kept on. "You can stop looking like that. What'd you do, Danny, swallow down the sorrows of the world while you were in your cell? Your eyes are sadder than that mongrel's. You ever smile? Know what that is?" He was close, now, spreading a hand across my jaw to form my muscles into some grotesque farce.

Ballast wagged his tail appreciatively.

"By the by, you really should lock your door, *cugino.*"

Cousin. There was a word I'd never expected to hear again.

"Locks don't keep the rabble out," I said dully. This, we both knew.

He dropped his hand, serious. "I know you're on the straight and narrow. But if you can muster one last job, the boys and I have one. We could use a man of your . . . skill set." He tilted the words in emphasis, as if they held special meaning. As if they were a joke. "Meet us in Nob Hill tomorrow night if you're in. You remember the spot. Quick and easy, empty house—nobody to get hurt."

Was that regret I heard in his voice? That was something new.

"Might get a good bit of money to help her out, eh?" he said.

And with a wave, as if this had been a casual, everyday encounter and not the first glimpse I'd had of him in six years, he was gone.

In the dark, I was alone. More than ever before. I pressed my eyes closed and willed an image to appear: that of my mother.

Sounds whispered in . . . the flutter of pages, the dance of her voice.

My muscles remembered the oddest things—the way my young feet would slip on a stray bit of flour in our small kitchen as she cooked up fresh batches of pastry. The feel of her arms beneath mine as she saved me from that fall and spun me around, setting me to flying.

Her laughter. The sense of everything bright and good.

I closed my eyes tighter. Willed the image harder. The form of her, the smile I knew would be there, the light in her eyes.

But still, it would not come.

And the empty place that was my visual imagination these past six years dug that hole deeper. Every grief, doubled. Lost in true life and lost again to this wall between me and the once-simple act of picturing things.

But though I could not summon her image to my mind, she was out there in the real world, this moment. And bearing a dark cloud herself . . . because of me.

"*Move along home quick,*" the officer's words tumbled in, and I gripped them with resolve.

Tomorrow. Tomorrow I'd go and do what I'd been too much a coward to so far: show my face in my home neighborhood. And see what could be done.

3

Donning a news cap and ducking my gaze, I departed the safety of shadows among Washington Square Park's evergreens.

I was no stranger to this borough—"Little Italy," as my uncle had taken to calling it. I just hadn't ventured here in the light of day for a good long time. But even the times I'd come at night, it echoed with memories. Clothes flapping like victorious flags on lines, mamas hollering at children playing in the streets, the clamor of feet as they all jostled past the side door of our *trattoria*, where my mother used to dole out morsels of day-old *cannoli*. Ground floor shops and homes stacked in rooms on top, like blocks of life sent over direct from the old country.

Part of me wondered if home ever stopped being home, even after you'd left it behind. This place, its people, had raised me. One of its residents, in particular—a resident who was the very heartbeat of the neighborhood. Flinging her door open wide to all those cannoli-carrying children, wiping their hands when they were finished, filling those hands with colorful volumes from her own bookshelf. Telling them tales so legendary they leaped out of history, across the water. Tales of Casanova and his infamous escape from the inescapable prison. Tales of a mysterious child found floating in a basket on the canal waters as a baby, like Moses himself.

Tales of Marco Polo and the one-horned creature he discovered—a unicorn, he'd called it. When she opened a volume to show a picture, and they discovered Marco Polo's "unicorn"—the "ugly beast" he described as delighting to abide in mud and mire—was, in fact, a rhinoceros, they'd laughed uproariously.

She made the Old World feel magical, and in doing so, made our own lives, right here in the New World, magical, too, with the thrill of what our futures might hold. She'd let us hold colorful little birds and horses of blown glass, created in our own family's furnaces on a tiny island in a lagoon across the world, which I would never see. Holding those creatures had felt like stepping into a fairy tale.

What I stepped into now was no fairy tale. It was a sidewalk, hard and high, carrying me to the bank's gleaming window. I slowed near the door's alcove and nearly pulled my hand from my pocket to reach for the door . . . then shoved my hand back inside my pocket, picked up my pace, and kept walking. I paused at a window at the edge of the brick building and feigned a study of the posters inside. I read the words, letting them buy me some time—and hoping that time would buy me some courage.

TO LET: TWO ROOMS. The first notice, scrawled on yellowed paper, had been there for months now. I'd seen it before, knew the address to be the flat above the butcher, and knew his infamous temper to be the reason the place was still "to let."

FOR SALE: BICYCLE. WORKS EXCEEDINGLY WELL. This, I knew to be the spectacle leaning against a tree in Washington Square Park for a good many weeks, missing a good many spokes, and asking a good many dollars.

And a new one: *WANTED: AUTHENTIC ITALIAN ARTIFACTS. TRANSLATOR. MANUAL LABORERS. INQUIRE WITHIN.* I pretended intent study of the post with its odd array of inquiries, but registered none of the words that followed.

"Looking for work?" a voice beside me said.

No. I kept back the reply. I could scarcely afford to be here today, missing a shift. If I could barely hold down one job . . .

26

I turned to face the speaker and give a brief *"No, thank you."* A man with a rounded bowler hat and an even rounder belly waited with dark brows—the sort that manifested an impressive presence—raised in anticipation.

He nodded at the poster. "We're still looking for a few good men. Digging, mostly. Canals, if you can believe it. Down south a ways."

The man in the bowler hat shifted his weight, and I realized he was awaiting a response.

I apologized. "I'm . . . afraid I don't have anything to offer." It was true. No artifacts, no need of employment, although the work of digging earth held a distinct appeal compared to soldering cans and affixing labels.

"Well, I'll be here the rest of the day," he said. "If you're interested. Wharton. Edward Wharton. Come see me if you'd like to talk it over. I've set up camp in the rear of the bank, the side entrance. I'll be leaving the area again tomorrow, but I might have a spot or two left if you change your mind." He tipped his hat. I managed the same, offering a distracted thanks, and turned toward the bank.

I filled my lungs, looked at my reflection in the glass, mouth grim, and resolved that even if there was the slimmest hope, it was worth facing this moment.

I kept my head low until I'd crossed straight to the banker's desk. Trying not to think who he might summon if he recognized a thief.

I sat down, hands folded on the desk where he could see them, see that they were empty, that they meant no harm.

"I'm so sorry," Mr. Giordano said somewhat absently. "I've an engagement in just a few minutes, but if you'll see my secretary, Mr. . . . ."

He looked up for the first time, his easy smile freezing in faded recognition, eyes reading my face. I could only imagine how it must be to see me now. The boy he'd once known, the hopeful youth, replaced with this face of hardened lines. New sorrows. Old regrets.

"Mr. Giordano," I said, voice raspy as it came from its shadows. I cleared it and continued in a steady cadence I did not feel. "If I could beg just a moment of your time."

He placed his pen down, straight alongside his ledger. This was a man of weights and balances, in a world where things had to add up.

Nothing about me, here at his desk, added up.

"I'm very sorry to inconvenience you, sir," I said. Apologizing for so much more than my unannounced arrival. Apologizing for—me. And hoping he would understand. "I wondered, sir, if there was anything I could do on behalf of—"

The door opened behind us, a pair of suited men talking low. I straightened the worn lapels of my own faded tweed suit. Lowered my voice and nudged my chair forward with my foot.

"Of Mrs. Goodman," I said. Wishing to frame her in honor and respect. Not the tainted association of me, if I had said *my mother.* "She doesn't know I'm here," I said, tripping over the quiet words and feeling like the boy Mr. Giordano used to toss baseballs to out in the streets, even giving me his own worn glove. "I learned that she had inquired with you . . ." I trailed off, my silence a plea for him to pick up the rest of my meaning.

His quiet study turned to sadness, and he looked down. "Ah." He adjusted his spectacles, the wary concern on his face morphing into something more akin to . . . respect. Or pity? "Mr. Goodman—"

I bristled at my name. He noticed.

"Daniel," he said, his voice lower. Kinder. And I could almost feel him lofting that scuffed ball with its ragged stitching my way. A gentle launch, so that I'd be sure to catch it. "As much as I'd like to help your mother . . ." His gaze darted toward a desk across the room, where a man in pinstripes studied his newspaper with deep concentration. "It's not just up to me. We've had to take on a partner, you see. He does quite a bit of research on any potential borrowers . . . and their connections."

Their connections. Which—if Mary Goodman was asking— also meant her son. The convict. And her husband, whom nobody talked about, for the pain it caused her.

"Mrs. Goodman is a wonderful woman," he said. "Well-loved by everyone. She'll land on her feet, I know she will. All of us do, even in hard times. We look out for one another."

His words smote me, though he did not intend them to. "Do—you know what she needs? How much, I mean?"

His jaw worked as he considered his position. "I'm not at liberty to disclose . . . but, son, the best thing for her now would be to sell the building."

"Sell." I parroted the word dumbly. It made no sense. For all my father's faults, he had provided that roof over her head. Her inheritance, the old family building, once he'd been gone. And there, when the winds of life would have tossed us both out to sea, she drove our roots deeper still.

It had been more than our home. It had been our anchor. Her lifeblood, where she had stood in the street and studied the printing on the awning: *Goodman's Fine Italian Hats.*

I remember feeling her sadness, the way it wended down into me and settled, heavy. Sidling up to her and slipping my hand into hers. *"What is it, Mama?"* I'd asked, my voice young, small.

She'd pulled in a shuddering breath. Put on a smile. Pulled me close by the shoulder into her warmth. *"Hats,"* she'd said. *"What an easy word to change. No?"*

And she had. She had rubbed it clean until traces of flaked white paint clung to her hands. And with care, she had stenciled in a new word: *Treats.*

And thus, with the birth of her bakery, she had woven grief into hope. She began to rise before the sun, working magic with sugar and flour, which swirled out into the square and beyond, summoning weary hearts and hands to savor a confection and to leave with their spirits lifted.

She made ends meet through pastries baked, trousers mended, lessons given, shirts laundered, and even books balanced for other businesses around the Square.

Above the shop, up a spiral stair, were our simple living quarters. A bedroom, a kitchen, and a small sitting room in a round corner window that protruded out over the sidewalk below like an overhanging nest. Above it all, tucked beneath its low ceiling in a tiny gable room that was my own corner of the world, was my bed. And walls covered, floor to ceiling, side to side, with drawings. Places far and near, spectacles real and imagined. An entire universe. And then there was the ever-changing water stain on my gable ceiling that had shifted shapes when it rained and had grown along with me. I'd invented shapes and stories around it for as long as I could remember.

It was not a sprawling estate—but it was ours. *Hers.* The same place she'd opened wide to all the neighborhood children.

"She can't sell," I said, throat hot. "Where would she go?"

"Hard times all around here, I'm afraid," he said with all the compassion he could infuse into his voice. Something made him pause. He lowered his voice and leaned in. "I cannot give numbers. But I will say . . . springtime is a season of change." He paused, summoning my gaze up with a weighty look. "If you catch my meaning."

Springtime. She would need a large sum of money within a few months' time.

My fingers tapped on my knee. "If she were to sell," I said slowly, weighing my words, weighing his position, "how much do you think she would have in her pocket?"

The air between us pulled with understanding: whatever he said, this would be an amount to aim for.

He named a sum. It knocked the wind out of me.

"If I may, Mr. Good—" He stopped himself, took off his spectacles. Sighed, and looked at me as one who knew me well. "If I may, Daniel. Reduced bank notes are a sight different in number from selling prices." He meant to give me hope. "But . . . what she needs, more than any sum or loan . . . is sight of you."

My chest constricted. I was so close to being able to come home, as clean-slated as I could.

I nodded. "If you could keep this between us for now," I said hoarsely. "I want to come at the right time."

He held up his hands. "Say no more. As for the right time . . . do be sure it's before April."

Outside the bank, I rubbed my temples and did some quick figuring as a horse and wagon passed, followed by an autocar whose engine revved thoughts up my spine. *April.* It was January now.

An invisible clock began ticking. It reached into me, gripping my lungs. For so long, I had worked toward something so close I could almost touch it: a return. A restoring of what I had taken from my mother—honor. A good name. And, if I could, a repaired roof.

Now . . . the roof over her head could be snatched away. And I knew, whatever it took, I had to keep it there for her. She'd done that for me, when my world had been shaken and "home" was the only certain thing I knew.

Emilio's offer flitted before me, tempting. Quick and fast, and it'd all be done. But I'd never be able to look her in the eye . . . and she'd never accept help that came in such a way.

Leaning to see between the bare branches of the winter trees, I caught just a glimpse of the place. Blue, a little triangle of a building there on the pie-shaped island of city between Union and Columbus. *"Perfect for a bakery,"* she'd once said. *"We're even shaped like a slice of pie. Aren't we lucky, to get to live in a triangle? Nobody else gets that, they all have boring old four walls!"*

This had been the cheery optimism she'd framed my whole life with.

Who had she on earth but me? The injustice of that smote me.

"Yes, good," a voice said around the corner. *Her* voice. "Thank you, Mr. Wharton. I understand. Here." The sound of parchment paper—I'd know it anywhere—as she doubtless handed the man in the bowler hat one of her pastries.

I dared a glance around the corner toward the bank's back entrance and saw her. Dark hair, threaded with whiter ones here and there, piled atop her head in a twist. She was as lovely as ever. Skirt of blue, shirt of white, and an apron tied around her waist that attested to the fact she'd stolen this moment away from the trattoria.

Regret flooded me, ushering action into my feet and then proceeding to shackle my ankles. *Go to her*, it said, immediately followed by *Don't you dare*.

I forced one foot in front of the other, instead approaching the door Mr. Wharton had retreated into.

With my mother safely across the street and nearly back to the trattoria, I knocked on the doorpost and ducked to enter the still-open door.

Mr. Wharton looked up, round face pleasantly red and expectant.

"Ah, my window friend! You've come to see me after all. Very glad of it, young man. Have a seat." He gestured at the caned chair as he sat in its creaking twin across a wide oak desk.

Something caught his attention out the window, and he chuckled. I turned to see what it was and spotted my mother, stooped before a girl in braids, handing her another parcel.

"That woman's generosity will be her undoing," he said. "She'll put herself out of business! But it seems the neighborhood's all the better for it. Have you eaten there?"

I shifted in my seat. "A long time ago, yes."

"Wonder of a place. They serve this dish—famous for it, actually. I can't recall the name. A tall cake, golden and buttery and topped with Swiss chocolate. Swiss chocolate, on an Italian cake! What a combination!" He slapped his stomach in deep appreciation. "I can't remember what they call it—*pancetta*? No, no, that's wrong. Pan—pan something. Pan—"

"*Pandoro*," I offered.

"Pandoro! Ha!" He raised his finger victoriously. "That's the one. Thank you. It doesn't get better than that. You should eat there soon if you can because—" He seemed to remember himself, perhaps some confidence he shouldn't impart. "And when you do, sit at the south window."

I tried to picture it. Couldn't. But felt around for it in my memory, for the facts of it. "The window . . . that opens up to the alley?"

"Mmm," he agreed around a sip of his coffee. "Most extraordinary thing. They say they used to have a view down to the water—

before they filled in the land and built the wharfs, you know. And then someone purchased the lot beside them, built a brick monstrosity, and just like that—" he snapped his fingers—"no more view. Until a boy—a *boy*, of all things—took it upon himself to restore what he could. That woman, Mrs. Goodman, she told me that her son borrowed a suit from a cousin, went next door, obtained permission from their new neighbor, and proceeded to paint an entire mural upon that wall. The very water scene that they had once had a view to. It's remarkable, I tell you. I could use a talent like that for a task or two for our project."

He knocked his knuckles on the desk absently, then leaned forward with a sudden burst of focus. I didn't have the heart to tell him that boy was long gone, and his paints too. Even the cousin, the source of the borrowed suit, was long gone—back to Italy, when his twin, Emilio, began to "get into scrapes" and he tired of being mistaken for him. *"Twins run in the family, but trouble doesn't have to,"* he had said to Daniel once long ago. *"Remember that."*

"But you didn't come here to hear about murals. Let's talk about the digging. You've reconsidered? Good strong backs, we could use them. It is the chance of a lifetime. To be a part of something grand, something that will change history and bring even more beauty to the auspicious state of California."

My brain was having trouble keeping up with him as he gained momentum, sliding a map toward me. It appeared to be a stretch of coastland far south, closer to Los Angeles.

"My employer, Mr. Kinney, intends to develop this land—the very land you see here"—he infused a great amount of enthusiasm into his words—"into a center of cultural and academic greatness. The Venice of America, as it were."

My brows furrowed as I studied that area. It looked to be rather a desolate place, marshy by its depiction.

"Ah, you see that? That feeling, one of . . . confusion, I'd venture to say? *That* is the element of surprise. It's part of the magic. Right here—" he tapped a place on the map, where the land met the sea— "will be a great canal, stretching into a whole network of them, inland. Bridges! Bridges! Bridges!" He exploded his fingers three times—explosions that resulted only in three frames of *Blank! Blank! Blank!* in my mind, rather than the imaginary panorama of snapshots he intended. "Gondoliers, rowing—imported from the motherland of the true Venice, of course." The man lifted his brows impressively and waited.

"Of course," I said, unsure how to respectfully interrupt him and inquire what my mother had seen him about.

"And—" He paused dramatically. "Piazzas and plazas in the style of St. Mark's Square. Columns, covered colonnades, and buildings for the Venice Assembly."

He spoke as if I should recognize the name of the event. Then, realizing I did not, he shaped his voice into one of compassion.

"I'm getting ahead of myself. Sixty days—*sixty*—of lectures and symposiums. Season tickets, and The People"—he shrouded the phrase with awe—"can come for lectures."

Genuine interest began to stitch me to the man's vision. "Lectures on what?"

"Why, everything! Philosophy, politics, religion, travel—all of it, right there on the beach."

I considered this. "It's certainly . . . different," I said, infusing respect into the word.

"Different! I should hope so. None of this seaside frivolity, piers filled with amusement rides and whatnot. Do you know the definition of *amusement*?"

I did a quick etymological calculation, remembering the onion-skin thin pages of our dictionary, growing up. *A*, from the Latin for *not*. *Muse*, from the Latin for *think*.

"To not think."

"Precisely!"

I flinched as the man jabbed his finger into the air for emphasis. "People can go any number of places to *not think*. And certainly, we'll have our share of happy entertainments, as well. For the families, you know. Sea lion shows and performances. Carousels and ballroom dancing—dizzying things, but people must spin." He shrugged and gave a befuddled laugh, as if it was one of the great mysteries of life.

"It's ambitious," I said, truly impressed with the imagination behind such an endeavor.

"Mr. Kinney is an ambitious man." Mr. Wharton laughed. "He has the resources, and a personal history in Venice that—well, I'm getting sidetracked. The proprietor here at the bank is an old friend and has kindly allowed me to meet with the fine people of this neighborhood to see about procuring artifacts from the old country, hiring those who will move this earth and form the canals. Our traveling roles are almost assigned, but that's of no consequence. We have many already in place from our own neck of the woods, so to speak, but we do have room for a few more. You have a good strong back. I see a light in your eyes—you're catching the vision for the place, aren't you? I bet you can just picture it."

Blank canvas.

"We can pay a fair wage. . . ." He thumbed a stack of papers and landed on one that listed pay for the diggers, and for two other positions as well, though their titles were covered. They had significantly higher . . . *remuneration* attached to them.

"You mentioned traveling positions, sir?"

He lifted his eyes and studied me, his look morphing into one of compassion. "Well, yes, we're narrowing our candidates for two very particular positions. As I mentioned, we need men on the ground in Venice—or on the gondolas, rather. Not much 'ground' there to speak of." He chuckled at his own joke. "We'll be sending someone to track down the artifacts we haven't been able to procure here, and that person will need a thorough grasp of the Italian language, both written and spoken, for navigating the city and for translation work. And the other will need to be of an artistic persuasion. Someone who can capture the sights of Venice and bring them back for us. We'd like to have original drawings, you see."

He waved off the talk. "Now, about that digging position . . ." He named a sum and began to discuss lodging, as my mind hammered out another set of calculations. Though the work was admittedly appealing—good, hard, honest work out in the sun, not closed up in a cannery—the wage would still not yield anything close to what was needed.

"Did you say . . . you were in need of artifacts? Is that what the woman before me was in about?"

"Oh, yes, she came with a list of books she has. But sadly only one or two of them fit with the vision for Venice of America's own library."

"There is a list?" An absurd hope sparked, as if a book could fetch the sum I needed.

"Yes, and Mr. Kinney will pay handsomely for genuine Italian copies and their English translations. He plans to display them side-by-side, so that visitors can enjoy the full beauty of their original form, as well as read and understand parts in their own language." He slid the list over, and my eyes scanned the familiar titles:

Divina Commedia, Dante Alighieri. Two checkmarks there— apparently he'd found both Italian and English.

Preclarissimus liber elementorum Euclidis in artem geometrie. No checkmarks, and it wasn't any wonder.

"Hard to come by *Euclid's Elements*?" I said, offering what I hoped was a commiserating smile.

Instead, his face froze. His fingers, which had been carrying on their general cadence of drumming enthusiasm, stopped. "You knew what that said? In English?"

I nodded and read the next few titles on the list, checkmarks scattered. But it was the last item that stopped me.

Piccole Storie de Venezia, from Piccolo Press. I leaned forward in my seat. The small histories.

The very ones given to me, while locked way, while unworthy, by my mother. I swallowed.

"Did the woman who was in before—did she not speak of these?" I tapped the title on the list.

"Oh, we spoke of them," he said. "She even knew of someone who has many of them! But she would not give a name, no matter how I pleaded. She said she would never take them from that person, not for all the world."

"But . . . you have need of them?"

He tilted his hand in a somewhat-yes, somewhat-no fashion. "They are plentiful enough," he said. "Do you know of a set?"

I swallowed. "I have one," I said slowly. The only thing I had, really.

He narrowed his eyes. "Which volumes?"

"All of them," I said.

His jovial expression turned serious. "How many . . . is *all*?"

I had to think. Recall their contents, the facts that had once marched color and fantastical imaginings into my youth. Facts were like ladder rungs to cling to when climbing an invisible image I could not grasp.

"The Book of Glass," I said. Mr. Wharton nodded, ticking it off on his finger. "The Book of . . . Isles," I said, and he continued to count. "The Books of . . . Gondolas, Ink, Masks, and—" I halted, reaching in the dark for what the next one was.

I couldn't picture its color, the typeset or embossing of its cover. But I remember it had made me feel . . . entranced. As if I were traversing a spider's web, crossing an intricate pattern—*weaving*. That's right. It had been about the lacemakers of one of the isles. "The Book of Thread."

And the last. The one whose spine had worn nearly smooth as I'd run my hope-hungry hands over it, so many dark days. I could not bring myself to mention it. It felt so much a part of my own story . . . which was not a story worth telling.

His face fell. "Ah."

"Not . . . what you were hoping for?"

"There is a rare volume that we've had trouble procuring. The . . . Book of Waters?" This, tentative, held out like blown glass itself, ready to shatter.

I hesitated, something catching inside.

He noticed. Shrewd man.

Leaning forward, and looking around, he asked, "You know it?"

Intimately. And not at all. Pulse thrumming, I swallowed around the memory of its feel in my hands—the very last book my mother had sent, when I was locked away. *The tale with no ending, Daniel,* her letter had said. *To give you hope. Remember—though it may feel as if it is, the story is not over yet.*

And it was the blank pages at the back of that book, waiting to be filled, that were like oxygen to me. I waited to read it for a day, and then a week, and then—always. For every time I opened the cover, a clock began to tick, as if counting down toward the end of hope. If I came to the end of the unfinished story . . . what then? Where, then, was hope? As long as it waited, ready to be read . . .

The story isn't over yet.

"Precisely." Mr. Wharton's eyes grew wide. I hadn't meant to speak that out loud—that phrase my mother used to offer with a wink when I was young, any time I came home dejected or upset with myself for a failure. "So, you *do* know it. The unfinished tale."

I wanted to hoard it. Clench tight my grip around the impossible hope of an unfinished story. But I wanted something else more.

"If I did," I said, and watched his eyes spark, "it would be of value to you?"

"Yes, and no," he said, and my stomach sank. "We intend to procure one of the rare editions, yes. But it goes farther than that. We are hoping to procure the handwritten first draft. To show its progression from idea to book. The hope being to inspire others, show a bit of the process, spark imagination of what can be possible when one takes hold of an idea and runs with it."

"Like your resort."

"Very much like that. And there is some speculation that—well, the printed edition feels less . . . complete than its counterparts. Unfinished, as a matter of fact."

I sat straighter in my chair. "That's true," I said, placing everything I had on the line.

"So . . . you *do* have one?" He looked wary. I didn't blame him. Gulping, I reached into my sack, my practiced hand knowing just where to find it. I pulled it out, slid it onto the desk between us, where it seemed to beat like a living thing, there between us.

He stared. At the book, then at me, and at the book again.

"May I . . . ?"

No, I thought. "Yes," I said.

He picked it up with almost a reverence, pausing to study the woodblock illustrations, the foreign words.

"Remarkable," he said at length. "We've wondered if the original might hold some clue as to its rather abrupt ending. Legend says it finishes the story, but Venice is a land of legends, and one never knows . . . well. When we find the man to send over, I'm sure he'll have better luck procuring it in its motherland. I don't suppose you'd . . . part with the volume? For the right sum, of course." All talk of a digging job seeming forgotten, the man was suddenly all business.

"I'm afraid not," I said. It meant too much—and not just to me.

Crestfallen, the man nodded.

"But . . . if I might propose something . . ."

He lit. Palms up, gesturing. "By all means!"

"Translator," I said, quick as lightning. *Slow down. Full sentences.* "I can take my book, procure the original, work your translation. . . ."

"This book changes things, son, I will say that. But you must understand, we're in a difficult position. We've already identified a man for the job, his credentials quite extensive." His mouth pulled to the side. "I don't suppose you . . ." His tact left the unfinished question up to me.

"I don't have credentials, sir," I admitted. No letters after my name, other than *convict*.

A clock struck in the main bank. He looked flustered. "Is that the time? I—I have an appointment I cannot miss." He fixed his eyes on the book, not me. "Perhaps we could negotiate a raise in pay, if you're willing to lend it, say, and take the excavating job. Let me get your information."

He took down my name, pausing only briefly as he wrote *Goodman*. I didn't know how to give an address for a shanty out in the Great Sand Waste.

"If you change your mind, please," he said, setting that last word with a passionate buzz, "come back. I'm off first thing tomorrow, and we'd be glad of your help down south. We can share a railcar, if you like. The company will pay your way!" He shook his head, his mind having transported him to the imagined train. "I do love a good railcar, don't you?"

I stood, nodding. "Very at home in them." I took his offered handshake. How had the man, in less than half an hour, made himself feel an old friend and managed to dash my last hopes simultaneously?

I was off, back striding among shadows. The drumming of Mr. Wharton's fingers had embedded in my mind. Driving me like a militiaman, bent on purpose, formulating plans.

I traversed the city in a long blur, that plan overtaking me with every step. At last, entered my railcar and beheld it in the full light of day. Forced myself to see it as it was.

This . . . was my life. An empty chamber. A glorified crate carved out to make way for atonement. Capture it, cage it, live it. And yet, across the city, the one I had wronged the deepest was about to lose everything.

The walls constricted. My throat too. Pressure, as time and hope grew small. There was something both dangerous and beautiful about the reality of dwindling logical solutions. It broke chains. Made a man entertain the impossible, give credence to the illogical . . . and risk it all.

This place was built to atone?

Let it atone.

With the clock ticking and my chest beating, I made swift work. Tore the sketches from their nails, each with a small rip that severed my soul from this place, stitch by stitch. I pulled out the jar in the sand, emptied its meager coins into my hand. Retrieved the set of books. Held the glass pen in my hand, deliberated. Stuck it back in its safe and shadowed cavity in the floorboards. Beheld my food stores, their wobbled tower. A cheerful trot-trot-trot sounded as Ballast climbed the splintered porch and sat beside me, both of us eyeing the stack of food like admirers at an art museum.

"Today's your lucky day, old boy," I said. I tossed three cans in my knapsack—any more than that and I'd clang like a bell through the streets—and cranked the rest of them open, setting them on the floor for my canine companion, who needed no further invitation to dive in with glorious, ravenous abandon.

And that was that.

With a last look around, stroking Ballast slowly with a growing ache inside as he wagged his tail in happy, gluttonous oblivion, I filled my lungs with determination.

I would offer everything I had, and it still might not be enough. But I could not go on if I didn't at least try. Turn over every stone, offer every meager shadow of this life that I could. I gathered up the empty cans, placed them in the trash bin. Strode toward the door and—at the last second—returned to the floorboard and snatched up the box containing the old glass pen. I didn't have to use it, but I could at least bring it. It deserved not to be left behind just because of my sorry mistakes.

I took the creaking porch steps one at a time, Ballast trotting happily off to his next adventure.

A lonesome west wind slipped through the cracks, keening a mournful song as if to warn me away from imminent failure.

I closed the door, trapping its warning inside.

4

It was dark by the time Columbus Street took me almost all the way there. I stopped at Lombard, looking right and far into the rises ahead. Up there, somewhere, Emilio and his crew would be gathering soon.

A quick job. One last time. Enough to set my mother right, fast. And pay the last of my own debts. *Freedom.*

The siren call was strong, summoning some deep memory in my muscles to turn that direction. Take a step . . . and another . . . and with each step, the old familiar refrain came back strong. The words I had beat back a thousand times over the past years. *Quick job.* Even quicker, if I was there. That was my strength—assess a building, find the perfect combination of "quick and obscured from view" based on the architecture of the place. Sometimes a basement door, sometimes a window reached by fire escape or sheer insanity. I could look at a place and get a sense for what it held within, as if I were in the mind of the architect of yore. Science and art, that was the breathtaking symphony of architecture—and I'd made it sing for us, time and again.

One more step. *Just one more time.*

The cans in my knapsack slid against each other, metal-on-metal. For all the world, the sound of shackles.

And it was enough to stop me.

I heaved a sigh.

This was crazy. I had no guarantee of Mr. Wharton even listening to my proposal, let alone going along with it. By the time I had his answer, I'd be too late to join up with Emilio. For all I knew, Mr. Wharton would send me packing—he'd have every reason to. He already had someone in mind for the job, he'd said as much. I'd be back to my railcar, with my empty jars and now-vanished food stores and no way to give a home to the very one who had *been* a home to me, even when I'd least deserved it.

And with the way the man came alive at the idea of "doing things differently" . . . well, I was banking a good deal on that thing inside him, whatever it was, coming alive at my idea. It was foolish to risk it all in this way.

But it was the good way.

I turned. Rerouted my wayward feet back up Columbus. Away from Nob Hill.

"Sorry, Emilio," I said, and felt a strange mix of doom and freedom as I walked away from the only sure thing.

I was close to out of breath by the time the familiar jut and jaunt of city blocks and alleys took me once more to North Beach. With the twilight fast turning dark, I hurried. The rain was taking a rest, though it had summoned spice from the patch of grass in Washington Square. I paused beside a tree to catch my breath. And more, to try for a glimpse of the old home . . . and the beloved soul who occupied it. Movement in the apartment above the trattoria across the street silenced my thoughts.

There was Mrs. Mary Goodman. My mother.

I watched as she set a kettle on her stove and waited for it to boil. *"Listen to that water inside, Daniel,"* she used to say, beckoning me to still my playing and hear the roil, the rumble and pop of water within. *"Just bursting to life . . . and destined for your belly!"* She bent and tickled me, punctuating the sound of boiling with my laughter.

Now, in this chasm that stretched between us, there was only silence. The warmth of her small window reached into the night, an invitation to all the good things I could not deserve. She lifted the trusty kettle and pulled down her cup from the cupboard above—the same one she'd always used. A small white teacup with roses painted inside, and a chipped saucer to match.

She reached up again and lifted the only other cup there—one that portrayed, in red and white, a ship tossed at sea. Mine, a relic brought over from the old country long ago by my mother, before I was ever a notion on the wind. She set it on the counter next to hers. Poured her cup, moved the kettle to pour mine and stopped short, as if awaking herself from a daydream. The sudden movement caused a splash to land on her hand, and she set the kettle down on the stove in haste, clutching the burn.

I winced, watching.

But it was not the burn that brought her tears. She pumped cool water over it, as she had done for me and my boisterous accident-prone wounds countless times. Then, leaning against the counter with her hands clasped, she beheld my storm-tossed china cup. She picked it up slowly. Held it close to her heart, and then replaced it into the cupboard, where the door enclosed it again into darkness.

This . . . was what brought her hand to her eyes to wipe tears.

My throat ached, and the ache went deep. With new determination and a furtive look around, I crossed the street to the bank. The doors were locked. I went around back and discovered the same—but the green glow of a banker's lamp illuminated the face I hoped to see. I knocked softly, loathe to summon anyone's attention but the one man who held my destiny in his pen-twirling hands.

Mr. Wharton appeared, looking a bit disheveled and far less polished in his shirtsleeves. No coat, no hat. But when he saw me, hope lit across his round face.

"Mr. Goodman!" he said, and I thanked the heavens his voice was muffled behind the glass window.

He opened the door. "You've reconsidered? I've wired Mr. Kinney, and we are prepared to offer quite a healthy sum for the book if you'll sell it."

But I didn't need a healthy sum. I needed a miracle sum.

"Send me," I said, breathless.

Understanding dawned on his face, followed by compassion and a search for how to let me down. But I wouldn't give him the chance—not before I'd made my case, crazy as it was.

"Sketches," I said, pulling out the houses from my wall. I didn't mention that they were a veritable boulevard of broken-into homes.

He shuffled through them, his brows raising in pleasant surprise. "These are yours?"

I nodded. "But you needn't take my word for it. Name anything—anything within sight—and I'll sketch it for you."

He poked his head out the door, searching the walkway for people, or possibly for understanding.

"I've gotten ahead of myself." I pulled in a deep breath, starting again. "Mr. Wharton," I said, fixing my eyes on him with sincerity. "I can offer you the services of a sketch artist and a translator, all in one man. It would cut travel costs in half for you."

He looked dubious.

"And—instead of having to pay two men wages, you'd be getting the services of both men, for the cost of—" It felt presumptuous. *Replace roof.* "One and a half."

This made him laugh. "One-and-a-half men, eh?"

I gave a serious nod, ignoring the heat crawling up my neck. He was right to laugh. But there was no turning back.

"It's an intriguing proposition, Mr. Goodman," he said, and the name seemed to jostle a question loose from his memory. "No relation, I suppose, to . . ." He tipped his head in the general direction of the trattoria.

I nodded.

"And the mural . . . ?" A spark lit his eyes.

"That was me," I said. "A long time ago."

"You'll understand," he said uncertainly, "if I must ask for proof. Come in, and if you can sketch a likeness to the mural in question, perhaps we can talk."

My collar grew tight. *Blank canvas.* I could no more sketch that mural's likeness than paint the *Mona Lisa*.

I gulped. Reached for phrases that put a gloss on the truth.

Don't have the capacity to . . . unable to visualize without seeing the grandeur in person . . . desire to do it justice by seeing it before me . . . but the shiny words all piled up in a choke point, fell to the ground as the plain truth came out. "I—can't."

His face fell. "I see." His fingers drummed on the door's edge with none of their earlier enthusiasm. "Well, Mr. Goodman, I'm afraid I can't—"

"I'm sorry," I said, feeling this last chance slip away and grasping for it, desperate. "I don't mean to interrupt. It's just—I can't draw what I cannot see."

"How unusual," he said, his interest piquing. "Tell me more."

"It's . . . fairly simple . . ." I tried to boil the tale down to what was relevant. "I fell, several years ago. Hit my head."

Fatherly concern pressed his brows together, and his expression landed inside me with a pang.

"I'm all right," I said. "I just . . . lost the ability to imagine, visually. My mind's eye, so to speak."

"But you can still draw what you see."

I nodded, stuffing my hands in my pockets and feeling the burn of my cheeks. I knew how boyish that particular tendency made me look, and Mr. Wharton was looking for a man. One and a half men.

"Please, Mr. Wharton. I know I'm not the most obvious person for the job. I don't have the right suit, the polish—"

He shook his head and stretched out a gravelly "Well . . ." as if to say, *"not a bit of it, son."* But we both knew it to be true.

"But if you'll give me a chance. Is there something here I could draw?" I turned, gesturing at the square, the neighborhood.

I wouldn't have blamed the man if he'd closed the door right then and there, sent me on my way. There was nothing reasonable about what I was suggesting.

But perhaps it was the very unreasonableness of it that gave him reason to be intrigued. For though his expression bore a good dose of wariness, there was a cunning spark there too. "The cathedral," he said at last. He took his coat from a hook, donned it, and stepped into the night. "Can you draw that? Very like what we'll be needing sketches of, in Venice."

He pointed up the gentle rise of Filbert Street, where the twin white spires of Saints Peter and Paul reached up. I'd given churches a wide berth these past years, more out of respect for them than anything else.

"I'll give it my best," I said.

We crossed the silent square and made our way past homes—some slumbering, some with lantern glow spilling out into odd shapes and shadows over the street—and reached the church. My insides tumbled and I reached for something to break this apprehension creeping up the sinews of my arms.

"I used to think this place was named for my great-grandfather Pietro," I said, chuckling.

Mr. Wharton rewarded this with a hearty laugh. "Santi Pietro e Paolo," he said.

I grinned. "Perhaps you don't need a translator after all. You know Italian?"

"Oh, no, no, no," he said, making descending stairsteps of the words. "Just learning through this project, you know." He pointed at the church, the winged angel at the top of the steps that looked ready to take flight. "It seems to me it would have made a splendid border to the square, with the green in front of it. I wonder that they didn't build it there."

I had thought the same. Perhaps the square had come later. "Maybe if they had it to do over again . . ."

He laughed. "Indeed. That's not likely to happen, is it? In any case, it will serve well for our purposes now, eh?" He eyed my sketchbook.

This was it. The weight of all that rested on this moment descended, pressing that blank canvas deeper inside me. My mind raced into a tangle. My fingers flexed, protesting what I was about to do. *We can't*, they seemed to shout. But if I couldn't do this one thing . . .

I took a deep breath. Set pencil to paper. And let the graphite etch the form before me, line by stiff line. Unimpressive, rudimentary.

Soon my concentration gave way to something deeper, more

instinctive, as the lines joined into angles, one dimension became two, shadows lifted corners and crannies from the page. I forgot, for a moment, that I wasn't alone.

Soon I was copying the words that had engraved themselves, banner-like, around the façade of the building:

La Gloria Di Colui Che Tutto Muove Per L'Universo Penetra E Risplende

As the sketch neared completion, the cloud of creation lifted, and I became aware of a heavy silence beside me.

Mr. Wharton's face was schooled carefully into one of detached study. He stroked his chin. An owl hooted somewhere across the street.

"And . . . the words?" he asked. "Speaking Italian is one thing, but the nuances of translation are quite another. How would you translate the words on the building? Convey not just their meaning, but their tone, their composition. The way they hit a person here—" He thumped his chest. "You know."

I did know. I looked at the words—from one of Dante's cantos. A book the man would know well, probably, as it was on his list of important tomes.

At the bottom of the page I wrote their literal meaning: *The glory of the one who moves everything through the universe penetrates and shines.*

I pondered them and made a few tucks and trades, to better convey the lofty but poignant words with which Dante ushered his reader into the realm of *Paradiso.*

The glory of He who . . .

I scratched it out. He and Him were small differences but changed the feel of it.

The glory of Him who moveth all doth penetrate—

But that wasn't right. It was correct in the literal sense, but penetrate bespoke only piercing. Nothing of the saturation, the flooding, that the lines conjured meaning of. I scratched it out.

Permeate the universe, doth shine.

I lingered over the words and the sketch a moment longer. Then tore it carefully from the book and handed it to Mr. Wharton. A ticket to my future.

He whispered the words aloud. Traced the peaked roofline of the church with his thumb and looked across the avenue to compare. He was all seriousness. Nothing of the jubilant man I'd met earlier today.

My heart sank.

Those fingers, the ones scarred and callused from the cannery, had attempted something too lofty for them . . . and failed.

"It's all right, sir," I said. He had been so forbearing, coming out into the dead of night with me on a fool's errand. "I understand. Thank you for the chance." I extended my hand, wishing to spare him the unpleasant task of telling me what I already knew. I wasn't fit for the job. Or *jobs*. "I wish you all the best—"

"Remarkable," he said at last. He took my hand and shook it absently, old habit. Then he dropped it and gestured at the church. "Do you know that your translation is nearly identical to the one largely regarded as the best embodiment of Dante's skill and intent, his meaning and his tone?"

I shook my head, not entirely sure what he meant. I knew little of Dante and even less about translations.

"Longfellow," he said, his old fervor returning. "You can do this for any building?" He gestured to the sketch.

I nodded. It had nearly done me in, doing this one. "Yes."

"And you can translate like this . . . for any bit of Italian? Or Venetian?"

They were alike, the two. But they had lifts and twists that set them apart. *"Like the canals,"* my mother had told me. *"You never know where they will turn, where they will take you."*

"Yes, sir. I'll give it my best." I meant it.

Mr. Wharton shook his head, shifting his gaze between the paper, the church, and me. The last bit of reservation teetered between us. Desperate to push it over, I spoke before I could stop myself. "And once the translation is done . . ." I said, breath catching, "I will send the Book of Waters. My copy, for display in your Venice Beach."

"Venice of America," he corrected absently. He puffed out his cheeks, shaking his head and offering a handshake. "You've got yourself a deal, son."

It was foreign, this lift beneath my feet. That ran up inside of me, all the way into my chest. Gratitude? Hope? Joy, even? It was foreign, and it was wonderful. It carried me through the night, making preparations. To the oak desk to sign papers. To receive, wide-eyed, a small fold of bills. A stipend, Mr. Wharton explained. For the trip over the ocean.

The ocean that had bound me in, been my border . . . was to carry me off.

But not before I took care of one last thing.

When *Goodman's Fine Italian Treats* was dark at last, I clambered with old familiar stealth up the fire escape ladder around back and made straight for the water spot. A growing ulcer of a thing, intent on collecting all of the mournful sky's castaways and dripping them into that warm refuge below. I set to the familiar work, releasing the old umbrella, its skeletal frame inverted and its dome blown away in the last wind. I set it down and lined up my supplies. It would be built to last, as best it could.

Many a night had I come here, unbeknownst to my mother. Whenever the rain was heavy, and especially if the wind was up too. Sometimes, in the thick of the storms, I held the open umbrella myself, for no amount of fastening it this way or that would keep it long against the winds that tumbled over rooftops.

Always before leaving, I'd anchor an umbrella by lashing it, open dome and all, to some old metal loops I'd pulled off of a black-and-gold wood scrap from the Sand Waste, the hardware probably a vestige of the men half a century before who'd packed the harbor with ships and abandoned them in gridlock, eager to chase after the gold in the mountains beyond.

Little had the prospectors imagined that one day, the smallest bit of their ship would be nailed here, above a woman who was trapped with grief for a son who had betrayed her. And that same lost son, whose whereabouts she did not know, planted one floor above, holding an umbrella over her.

The spot was growing. The roof below, soft.

Rolling up my jacket into a wad, I used it to sop up the puddle already collected. I lay the new umbrella open on the ground at a cheerful tilt, securing it with a coil of rope, repeating the process with two other new umbrellas, until they formed something of a bouquet. Or a circle of warriors gathered in battle, facing shields outward—or domes upward, in this case. Each of them secured to the roof, each secured to one another, each anchored over the top of its arch with yet another length of rope. The stalwart circle topped with one final umbrella, roofing their makeshift structure in. It would last for a few weeks at least, I hoped.

The days that followed were a flurry of travel and preparations: Tendering my resignation at the sardine factory.

"We'll not hold your spot, you know."

I knew.

Accompanying Mr. Wharton back down south. Being pricked and measured and all manner of things that made me squirm, fish out of water, as three suits were made.

"You'll be representing our entire operation, you know."

I knew.

Procuring paper, pencils, a travelogue on Venice. Last, but not least—the Book of Waters. Mr. Wharton held the volume in his hands, its gilded title scratched, letters blocked and adorned in filigree. *"If we can just find the ending . . . well. You'll find it. It's a singular tale, you know."*

This . . . I knew.

And my pen knew, too, as I scratched out those first storied words upon the deck of the ship, the old boundary-shore that had always hemmed me in, fast disappearing as waves rose and fell beneath.

Everything I'd ever known faded into specks upon the shore, and I pulled out the book. It was just me and it, now, and to open it felt like the unlocking of so much. This, the one cover I had refused to open for so long. Keeper of lost hope, which threatened to fly away into the wild the second I opened this cover.

Hauling in a breath, I did just that. The spine creaking with the song of another time, another life. Letters lining up into Italian words. Whether this act would draw me closer to hope or vanish it once and for all . . . only time would tell.

I took pen in hand and scratched the first words:

Ancient waters rippled in moonlight. . . .

THE BOOK OF WATERS

The Basket That Changed a World

1807

Ancient waters rippled in moonlight. Waters born before the fall of any creature's foot upon soil. Before man breathed his first.

But here on these dark waters, a tiny babe did breathe his first. Alive in the world only a sprinkling of days and tucked into the folds of a blanket with care. Small chest rising and falling shallow, like the black canal beneath his basket.

Newborn clouds shifted above. Moonlight, aged companion of these waters, glinted over ripples like silver. In a city of black gondolas, long and grand, the babe's vessel was small, humble. Tightly woven of reeds by a hand who could never have imagined what cargo it would one day bear, an embrace around this child.

Where the baby had no cradle, no mother's hand to rock it, the canal played the part with walls and embankments all around. Palazzi and porticos, marble carved by hand just as a father's hand might have carved a cradle. But a father's hand had not known this child, and like a baby once long ago in Egypt, the water carried this babe to a last hope for a good life.

Ahead lay the orphanage, three or four windows glowing amid myriad dark ones. Light tossed from them into liquid avenues, as if to draw the basket in.

But there—just in that last stretch of space between the babe and the building, a wind tumbled through, unfurling down the canal and pushing him back, back from the threads of light, into the shadows.

The basket bumped against the lone gondola moored to the quayside, where it was found once a month, upon ordinary Tuesdays. It bumped again, this time a little harder. And isn't that the way of miracles? Something extraordinary because of the faithful ordinary.

A figure rose from within the larger vessel, solemn and silent, scanning the water with eyes well-accustomed to the practice and stopping at the sight of the basket.

The man leaned forward, pulling back the swaddling within. Studied a moment, then drew back in sudden realization with a whispered declaration.

Those well-trained eyes read the scene before him like a story. A solitary baby. An orphanage in the offing. And his own blistered, wind-chafed hands . . . suddenly holding somebody's very fate.

Hesitation lingered like a mist and blew away as quickly as he reached into the dark canal and pulled the bundle into his keeping.

Bells rang in the distance, marking the hour. Ten o'clock.

Though the man could guide a gondola with practiced grace and strength, the small basket caused his every nerve to tense. He held it out in front of himself like the fishmongers carrying their goods to market. . . .

"But you do not stink like the fishes," the man Giuseppe said. "You are a deal better looking, too, small one. No scales or slime. Maybe . . . more like a crab than a fish. Ah! You take no pleasure in my jokes? Though you sleep, you wrinkle your face at me so? You are a crab, indeed. But I like you." The absence of scales and slime seemed to hold great magnitude for the man, for he adjusted the basket, hoisting it up into a closer embrace, and stepped with careful balance from his rocking boat onto the *fondamenta*. "Come," he said. "Meet the rest. You will like them. They are very likeable! Mostly."

He walked toward the orphanage, but as he approached its

stone walls and the wheel upon which children—orphans or those born out of wedlock or those whose parents believed a better life awaited them within—were left and rotated through a door to ensure their warmth and prompt discovery, he veered to the right instead. Down a narrow alley, where the smell of the canals eased into the smell of honeysuckle climbing over the edges of window boxes and spicing the night air.

After a few turns more, until it seemed the city should have swallowed them, and that they should have crossed their own route three times over in the circuitous paradox of Venice, he paused.

He approached a door where a torch had gone out—or was put out—above it. On the door, a brass-forged coat of arms showed its age and gave the paint-chipped backdrop a storied air. The place had the feel of a *palazzo* once grand but long abandoned. Its bones seemed to creak with tales untold. Or tales held captive—like Venice herself, these ten years since Napoleon arrived and soldiers poured in—first French, then Austrian. Ending the Republic's long and illustrious reign as an independent power.

With a careful motion balancing the basket, Giuseppe pulled a key, scrolled and tarnished, from his pocket and inserted it with a resonant click that echoed with craftsmanship from an era gone by.

Inside he was greeted by the ghostly sight of furniture draped in white cloth. Placed there many decades ago when first this place had been shuttered. He traversed the corridor, quieting his footsteps in the echoing chambers of the high-ceilinged palazzo with its parquet floors and its reaching columns and painted frescoes veiled in dust.

Through a maze of passageways he went, guided by memory and the soft glow of a door ahead holding promise of fire and warmth. Out of the palazzo's grandeur, into the obscurity and delicious smells of the kitchen.

It felt very strange, he thought, the reach of warmth, the glow of light, the sweet smell of fresh confections here in this abandoned place. But after all, was that not why they came month after month? To preserve life, no matter the condition of the palazzo? Or, more importantly, the city beyond it?

The infant stirred, as if it—he? she?—sensed a homecoming as well.

Had he done right, pulling the basket from the canal? He thought to his own upbringing in *ospedale* before Dante's grandparents had come for him, thought to the orphanage's cold and runny polenta. Though the sisterhood did all in their power to care very well for the children, there was a limit to what they could do for scores of them all at once.

Before him, three familiar faces spoke in hushed tones, pausing to take bites of *fritole*, fritters fried golden-brown and dusted with sugar.

There was Pietro, the scamp, his hair pointed haphazardly as if he had been in twelve different street fights today. Knowing him, it was not unlikely. He was a walking contradiction—conducting himself with utmost care beside his Murano glass furnaces all the day, the picture of precision. Then bursting forth on the waiting world at night to release his pent-up energy with all manner of mischief—mischief tempered, thanks be to the heavens, by a good heart inside of him. Beside him sat his dog, whose fur likewise looked as though it had been attacked by mischievous gulls. Pietro ruffled the dog's fur, and his grin pulled up crookedly, his cheeks stuffed with fritole. Sugar dusted the man's face in funny streaks like snow.

There was Elena, strong and still. Her quiet ways often masked the fierce resolve she bore. She could well embody the name of their beloved Venice herself: *La Serenissima*. The most serene. Looking up and tilting her head at his basket, ever-perceptive even for one so young. Having lived only twenty years, just a girl when Napoleon came, she embodied the wisdom of a soul much older. She lifted a hand and gave a warm smile.

And Valentina. Twice the age of Elena, growing more beautiful with each passing year. Hair streaked with silver, hands strong from a lifetime of working the lace in her beloved *Isola di Burano*. And yet, for one who lived among the kaleidoscope cottages of the fishermen there, she had a distinct dislike for fishermen. Or perhaps it was just fishermen by the name of Giuseppe.

56

But one was missing. "The auspicious guild has convened, I see," the bearded fisherman said, winking as they all turned his way.

"Giuseppe!" Valentina looked aghast at him and his sleeves, wet from their dip into the canal to obtain the basket. "What has become of you? Did you fall into the canal?"

He feigned offense. "A man of the sea like me? The water is life to me. I would never fall unless I meant to fall in."

"Then why?" She feathered her hand in his soggy direction. He could almost picture lace spinning from her fingertips in the gesture. Casting a web for him. "And what is in your basket?" She began to look suspicious.

"I shall tell all. But where is *Signor* Cavellini? We must all be gathered for this." Giuseppe pulled the basket away from her view, and the child sighed deeply.

Giuseppe released a man-sized sigh to cover it. Valentina's eyes shifted from him to the basket and back to him, narrowing. She was seeing into his soul again. Maddening woman. Bewitching woman.

Giuseppe cleared his throat. "Where is the rascal Dante Cavellini?" He repeated the question, hoping it might disarm or distract her. It accomplished neither.

A shuffle sounded behind him, footsteps approaching. The man appeared from the shadows.

"Here," he said, a little out of breath. "I am here."

Giuseppe turned to face the younger man. He gave a sheepish smile, which looked out of place on his always-serious face.

"What is that?" Giuseppe said, leaning closer to the younger man.

"What is what?"

Giuseppe lifted his chin to gesture at Dante's smile, since his hands were occupied. "This thing, upon your face. It looks as though you fished a drowned smirk out of the waters and slung it over your head."

The drowned smirk froze in place and melted into a scowl. "I? I am not the one who has fished something out of the canal this night. I saw you pull that basket onto the bank as I came. What is it?"

The others drew near, and soon, amid a chorus of exclamations and urgent hushes from the ladies lest they wake the sleeping child, five faces were bent over this small life. If it awoke, it would have a sight to behold and would be startled all the way up to the Dolomites and back.

"Gio. What have you done?" Valentina whispered. If he had not held the basket, he was certain she would have hit him with the back of her hand.

"Done?" Giuseppe said, his voice reverberating down the marbled corridor at their backs.

"Shhh," Elena said as the child's face pressed into an expression that indicated it might soon implode. She reached in, pulling the little bundle into her arms and to herself. Clasping small hands inside hers, breathing softly on them to bring warmth. Watching the creature's breath carefully.

"*Done?*" Giuseppe repeated, this time in a whisper. "I have rescued this child from a life of loneliness, that is what I have done. Where do you imagine this basket was floating to? Directly toward the ospedale. Where the babies line up by the numbers and the rooms are colder than ice."

Valentina's hand reached up, and he pulled away, thinking this time she surely would hit him. But she rested that hand on his shoulder, the lines around her blue eyes softening. "But where did it—he or she?" She paused and directed the question at Elena.

After a momentary pause, Elena pulled the blanket back slightly. "Boy," she said quickly, her cheeks flushing as she quickly bundled the little thing back up and began to sway, coaxing the child back into a deep sleep.

"Where did he come from?"

As if in answer, a small object tumbled from the folds of the blanket. It fell to the floor with a metal ding and danced there upon its axis.

Pietro, the wild-haired scamp, dove for it. Dante grabbed a candlestick, pulling it close to illuminate the form of a coin.

"What is it? It isn't Venetian," Pietro said, scratching his unruly head. "*Lira? Franc?* Perhaps it will tell us something of the boy."

Dante's jaw clenched, his face grim as he studied the etching on the coin.

"Ah," Valentina said. "Austrian? Something to do with the Habsburgs. Perhaps one of the guards around the city."

"No," Dante said and filled his lungs, drawing himself up. "It's nothing."

Elena stepped close. "Come, Dante. What is it?"

He faltered. "If—if it tells us anything, it's only that he was meant for life."

Elena's hand slipped into his and withdrew the coin. She blanched at the figure embossed there, her typical countenance of joy shadowing into concern as a swallow traversed her slender neck. "A skeleton," she murmured.

Valentina plucked the offending object from her hands. "Skeleton! With a babe like this! Who would do such a thing?"

Pietro now took his turn, studying it in firelight. He, an artist to whom everything was a story, turned his mouth down and shook his head, dismissive. "It is only a start."

"A start," Dante repeated, voice gruff.

"What is a skeleton but the bones of a life? This young thing"— he waved his hand at the child—"has nothing but life in front of him. Flesh to put on bones. It will be a full and good life."

Valentina tsked, shaking her head and peering inside the basket, pulling something more out.

"How do you know?" Giuseppe asked, turning the basket around in his thick arms.

"Because he is ours," Pietro said, lifting a shoulder in a matter of course. "What else?"

"And he has a name," Valentina said. She held up a small parchment, rolled into a tiny scroll as if it were an emperor's decree. But it held no grand law or declaration. Only a small note in meticulous but shaky hand.

He is called Sebastien. He was well-beloved. Please give him a good life.

Elena's hand went to her heart, eyes shining with tears. "Such a legacy already," she murmured, stroking the slumbering child's cheek.

Dante looked on, observing the scene with depth to his gaze and silence to his presence. He bowed his head, averting his eyes as if he had just witnessed something so intimate it necessitated such deference.

"Tell us all that happened," Valentina said.

"As I said! There came the basket, floating down the canal. The wind blew it to the side of my boat—just as if it was delivering the child straight to me. Do you think the wind was mistaken? I ask you!" Giuseppe's voice was climbing again, and this time it was Dante who laid a hand upon Giuseppe's arms. What did these people think, that he was a musical machine to be turned down? Giuseppe was no machine. Did not a heart beat within his chest? Was that not why he rescued this child? His blood began to boil.

"What do we do with him?"

Valentina looked at Giuseppe. Dante looked at Elena.

Pietro ruffled the fur of his dog. "Is it a question?" he asked, his boyish features sincere. "Is this not why we are here? Venice is a refuge. It is why we meet today. It is the work that we do, is it not?"

Elena nodded. "We carry on the work of Venice," she said. "Pietro is right. He needs asylum. We are here to give it. Yes?"

A hushed chorus of affirmation, fading into Pietro's lighter tone. "Ah, the *bambinos*, they are bushels of fun."

He spoke knowingly. He had seven younger siblings bursting the seams of his family's cottage with bodies and with squabbles and, most of all, with joy. Sometimes Giuseppe imagined he could hear their merrymaking all the way across the lagoon, from Murano to his humble, silent abode on the Giudecca. "He will need to eat soon, you know. They are always eating. Should I fetch something? There is a little fritole left. We saved it for the two of you, but surely you would not deprive such an innocent thing of this splendor."

"He'll have no teeth," Dante spoke. He looked upon the baby with an air of tenderness entirely new. Dante, the man of letters and books, was not accustomed to children—or to any family, for that matter. "Should I find him something? Some broth?" His face flushed as he quickly seemed to realize he knew nothing of what he spoke. The stoic and unshakeable Dante had never looked so . . . tentative. It was a very good sight to behold. Giuseppe wished to laugh but valued his life too much. "What do they feed the bambinos at the ospedale?"

"I know someone," Elena said quickly, with a note of hope. "A friend . . . who has had a baby. I am sure she would help."

"A wet nurse," Valentina said. "Of course. You should take him. He may wake soon."

"But what of our meeting?" Giuseppe said.

"Shhhh!" A chorus, this time, the four of them.

"You intend to baptize him with your shooshing? You'll be the ones to wake him!" Giuseppe said in a whisper. "What of our meeting? We cannot wait another month. We have the room to prepare, papers to make, supplies to lay in. The Visitor is set to arrive in weeks, unless they are—" Giuseppe stopped abruptly, giving a grave look.

"A week," Dante said. "We'll meet in a week's time. Is that agreeable?"

"Proceed without me tonight," Elena said. "Giuseppe, can you bring me word of what is needed of me for the Visitor?"

Before Giuseppe could agree, Pietro waved both hands out in front of him to stop the notion. "We do not proceed without one of the guild. Do we want another incident like—"

Four sets of eyes silenced him. He had meant it in jest, but mention of the event that had shaped the course of their lives, and so many before them, blanketed them all with thick silence.

"A week, then," Elena said.

THE BOOK OF WATERS

The Boy Who Was Found

1807

The boy grew. Sebastien Trovato—man in miniature, carried from the canals out to the far-flung isles of the lagoon. A world away and yet so close.

Named for a saint of soldiers, for an army he would never command, a life he would never have, by a family he would never meet.

A month passed. A year, and then more. Sebastien grew and he grew, a most ordinary boy with a most ordinary childhood, learning at the knee of his parents, building his skill to one day grow into a man and step into his role in the family business.

Only—there was one thing very unordinary about him. He did not have a family business. He had five. He did not have one parent, or two, as others did. He had five.

"Who are we to say which of our trades will be his?" Giuseppe had posed his question like a proclamation, in all his passion. "We are the ones who Venice delivered him to. We are the ones who shall raise him! Every one of us. Is he not an exile in his own young right? And have we not sworn, with our very lives and livelihoods, to aid such? We have done so for strangers, time and again. A month here, a rendezvous there, all for those in need of asylum. Can we not do the same for the boy over the course of his whole life? Is it not what Venezia did so long ago for our forefathers?"

Elena had been reluctant to embrace this idea in its entirety, for the boy had dwelled on her island and in her heart for his youngest years. He'd plunged his tiny hands into the soil alongside her since he was old enough to sit. Many were the times he funneled soil to mouth, only to have Elena fly in and snatch him up, lifting him to the sun and spinning him around. "Why eat mud, Sebastien, when you can fly amidst gold?"

Too small to understand her words, he understood well the warmth in her laugh and tossed his laughter back out, their voices mingling in a language with no words—only joy.

She would have been happy to keep him there, always. Beside her, tending the garden, bringing carrots, onions, leeks, and garlic to market, chinking cracks in their cottage. But even she had agreed, once he was older, that an education in all of their trades would serve him well. Indeed, he might well be the first Venetian in all of time to have his choice of artisan trade. In this land of guilds and oaths, where familial heritage and pride of a craft passed from father to son, a gilder's son was always a gilder; a glassblower's son was a glassblower. Kind after kind, time after time.

Until Sebastien.

So, his education began. In the summers, he lived upon the isle of Murano, where the glass was blown. Life was a kaleidoscope, lit by the Mediterranean sun through colorful glass in shop windows. Inside, inferno fires created that glass, trapping light in liquid form, keeping it for always. Sometimes a Visitor would be there, aiding the work of the forge in the back. Sebastien would hold the *parchoffi* or steady the yokes for Pietro, wide-eyed in tandem fear and wonder as glass entered the furnace, glistened molten as air was blown, given from earth to the smaller universe within the glowing, twisting bit of glass until it became a vase, a pen, a sculpture. But to Sebastien, the tiny worlds of air suspended within glass were the preservation of that moment incarnate. Born beside a fire and destined to be transported to another place far away. How, he wondered, could moments be transported so far, but he could not?

But in this he was consoled, for though he did not travel far, he did travel farther than most. There were many who were born on a Venetian isle, toiled upon that Venetian isle, and entered their eternal rest upon that Venetian isle without ever setting foot on the other islands dotting the lagoon, much less the city itself. They would leave only to claim their resting place on the newly declared burial isle of San Michele, there to stay, always.

But Sebastien moved, like one of the migrating birds, each season.

In the autumn, he spent his days and nights tucked into Valentina's Burano home. In the street outside, colorful houses lined up in rows, colors radiant enough to rival Elena's summer bouquets. Elena brought him, clutching his young hand in one of hers and one of her famed bouquets in the other, and tucked him in his first night there with stories of adventures that awaited him in this place of quiet and light and lines.

"So many lines, Sebastien!" She whispered it like it was a grand secret. The men taking their spools to the sea and casting lines there, the women taking their spools up with deft hands in an art that whispered over the island. Where one could nearly hear the needles murmur, swift and sure, weaving threads of precious silver and gold into *punto in aria* —points in the air.

The craft was a mystery to Sebastien. He watched Valentina's fingers fly as if they played the notes of a silent symphony she knew by heart. Out came the spinning of something as delicate as a spider's web, but with form and pattern to rival the domes of St. Mark's. The closest he ever came to it was when he was entrusted with a length of it to deliver to Elena in Valentina's kitchen. Ten steps and no more, where he handed it over and watched, wide-eyed, as Elena folded the risen dough of a bread loaf over it.

"Stop!" his young voice said, troubled that this work of Valentina's, which he had witnessed her toil late nights over, was to be laid waste in such a way.

"Do not be troubled," Elena said, kneeling and taking his hands.

"The lace is . . . like a letter. The stitches and shapes, they hold certain meaning. It has a very dangerous journey ahead to make it to the family who awaits word from their father. The bread will be—" She furrowed her brow. "It will be a safe way for it to reach them. And Valentina has worked magic." Her eyes sparkled. "After it has delivered its message, this family may sell it and eat well for a long time to come!"

"All because of lace?"

Elena nodded. "Food . . . from thin air! Valentina is a magician, no?"

"Look, Sebastien," Valentina called him back over to view her new work. "When it is finished, it is bound for the finest palazzo on the Grand Canal, and you shall never see it again." She wore a smile and leaned in, her aging voice infusing the name with magic, indeed: "*Ca'Fedele.*"

She told how it was not one palace, but two. How the first was built five hundred years before. How two hundred years later, another grew up, brick by brick beside it, so close they shared a wall. How the family of the tall house—the second one—wished for more room, only to realize what every good Venetian knew: space in the city of stitched-together islands was precious. They could not sprawl outward, lest they fall into the canal. They could not reach farther upward, for they had gone as high as they could without taxing the ancient poles creating the island beneath them. So? They had looked at that fine, wide palazzo next door, only knee-high to them, if theirs had been a man.

"Waist-high," a voice scoffed. Giuseppe had stopped in for a repast, as he often did while out fishing. "At least!"

"Waist-high to a short man like you, Gio," Valentina had conceded, being rewarded with his laugh before carrying on with her tale. The owners of the newer palazzo asked if they might build upon the empty space above the waist-high house—*palace,* they called it, so as to avoid offending the very fine family whose favor they would need. Permission was granted with a handful of stipulations:

A certain sum.

A contract, signed and witnessed, that no marriage would ever take place between the descendants, lest the two palaces become one, and they forfeit the benefit of two voting noble families.

A demolishing of the wall between their gardens, that they might together boast the largest private garden in the republic.

And the *sotoportego*, a walkway tunneling through the ground floor from the canal side to the garden behind the palazzo, that any of either family's visitors might share in the enjoyment of those expansive gardens.

Thus the two palazzi had stood, time without end, until "the dark days," as Valentina called them.

"What happened then?"

She had patted his hand, smile gentling even as the heat of the fire snapped through her rigid movements. "Never you mind, my boy. You'll not set foot there, though our work shall, and I hope it does you proud. They are very good customers, *la famiglia Fedele*. The master enjoys spoiling his young sister."

They were stories of another world, but Sebastien did enjoy hearing them. To Valentina, he tried to be of help, keeping the fires burning and the lights bright for her stitching and weaving. But Valentina often ushered him out the door after a time, where he would inevitably amble his way down to the docks, to a small boat, and row himself the short distance to Torcello. Here he would enter the Assunta and turn slowly, taking in the myriad mosaics that adorned the cathedral.

It was empty in so many ways—this most aged structure known to the lagoon. Bits of it were gone, the crowds it once knew vanished since plagues of the past drove them away. He did not know all of the stories these walls had seen, though they were themselves adorned in story. Mosaics composed of a million broken pieces depicted scenes he knew not how to decipher. The domed apse above him, gleaming in gold, caught the light upon the thousand edges in a way that made it seem moving and alive—so different than if it had merely been painted solid gold.

It was the brokenness, he realized, that caught the light. And its emptiness seemed to await him. Could it be that such a place held as much purpose for a solitary soul as it had for the masses who had passed through it in the ages before him?

On the island also stood an ancient stone seat, perfect for perching upon and watching the clouds.

Valentina laughed heartily when he told her of this practice. "Watching the clouds from the Throne of Atilla!" She shook her head. "Imagine." And then her voice grew earnest, and he couldn't tell whether she jested. "Take care, young Sebastien. One does not wish to follow in the footsteps of such a tyrant."

Giuseppe said it was "hogwash," that the dreaded attacker of their ancestors never set foot on the isle. That it belonged to some governor or bishop, and that there was none better to sit in a place of authority than "our Sebastien."

In the winters, Sebastien left the outer-flung *isolas* and dwelled by three hearth fires: Novembers with the monks of San Lazarro, apprenticed in a fashion to learn the printing presses they operated. Decembers—and quiet Christmases—with Dante, who dwelled in the Campo Sant'Agostin, tucked into his shop where he printed books and letters, things of great import and occasionally even intrigue for the people of Venice.

There was a peculiar magic in Dante's home. The smell of ink and wood, paper, and the sense that invisible ideas pushed against the walls to be let out. This was the alchemy of printing, Sebastien learned. The harnessing of intangible worlds, ideas that could change the course of history and affect lives two or ten generations from now. The lining up of letters, the rolling of ink, the pressing of paper—and *presto!* The intangible worlds and invisible ideas left their shop in the form of books and memorandums. There was a span of time he even heard the world-changing click and slide of the press late into the night, weeks on end, during the month that a Visitor had made camp in Giuseppe's attic room in Cannaregio and wrote for hours and days at a time sequestered away there. Dante brought the man's papers home by the armful and worked them through his press only by night.

Other evenings, they were joined by a silence that seemed so full, for the man was thinking, always thinking. Often with his eyes resting on the boy. "Come," he would say sometimes. "Let's meet with Galileo." And they would climb the stairs of the building, past Dante's ever-present collection of colorful paints in jars, until they arrived in a tiny attic where an old telescope lived. A trapdoor in the ceiling, painted long ago with a scene of the constellations, opened to the roof above. Dante crouched, let Sebastien climb upon his shoulders until he touched the stars of the fresco and pushed the panel free. He clambered up to the red-tiled roof, reached back down to pull up the telescope, attempted to raise it quietly, and, without fail, caused a clang in the effort as it collided with an edge. Dante then pulled himself up, and together they watched the stars.

"Imagine," he said. "People all over the world, looking at the same sky, even now. Scholars and students. Boys on ships away at war, fighting Napoleon. Even Galileo—see?" He pointed across the skyline, where the peak of the *campanile* in St. Mark's Square was just visible. "That is where he first demonstrated this wonder—" He touched the telescope. "Right in that tower, so many years ago. Note that tower well, Sebastien. It was built for keeping watch over oceans . . . and became an ascension to the stars. A person never knows how far their life might reach." He paused, deep in thought, as he often did. "Courage keep, and hope beget . . . the story is not finished yet."

He did this sometimes. Slipped into rhyme, as if to record for Sebastien, somehow, the things he could not write down for the boy. Dante, Sebastien would learn, had good reason to be often thinking. He was a man of highest intellect and deepest heart, with nowhere for those two strong threads of twining thought to go. For the man of letters . . . could not read and could not write. It was a deliberate choice, essential for his livelihood. He could set letters with greatest care and had a steady flow of customers, for there were those who wished their printer not to know the contents of their missives and manifestos.

So Dante had a world within him, a universe without him, and no bridge between the two except for Sebastien, who had learned at the knees of the monks to decipher letters. A secret he would not tell, for fear of harming Dante's business. He could lay the letters, ink them, and run the shop, even while Dante was sometimes long away on other errands. What those errands were, he did not know. They took large portions of his days, but he sometimes brought home delicious foods to lay across their table, already cooked, and that was answer enough for Sebastien. Meals over which Dante would regale him with tales and rhymes. For though the man could not read or write, he made magic of words.

"Ancient waters, secrets keep, of *rios* long and places deep. Hear them ring in kindest dreams, let them sing you off to sleep." He spoke the simple lines over Sebastien each night, the whimsy of the words taking on gravity in the man's deep timbre. Dante taught them to the others as well, that Sebastien might have at least the same spoken lullaby, no matter which bed he slept in.

Februaries were Giuseppe's, the gondolier whose strong grip had first pulled him from the waters. The winters were heavy and quiet, with visitors staying far away until finer weather. To atone for this shift, Giuseppe moored his gondola and took to the lagoon in his *sandolo*, the trusty fishing boat. Traded in his traditional gondolier attire of striped shirt and black hat for the fisherman's cap and *galosse* for his feet, Sebastien in charge of bringing the blanket and the sail. Sometimes they brought an extra blanket, to sleep the night out upon the lagoon. Sometimes they returned to Venice for encampment in Giuseppe's flat. But always, the man took with him his song and his passion.

"Fish are freedom!" Giuseppe loved to exclaim with vehemence. "They stink to the heavens and dwell in a slimy flesh, and I declare to you, young Sebastien, that there is no more angelic creature in all of God's creation." Sebastien used to wrinkle his nose at the description, but now he knew what was coming next and would jump in to finish Giuseppe's discourse. "Fish are food! Fish are freedom! Coin in your pocket, that you might walk proud and free. Whatever the soldiers might think." This last bit with derision, spitting into the lagoon in the general direction of Austrian soldiers patrolling the Lido, which was the outermost isle, a long strip of land that played barrier between lagoon and sea.

Giuseppe would send him off with a bushel full of that scaly freedom in the spring, when he continued his migration.

Spring. The season of home, for this was when he returned to Elena's isola. An island where she and her chickens were the only residents. A veritable Eden, the foliage lush in thanks for the woman's constant care. Here, stepping upon the quiet shore was like one great exhale. Here, Elena waited with a smile that grew deeper with each year. To the cattail forest that once towered over him by heads and shrank, somehow, each year he returned. To the saltwater creek that escaped the lagoon and snaked to the center of the isle, carrying a boy upon his stick-constructed raft too many times to count, until it flowed straight into the heart of an ancient and ruined abbey.

Elena and Sebastien kept those walls well hidden in trees, with extra vines and shrubbery planted all around as well. They did not want the soldiers to commandeer it, as they had so many other of the former abbeys and monasteries, claiming them as outposts and arsenals. True, there would be little for them to claim—only a handful of decrepit walls, and a few vestiges of times past. But they wouldn't risk it.

With Elena, he did not turn glass, nor stoke fires, nor ink letters, nor guide rudders. Here, he learned the earth. To keep the island, to guard its history, which crumbled by the year at the heart of it in those hidden ruins. He learned to grow carrots and tame weeds, feed sheep and herd chickens—if chickens could ever be herded. He dug and built miniature canals in a marshy corner of the ruins. His own kingdom of mud, with a humble bowl given by Elena, used for sculpting palaces and creating mountains, wondering about the people who lived in such far-off places.

Elena's work was that of life-keeping. Treading paths that others, long before Sebastien, had treaded. Many *metres* below stood poles—or piles—pounded deep into the soft marshy earth and packed in tight next to one another, making strong ground to build upon where once there had been only silt, water. This walking upon earth upon trees bound by mud . . . and thinking, too, of the ones who would one day come after them here.

Sebastien's heart began to beat for this place. For a few years, when he bumped along into the upper reaches of boyhood, where soul dreamed big, form grew lanky, and spirit ran free in the dregs of childhood, the island became so familiar to him that parts of it became ordinary, invisible.

Piece by piece, he spent mornings building a boat of the remnants left by those lives before him. An old floor plank, a planed piece of driftwood, the pieces that remained from his boyhood raft, a broken oar from Giuseppe, a storm-tossed signpost. The lagoon brought him the pieces, and he assembled them together until one day, he had a boat and could row the full circle of the island and greet the shadow of his younger self, who had relished walking that same circumference.

When the boat was complete, an entire universe opened unto him—the lagoon. He grew to know it as a friend, to love it. To walk upon it in winter when it froze, to swim within it in summer. It was his homeland.

The lagoon was flung not only with islands, but also with thick poles, protruding tall from the surfaces, as if a giant dwelling in the sky had tossed spears down in hunt of fish and left them there. They lined up in watery avenues, marking for the ships the deep places, warning them of the shallows.

Sebastien rowed these, weaving among them, wading those shallows until he had found a long-disappeared island just below the surface, where old foundations rose rough beneath his feet as water sloshed around his ankles. Where an altar—little more than a wooden box sitting atop a post akilter from one too many storms—lay abandoned. In times past, some had erected such water altars in tribute for the island's namesake. And now, with no island, what purpose did the water altar serve? Was faith so easily forgotten? Abandoned?

. . . as he had been?

A question driven further when one day, on his rowing journey, he discovered an inlet that led to that stream he had floated long ago upon his raft, and rowed again into the heart of Elena's island, that old abbey. It came to life in a new way, in this new season. Beckoning him, echoing with stories long silent and songs unsung.

The rocky ruins became his private retreat—a place for the hard questions. A single place among all his many isles and homes that he could call truly his own. Here he would lie and watch the clouds, comparing them to the view from Atilla's throne. Imagine ways to one day rebuild this place, and all of the fallen places of the islands. How to do so despite the soldiers who patrolled the corners, crannies, and borders of this many-edged lagoon.

How one day, he might save the city that had once saved him.

It was a singular childhood, he gradually came to understand. When the *Festa del Redentore* happened in the city and he watched the other children go home after the fireworks, always to the same house, the same *sestiere*, the same parents, understanding sparked to life.

"Why do the other children not change homes?" He asked this, ten years old, of each of his homes and parents.

"Why, they are boring, that is all there is to it," Giuseppe had said. "Just think of it—your life was changed by a gust of wind and a matter of six meters! Bound for the orphanage, and trust Giuseppe, it is not the ideal life." Sebastien laughed, but his answer did not fill the growing void.

"They are not as lucky as you," Valentina had whispered her answer conspiratorially. "Only one roof to live under all your life? Imagine!" And she clicked her tongue and shook her head with pity. There was delight in her answer, and he felt it and knew the wealth she spoke of to be true, but the question dug farther inside him.

"They are surely jealous of you, Sebastien." "You are no ordinary child, Sebastien, and God above knew you needed no ordinary family." All of these, offered with eyes that shone with love, in the safety of walls that felt like home. Every one of them.

But it was only Elena who answered his question not with words, but with an embrace.

"Why do the other children not change homes?" he asked, just as he had with the others. And when her gaze beheld his and he saw a very deep longing in her unanswering face, he drew in cour-

72

age to ask the question that had rumbled around the very soul of him, but never found strength to be uttered.

"Who—" The word stuck in his throat. "Who am I?"

That was when she embraced him. Folded him in, held him fast. Not with words, but with an answer that seemed to grow deeper than words.

She held him long and tight. As if her arms might infuse an answer into him where words failed. As if by exuding strength, she might arm him for the answer that would one day come. She bent her head over his and kissed him, pressing her cheek upon the top of his head.

"It is a very worthy question," she said at last. Softly. As was her way in contemplative matters. "One that I know will not go away. Nor should it. I can only tell you that I will stand by your side as you grow, and I will help you search out that answer one day." She hesitated, then added, "But you may find, in time, that though your question is a very good and important one indeed, it is not the most important one of all. In the meantime, Sebastien . . . who are you? You are loved. You are *you*. You are full of good purpose. You were made for this, your time, and this, your life. There is none like you, and I see the fingerprints of a mighty and good, kind, loving God in your good, kind, loving soul. You are full of honor and goodness. There is no one in this world with such a big heart as you. I see it in the way you tend to each of us, always watching, always helping. You, Sebastien, are a man who loves well."

He grew uneasy beneath her shower of praise and shrugged a shoulder stiffly. "It's only the same thing you do for me," he said. "All of you."

"That is because you belong to us, and we belong to you— always. You came to us on a dark night, and we didn't know, then, how much we needed you. Each and every one of us. So when you feel lost, my love . . . remember—you are *found*."

His shoulders had slumped. "A foundling, I know," he said. He had heard the neighborhood children whisper as much about him during games of kick-the-ball on Burano.

"Foundling," Elena said, lifting her eyebrows. "A word that makes you seem only a creature by the wayside, taken pity upon. That is not your story, Mr. Trovato. And that is why we gave you the surname that we did. *Trovato*."

He nodded, hoping he seemed older. Sticking his chin out, hoping he seemed braver. "Many of the orphans have that name. I understand."

"We gave you that name not because you were an orphan, but because of the story it told. One of great treasure, whom any of us would do anything for. Do you recall, Sebastien, the parable of the merchant searching after fine pearls? He found the most precious and valuable one of all and gave everything he had to make it his own. *Found* means someone was searching for you, running after you. You, the greatest treasure in all the world. *That* is what *Trovato*—Found—means. Sebastien Trovato, you are Found. Always and forever. Gathered up into Giuseppe's great big arms and carried into our hearts from that moment on."

Sebastien didn't entirely understand her answer. He wanted to. Could feel how much it meant, in the fullness of her voice, the way her eyes brimmed. But he knew enough to know that the comfort her voice gave was wrapping around him, wrapping his unanswered questions with promise and home and a safe place to land, if not with all of the answers themselves. Whether those answers would have been better, he did not know. And as the mysteries surrounding his life grew right alongside him in a quiet place deep within, so, too, did Elena's allusion that there was more to his search than just one question.

Perhaps that was why she did not tell him, in that moment, what she believed the most important question to be. Perhaps she knew that it, too, would nestle like a spark, offering the warmth of promise, taking the edges off of the unknown, and making the land of unanswered things a place less formidable.

Whatever the case, the night she spoke these words to him, he lay upon the old stone table in the middle of the roofless, ivy-covered ruins. The plucky wending vine felt like a companion somehow, some living thing to keep him company until something—or someone—else arrived. An as-yet shapeless being he had the distinct conviction that he was created for. It had him often watching the shores, searching strangers' faces in the city, wondering, *Is it you?*

As he looked at the ageless and knowing stars above and listened to the steady ribboning song of the stream beside him, it was very strange that Elena's answer to his question was the one that brought the most peace—and yet it gave birth to so many new questions.

Far across the lagoon, he could hear the midnight bell ring out from St. Mark's campanile. Slow, steady, mournful as it presided over the shift of today into yesterday, and tomorrow into today. Burying lost hopes, summoning fresh ones. With each toll, his question rang out across those waters:

Dong . . .

. . . *Who am I?*

Dong . . .

. . . *Who am I?*

From that night on, his life marched to the beat of unanswered questions. He went on stoking Murano fires and walking the colorful hush of Burano streets, tracing nonsense maps in gossamer lace, marbling bookend pages, and inking letters to press.

And always, in the distance or all around him, the city rose from the sea in a hundred and more fragmented pieces, cobbled together with bridges and boats.

I am like you, Venice seemed to say. A patchwork life, whole and yet broken.

7

DANIEL

VENICE, ITALY
FEBRUARY 1904

ho am I?

W Sebastien Trovato's question knocked around inside me with the rhythmic clack-clack-clack of the train. I couldn't tell who he was, either. Man? Myth? True account or Venetian fable? The translation was slow going and had helped the time pass on the voyage. But the more I dove into the work, the more the story gripped me.

My eyes narrowed, taking in the sights outside the train window with an intensity that would, I hoped, burn them into memory. Islands, packed with shrubbery up to the very place where they dropped into the sea. *Lagoon*, I corrected. Smaller islands, bare of anything but mud. A fisherman, his boat rocking to the side when he leaned to pull in a catch, victory written on his weathered face. And in the distance—Venice. Rising like a fistful of jewels from her watery surrounding: domed cathedral roofs, red bell tower campaniles spearing the sky, and architecture woven into lace from brick and stone against the coral sky above.

Such a vivid scene, and yet the old void greeted me with darkness when I closed my eyes and tried to summon the scene. And still, I would do things right this time.

"*Sei un medico?*" An older woman, dark hair twined with white and braided over her shoulder, spoke from the opposite seat. She gestured at the black bag on the seat beside me.

The language was music, its rolling stretches and punctuating peaks like warmth from a better time. I'd grown up with the jaunty melody of Italian in the neighborhood, and while Venetian was similar, there were slight variations that met the ears with a lift of surprise.

I was not a doctor, and told her so. She smiled brightly in question, an invitation to explain myself. How to answer . . . thief? No. Artist? Not really, no. There was no simple explanation for me.

She tilted her head.

"Just a . . . traveler." I winced, realizing I'd forgotten to translate. "*Solo un viaggiatore.*"

"American, no?" she said, her accent drawing out the words. "What brings you to La Serenissima?"

The Most Serene City. The name rose up before me like scrolling gates sent to keep the riffraff away. What brought me to such a place? Outrunning the past. Embarking on a mission I had no business embarking on. Looking for a lost thing in a city with more secrets than history could count.

"I'm here on behalf of my employer," I said, and still couldn't believe the truth of it. I explained briefly about the Venice of America, and Mr. Wharton's mission to procure original books and sketches.

"Ah. Good! There is much to see and remember in Venice." She began pointing at sights out the window as we approached. Our view just now was limited mostly to the farther-scattered isles, but she knew them each by name, like a mother with her children.

"San Segondo." She pointed to a diminutive and forgotten place, where the ruins of what looked to be a military fort stood in exhausted guard. "Isola Campalto." She gestured toward an isle emerald green and bursting in foliage bent on escaping its island bounds. "Murano you will have heard of, with the glass blowers.

You will of course see it." I thought of the colorful glass menagerie at home, Mother running those streets there as a young girl, and something quickened inside.

Another island lurked in the distance, where a mist seemed to beckon it away from the city. Her eyes settled on it for a moment, and she shifted in her seat but said nothing.

"And that one?" I asked. Something about it drew me—the way its trees cast blurred shadows into the lagoon, the way it stood like an undiscovered thing beyond these friendly islands with names.

"We do not speak of that one very often," she said, infusing false lightness into her voice. "It once had a true name. Now we call it only—" she hesitated, lowering her voice—"*Malodetto*."

I shook my head slowly. "I'm afraid I don't know that word."

She looked to the aisle of the train, then leaned in, whispering, "Doomed. Or rather—cursed. A very dark history, there." She straightened up, shaking off the chill in her voice and returning to her warm way. "You will have much to see elsewhere, anyway. *Benvegnù!*" she said, and I noted that her welcome differed slightly from the typical Italian *benvenuto*.

I smiled my thanks and let my gaze drift back to the isle of Malodetto, where its reflection now shivered over evening waves.

The train began to slow as it approached the platform. The isle of Santa Lucia—once a convent and church according to the travelogue, now a bustling depot with trains coming and going all the day long. The train squealed and huffed, steam releasing into the air, mingling with the ghosts of evening vespers long silent.

Exiting, I brushed the travel from the suit I wore. I could not bring myself to call it my suit, for I felt entirely an impostor in it. But Mr. Wharton had insisted that if I was to represent the company and the future Venice of America, I had best do it "looking sharp."

I unfolded the typed itinerary he had prepared for me, with the name of my quarters stamped in crisp black ink: San Giorgio Maggiore.

The platform blurred with people—visitors speaking English, French, an entire symphony of languages. Dressed in laces and hats, with canes and monocles. Merchants hoisting crates and traversing the planks quickly. I turned, just in time to see one of those crates come straight at my chest.

Twist, I could hear the voice of Emilio hiss at me in a whispered memory. The name of one of our heist schemes. He may not have been a shining moral example to me, but when my father found himself locked away in the military citadel on Alcatraz, Emilio, five years my senior, had stepped in as what he presumed to be patriarch, at least among the passel of cousins who darted about our neighborhood. What was more, he named his schemes in a way I could understand, after listening to me drone on about books every week at dinner. This—the collision—would have been the perfect circumstance to pickpocket like Oliver Twist.

Old instincts sprang to the ready, and though I had no intention of acting on them, I made to assess the location of the collision culprit's trouser pockets—and saw instead a skirt. Blue, much deeper than the turquoise lagoon, dusty at the hem, pooling as the young woman stooped to gather her fallen cargo.

"Let me help," I said. The rehearsed words coming out, but this time I offered them in earnest. No plan of securing trust in order to rob the target.

A string of foreign words began, and while the cogs of my rusty translation machine inside my brain could not keep up at that speed, the tone of urgency was universal. She plucked fallen items from around her—books in muted hues of blue, green, deep red, all laying among splayed straw. She seemed not to register my presence, and I stooped to help. Unsure how to communicate as her diatribe continued, I stacked books silently, then reached to secure them in the wooden crate, where straw packed the gaps for what appeared would be a journey ahead.

She reached in, too, and seemed to register my presence for the first time.

"*Uffa!*" she exclaimed, hand flying to her heart. She stared, her eyes warm brown, framed by dark curls that had come loose from her braid.

I, too, froze—caught in a moment with trains and people on

the move, she and I in the eye of a storm, there upon a platform and vespers of ages past.

I forced myself back to the present and eased my books into her crate. "I'm sorry," I said, hoping my expression might convey my apology. "*Mi dispiace.*"

She placed the last of the books in the crate with a thud, sliding a folded scrap of paper from beneath one and looking at it, perplexed.

That paper, worn and minuscule as it was, was mine.

"You are American," she said, slipping into accented English and eying me warily. "Your accent, you know. Thank you. But I must go, these books, they are to be on the next train to Verona, and I am already behind—"

Her words coincided with the departure anthem of the train down the platform, chuffing to life in a cloud of steam.

The girl scrambled to her feet and began to run. "*Fermarsi! Aspettare!*"

I picked up the crate and ran after her, but the train had no care for the unlikely duo we formed. It grew smaller and quieter as it left the station, bound for the mainland.

My partner in crime—or rather, in train-chasing—let a hand fly to her forehead, shoulders rising and falling in defeat and disbelief.

I stood a few paces behind, waiting. Not wishing to intrude, but knowing I was the reason she was in whatever predicament this was.

The platform was oddly still now, with passengers having dissipated and no running trains awaiting movement. For the first time, I heard the sounds of Venice. Waves, lapping a gentle welcome. Bells, from many directions, as if they spoke to each other from across the city.

"Miss?" I said at last. "Is there somewhere I can take these for you?"

She turned, surprised. "You are still here?" Her dark brows furrowed over delicate features.

"They look important," I said. "The gilding . . . And some of these pages have never been scored." I ran my hands over the deckle-edged pages, where some had been torn open by letter opener to be read, and others held fast their secrets like treasures.

Her look of puzzlement deepened. "You know books?"

"You might say that." I did not often speak of myself and books. It didn't make sense to people. "I'd be happy to carry these for you," I said. "It's the least I could do."

The phrase seemed not to carry meaning, and I wondered if it was unique to English. "I am sorry," I offered instead. "For running into you. I should've been paying more attention."

"I am at fault," she said. "Always I am running, and always they are saying, 'Stop running, Vittoria!' And always I promise I will be better, plan better, and not have to run, but I—"

I tried to stifle a smile. She had slipped into conversation with herself, and I was a mere spectator. I eased back on my heels a bit, ready to take in the full performance.

She noticed. "There I go again, only this time it is my mouth that is running." She gave a sheepish smile. "What was your question?"

"Can I carry these somewhere for you? I owe you that, at least."

She dismissed the thought with a wave of her hand. She seemed to speak with her hands too. She was something entirely new, this Vittoria.

"No need," she said.

I faltered. How to ask for a scrap of what looked to be rubbish? "The, um, paper . . ." I nodded at the slip in her hand. She seemed to recognize its presence for the first time.

She seemed to be biting back a retort—something assured and indignant, perhaps, about being perfectly able to dispose of garbage on her own.

"It's—it's mine," I said. Holding my gaze, she slowly handed it back. Tension eased from across my back, and it was ridiculous. But I could almost hear the whisper of pencil marks in a confined space, how they had been for so long the lone voice of hope. I tucked the paper into my jacket, deep inside an inner pocket, and thanked her.

"Are you sure I can't help?" I gestured at the crate. "I've read

that the city is difficult to traverse, and if it would be a help, I . . ."
How to finish that? I tried not to listen to the sparse collection of
change and bills in my pocket, crying out in protest. The suit they
dwelled in bespoke wealth, but it was only a whitewashed tomb, an
empty advertisement. I could hire a gondola, but with my financial
constraints, I was destined for the more public transportation of
the *vaporetti*, the water buses. I swallowed my pride. "I would be
privileged to pay your way on the vaporetto."

She laughed. "You did read correctly. But walking this city is as
natural to my feet as breathing air is to my lungs."

"You mean running."

She tilted her head in question.

"You said walking. I think you meant running."

The corner of her mouth attempted a smile, but she stopped it
quickly. She reached out and took the crate from my hands. With
very measured, slow movements, she moved past me.

"I mean"—she took two very pronounced steps—"walking.
You would do well to hire a gondola for your own self, though,"
she said. "La Serenissima, she will swallow you up into her alleys
and never let you go."

She kept her measured pace as she disappeared down the platform, her speed picking up until she stumbled. I lunged as if I could
close the space and catch her, but she righted herself and refused
to look back, resuming her harnessed walk until, at last, she was
gone. Vanished into the sea of red roofs and shadowed places.

A book lay open on the ground where she'd stumbled, its pages
riffling in the breeze as if to summon me. I picked it up, tucked it
into my jacket, and determined to find a way to do right by this
one, at least.

And then it was just me and Venice. The thief and the jewel
of the Adriatic.

What an adventure this would be.

8

February cloaked Venice in a suspension of opposite things. The odd snowflake falling through a shaft of warm-hued light. Canals that once bustled and brimmed with boats were now laced with a hovering air of expectancy that the whole city was waiting, holding her breath for something imminent on the horizon. The roll of waves, tossing light back upward here, there, then again pinging its way back and forth in the upward avenues of buildings.

In all of this, Venice ushered me into another time, a timeless place of brick and water, every corner sculpted into story and meaning.

The buildings sidled up to one another, seaming themselves together. Standing so close they gave the impression of a choir, shoulder-to-shoulder. Some leaning slightly, some holding their choirmates up with a steady stance, all with eyes wide and mouths agape in the form of arched doorways and windows. What song they sang, I could not tell, but it was one that echoed back and back, making me feel minuscule—a sensation to which there was a strange peace.

I was thoroughly outside myself. Where I was accustomed to the steep rise and fall of San Francisco hills, here the streets were water, flat stretches that only rose with the tide. And where the most aged building I'd ever seen in America was no more than a century old, here every palazzo and cathedral was hundreds, if not thousands, of years old. They looked upon me like sages condescending to notice the infant who now attempted to breathe their same air.

Venice was a paradox.

The captain of the vaporetto eyed me warily, and that wariness traveled up and down my suit in search of something. His forehead furrowed deeper after his assessment.

"You are American," he said.

It seemed a statement, but his silenced stretched.

"Yes," I responded at length.

"And that is a very fine suit!" His face, so animated it might well have been another passenger, lifted in happy approval.

"Thank you," I said, unsure how to respond to him. I knew I could be stone-faced to a fault. I tried to take his cues and summon some expression to my own face with a smile that felt forced and awkward. And no wonder, for my face—my soul, too—was very much out of the practice of smiling.

The boat plowed slowly through gentle waves, and he returned his gaze to them. "Forgive me my confusion," he said. "But the foreigners, the ones dressed so fine like you, they do not often ride the vaporetti from the train station." He removed a hand from the helm and gestured affectionately at his ferry. With great feeling, he continued, "Do we have the room for them? *Sì!*" He raised a finger to punctuate his point, then returned it to the wheel. "Do I know Venezia and does she know me? Sì! She raised me!"

His treatise continued, and I listened hard to try and find my place in all of this. "I know her better than any of the gondoliers splashing about these canals like so many minnows. Are my seats fit for the Doge himself?" He raised his hand, as if to punctuate with his finger once more, but froze. "*Forsi forse.*" He flattened his hand and tilted it back and forth in a "maybe" motion. "But it is the gondolas, the gondolas, always and always the gondolas, which they must take."

He blew out his cheeks and shook his head, then pulled a conspiratorial smile with a sideways glance. "But they always find me," he said. "You will see. When their coins grow quiet in their pockets, they will ride Vaporetto Line Two." He spoke with pride.

"And see what they have been missing. It happens to them all, especially the young men. You are on the Grand Tour, yes? But you are traveling with very little! The young men on the tour, they come with trunks and servants, and they may as well bring an army! Napoleon certainly did!" He laughed dryly. "And he took away with him the heart of this great city—or so he thought. But he did not know us, did he?"

Again, I didn't know how to answer, but I was learning the man did not require much from me in the way of conversation. Indeed, it seemed he had raised himself internally to a boil, the pleasant but vehement popping of bubbles escaping in the form of words.

"Ah." He swatted away the word like a fly. "But we are long done with Napoleon. You haven't come for history lessons, yes?"

"Yes."

"Yes?!" Up went the lines on his forehead.

"Well, not precisely, but I wouldn't mind—"

Again he waved. "You are right. A new century has begun, and you are here to see it, young man. Not our history books." He assessed me again, and this time one brow furrowed, while the other rose in tentative approval.

"I am Jacopo," he said, and offered a grin that seemed to seal us as friends. "And what is your name?"

"Daniel," I said. "Daniel Goodman."

At this, he flung his face to the evening sky and released a laugh rolling with gravel and gusto.

My face burned, and I was thankful again that there was no one else aboard. I knew the irony of my last name, but how could this man know . . . ?

"Daniel!" he said, and this time his punctuating finger jabbed in my general direction. "In the city of lions!" His laugh waned as he shook his head, though his grin remained.

"I'm afraid I don't take your meaning," I said.

"Look around you, Daniel Goodman. There—" He pointed at a door knocker as we passed it, shaped like a lion with the gold ring hanging formidably from its mouth. "And there." He slowed as we passed a statue in a courtyard—*campo*, I'd learned—a pair of lions stood guard at each side of an iron gate. One of them had his mouth open, a most formidable mail slot.

"And . . ." The man lifted his chin toward a bridge, where a scarlet flag hung from its railing. The flag was stitched in gold to depict a winged lion, sword raised in his great paw. The fabric rustled a caution as we approached, the tassel-like ends of it rippling one after another like fingers.

Despite myself, I gulped.

"Ha! It is alright, Daniel Goodman. Remember the fate of Daniel, after all. And I think you will find that your name is a most loved name in our city too. But all in good time, for there is much to learn here. Venice is history come alive! So. Daniel Goodman." He said my last name as if it were two words—*good man*. It fell as a reminder that this was a chance to live up to that name for once. "Where are all of your trunks?"

I cleared my throat, looking at my lone black bag, which contained all my worldly possessions. "This is it."

He released a low whistle. "You are like the monks, then. Is that why you wish to stay with them?" He knew my destination was the island of San Giorgio Maggiore, where an ancient monastery would be my home for the next month. "What other call has brought you to our most serene city?"

I cleared gravel from my throat and shaped the unfamiliar word into life: "Business."

"You are a . . . let me think . . . banker?"

I shook my head, holding back a dry laugh at the irony of that.

"An ambassador, then."

Again, no.

We entered a stretch of wider sea—or canal, rather. "The Giudecca Canal," he explained. "It separates Venice from your monastery island, and beyond that? The open lagoon." He nearly whispered the last three words, infusing the expanse surrounding the city with a sense of mystery not naturally belonging to the word *lagoon.* "Now. If you are not a banker or an ambassador, you must be a writer. They are a strange breed, you know." He rounded his dark eyes as if describing a fabled sea creature that occupied the deeps. He assessed me up and down again, then gave a decisive nod. "Your Mark Twain was here not so very long ago."

I laughed. "I'm no Mark Twain. And I'm no writer." I had read Mr. Twain's account of this place and was having trouble reconciling what I saw to his description of a place without poetry, needful of the moon to cover over its blemishes.

The buildings were old, certainly, and parts of them stained as Twain said. But the scars bore tales, and the tales bespoke depth. It held more than poetry. It held . . . hope.

Jacopo's impassioned love for the city depicted a place very much alive. "So, what do you do here, then?"

"I'm here to find a book on my employer's behalf. And I'm . . ." I hesitated, feeling every bit the imposter. "I'm here to make likenesses of some of the views around Venice." I couldn't call myself an artist. Perhaps someday. But for now, I was just a man with a pencil, some spare change for paints, and a second chance.

Jacopo did not share the same qualms. "An *artista*! Very good, and you wish to begin at the monastery? From there you can see across the Giudecca to San Marco Square, the Doge's Palace. You can watch the boats come and go." He named several of the places Mr. Wharton had listed for me to depict. But that wasn't why I was headed to San Giorgio Maggiore.

"The monastery is just . . . where I'll be staying." It was a deal more affordable than the fashionable hotels and palazzos typical of those on their Grand Tour.

"You are a paradox, Daniel Goodman," he said. "Very much like our city, I think. Something to impress on the surface, but mysteries within. Here you go." He handed me a rope matter-of-factly. He slowed the boat and a columned white building rose from the blue. "Your monastery. Come!" He crossed the threshold of the boat to the quayside and tied the rope, gesturing for me to follow.

The building towered high above me in a classical façade. It had a peaked roof like the American churches, but instead of a steeple, a tall, four-sided bell tower rose from somewhere behind the church. Even the ground beneath us was adorned, stonework laid out in an intricate, expansive latticework of grey and white.

I moved toward the columns and placed my foot tentatively on the first step.

"Psssst!" Jacopo hissed from somewhere to the right. "This is the door for you, Signor Goodman." I veered right, face heating at my mistake. Of course the gleaming church was not the building for me.

I approached where the white building joined with the stucco coral of the next building, plaster chipping and cracking away to reveal snatches of bricks beneath. The blue door opened slowly to Jacopo's knock, and a monk stood enrobed in a dark wool tunic, hood hanging down behind him.

Jacopo, bless him for his effort, attempted a more reverent volume, but his internal boil remained. He spoke in Venetian first, then in English, for my benefit. "This is your new man!" he said and held out an arm toward me as if to say, *behold!*

The monk looked at me. I looked at the monk. Both of us with a look of masked horror for the implications of Jacopo's words. We needed no translation. I raised a hand in an effort to show there was an explanation, that I was not freshly arrived to be transformed from the suited man of the world before him into a holy habit. This, I had practiced. "I am thankful for your hospitality," I said.

"Ah," the monk said, and with gentle creases around his smile offering welcome, he opened wide the door. Before I followed, Jacopo gripped my arm.

"You come and find me, young Daniel, when you need anything in this magnificent city. Jacopo knows!"

I nodded my thanks, and then stopped. "You don't happen to know about a girl—a young woman . . . ?" It wasn't likely, but I still felt I needed to make up for the fiasco on the platform. "She was . . . about this tall." I motioned slightly above my shoulder. "Long dark hair and—"

I couldn't picture her. I knew the facts of her, but that was as far as I could describe, other than that she had blown in like a bright place in my shadowed world and called herself something queenly. Elizabeth? Mary? "Victoria." It came to me. "I think that was her name." I was beginning to realize the foolishness of the question. "Never mind," I said. "It would be impossible to find her again."

"Ay, ay, ay," he said, shaking his head slowly. "Which is it that you do not understand? That Venice is one great village, or that Jacopo knows it all? We are like a garment, and the canals and *calli* are the stitches that bind us together. Every corner is its own world, every sestiere with its own flavor, but together, we are all Venezia. Come. Do tell me your question. If I do not have an answer, I will throw you into the canal this moment."

"You mean you'll throw your*self* in?" A brief image of Jacopo taking a swan dive floated in my imagination. "If you don't have the answer?" I knew it was a joke but felt the need to assure him there was no need.

"No. I stay above the canal waters. Do you know what is in them?" He waved a hand in front of his nose. "No? Consider yourself lucky." Jacopo was in the habit of answering his own questions. "I am not crazy." He swatted me with the back of his hand. "I mean what I say, and I say what I mean, Daniel. So speak!"

With little choice, I took my life in my hands and obeyed, praying the man would indeed have an answer and that this day wouldn't end with a tumble into the murky waters that, despite the glinting of sun upon waves, indeed held all manner of waste in its keep.

"Well . . . she would have been delivering a crate of books. And feeling very . . . passionate about them. She left one behind." I failed to mention that it was my fault, that I'd caused the girl to explode in a cloud of pages. I patted my inside jacket pocket, which happened to be sized to accommodate a book—a very particular book—but which also now housed the unfortunate casualty of the train station fiasco. I tried to think if there was any other way to describe her. Where my mind's eye was blind, I had begun to construct comparisons around things in an attempt to remember them by feeling, if not by image.

"She was sort of a—a gust of wind," I said.

He threw his head back and laughed. "Ha! *Vittoria*." He crowned her name with zest. "How is it you have already encountered the Garbin? I will take you to her tomorrow. The Number Two Line, remember." He tapped his head and turned. Engulfed in a cloud of monastic chanting that floated from within the cathedral, the man lumbered off with a swing in his step and a whistle on his lips to his empty vaporetto, while behind me, stone walls that had stood lifetimes longer than I had been alive waited to give me shelter.

Within the empty walls of my room, for the first time since I'd stood on the beach with Mr. Wharton, I stopped. Stopped moving, stopped this endless forward motion by boat or foot or train, always in pursuit of a looming destination. And yet now that I was here, now that I sat upon the simple straw mattress and watched the day's last breath filter in through the small window, I was overcome by the distinct sensation that this journey had just begun.

I pulled the scrap of paper from my pocket and, in the safety of solitude, opened it. I could almost hear the whisper of pencil scratches. One line each day, until they'd begun to form something. Some men kept tallies to mark the passage of time in the confines of their cells. I couldn't bear it—I already stared at bars all the day long. Why would I wish to draw them too?

And so, each day I'd etched a single mark, a single element of a scene that I could barely glimpse from my window, until it became a landscape. A beach that stretched on, disappearing around a bend, boundless and waiting. I set it on my windowsill now, rudimentary against the dazzling sunset outside. Waves lapped, as if applauding the paper's homecoming.

My bones ached to rest, and my body lay still in the simple bed, but my mind would not comply. Venice, in her tight tangle, seemed to beckon me to unravel some great mystery. I was skilled with locks, and knots, with entering forbidden places . . . but this was different.

I pulled out the only semblance of a key to this locked place that I had—the blue book of puzzle pieces. I set to work, scratching a pencil over a blank page as words took form and only deepened the mystery.

THE BOOK OF WATERS

La Famiglia Fedele

It came to pass, many years ago, that a certain noble family produced, at last, a doge. "The Doge," one might say, with all the venerated reverence the city's leader deserved. France might say, "The King," and England might say, "Her Royal Highness," but Venice had her Doge. A duke, a leader elected, who would lead with wisdom until the end of his days.

If a family had a doge in their bloodlines, or even better, two—or heaven be thanked, three!—you can be sure they would educate you upon this needful fact upon meeting you for the first time. "The first doge in our family was very keen on oranges," they might let slip handily. "Not like the other ones," they might add, and let you formulate your own royal mathematics.

But then there were the Zanettis. A family whose roots went back to the very founding settlers. La Famiglia Zanetti had Venezia in their very veins. They faithfully championed their noble peers and made discourse among the Great Council and yet never, not in the hundreds upon hundreds of years of Venice's reign, did they produce a doge.

When one must wait inordinately for something to happen, and then that much-awaited fate comes to pass at long last, it is relished, cherished, treasured, and more.

Paulo Zanetti, son of a son of a son of a son for generations back in

La Serenissima, was at last elected Doge. It was, indeed, a role relished, cherished, treasured, and more. So much more, in fact, that the title of Doge seemed to pale in comparison to that of the emperors, kings, and highnesses of the world.

Mocked at times by the peers he had so long served, whose fathers his father had upheld and championed, an idea sparked. What would Venice do under the rule of something more than a doge? Something more powerful, something not dependent upon the Council of Ten or even the Great Council?

What would Venice do . . . with a prince?

A plan was made. A coup d'etat. It would cost the lives of those peers, but it would be for the better, he thought.

The peers did not agree, when in the city of secrets and spies, his plan became known.

The peers, in short course, executed him. And what was more, in a city of veneration and remembrance . . .

They erased him.

DANIEL

I awoke amid a fog outside and a fog within. Heaviness lingered from the point of the tale where I'd laid down my pen. *Erased?*

A man's entire life, erased.

It was strange and yet unsettlingly familiar. Was I not attempting to erase parts of my own life? But no. They were spots that would not come out. I couldn't erase. I must atone. Find the original book. Translate. Copy likenesses of buildings. Something I could do. Get paid. And last . . . make things right.

Every time I recited these things in my head they formed like links of distant shackles, giving a phantom rattle. I welcomed it. Sebastien Trovato had his midnight bell to remind him of his question. Perhaps the jingle of my shackles could be my own anchoring anthem: *Atone.*

The water was cold as I splashed my face from the pitcher on my basin and tried to formulate a plan for how to do that. It all came back to this Book of Waters. I was beginning to learn that its lack of an ending wasn't the only thing profoundly puzzling about it. First, a baby on the water . . . now a traitor-king. *Doge*, I corrected myself. Scores of years apart, it seemed. Was it a book of fables? It certainly seemed the stuff of fairy tales.

But one look outside my window reminded me that I was standing upon an island that once never existed, in a land known for costumes and masques. A living pageant—or at least it once had been so.

Impossible to tell what was real here.

I opened my window, letting in a tumble of salt air. *That* was real enough, and the squawk of gulls pitching and diving was enough to shake me from my fog. Today's mission was both simple and ridiculously complex: *Find the missing original Book of Waters.*

I'd been sent with a list of libraries and private collections to start with, places to inquire. But as I shrugged into my jacket and felt the weight of the book from the train station in my pocket, a different idea took form.

Two ferry rides, an ill-fated venture into the wrong sestiere. Directions from two boatmen and one bemused seller of trinkets, and at last—two and a half hours later than I'd planned—I stared at my destiny. Time was kept by bells, not man, and I was beginning to suspect it was because man could not be ruled by time here.

I stepped from Jacopo's ferry onto the fondamenta and reached for my pocket to pay. Jacopo waved me off. "You don't pay," he said between his teeth and made to depart once more. He had other passengers, and his attempt to communicate subtly with exaggerated waggling of his dark brows was quite the show.

"But you deserve—"

"Ah!" He snapped his hand closed, like an animal clamping down upon prey. In this case, my words were the prey. Lines on his forehead rose, daring me to challenge him. "Are you the man in charge of this boat?"

"No, but I—"

"Mmm!" Again, the staccato noise cut me off.

"You do not pay, Daniel," he hiss-whispered. "You are too . . ." He shook his head, mumbling low words in Venetian that I didn't catch. Finally, he pushed out his lower lip and shrugged, as if he had made his point, and there were no adequate words to finish his sentence.

What was I? Too poor? How could he know. Too lost? So was every visitor here, by instruction of every travel guide in publication. *Lose yourself in the maze of the calli and canals,* they instructed. *For there you will find the heart of Venice.*

I realized my own brows were pushing in, in Jacopoean fashion. "You look like you've lost something," he said. "Those who search? Do not need to pay. It is my policy." He raised a hand as if releasing a bird.

"Since when has this been your policy?" I asked warily.

"Since now! Go. Go see the lady about the books. You will need your money there!"

I thanked him and looked to the right, the left, and in front of me where an aged black iron gate stood propped open, a vine clambering around its poles as if holding on for dear life.

"That way!" Jacopo hollered from yards down the canal, waving me into the gate.

I entered, studying the doors in the three walls surrounding the small courtyard. A well stood in the center, and a boy aged perhaps seven paddled a rubber ball up and down.

"Hello," I said. Then, continuing in Italian, "Do you know where the bookshop is?" He tilted his head, seeming to consider whether I was worthy of such information. At length, he finally pointed to another gate, in the far-right corner of the campo.

Thanking him, I proceeded, ducking beneath the low arch and entering an alley so narrow I had to turn sideways to fit, shuffling my way awkwardly through. Was this a trick? A passageway they sent unwanted imposters to, where a jailer awaited in the shadows at the end? I thought of the cells in the lead-ceilinged prison of the Doge's Palace, the Bridge of Sighs and all its lore of prisoners taking one last, mournful look at the city and sighing before being locked away for the rest of their days—or sent to a more sudden end. Like the doge from the book.

I shuffled faster. Something eerily soft alighted on my face and I sputtered, swatting away a cobweb or spider's web. Was it my imagination or did the walls grow closer as I neared the end? My feet sped, not willing to find out. The stones were rectangular, laid end to end, paralleling the walls and giving the disorienting impression that the lengths stretched ahead into distant, far-off endings. An ending I leapt toward as I neared it.

My face burned. I wasn't a child, and yet here I was, letting childish fears drive me. I faced the alley I had come from, certain that opening was narrower than the first had been. It hadn't been passed through in some time, judging by the webs clinging to my sleeves and ankles. Backing slowly away from the alley, I ran into something hard. I spun, readying my excuses for the jailer.

But the "jailer," it turned out, was only a lamppost, tall and flickering with last life. I looked around, finding myself in what looked to have once been a garden, though to which house I could never have guessed.

If this was the way to "find the heart of Venice," as the travel book indicated, then I wasn't sure I wanted to know where—or who—that shadowed heart was.

"Who . . ." a voice said, mellow and odd.

"Exactly," I muttered, then froze, searching for the source of the disembodied voice. Pinpricks traversed my spine, that distinct impression of being watched. A slow turn assured that I was indeed the only one in the campo, and yet that feeling at my back, whichever way I turned, remained.

But there was no one. The walls around the courtyard looked on from Byzantine windows, capped in their triplets of rounded ruffles reaching into peaks.

I rubbed a hand over my eyes. It was all this travel, the aching tangle of my mind as I hopped between languages and tried to find my land legs in a place built on sea. . . . I was just tired.

But I'd known tiredness before, a soul-tired that had once bound me to depths I hadn't known possible. And even there, fatigue had never manifested as imaginary voices. So, then, who . . . ?

"Who . . ." the voice said again, behind me.

I turned slowly, as if I could fabricate some camouflage.

There, a sign hung from an iron arm, which jutted out in scrolling metal to attach itself to the wall. It read, *The Second Story*

Bookshop. The pun, presumably intended for the steady stream of English-speaking visitors, greeted me like a friend, summoning something maybe even close to a smile. Beneath that, in scrolled, gold lettering, a name for the shop in its native language: *Libreria Grande.*

There, perched upon it like it was a branch in the middle of a forest, two yellow eyes drilled into my soul, round and unblinking.

I swallowed. The grey-feathered owl was ageless. Sage. Indignant that I dared to exist.

I had the sudden urge to apologize—or perhaps grovel?—beneath the scrutinizing gaze.

"Ss-sorry," I muttered and took a step back from his majesty the owl. Or *her* majesty?

A teal door marked the entrance, gothic in its peaked arch and with lines of rust running from rounded nail heads. A tin sign hung there, painted white with black letters, translating roughly to "We will return soon."

I tried the doorknob and found it locked. How soon, I wondered, was "soon" in Venice?

Near the lamppost in the center of the campo stood what must have once been a well. It didn't appear to be an operating one, a cover in place and its edges rounded in stone. Settling in on the makeshift bench, I pulled the Book of Waters from my pocket and returned to the story.

. . . They erased him.

Damnatio memoriae, they called it, but only in whispers and shadows, for it was a fate too horrible to speak: condemnation of his very memory.

In the Hall of the Great Council, they removed his portrait from among the other doges and, in its frame, painted a shroud of deepest black. Lettered in Latin upon the veil, stick-straight and stark to stand for the rest of time, were the words:

This is the space for Paulo Zanetti, beheaded for crimes.

Paulo Zanetti, beheaded for crimes. Five words that would carry that condemnation not only over his memory, but over his living legacy as well.

Merely to speak his name was punishable by death. Who among his children, and their children, and beyond, could live a life in this city, bearing that name now?

Nobody could.

Nobody would.

His descendants and heirs disowned themselves of him and extended the erasure of the man to his very name. They renounced the name of Zanetti. Claimed another surname for themselves, one meaning "Faithful," and set out to prove themselves the very epitome of the name. To atone, if it could be done, for the Unremembered One and his unforgivable deeds.

And so they returned to the ways of their obscure forefathers: serving their patrician peers. Assembling for the Great Council. Filling the coffers of the new doge, commissioning for him a statue of Justice, winsome and lovely in her triumphant form, for his *bucentaur*, the royal barge. Brokering relationships between powerful alliances, collecting secrets to ingratiate themselves with those whose sins they guarded. Making themselves a living vault, indispensable to those in power as the greatest supporters and greatest enemies, all at once.

Their lives became a vast and reaching game of strategy, crowned with the purchase for themselves of a new title, a place once more in good standing, written even in the Book of Gold.

All of this, and why?

They had their own guarded secret. A plan. The ultimate symbol of atonement, of triumph over the Unremembered One, of victory over disgrace.

They would produce another doge.

Whether it took ten years or ten thousand, this would be their purpose. To earn the trust of their land so much, to build beneath themselves a scaffolding so intricate, that one of their sons might one day be elevated again. Granted the honor and privilege of leading them once again.

Generations poured their all into this end until it was finally within reach. It had to be. They would do right by this city once and for all.

But even plans generations in the making can be dashed to pieces in the blink of an eye.

One night, an emperor from the north invaded with his army, laying claim to the republic—and disintegrating it. Obliterating, once and for all, this shining jewel of the Adriatic. With the arrival of Napoleon Bonaparte as the century drew to a close and a new era lingered in the offing, the last Doge of Venice abdicated.

And the family of the faithful, for all their long striving, were thwarted. It was a dark blow. A violent rending of their hope, their souls, their future—until one small word was whispered in secret one night.

"Unless . . ."

My pen moved fast, the account's grip on me so strong I lost sense of my surroundings.

My insides clenched, heavy with knowing the hot brand of a verdict to a man's soul. Mine had not been a sentence unto death like Paulo Zanetti's, but there had been many small deaths tied up in it. Honor, trust . . . family.

This portrait, this symbol of a life blacked out, it was the sort of thing I would have once pictured, and by old instinct, my pen moved to sketch it. I knew what a shroud looked like—a swath of fabric in some shape or another. And I knew what a portrait looked like. But *knowing* and *picturing* were two different things.

My pen scratched out a rectangle and swooped a swath across its width, swooped other lines below it like folds of fabric.

I could not see it, but I knew the science of shadows, the pull and play of them. Knew they would all fall at the same angles and give the image dimension, life. Lift it from the page and into its own form. Instinct, which had once come from my head, now burrowed somewhere inside my chest, pulling each line onto page as my mind watched on and entered the equation in a new and foreign way.

I lifted my eyes to the owl perched upon the sign, to the way a shadow from the building fell across it. I fixed upon the shadows and let my pen move blindly, applying shades at the same angle to the paper, using the tools before me to form the shape of a black swatch over a canvas. I shifted my focus, mimicked the reach of the darker places beneath each fold of fabric—and gulped.

It . . . was a picture. Form and shape and pieces that, while nothing to boast about, were something to start from. This—a thing imagined—was what I had once been able to have in my head. And here it was, on paper.

A starting place.

The very thing I'd lost . . . in a new and foreign form. Rudimentary and maybe even piteously loveable in all its fledgling scribbles, but still. A strange spiral shot through me, zipping around and exiting again with a sound so foreign . . .

A laugh. Small, just a huff of breath, really. But with it came a strange sense of life. Angels did not trumpet and the sky did not splay with sunrays of revelation, but the newness of this . . . *thing* . . . settled in and stared at me from the paper.

The owl hooted, and a creak sounded, startling me from this wary reverie so that I slammed the book shut.

The turquoise door opened, its shadow extending to meet my feet.

"Robert Browning, you scoundrel!" a voice gave a fond scolding.

Four words I was certain the poet had never heard in his life. I stood. The owl turned his head slowly, deigning to lend a sliver of his royal attention to the voice—a woman's.

I couldn't see her from where she remained inside the door, but there was a familiar zing about her manner.

"Are you frightening away our customers again?"

The estimable and avian Robert Browning ruffled his feathers in response.

"I'm sorry," she said, emerging through the door. Vittoria, the blustery being from the train station. Bedecked in a blue-and-black striped dress, twisting a long, thick glove over her sleeve and reaching up toward the sign. "He is usually not awake at this time, but he does become rather jealous if—come, Signor Browning, jump aboard," she coaxed, seeming to have forgotten about the man in the courtyard. The owl lifted his face and closed his eyes, aloof.

"I don't believe that for a moment." She disappeared into the shop again, this time emerging with a three-stepped stool and climbing it with such swiftness and such little attention to her feet I found myself at her side, offering to steady her.

"No need," she said. "He's just being stubborn. If he will only—" She lifted her heels, posing her booted feet on the tips of her toes and leaning, leaning, to reach him.

"Please don't move him on my account," I said, and for the first time, a chord of familiarity seemed to strike her. She peered down at me, eyes narrowing much as the owl's had. "You," she said, her voice perplexed. In the same moment, her balance betrayed her, sending her toppling.

I lunged as she fell with a whoosh, catching her light form, the material of her dress simple but soft. I had long known the ironic comfort of worn fabric made to stretch past its time—known it all my life, really—and knew it again now, as I set her feet on the ground and found myself looking into two questioning faces.

The winged Robert Browning alighted on her shoulder, quirking his head.

She, too, tipped her head, inquisitive. "What are you doing here?"

I opened my mouth to answer but was cut short by the tinny sound of a small bell from within. Vittoria winced, as if she'd forgotten something that had the urgency of a dish left upon a hot stove. She flew inside like she was the one with wings, Robert Browning disembarking and landing on the window box.

I followed Vittoria inside, ducking slightly to fit through the doorframe, and found myself in the middle of a room stuffed with books. In form, it was very unlike the home I had shared with my mother—and yet the smell of the aged tomes, the way their straight spines and flecked gilding murmured magic and bespoke eons of history beyond this moment—*that* was the same. Bookshelves became avenues of lives, history, epics, fairy tales, all standing silent and waiting to be cracked open.

A spiral staircase climbed in the corner, friendly and serpentine in scrolls of black iron. Its first stop was a landing, where a railed walkway skirted the room and wraparound shelves. It climbed, then, to a second floor, where a glass-doored balcony spilled light down onto the books and projected rippling reflections from a canal below onto the copper-tiled ceiling above, giving the whole place a feeling of movement and magic. As if the books resided in a shimmering sea, without threat of wetness. In the shafts of light that speared downward from the sun, dust mites danced like fireflies.

I turned slowly to take it all in and startled when I came face to face with the yellow-eyed stare of the curious owl.

"Sorry," I said.

"That is almost always what people say to him," Vittoria said, materializing from behind a dark-wooded bookcase, a slim volume in her hand. "I cannot think why. Poor soul. Can you imagine? What it must be like to live life with nary a 'hello' or a 'how do you do.' A worse fate than the real Robert Browning. He had plenty of admirers here. He lived in Venice. You might have passed by his rooms on your way here and not even known! You know him?"

She spoke so swiftly, hopping from thought to thought like a delighted frog on a sea of lily pads, that it took my mind a moment to catch up. "Know Robert Browning . . ." I said slowly. "Only on page."

"That is one thing we share, at least." She stroked the owl's chest with the back of her finger. "Poor owl, never greeted, always getting wary looks from people." The owl fixed his eyes on me, and I felt a sudden kinship to the creature.

But of all the stories lining the walls of this place and harboring history and hope, my own story was not one that belonged here.

"I'm sorry to intrude," I said.

"There you go, apologizing again," Vittoria said, making me shift my stance, uneasy. Every time I opened my mouth around this woman, my words landed in all the wrong places.

"I felt badly for the collision yesterday, and—"

"Collision," she curved the word in confusion, the warm brown of her eyes searching. Whether for the meaning of the word or for remembrance of the incident in question, I couldn't be sure. She lifted the top two books from a pile at her feet and shelved them, reaching for another. I jumped into the process, handing her the next, watching her method.

"At the train station," I said. What method was she organizing the books by? Not alphabetical, I saw as she stood a volume of Dickens beside a Hans Christian Andersen. Next, she placed Browning beside Browning beside Beecher Stowe. Not arranging by genre either, then.

Not by color or size . . . I studied the other companions: Brontë and Gaskell, several volumes of each. John Keats beside Percy Bysshe Shelley—and then I had it.

I observed the pile of books and saw them suddenly not as a haphazard hodgepodge, but as a brilliantly curated collection bundled by something intangible: friendship. These pairings were all authors who had known one another.

I searched and pulled four of my own countrymates from the collection, holding them out. Emerson, Alcott, Thoreau, Hawthorne.

She took the blue Emerson, shelved it, chattering on. "How is it that you speak Italian so well?"

I told her and offered the red Alcott, asking the same of her English.

"Half or more of our customers are visitors from afar," she said. "It is our business to make them feel at home by learning their language. And we Bellinis are, after all, in the business of words!"

She plucked up the Thoreau and the Hawthorne, examining their spines and setting them beside the other American volumes, stepping back to admire her handiwork, with a smile on her face, hands upon her hips. She blew a stray curl from her face and then froze.

"You did that," she said, pointing at Thoreau and company. "How did you discover my method?"

"I . . . just saw it." I shrugged a shoulder, eager for the attention to be off me.

"Nobody sees it. That is the point. I rearrange by theme every month or two—it keeps the customers coming in. Even the locals, and from every sestiere! They want to guess where the books have moved and why. It keeps them talking to me and—now don't laugh—" She leaned in as if to impart a great secret. "It makes them fond of the books! They become treasures, when searched for. Like . . . a rescue mission. For old friends."

"Like the authors," I said. "Old friends."

"Precisely. And I mean to have a dog here one day too. A friendly face and wagging tale, so that every customer who enters does have an old friend here, always." She kept her stance but looked me over, eyes narrowing again as if she didn't know what to make of me. "What brings you to Venice, Signor Train?" She seemed very pleased with herself at this moniker, and I smiled ruefully. "Are you here on your Tour?"

A customer entered from the door facing the canal, and as I brushed a stray cobweb from my sleeve, I rued the fact that Jacopo's route did not reach that canal. Vittoria darted away to greet a woman and child warmly, slipping into musical Italian and asking after the escapades of a cat named Franco.

Her question to me lingered, the same one from Jacopo on the boat, yesterday. An imagined life of the Tour tromped through my mind in sounds: feet planting firmly in mountain terrain, climbing the Alps, traversing aged streets of Paris and Rome.

And then, just as quickly, the sounds were overtaken by those that were my actual story, from a dusty cell. Feet tapping together to tick the months away while I read any book I could get my hands on—and refusing to read the one whose presence burned in my pocket just now.

Vittoria Bellini knelt to speak to the child and then led her to a corner I hadn't noticed before. There, a sculpted vine formed an arch over a blue garden gate in miniature. They entered together, Vittoria ducking to do so, and I watched her pull a red volume from the shelf, her joy palpable as she placed it in the young girl's hands.

My pulse raced. I knew that book. I shifted my stance as unobtrusively as possible until I could see its shelf. And there they were—The Books of Glass, Gondolas, Ink, Masks, Thread.

But no Book of Waters.

With the girl settled in to discover the book for herself, Vittoria ducked back out and approached with concern written on her face. "Signor Train?" she said, her voice entirely serious. "Are you all right?"

I nodded, swallowed. "Those books," I said. If she was always rearranging the volumes, perhaps somewhere . . . The hope was so slim, but I had to ask. "Do you have others in the shop?"

"The *Piccole Storie?*" She shook her head. "We have a difficult time keeping them in stock. The children clamor for them!" She noted the disappointment, the slight slump of my shoulders. "Do you have need of them?"

"Well, I—" How to explain? "I'm commissioned by a businessman in California to help him with a project. Draw a few likenesses of buildings. Procure artifacts."

Something shuttered on her face, and the warmth dissipated into an air of business. She cleared her throat. "Ah," she said. She appeared to be attempting to harness her tongue, her jaw working, dark lashes blinking increasingly.

"I've offended you," I said.

Her flushed face confirmed my guess. She drew herself up, setting her hands to shuffling books—the Gaskell in between the Brontës, then back again, running her hand over their gilt-lettered covers as if searching for another task.

In her haste, one of the books slipped from the counter. I stooped to retrieve it and laid it on an empty spot on the shelf, adding to it the book from my pocket I'd come to return.

"Thank you," she said, then realizing the book was from yesterday's incident, she raised her eyebrows.

"I'm afraid I'm just learning the ways of your beautiful city," I said, an attempt to apologize for whatever blunder I'd made to cause her to fall silent. "If I've done something wrong, I would be grateful to know what it is."

A pause. More jaw-clenched book shuffling.

"So that I can make restitution," I said.

Whatever storm was stirring inside of her reached its peak, and she unclenched her jaw to throw her hands in the air. "That," she said, gesturing both hands at the humble brown volume I'd taken and returned. "That!" she said. "This is what you do. You come, and you take, and you take, and you take—"

She paused, and heat crept up my neck. How could she possibly know . . . ?

"You just—you all come from afar and lay your hands on whatever you wish and take it away like we are some—" Her impassioned speech morphed from English into Italian, and my mind scrambled to make the switch too. "Some artifact! Only a curiosity! A relic, a dig site, and not a living and breathing city! Look at me," she said and pressed a fist to her lungs, her shoulders rising and falling in breath quickened by her passion. "Am I not alive?"

Yes, I wanted to say. She was more alive than perhaps anyone I had ever encountered. But every time I spoke, I made things worse. I gave a cautious, slow nod.

"Yes!" she said, slamming her open palm upon the desk and stepping from behind it to wheel her cart to a bookshelf. "I am, and so is Venezia. You come to *procure artifacts*," she said, enunciating the words until they were as pointed as swords. "As if the stones of this city were not carved by the very hands of our ancestors. As if they were not placed upon islands made to give us refuge, and safety, and—and *life*." She took a breath and lifted her dark eyes to mine for the first time since she'd begun her speech.

"Why are you so calm?" she said. "It is making me feel calm." She folded her arms across her chest, then shifted her shoulder into a shrug. "I don't prefer it." Those eyes flashed challenge, her mouth frozen, refusing to speak again until I responded to these allegations.

"I should have spoken with more care," I said. "If it helps, the man I work for—he loves this city. So much so that he wishes to construct something of a tribute to it in America. To give a taste of your arts and canals and culture to those who will never be fortunate enough to experience them in person."

She drew back, surprised at my answer. The sharp edges surrounding her presence softening, just a bit.

"A little of this living and breathing . . . heart-beating city," I continued.

The pause was so silent I could hear water lap from the canal outside, the ruffle of owl feathers from somewhere in the store.

"You used my words," she said.

I nodded.

"You listened."

"Yes." That, at least, was one thing I had learned to do. I had had enough of jumping to conclusions, concocting plans, and dashing headlong into haphazard schemes before taking the time to understand. And understanding, I had learned, came more often through listening than only by seeing and drawing conclusions.

"But I never said 'heart-beating,'" she said shrewdly.

"No." I dared a soft laugh. "But you lived it. You care deeply for your home. It's . . ."

"A great deal? *'Vittoria, you are a great deal.'* My papa used to say this, always shaking his head and—"

"I was going to say, it's admirable."

Her eyes grew round. She mouthed the word silently—*admirable*. She looked to the side, for the first time unable to make eye contact with me. A flicker of a smile cracked through her stone-strong stance, but she hid it quickly.

"Truly," I said and watched her cheeks color as she finally met my gaze. "I apologize. You are right—your city is remarkable. Incredible, really. And I need to apologize again for yesterday. I came to deliver your books to the train for you, if you haven't already done so."

She looked perplexed. "My books?" She scanned the rows of shelves, as if wondering which ones I meant.

"The ones I caused to . . . explode. When I ran into you?"

"Oh!" Now her countenance shifted, a sheepish smile curving into dimples. "Would you be surprised to learn that wasn't the first time that has happened to me?"

"Really," I said, lifting a brow in mock surprise.

She gave a rueful look. "We have names for the winds here. The Scirocco, from the southeast—it is damp, and warm. The Bora, from the north—it is cold, but dry. And then there is the Garbin, from the southwest."

"And what does the Garbin bring?"

"Fog." She leaned forward, eyes wide. "Like you've never seen before. A great and mighty mist. Do you know what the stationmaster says when he sees me coming to bring a delivery to the train? 'Here comes the Garbin,' he says. 'Take care, ladies and gentlemen. A fog of books is on its way!'"

"A fog of books sounds like a very good problem to have," I said. And with this, any vestige of coldness vanished entirely from her.

"I might like you after all," she said. And then with more reluctance, "Perhaps I was too hasty with my speech. I sometimes get carried away. I . . . apologize." She opened a hand as if lifting the word to me as a gift.

"No apology needed."

A lull in the conversation caused my proposal to rise to the surface of her memory. "It was very kind of you to come," she said. "To return the book and to offer to take the crate to the station. But my cousin is traveling to *Terra Firma* later and will be taking it. So I suppose . . ." She met my gaze. "You are free to go."

I dropped my chin in understanding, but my feet remained in place.

"Is there something else I can assist you with, Signor—" She cleared her throat and waited.

I detested this part—the uttering of my surname. It felt like a lie, every time. "Goodman. Daniel Goodman."

"Signor Goodman, then. Is there something more I can do for you?"

"You . . . know books," I said, letting my gaze travel the room to help communicate my point.

"You might say that, yes."

"What are the odds that you might know the whereabouts of—" I tripped over the coming words. A needle in a haystack, that's what the odds would be. "Of one particular book?"

She raised her eyebrows. "As for odds, you will have to visit the casino for that. But I wouldn't recommend it. Many men in suits as fine as yours enter looking very happy, and leave looking"—she pounded her fist into her other palm—"crushed."

"Oh, I didn't mean—that is, I'm not here to gamble." I would have to watch my American expressions. "I just meant, is there any chance you might know the whereabouts of a very particular book?"

"It depends," she said. "I have all of these, of course. If it is one in our shop, I can show you the way. Or, if it's a historical text, it might be in the national archives. If one of the *very* particular books—my Zio Antonio repairs rare and antique volumes." She pointed to a corner where a workstation sprawled with bits of leather, strands of thread, stacks of spools, bottles of glue, and an empty stool waited. "We do see many interesting volumes there . . . but you never know what will come in. If you want the *Libro d'Oro*, you are a hundred years too late, unless you want only ashes. Signor Bonaparte took it upon himself to burn it."

"Napoleon Bonaparte burned a book of gold?"

"Napoleon Bonaparte was the cause of a great deal of mischief in our city. Look!" She pointed at a painting on the wall behind me, one of a man with a kindly face, painted in oil, holding an open book. "My great-great-grandfather. And look!" She pointed to a slash across the painting. It had been patched from the back and the seam painted again, but it still puckered in its scar.

"Napoleon did that?"

"No—it was us! We, the Venetians! Someone began a rumor that this shop was a sympathizer to Bonaparte. Why? Because we had a French literature section. See?" She whirled around and led down the next aisle, stopping at a shelf pleasantly packed with the likes of *The Three Musketeers*, *The Hunchback of Notre Dame*, and *Journey to the Center of the Earth*. She pulled out a deep green novel, planted her free hand at her side, and looked indignant. "Does this look like propaganda to you?"

I laughed, but saw she was serious. "No."

"Precisely! But there were those who feared anything French back then and took it upon themselves to ransack our shop." The pained look on her face was as if she'd been there herself, though it had been well before her time. "Dumped books into the canal"— she waved toward the window—"tipped over shelves, slashed paint-ings."

I gulped. Wanting to offer condolences, feeling like a hypocrite if I did. Had I not been the perpetrator of worse, in my own corner of the world, in those houses with Emilio?

"I'm . . . sorry," I said. For so much.

"Well. It wasn't you, Daniel Goodman. But thank you. Anyway, they did not stop Napoleon by drowning several hundred books. He came in and ransacked far worse. Yes, burning the *Libro d'Oro* and dashing to pieces our identity, our hope, and a great many other things. Some say he was a liberator to Venice, others spit upon his memory and what has become of our country since he seized us. It is complex. . . . Paris has many of our treasures now. It could be that your book is there."

I nodded, pondering. A new possibility registered, in the wake of her tale. Could what I sought be *in* the waters? One of the volumes dumped by the ransackers? What if the original was . . . and perhaps that was why copies were so rare? "This one was called the Book of Waters."

The volume of *Les Misérables* in her hand tipped as if craning its neck to see.

"Where did you hear of that?"

"Here is hope, Daniel. A story unfinished." The words of my mother's letter, stamped upon my heart. I gulped. "I can't make good sense of its genre, and when I translate—"

Her hand clamped down on my forearm, soft and warm. My muscles tensed, unused to the touch of another person. "You have a volume of the Book of Waters? In your possession?"

Slowly, I pulled it from my jacket.

She froze, eyes wide. "They say there were only ever seven volumes printed," she said. "How did you come to have one?"

Choosing my words carefully this time, I explained my purpose here, the source of the book, and my mission in attempting to lay my hands upon the original text, to gain the complete ending of the book, if there was an ending somewhere.

When I finished, I puffed out my cheeks. Her hands were clasped tight together, and I could see she was practicing great restraint to not reach out and pluck the volume from my hands.

"Go ahead," I said, offering it to her. "If you'd like to look . . ."

Her entire being morphed in an exhale. From statue to living, breathing, extremely exuberant person. And even so, she restrained herself, taking great care as she turned each page, ran a finger over a pen-and-ink illustration here or there, holding it up to inhale.

"There is nothing like the smell of books, no?" She closed it with care. "Now. Tell me, you have been sent here with no direction? No one to check with?"

I shook my head. "Aside from an address . . . no. My employer was told a man here might know something." I retrieved my notebook and showed her the paper bearing the address. Written in my mother's own hand, when she had visited Mr. Wharton about his need for books—and little imagining it would land in the hand of her lost son.

She leaned in to see. "I know the sestiere, but not the address," she said. "You are not far. You're going there next?" She proceeded to give me directions, and I kept up as best I could by drawing a hasty map in my notebook, then holding it out for her to approve. I couldn't hold landmarks well in my mind and had learned years ago that carrying a map simplified things.

She smiled in a mixture of approval and amusement. "What is it?" I asked. "Are my lines not—straight enough?"

"Oh, they are very rigid lines, Signor Goodman. Just don't be surprised if they . . . come to life in different ways, when you walk this route."

She looked longingly at the map, at the door, her foot tapping as her arms crossed in front of her. She bit her lip, and I could almost hear the wheels of her mind racing.

"Would you . . . care to join me? I might have a deal more luck finding the place with an expert along," I said, trying to make the invitation seem more natural by poking fun at myself. And knowing it to be entirely true.

A battle waged inside her as she dashed a glance at the clock and threw her arms to her sides in defeat. "I wish I could, signore! I would give anything to see what comes of this. To be a part of finding something so rare! But—"

The bell rang over the canal-side door, and in stepped an older woman, basket over her arm, face beaming. Followed by a shawled woman of similar age but taller build and cooler gaze, and a third and a fourth, one with a basket on each arm, and the other on crutches mellowed and warmed by the hand of time.

"My *nonne* are here," Vittoria whispered. "Not really my grandmothers, but they may as well be. Every week at this time they come and do their needlework and swap stories and—well, their coffee must be had!" She lightly touched my elbow, leading the way back to the campo-side entrance I'd come in from. "You go. But will you meet me tomorrow? I must know what happens! And . . . I have an idea." This last bit said rather conspiratorially.

"Should I be afraid of this idea?"

"There is only one way to find out, Signor Train. Meet me tomorrow morning if you can."

11

THE BOOK OF WATERS

The Seven Seats

BEFORE THE DAWN OF VENICE

Ah, but long before that once-great man was once-and-for-all erased . . . he, too, had a history. His, reaching generations before him, and generations before the land he had sought to control was even a land at all.

All those ancient years ago, from the mountains above, from the fields to the west, from the sea to the east, the people came across the waters.

There was nothing there, back then. No city, no bridges or bell towers, gleaming domes or frescoed walls.

There was swamp, and disease, and swamp, and insects, and swamp, and—safety.

For who among their attackers would follow here? Willingly beset themselves with affliction? Affliction that, by turns, acted as a safeguard to those who fled straight to its embrace. And so Venice sprang up, one hut at a time, one island at a time, until she became a jewel, there in the swamp. A prize of the world, over the centuries. A port of wealth and trade, a center of philosophy, art, music, literature.

. . . And still, safety. All from a swamp.

For among those who first settled there were seven families, who knew well what it was to tread the earth in search of home, only to have it ripped from beneath them by a fresh wave of attackers.

It was understandable, then, that when they settled the swamp, they were wary of trusting it too much.

Or rather, of trusting men, who had betrayed them time and time again. And so, with torchlight, trepidation, and not a little conviction, these seven formed a society. A guild, as they came to call it. Keepers of the heart of this place. Though they came from many backgrounds and entered many vocations, they held two things in common: Loss . . . and hope.

Loss of family, home, safety. Loss so deep and perpetual it had marked each of them and lit within them a fervent flame to safeguard future generations from such.

And hope. That they might be a turning point for those who would follow. That though life had taught them hope was a dangerous and fragile thing . . . Faith sang a different song: hope was as necessary as breath, and so strong that it carried its own heartbeat.

A heartbeat that drove them when they were tempted to give up. They were a remnant from those whose lives had been claimed by their pursuers, and they pledged in the honor of those same lives to uphold whatever was true and good in this place, their marshy promised land.

They were a hardscrabble band who flung themselves across isles and callings but held fast to this unifying vow. The Remnant, they called themselves. The *Scuola Piccolo di Resto*.

Time passed. Their shelters on stilts long ago grown into cottages on handcrafted isles, isles built atop trees pulled from the mountains above and driven into the lagoon into a platform of adjacent poles. Hope, fragile? Why, they lived where there had once been no land.

Hope ran deep.

For generations, they met at one table or another, or sometimes upon an island unvisited by others, where a stonemason from among them crafted seven seats and placed them in a ring. A metalworker from their midst crafted seven rings, to be worn by each member and passed down to next generations, in hopes that in the face of any wars, plagues, or other tribulations that might come, they would stand fast and do what they could to guard this land from corruption.

Their number climbed from seven to twelve, to twenty and beyond.

As the guilds grew in the republic, so did their governing. It became a rule throughout Venice that those of nobility could not hold power on a governing board within a guild. What, then, did one do when guild members grew into nobility?

They left. Splintered away, one by one, for as their power mounted, so did their conflicts. Away they went, in search of larger guilds or the Great Council, confraternities more illustrious than the humble hardscrabble lot they had once been a part of. Places where they could once again have a voice.

And who was left, then? The remnant, in reprise. Those who never attained nobility. A veritable Gideon's army of those who had never claimed power (but were not powerless), wealth (but were not poor), or acclaim (but lacked no purpose). Just a clutch of humble souls, intent on caring for their fellow man.

They had dwindled back down to the original seven, but the dwindling did not stop there. For one man, generations down the line, aspired to greater things, leaving behind the farther-flung reaches of the lagoon isles to dwell in the city and draw near to its center, its power.

Another of the seven, grave of heart at his friend's penchant for power, followed. Promising to keep watch and keep the wandering one in the fellowship of their promise, if he could.

There were five, then. Five, who met in the seven seats, and held fast the original intent of the guild: to guard the heart of what Venice sprang up to be—a keeper of lost souls. A refuge for those in need of safe harbor.

And then, even more generations down the line, that hardscrabble guild was delivered a lost soul into their very keeping one night.

Perhaps, for all the decades, the centuries, the clutching together and escaping and unifying grief—it was all for such a time as this.

For such a soul as this.

When ancient waters rippled in moonlight . . .

12

THE BOOK OF WATERS

The Boy Who Would Be King

A good many years before the ancient waters carried the child in a basket to his new life, the waters parted. And parted, and parted again—around an entire fleet, slipping into the lagoon with the intent to overthrow, overtake, overpower.

Anno Domini 1796. The waters of the lagoon were speared by ships from the Adriatic beyond. Lines and wakes interwove as if in attempt to arrest the offending vessels. Some of the boats puffed steam like dragons. Others had sails that punched against gusts in canvas applause, saluting their own arrival.

Napoleon's fleet. As the hours unfolded and cannons rolled into St. Mark's Square and pigeons and men alike took flight, somewhere down the serpentine curve of the Grand Canal, a son was born into la Famiglia Fedele.

Massimo Fedele, they named him. A name they intended as a prophecy— "The Greatest Faithful"—and represented everything the dwindling family had worked for, these many years since the Unremembered One.

The boy, with his head of dark curls and small lips shaped into an O, as if practicing his own name, was their last and greatest hope. Not only for the fulfillment of their family's mission, but now for the very life of their beloved republic.

For the night he was born, Venezia—The Most Serene Republic—was neither serene nor a republic. A gathering of the Great Council voted, and the last of their ancient pride crumbled.

They and the Doge would abdicate to a pro-French government.

The pillaging of art, architecture, and every treasure in between overtook streets and courtyards and left no shred of the infamous serenity. Fires burned throughout the city, setting the pinnacles of her bell towers alight in a yellow glow that seemed to plead with the stars above them, "Save us!" Mournful cries, the bells that tolled that night.

And somewhere, betwixt the voting and the pillaging and the fires and dirges of bells, that baby cried his first.

"There is hope," his mother said. His father nodded, his face still etched in despair after his return from the scourge of a vote by the Great Council. The man stroked the woman's hair, hiding from her the hollowness of his heart, the emptiness of his accounts.

The House of Fedele had given all, at last. There was nothing more to give—no coin, no acts of loyalty to prove their worthiness.

All around them, palazzos emptied. Canals rocked with waves wrestling against boats, barges, gondolas leaving in droves. In the midst of all this utter loss, a small word, dull and obscure in its sound until this moment, sparked suddenly to life. First as a whisper, then gaining momentum, picking up strength like a rising tide as it circulated among those left behind:

Quorum.

The minimum quantity of men required in order to conduct business and carry out votes.

So many had fled before the vote of the Great Council . . . that there had been no quorum. But the council had voted anyway.

And Signor Fedele's voice shook as it wrapped tight around the slimmest hope: "The abdication cannot hold." His voice began to steady, gripping that hope until it grew deep and rich with conviction. "It cannot stand. It shall not."

He stroked the silken cheek of his infant. "The Republic shall rise once more. It will take time, but time is what we are given. And she will need a leader yet."

The House of the Faithful was without coin, without friend, and looked upon with suspicion by the new leaders.

But they were alive.

They had purpose. They would gather about them those who believed, like them, in the restoration of the Republic. They would build again—as it was, where it was. *Com'era, Dov'era.*

Faithful. Fedele.

DANIEL

I closed the Book of Waters and set my chin. *La Famiglia Fedele* . . . It was not a name I'd heard. I hadn't seen it in the travelogue, hadn't witnessed any of the campo statues made in the likenesses of any Fedele men memorialized as heroes.

I didn't know what to make of the man's resolve, whether it would be used for ill or for good. But the fact remained that in the face of such absolute devastation and loss, when the living story resounded only in defeat, he dug instead for the tiniest slip of hope. And in doing so, hope became . . . purpose.

Had I known such a thing? I had purpose—I had my jars, the houses and people I was trying to do right by. But there was a knot forming in me, telling me it was not purpose born of hope, but regret. It was good, it was right, I needed to do it. But . . . something was missing.

I was juggling two looming unknowns: the way this story in my hands would unfold . . . and the way my own story would. The book was becoming decidedly less intimidating than my own account—and also uncomfortably resonant.

The knot inside cinched tighter, and I pushed myself up from the wall I'd been leaning against. I'd snatched a bit of time to translate a few pages, escape the task before me, but now what I was to do seemed a lifeline thrown to pull me out of questions I had no answers for.

I had arrived at the address indicated and decided to watch for a bit, to see what I might learn of the place. It was a door settled deep in a clutch of alleys and campos. Number 751, San Polo. Vittoria had been right—the straight-lined route of my map had curved into turns and twists where the house numbers did not ascend in natural form according to street, but by sporadic spurts assigned by block.

Number 751, San Polo, was a door of deep red winking back at me in diamond-paned glass from a window that was missing two of those diamonds. As if it had known I was coming and had begun hiding away its treasures.

I raised my finger to ring the doorbell and halted. It was a lion, captive in brass. Mouth open, voraciously awaiting the arrival of an unsuspecting finger. *You are in the lion's den now, Daniel.* I remembered Jacopo's hearty laugh. Pulling in a breath, I plunged my finger into the lion's mouth and wondered if it was a taste of things to come.

But nothing happened.

I pushed again, harder this time, and stepped back, hands safely tucked in my trouser pockets.

A woman pushed a cart of plants past me, the wooden wheels squeaking a wobbly song. She stopped and pointed to the right of the door. "Ring that one," she said in Italian, and I followed her gesture to find a long chain suspended from an upper floor window, swaying in the breeze as if taunting me. "The lion does not work."

"*Grazie*," I said, and she smiled to reveal several missing teeth and a hopeful look toward her cart.

"Ah?" she said. "In this city of stone, we must plant life, yes?"

I thought of my dwindling coin supply. My stomach rumbled. The chain swayed. It wouldn't hurt to present the person within— whoever it was—with an offering of presumptive thanks.

I purchased a small pot of ivy and rang the bell, waiting as the cart squeaked off into the distance. She muttered an ominous *buona fortuna*—good luck—as she walked away, with a distinct lilt of amusement to her voice.

A curtain fluttered in the window that the chain entered, but no other sign of life.

I knocked on one of the sturdier diamond panes.

"*Non c'è nessuno a casa,*" a voice from within rumbled. Nobody was home? The words landed with such dry wit that I immediately liked their speaker. It was something I'd be tempted to say myself, if someone knocked on my own railcar door—but which I probably wouldn't have the gumption to say. The plight of the polite hermit.

I deliberated. Should I ring again? The lion seemed to laugh at me with its mouth looking even wider-open than before.

I rang again and quickly confirmed that was the wrong choice. The chain rattled something above, unleashing the scrape of an object bent upon falling to its own demise.

A terra cotta pot descended. Out the window at a low arc, shattering beside me and exposing the roots of an ivy plant, or rather the crispy-leaved ghost of an ivy plant.

The little vine in my hands quivered in the breeze.

"Hello?" I volleyed the word upward. "*Buongiorno?*"

I could scale that wall in ten seconds, slip inside that open window, and be done with this.

But I was not that man anymore.

"I come with regards to a book," I hollered, tipping my head up and clamping my hat on with my hand.

Silence, the sound of a chair across a floor, and a white-haired man with bushy brows furrowed deep enough to sink Venice leaned out. Here was a tempest in human form, and all I had in defense was a quaking sprig of ivy.

"What book." It was a demand.

From my jacket I pulled the printed copy. "The Book of Waters," I said. "I'm in search of the original and was told you might have some knowledge of it."

For a moment, I could have mistaken the man for one of Venice's many statues. He did not speak, he did not move, and a shadow crossed over his stone being. But his face opened somehow, as if a memory had flooded in and pushed open the walls around him. He shook himself from the trance and said, "Impossible." Then a pause, as if reconsidering, followed by a shake of the head and a simple "I am sorry."

His apology took me by surprise in its sincerity, as it erased any edge to the man's voice and held only regret. He turned to go, my chance vanishing before my eyes.

"Signore, *la prego*," I said, tossing up the "please, sir" like a prayer. "Is there anything I can do? I cannot leave Venice without the book."

He reappeared, looking out over the square as if he could see through the walls bedecked in scrolling iron balconies and clotheslines waving. As if something out there in the beyond might give him an answer. His mouth twitched, and the light fell in such a way that it illuminated a scar upon the man's time-weathered cheek. Mouth to jaw, jagged and deep and from a time long ago, by all appearances.

"You want to see the Book of Waters?" he said. A flicker of something—joy? Mischief? "Come back with *Marangona*!"

Marangona. Marangona? "Yes, sir. But who is Maran—" The window shut, and my words rattled into silence, along with the diamond panes of the window's glass.

I closed my eyes, willing every bit of study I'd conducted on Venice to the surface of my mind—and discovered no Marangona. Was it a person? A food? A relic? One of the winds Vittoria Bellini spoke of? What was this fabled, formless key that would admit me into the den of the window-slammer?

More to the point—did I even want to be admitted to the den of the window-slammer? It was beginning to feel like a fool's errand.

As if summoned by my thoughts, the very man opened his window again, and a sliver of hope with it. He did not seem to respond well when I spoke, so I bit my tongue and waited.

"La Marangona. And with the ring!"

Another slam, another rattle of panes. My mind rattled, too, beginning to ache with the tangle of things.

"Uffa," I said, repeating Vittoria's expression of dismay from the train station.

I stooped to pick up the pieces of broken pot, well-aware that like most things in this city, the shards in my hands were likely older than I was. The white patina attested to that. I gathered the pot's pieces into my pocket to see what could be done about them back at my room.

I had been here less than twenty-four hours and already I had accidentally stolen a book, failed to obtain the book I was *meant* to claim, obstructed a delivery, and been the cause of an aged pot's untimely demise.

As I felt my way toward what I hoped would be the Grand Canal, I fingered the rustic pieces in my pocket and thought again of the story. If Venice herself had been shattered under the foot of Napoleon once—and if there were those who had seen hope for a way forward—perhaps there was hope for me yet.

14

THE BOOK OF WATERS

The Secret Burial for All to See

The House of Fedele was joined by others. Those whose hearts beat for the fallen republic, for all that Venezia had been and all that Bonaparte had taken. In secret meetings they were joined by the houses of Bellini, Mendeli, and more—until they numbered eleven in all. And called themselves so: The Eleven.

The Eleven who would give all for a plan that would outlive themselves.

"Pisa took over two centuries to build her tower. Can we not give the remainder of our lives to rebuilding an entire republic?" This was their anthem. So, they plotted and planned, all with careful movements beneath the watchful eye of the occupying armies.

Soon, Bonaparte decreed that a place for burial of the dead be found outside the city. The Eleven lost no time in orchestrating a proclamation that was incredibly public for their fellow citizens—and surreptitiously private, before the seeing eyes of the soldiers. A declaration of their intent, right beneath the noses of their occupiers, without them ever suspecting.

How? With all the pomp, all the expense, all the conspicuous ceremony of Venice's funeral traditions. Venice felt the loss of any citizen deeply. And because pageantry of the processions matched the citizen's station in life, not a soul could be caught unawares when the loss of a doge or dignitary took place. Bells rang from every church. Black and red ribbons of berobed officials lined the squares.

But now there would be no procession to a church. The burials were to take place on an outlying island, close to the city and yet a city of its own, a place of the dead.

The Eleven orchestrated a procession, complete with boats and canopies, trumpets and bells, all for the burial of a prominent "citizen." As soldiers watched on and took note that the new burial place was being adopted and utilized with respect, they, too, showed respect by keeping their distance.

They did not hear, therefore, when the officials spoke at the place where a headstone reading simply L. S.—La Serenissima—was placed over an empty grave. It was a way for all present to see who among them was committed to this plan. It was a keeping place, too, where any of them could visit without suspicion or question. Leave flowers . . . or hidden memoranda for distribution amongst themselves.

Upon the passing of any doge in days gone by, the most senior councilor had said, "With great sorrow we understood the death of the Most Serene Prince of such piety and goodness . . . but we shall make another one."

This day, they did not bury a doge . . . but a republic. And as The Eleven and those who gathered to hear this public proclamation circled the first headstone upon this isle, they bent those words with new resolve:

"With great sorrow we understood the death of the Most Serene Republic of such purity and goodness . . . but we shall make another one."

And so they did.

126

15

THE BOOK OF WATERS

The Boy Who Would Not Be King

Massimo Fedele, doge in miniature, grew up enthroned upon the annals of his city. His days were ensconced in tutelage of history, government, warfare, justice, trade, and above all, honor.

He toiled. Oh, did he toil. Until his eyes ached, his young mind hurt, his dreams danced with visions of masquerade and maneuvering, things long past in this city now occupied by Austrian soldiers.

His father watched during his lessons, and the boy toiled harder when the man's gaze fell upon him with so much hope and fondness—and a growing shadow of doubt too.

When he tripped over a word. Stuttered over a fact he knew, deep inside.

His father would lay a hand upon his shoulder, comforting. "Your time will come," he said, in a voice meant to console.

But instead of consoling, it drove him harder. He must do better. He was Massimo Fedele, the Greatest Faithful, the final hope. It was his destiny. He studied the heroic tales of old with fervor: the *Odyssey*, the *Iliad*, *Beowulf*. Tales of men who saved not just lives, but entire societies.

One night, beside the marbled fireplace in the *piano nobile*, he watched his father wage an internal battle. Seated in a chair of red befitting a royal, he held something small in his hand, tarnished but catching the glint of flame.

A coin of some foreign kind. It obeyed the whims of his father's fingers, twisting here, hiding away in a clench.

"Father?" Massimo drew near, stretching himself to reach the height of his father's broad shoulders. Shoulders so strong he was sure they could carry the weight of the universe. Massimo wished to know how to do this. He felt it sometimes, shadows of that weight, whispering to him that one day this would be his lot too.

It was important to understand how to carry heavy things.

"What is that?" Massimo started with a small question, hoping the answer would be very big. That it might hold all the secrets he would need.

"Hmmm?" His father straightened, summoned from whatever somber cloud had held his thoughts. "This?" He held the coin still, palm open, and studied Massimo, as if ascertaining whether his son was ready for the answer. Gave a small nod, which set Massimo's heart to soaring.

He was worthy.

"This is . . . a reminder."

"To buy things well?"

Signor Fedele laughed, tipping his head to one side, then another, as if weighing that answer. "To *live* well. See." He held the round object, tarnished in bronze, before Massimo. If he had not felt his father's study of him like a living thing, Massimo would have recoiled at the object. For there, in the place an emperor's figure would be embossed upon coins, was a skeleton. Bony and grotesque, horizontal on his back. Skull looking back at Massimo with an empty, gaping, questioning stare.

"*Mem—memento Mori.*" Massimo read the two words that traversed the curve of the coin. "What does it mean?"

"It's Latin," Signor Fedele said. "It is a memento of our mortality, my son. To help us make every moment matter, for our time here is limited. It is a gift—time is what we have been given. Whatever else our lot—whatever our legacy, our history, our burdens to bear—we have all been given time. And we must spend it well, spend it like it is gold, or better."

128

The words were strange to Massimo. They felt like hope and doom all at once, and he did not know what to make of that. Turning the coin over, a Greek inscription greeted him.

"And this?" He squared his shoulders. He would prove himself ready, whatever it meant. He ran his finger over the words, which looked like they held echoes and journeys in every character.

γνῶθι σεαυτόν

His father took the coin again and ran his thumb over it in a gesture as familiar as breathing. "Know thyself."

It twisted inside Massimo and felt like a warning. "Know thyself," he repeated, infusing his voice with conviction.

"All of the great minds have quoted it. Socrates, Plato . . . It was inscribed over the Oracle of Delphi."

Massimo could not recall what that was—a statue? A temple? It sounded important, though, and he responded in silent gravity.

"Know thyself, Massimo. Whatever may come." His father pressed the coin into Massimo's hand and closed his young fingers around it.

The boy would grow into a man who would one day remember this admonition and be inspired by it. But just now, he held that coin like a dark omen, a warning to live by.

Know thyself . . . or else.

He tried harder. Schooled his stutter every chance he could, practicing the hard words in front of a mirror of Murano glass. Practiced his posture in it, too, and attempted to stop the habit of biting his lip whenever he felt his insides closing in. Doges, he was certain, did not bite their lip. And if he would one day be Doge—the First Doge of a New Era, as his father told him, he would need to be ready. For the First Doge would not only rule, but inspire. Instill a defeated and weary people with hope. He would be as much a symbol of the republic as he was a leader. Had Massimo not been born the very day the previous Doge stepped down? If anyone was meant for this, it was Massimo. Nothing could be clearer.

Time went on. At ten years old, they took him to the Ducal Palace, where once not long ago, the last Doge had presided with pride and joy over his most beloved city. Cracking open the monstrous doors to the *Sala del Maggior Consiglio*, Massimo's small hands gripped the aged entryway and felt, in its heft, the significance of such a place. How vast it was, how small he was.

The very room where the Great Council once met.

The very room where that word, so tied to his destiny, seemed to float ghostlike amid specters of voting noblemen. *Quorum.*

And the very room where the portrait of a forefather, shrouded in a veil of black paint, erased the history of his condemned roots. The Unremembered One, face a banner of darkness, sent a chill down young Massimo's spine.

Stand taller, the obscured one seemed to speak. *Be worthy.* And last, unbidden, a warning that twisted the child's stomach: *Behold your future, if you should fail.*

This, from the man whose very failure had created the purpose of Massimo's life: to atone, in full. They were linked, the two of them. Bound in soul, separated by eternity and intent.

He became aware, through a pricking of that same spine, that he was being watched. That his father, and his father's friends, important in their suits of black, spoke in hushed tones that drifted in snatches.

"Not enough time . . ."

". . . better to start again . . ."

"Only one chance . . . Cannot risk . . ."

"New plan . . ."

". . . the child struggles . . ."

Then, heated debate. That there would be no guarantee with a new plan either. That it was better to stay the course. That there were "those who can lead, and those whose gifts are . . . elsewhere." That it would be cruel to demand more when it was clearly outside the boy's—

Massimo approached them, and the voices fell silent. Silence spoke volumes, and he understood.

He was not enough.

He knew it when the whispers continued at odd times, in dark corners. When his father would not hold his head high as he looked upon the paintings in their own library of his forefathers, back and back, stopping before they reached the Unremembered One. When his mother laid a hand upon his father's shoulder and said, "Who would wish such a burden upon their own son? It will be better this way."

When one of those dark-suited men offered up his own child, soon to be born, and sure to be a boy, as all children in his family's heritage were. When books began disappearing from Massimo's schoolroom and his lessons made his head ache less and his heart ache more—for it could only mean one thing.

They had given up on him.

Not even a man yet, and he had failed the destiny of his life. It descended upon him, floating down gossamer like a dark veil, like the man in the picture.

"Your time will come, Massimo," his father said again, noting the graveness in his young son's countenance. But the lad heard the unspoken too. *Our great hope has ended with you. You will serve another purpose.*

At night, those words visited him, submerged him like water: *"Your time will come."* He turned them, churned them, burned them onto his mind until they became not a motto of resignation but a proclamation of purpose.

His time *would* come. He would make this right. Prove his worth. Bring pride and not shame to his father and forefathers, who had already known enough of shame. He *would* be the one to resurrect the republic.

When next they visited the palace, Massimo lingered as the men moved into the passageway and felt himself small among the portraits. Doges past, who had faced armies, led through plagues, overseen the transformation of a swamp into the most prized palace of the world . . . and him.

Massimo swallowed. He looked at the black-veiled painting, where the Unremembered One would have been just at eye level. And in that moment, with the eyes of a thousand oil-painted saints from frescoes blanketing the walls as his witnesses, he felt a surge of righteousness. He had heard stories like this. A dark moment, a fallen man—original sin. And how later, another would come and atone. Was it not the tale enshrined in churches beyond number in this city? The song their bell towers reverberated?

Massimo shivered at the coming thought but felt a strange power in the brassy, shiny tones it took on, snaking up and through him. The man behind the veil was, to his family, original sin. He—Massimo Fedele—would be everything opposite that. He would not let his ancestors' sacrifices and sufferings be for naught. He would not let this city sink into obscurity . . . or himself either.

His fate was tied to Venice's. And, like Venice, he would rise again.

He held this revelation like a hot coal, tending it with care whenever he felt the shroud of failure descend in the weeks that followed. More so when the infant cries from the palazzo that they shared a wall with came in the dark of night, cutting him to the quick. That boy—only days old—now bore the cloak of hope.

And Massimo . . . was nobody.

THE BOOK OF WATERS

Quantum

> *Quorum* . . .
> *Know Thyself* . . .
> *Memento Mori* . . .
> *Time spent like gold* . . .

The words became invisible figures, marching to the thrum of Massimo's pulse, as he grew. There in the shadows, all but forgotten by his city—but never by his father.

It did not seem to matter to the older man that Massimo was no longer the great hope of the old Venice, the true Venice.

His father was no longer troubled when Massimo would trip over a word or fail to retrieve a fact quickly—but Massimo spoke less, so that it would not happen often.

With all expectation fallen away, they read the *Iliad* now for adventure. They laughed, together, when they read the *Odyssey* and its account of Odysseus triumphing over the cyclops Polyphemus. . . .

"*My name? It is Nobody,*" the king told the giant. The great man making himself a veritable nothing, that he might triumph even

133

trapped in a cave with a man-devouring giant. When he wounded the cyclops enough to make his escape, the howling giant's friends came running.

"Who harmed you? Tell us!" they said.

"It's Nobody!" wailed the giant, who, moments before, had been set to end the cunning king. And at his assurance that Nobody was after him, the friends fell away, all fear assuaged.

It was then, even amid shared laughter, that the phantom king Nobody entered ranks with those marching through Massimo's mind.

He was nobody. He must make his time matter, spend it like gold. *Know thyself* . . .

Massimo, in his shadows, began to understand that by the clicking of his numerical mind, his gifts lay elsewhere. He might not command armies, but he could make an abacus dance. He may not philosophize like the great Plato, but he knew the number of steps up the Rialto Bridge and down it. He may not bring stars to man like Galileo had for their city, but he knew the heartbeat of history in this place, and he could see, down the line, numbers adding up. He may not create the masterpieces of Tintoretto, but when he looked around the Palazzo, feeling deep within the emptiness of the adjoining house, he could calculate ideal placements for opening walls. Joining the two houses into one Palazzo—and someday, he would.

And he may not be the Once and Future Doge—he may have lost his family's hope of sanctifying their family name in such a way—but could he yet make numbers into a path toward reconciliation with the past?

The gift in being Nobody was that nobody was watching him. And therein lay his strength.

If *Quorum* was not to be the theme of his life, perhaps its neighbor *Quantum* would be. *How much?*

He pulled out a ledger and wrote at the top: *Quantum*.

Numbers, he understood. Numbers begat purpose. On the next line, he wrote: *The Price of a Man.*

He dipped quill into ink and considered. On the next line down, he scratched with care an equation:

Paid to feed a man: (price per meal) x (three meals per day) x (days lived).

A concrete number appeared, settling within Massimo with a delicious weight upon the invisible scale. Transforming abstract into tangible.

He did the same for the typical number of people in a man's household. The sum grew, and so did the swelling satisfaction.

With each dip of the pen and scratch of quill, filling the page with lines and dots that held actual meaning.

Paid to church . . .
Paid to scuola . . .
Paid to maintain merchantry . . .
Paid over a lifetime for Food . . .
. . . Drink
. . . Clothing
. . . Education
. . . House
. . . Charity

Faster and faster he wrote, letters in a flurry to keep up with the flying figures in his mind that clacked satisfactorily. Here, at last, the shadow that loomed before him began to take on shape. A number to lay hold to. Something he could grip and tally, something he could give his life to. The sum growing and growing and then—

A tremor of his hand as his breath came shorter. Ever-so-slight, but his thumb collided with the inkpot, Murano glass with swirls of color suspended around liquid black as it swiveled, toppled— and the ledger was splayed in black. Ink pooling. Swathing the careful calculations into obscurity.

Massimo's stomach twisted, the shining pool flashing before his eyes, into another black swath in his memory.

The canvas that was once Paulo Zanetti.

A man, erased.

And before him now, this ledger—on the cusp of showing a path to reckoning—hope, destroyed.

Massimo could calculate again, certainly. He could wield the only tool he mastered—that of numbers—to try to lay hold of a sum that might be earned, given, to reconcile the wrongdoing of Paulo Zanetti once and for all.

But the ink, creeping until it bled onto Massimo's fingers, was clear in its message.

Nothing could undo it.

No sum.

Massimo raised his blackened hand and stared at the marks upon himself. As if Zanetti himself had reached from beyond the grave to condemn him.

Lining up a string of numbers on one side of an equation, with the blight of a man on another, would never balance the scales of justice. Only payment-in-kind. One man, for another.

Zanetti had destroyed his line? Endangered Venice? Then Massimo must give himself. Save the city. One man for another.

Zanetti had given all that he might become Somebody? Massimo would forfeit all to become Nobody.

And like Odysseus of old . . . Nobody would be the cloak that would win this war.

DANIEL

I awoke the next day to the same melodic chanting that I had drifted off to the night before. The monks, it seemed, kept a revolving schedule of prayers and services.

I was no stranger to small, confined spaces, but my quarters here were clean and bright, if simple. A far cry from the dark cell I had once known, where sounds carried agony and madness. Here, it was different. The tones that drifted through my open window were at once somber and hopeful.

I watched as a rising sun cast golden fingers over the red rooftops of the city until they burst forth in spreading light. Bells pealed so close and loud that I jolted, and a flock of pigeons ruffled into a chorus of sudden flight, as if to join with the monks.

The sounds seemed a portrait of Venice. How the holy and storied things wove into the very lifeblood and heartbeat of this place, into ordinary things like feathered creatures and exiled prisoners far from home. There was shadow and song in every stone.

Pulling out my sketchbook, I opened to an attempt I had made to capture the domed Salute cathedral that stood on a pointed piece of land between here and Saint Mark's Square. An icon of the city, it was prominent on Mr. Wharton's list. It stood larger than life outside my window—and it stood lifeless, stiff, on my page.

There was nothing of its soul on the page. *"Capture its essence,"* he had said. *"Like your translations. The perfect combination of technical skill and artist's soul."*

I had nodded, gulping.

I gulped now.

There was no soul evident on this paper.

I closed my eyes. This is where I used to picture things—take the image, pull it from my mind with each stroke of pencil, my arm a bridge from mind into being. And without that bridge, the dark chasm it once crossed threatened to swallow me whole.

The chorus of sounds played like a symphony, here in crescendo, there in rest, and traversed the bones of my arm until they swelled into a vague shape on paper. A scribble at first, so shapeless it smote me, but I kept on. I knew that outside, at a point of land between me and Saint Mark's Square, a grand domed cathedral stood. That it had once been built as a plea for salvation from plague. I felt the grip of the people's desperation in my gut, and let it drive my arm.

Opening my eyes, I laughed dryly.

Was there soul on the page now? Perhaps . . . if "soul" looked like a tangled cloud of nonsense. But it was a start. I set the page beside the technical piece I'd done the night before, laying it to the right.

On the left was a picture that made sense but had no spark.

On the right was an impassioned attempt to capture a feeling but had no form. But it held shadow, and light, and a vague shape to it.

If I could but bridge the two . . .

But I had an appointment to keep. And I wouldn't miss it for the world.

After a simple meal of bread and water, the same monk who had first greeted me gave instructions that a hearty lunch might be found farther down the Giudecca at the market where fishermen and dock workers congregated, rather than the tourists and visitors to be found along the cafes of the Grand Canal.

He eyed my suit, which I had brushed well and hung to air outside my window the night before. I was an enigma, I knew; monk-like in my simplicity of possessions, and yet those few possessions bespoke wealth. "Perhaps you prefer the cafes, though?" he asked, as if trying to ascertain which world I belonged to.

I had no answer for that, for I had no inkling where I belonged. I thanked him for the bread and inquired as to the Palace of Letters and Sciences. It was one of the places I was to sketch, and I meant to make use of their archives while there, to see if I could ascertain anything about a guild of artisans and a boy in a canal, or a family by the name of Fedele.

Once there, I was successful only in capturing the sketch—another of the lifeless sort. When I inquired within as to whether they housed any material regarding the history of guilds—*scuole*, I learned—the clerk harbored an amused spark and led me to rows upon rows of books and ledgers, information that spanned centuries and vocations, charitable work and more. It would take months to comb through them thoroughly. At one point I nearly leapt out of my skin when I read that their regulations had been called *mariegola*. The weathered voice of the man at the flat yesterday materialized, formidable in my mind, and I smiled to the heavens, thinking to have found the item he'd required.

"Mariegola." I tried the word out, and it fell flat. Close, but something was off. I flipped through my notes and read the word he had said: *Marangona*.

I braced myself to again face the clerk, this time asking about this word.

"Marangona?" the man repeated. "Si, signore." He looked on me with pity, spotting the map in my hand. He unfolded it upon his glass counter and pointed to Saint Mark's Square. "May I?" He held up a pencil, and when I nodded, he circled the place where the campanile stood. "One of the bells, you know." He shook his head sadly, though I couldn't think why.

I thanked him heartily, noting the time and gathering up my materials as a noon bell summoned haste. I was to meet Vittoria soon at the very campo in question, and I was beginning to learn this city needed more time than expected to traverse. Not just because of the ferries and canals, steps and bridges, and its aptitude for swallowing wanderers into forgotten waysides, but because the people, too, were islands of time. Happily so. Stopping to chat on the way to the market, stopping to chat on the way back home, marking the time not by clocks or shadows but by who was where and when.

When I arrived at St. Mark's Square, I passed through the double-columned entrance and a hallowed shiver traversed my being. Soon, I would round the corner and see the renowned form of the campanile tower. Hope sprang into my steps. Perhaps this, the place that marked so many historical moments, would be the thing to help bring the spark of life back into my sketches, and—

I turned left, lifted my eyes. There was no tower.

Had I missed it?

I turned and turned again. There was the Doge's Palace. The intricate archways lining the square, the basilica, the deep cerulean clock with its gilt numbers gleaming and the golden form of the lion atop.

But no tower.

Which made no sense. I had seen Campo San Marco sketched and expounded upon in my volume of travel essays. It was written on my list of landmarks to sketch: the Doge's Palace, its courtyard, the basilica . . . and yes, the four-sided tower that reached above the square, platform to bells that pealed declarations of hours, occasions, intrusions, celebrations . . . all the joys and sorrows of life.

But the watchtower, proud and victorious for longer than my own nation had been a country, lay in a pile of bricks upon the ground. My stomach tumbled, and I could not account for this bereft sense of loss of something I had never even seen.

Footsteps, carried on wings, drew up beside me. Vittoria.

"It fell," she said. "Not quite two years ago." Her serious tone cradled the facts in grief.

I turned again, slowly taking in the arched colonnades, the ornate stone adornments of the palace and the steps rising up to it, the neatly stacked windows where, for centuries, black-robed members of the Great Council took apartments and retired from their sessions. What ideas, what deliberations, what sleepless nights had those walls played witness to?

All of these buildings stood timeless and tall, with no traveling cracks or toppling spires attesting to any great calamity that might have overturned the tower.

"What made it fall?"

"So many things," Vittoria said, her voice drawing my gaze. She was in a yellow dress today, and sunlight reached for her as if reclaiming one of its beams. "One can only be struck by lightning so many times, and be shaken by the bells you were built to hold, and be hammered and fortified and patched together for so long before finally all the blows give way to catastrophe." She shook her head, eyes glistening with feeling. "I remember which book I was pulling down at the shop, for a little girl. One of the *Piccole Storie*. It was bright and green, small and perfect for her hands, and as I placed it there . . ."

I could feel a memory tug at me, the slip of a small volume into my own hands. The Book of Isles, the green one was. Tucked into my hands as a boy, from my mother. Tucked into my cell, as a man, sent by mail from those same hands.

"There came a low rumble. The whole city seemed to shiver. But we have a saying, since it fell. We will rebuild—com'era, dov'era. As it was, where it was."

As it was, where it was. The shackles deep in the shadows of my mind grated at that. Could anything ever be restored so perfectly?

She inhaled sharply. "But you did not come for the bricks. Tell me what you learned. Did you discover the book?"

We sat upon a bench, and I told her of the ill-fated encounter with the man at the flat and the little I'd learned this morning.

"Marangona," Vittoria said, eyes wide with mirth. "He asked you to bring him a bell?"

"It would seem so."

She smiled. "The bells are monstrosities! And most of them were destroyed in the fall. Who would ask such a thing?"

"Someone bent on getting rid of me, I'd say. A . . . wild-goose chase."

She responded with a laugh that had a ring all its own. "I enjoy the chasing of geese." I could well believe it. "Come. We will see what can be done."

She launched herself up and strode with purpose. I stood, too, pausing as her skirt swished around her ankles and a question swirled inside of me. She turned, sensing I was not with her. "Coming?"

I hesitated. She tilted her head, listening.

"Why would you help me?" I blurted, ruing the lack of polish in my speech. "You have customers, deliveries, a full life . . ."

She retraced her steps, returning to me. "Do you remember what they call me at the train station?"

"The Garbin," I said, and she looked surprised at how quickly the answer rolled from my tongue. But the wind had a homeland in me, and she didn't know that.

"That is correct," she said. "Zio Alonzo told me that the Garbin comes in and floods this place with fog because it is always looking for the place it belongs. It finds Venice and sets down its baggage because it belongs here." For the first time, I saw in Vittoria a flicker of uncertainty.

"The Book of Waters," she continued, "it has always been my favorite. It seemed beautiful to me that, in a world full of books, there is still a story that has no ending. It makes it feel like . . ." She twirled her hand in the air, looking for the words. "Like anything is possible." Breath froze inside me at her words. The very same as my mother's.

"Yes," I said. She watched me, waiting. Pulling words from their buried place deep inside. "It—it almost makes me wish to preserve it that way." It felt like a confession. Painful and yet somehow freeing too. "The ending could be a good one, or it could be . . ."

"I know," she said, catching my uncertainty and receiving it with her own look of understanding. "But to help something find its wholeness . . ." A corner of her mouth tugged up into a smile, dimpling with magic. "Plus, there is the matter of . . ." She clasped her hands in front of her. "Well, I have a proposal for you, Signor Goodman."

"You didn't say 'Train.'" I narrowed my eyes.

"I did not," she said with exaggerated gravity.

"This makes me nervous."

"I have a proposal for you, Signor Train."

I laughed. "Go ahead." I spread my hand out in a half-circle of invitation.

"I, Vittoria Bellini—"

"The Garbin," I interjected.

"I, Vittoria Bellini, the Garbin, offer my services as local Venetian expert and keeper of various bits of book facts in return for . . ." She slowed her words and took a deep breath.

"Yes?" This offer was beginning to sound appealing, for many reasons.

The next words came out in a speedy gust. "For a copy of the original text once you have completed it and translated it." She finished, breathless, biting her lip as if she wished the words back.

This volume—the one I hadn't had the strength to open for so long—was now opening doors I had never imagined.

"Yes," I said, without hesitation.

She gripped my hand in both of hers, clutching it in excitement. "Grazie! Oh, what it would be to have that volume . . . and the people who would come to see it! You cannot know, Daniel Goodman, what this would mean to them all. They have grown up with these tales, and so many have wondered and wondered why there were so few of the blue book, and what the ending was, and what it all means. Not to mention, the funds it would bring would be—well, we *are* in need of some spots on our roof patching—"

I laughed at the uncanniness.

Her face went stoic. "Is that funny? Did I say the wrong word? I cannot think why water spots from a leaky roof would be funny. *Roof.*" She emphasized the word, rolling her eyes up in question, checking her internal dictionary. "Roof? Roofs. *Rooves.* Rooves? It all begins to sound wrong. I—"

"You have it right," I said, lifting my free hand around hers.

This seemed to remind her she still held my other hand captive and she dropped it like a hot coal, her cheeks blushing.

"I have been carried away again, haven't I?"

She was the one doing the carrying. She was captivating, and it just was entirely ironic in a strangely beautiful way that this might help her fix her roof.

"You are . . . just right," I said.

And for once it seemed that what I had said was just right too. She lifted her shoulders a bit and stuck out her hand. "Americans do business with handshakes, no?"

I shook her hand.

"Now, about La Marangona." She turned, and I followed her cue. Rising before us was a building constructed in a lacework of stone. Pillars and arches alternating all along the ground floor, the meeting of strength and delicacy.

"Do you know where we are?" she asked, smile dimpling.

"The Palazzo Ducale?"

"Correct!" Vittoria said. "The Doge's Palace. You have done your studying, signore. While you are here, you must visit the *biblioteca*."

Something quickened inside me. "A library?"

"Turn around," she said, and gestured to the building across the campo, facing the palace. "The *Biblioteca Marciana*. At least for a little while longer. They will be moving the collections soon, but it is one of the few institutions that our beautiful republic formed when she was in her glory, whose heart beats still today. You can see why St. Mark's Square is said to be the heart of Venice."

"It seems a great many places are the heart of Venice," I said.

She looked pleased. "Ah, perhaps you are more Venetian than you think! Very good. So. You will want to inquire at the biblioteca about your Book of Waters. They are the keepers of many of our important manuscripts. And their reading rooms will do well for you, if you should need a place to work as you translate. You will doubtless hear the tower workers, and those restoring the palace—it has gone to shambles these last hundred years. But beneath all that dust and disrepair, Venice still gleams." She turned again to face the palace and led to the left of the building, where between it and the basilica next door, a narrow gate joined the two buildings. Marble twisted and pillared its way around statues of four women, enrobed and winsome.

"Prudence, Hope, Charity, and Fortitude," Vittoria named them. "You see? So that the criminals who passed through on their way to their trials might be reminded of what is right and good."

I swallowed, unable to do more than nod as I walked between the white marble monuments.

"Why—" I cleared my throat as I passed through, noticing the lion of St. Mark and the kneeling man residing statuesque in their place above the gate. "Why are they so much brighter than the other figures?"

Vittoria backed up, gazing at the figure of the kneeling doge. I wondered, briefly, what it must have been to reside in such a role. To bear the entirety of a powerful republic.

"The French, you know. You will notice their mark all over the city. For when Napoleon's armies invaded, they were intent on erasing any reminder of Venice's former power and pride. They destroyed the lion and the Doge Foscari statues you see there—and then?" She released her hand into the air. "Decided they no longer wanted us. They realized, perhaps, that they could never erase Venice only by removing some of our crown jewels. And the lion and doge were re-created soon after they left. We do not so easily forget, you see. Come." She proceeded through the gate. "You will feel quite at home beneath this gate, of course," she said, facing me expectantly.

My stomach twisted like the marble above me as I passed through. This place so symbolic of justice branded me all over again. Perhaps she knew. It seemed sometimes that my past hung upon me like a cloak, proclaiming for all. "I suppose I should explain," I said. *Confess* would be a better word.

"You already did." Her expression morphed into one of perplexity, her dark brows drawn down. "About the text you are translating? I meant it as a joke, but I see it translated poorly. This is the *Porta della Carta*. The Door of the Paper. There once resided a scribe at a desk nearby, who would write letters and contracts for those who could not do so themselves. If the desk remained, wouldn't it make a perfect spot for you to conduct your translations?" She looked delighted with her proposal, and I breathed easier.

Ever so briefly, we passed through the halls of the palazzo itself. Though absent of people, a million mites of dust spun in golden sunbeams, illuminating the place enough to feel the stony stares of the figures adorning doors and halls. From Atlas, to the saints, to ancient faces I could not place, they watched on in silent consideration. The place dripped in gold and history.

We passed the open door to a sprawling chamber, where Vittoria explained the Great Council once met to deliberate and decide the fates of people and nations—meeting for the final time to decide the fate of their floating, invaded city. The chamber, empty now, echoed with unseen arguments, impassioned speeches, arisen souls who by no means agreed with one another. Who carried the fates of their children, grandchildren, great-grandchildren, and the yet unborn great-great-great-descendants.

Every last inch of the walls and ceilings of the chamber were covered in frescoes depicting scenes in a spirit of cosmic drama: struggle, defeat, victory, bound in by tarnished golden millwork.

"Here," Vittoria whispered. I hadn't realized the slowness of my pace as I took it all in, and she was now ahead of me, waiting at an arched door to the courtyard beyond. I joined her, and she gestured to the scene outside, where a few men stacked bricks and went about their work.

"Here is what you need." She peered at the small watch she wore pinned near her waist and winced. "I am sorry. I must go, but—buona fortuna, Daniel." She gave my hand a squeeze. "You must tell me what happens!" She turned to go, her skirt swishing as she did and catching my ankle as she passed.

"Wait," I said. "Aren't you coming?"

"I cannot!" She bustled on, a glint in her eye. "I am needed back at the shop."

"But—Marangona. How will I find it?"

Something crossed her countenance. Whether it was delight or mischief I could not tell, but it was lined with a twist of magic. "You are closer than you think." And with that, she was gone.

I watched her go as she glided with ease and speed past the watchful works of art.

I turned and let out a rueful laugh. A thief and a palace. What a joke I must be in the cosmic realm.

A breeze gusted about the courtyard as if trapped, making circles of leaves and causing a man to pause his work creating neat rows of the heavy pieces. He lifted his tanned round face to the breeze for reprieve.

I greeted him in Italian, inquiring if he might know the whereabouts of this Marangona.

He looked at me as if I'd taken leave of my senses. "But she has been silent since the fall," he said. "Hardly a soul has come to see her. Why would they? She does not sing now, though there is none like her. If you wish to see her . . ." He dusted his hands on work-smudged trousers and led the way through a maze of several platforms stacked high with the bricks of the fallen campanile.

"La Marangona," the man said.

There stood the bell. Odd and otherworldly, much taller than I. Standing there with no hours to mark or sentences to announce, and if it could shiver in the cold for want of its tower, I think it would have. Instead, its silence dashed a shiver down my own spine.

"The only bell to survive the fall. She breaks my heart every time I see her." "She" hung not two feet above the courtyard, suspended from a thick-beamed tripod. "A tragedy," he said. "She served her city for many lifetimes, sending song into our darkest midnight hours. So faithful, only to fall from the sky, watch her sister bells become shards, and then stand here alone and forgotten." He placed a hand on the bell almost reverently. A grown man's hand, dwarfed by the breadth and height of this bronze behemoth. Latin words were etched upon it, flourishes adorned its circumference, as if their engraved beauty might ring out with the steady notes she was cast to roll over the city's sea of red rooftops. "But we will build her tower again. We will mend her sister bells. Venice may fall, but she does not rot. She rebuilds."

Like Vittoria, the man was almost zealous in his proclamation.

I removed my hat and pressed it to my chest, a gesture I hoped would show the respect his speech seemed to warrant.

And then, as he resumed his work with a wary eye on me, I stared up at the Marangona and wondered how, in all of creation, was I to bring this to the man who lived at the center of a maze. I recalled the narrow alley, the gates, the odd windows cut into the bricked-in doorways.

The bell may not be defeated, as the man said. But I was. It settled over me, heavy and final and silent.

That evening, I returned to my quarters after a day of lifeless sketching and combing the shelves of every bookshop, library, and archive I could find. Climbing the stairs to my room, the bells of San Giorgio tolled a melancholy peal, ushering the monks into their vespers.

In the hallway, my friend the monk asked if I would join in. "The evening prayers . . . they lift a weary heart."

For a moment, I was sorely tempted. To be among people, to be lifted from this dark defeat . . . but prayers were for the holy. I thanked him and shut myself away in the quiet of my room.

The monk was right. This heart was weary. More than weary. It had wandered and lost itself, toiled to right itself, journeyed to justify itself, and here at the end of that journey was on the verge of crumbling.

My bones ached to collapse into the bed, so perfect in its simplicity. But its simplicity was *too* perfect for the tangle I'd made of it all.

At the window, a small desk bore the weight of its solitary occupant: the folio in which I was translating the book. An oil lamp protruded from the wall, and evening light unrolled like a scroll over the oddly geometric islands speckling the lagoon like haphazard stepping-stones.

I had nothing left to give—and yet here was something, however small, that I could set my hand to.

Those last words I'd translated blew into the room, the story of another who meant to atone. Massimo Fedele, who had tasted defeat.

The pang of my own defeat eased a bit as I thought of the boy so young, watching his own future crumble and determining that—how had the book put it?—like Venice, he would rise again. I opened to find the last words:

Massimo . . . was nobody.
But it would not always be so.

I sat. Picked up my pen. And began to write.

THE BOOK OF WATERS

The Guardian

The baby next door to Massimo Fedele had been born unto wealth, born unto a family fated, born unto blood that reached back into the souls who settled this lagoon and built refuge from refuse. Even his name was one that honored doges of the past: Sebastien.

Upon Sebastien's birth, he received an unusual inheritance. Not from his parents, nor his forefathers, but from the older boy next door.

In the watches of the night, a title lifted from Massimo Fedele. Arose with all pomp and mystery, swirling through the passageways and walls and settling upon the tiny shoulders of Sebastien Mendeli: heir apparent. Once and future ruler. Unelected, and wholly unsuspecting. All while the boy next door became, to his dismay . . . unremembered.

The doge who would save Venice—a baby? Who would be trained, groomed, prepared, and, when the time was right, installed as the great leader to pave the way for a fallen Venice.

It was to have been Massimo's role. A dark seed of bitterness took root within Massimo Fedele. But deeper—a dark weight of failure. Had he really failed so much that they imagined starting afresh with an infant—an infant!—gave them more promise?

But the baby received another inheritance too: that of loss. For Sebas-

150

tien Mendeli's father was snatched away in a wave of a plague before ever meeting his son, his dying wish for all preparations to be made. That if he could not be there to provide for and support his son, every infrastructure he could arrange from his bedchamber, in his last hours, would be. A schoolroom, hidden away, lest the occupying Austrians suspect. Tutors, all *simpatico* in their hopes for Venice's future. Books, crammed onto the schoolroom shelves. A map of La Serenissima, that the boy might behold the hundreds of islands, stitched together in bridges, and learn to love it. And a guardian, devoted to the Mendeli family as if it were his single purpose. A man Signor Mendeli trusted more than his own breath. It grieved the soul of this dying father, that if his one son would bear the fate of a city on his shoulders, he would not be there to hold up his arms in the duty. But he could give him a name and give him all that he was able. There were others who would rally and lead the boy into manhood, teach him of the need for a good and true leader. They would pour the best of themselves into him, and when he was of age, he would offer back to Venice all the good that Venice had given to them in all of her years.

"And if it is not a son?" his wife whispered through tears.

"It is." Two small words. No explanation, and every conviction.

"And if he is—not fit to be doge? Look at young Massimo," she said with compassion. With all the love for her unborn child, a swelling of protectiveness rose. "If our child should not be meant to carry such a future either . . ."

But there was no answer. The plague took this father, and when at last the baby was born, the hand of fate visited the house of Mendeli again. In the months that passed between Signor Mendeli's death and Sebastien Mendeli's birth, much changed.

The plague took the lives of many. Allies and those who were to have infused the coming child with their tutelage and wisdom, taken by the pestilence or driven by it to the mainland and the mountains beyond. Before his life had even begun, it was turned upside down.

His mother, strong of soul, knew it before the doctor and midwife did. Something amiss, after the boy's strong cry rang out. For as he took in his first breaths, her own became more difficult.

She did not have as much time as the boy's father did, upon her deathbed, to make arrangements. But she did make one.

The boy's guardian—family friend and faithful servant for as long as either of their bloodlines could account for—would deliver the boy to safety. She whispered her plan to the man, keenly aware that their allies were dwindling and her innocent son could soon be a target. And when his brows drew down deep in concern and confusion and he asked, "Are you certain?" . . . she gathered the last of her strength and said, "Never more so."

And so, when she had gone on to eternity, he bundled the child up. Left the child's side for mere moments to arrange the gondola for himself—no boatman would accompany. No witness would be allowed.

When it was time, the guardian slipped out into the night. Followed the maze of canals until he was placed just far enough to cloak his identity and be sure of the child's destination whilst remaining in the shadows himself. Though Venice was quiet, her stones were alive, sending a shiver up the man's spine, making him feel watched.

He stooped, held the baby for the first and only time—this wee man whom it was his life's purpose to guard—and whispered something of waters and secrets beside the tiny ear. Nestled him into the vessel of a basket and watched him go.

The house of Mendeli ended once and for all that night.

And the house of Trovato . . . began.

THE BOOK OF WATERS

The Girl upon the Mountaintop

In a twirl of frost and wonder, oceans take to the sky and dance again to earth. *Snow.* It resides across the lagoon, high above Venice, and in the mountains beyond.

Years after Sebastien floated in his basket, across those same waters came a girl.

Hair yellow as sun, eyes blue as sky. Even her countenance seemed as if it might be more at home among the clouds than here on the earth— something ethereal in the way she watched the world, as if trying it on to see where she might belong.

Over sea and land she came, until a carriage took her on the Alte Vie. From that high path she watched the sea disappear and the mountains rise like giants before her . . .

Mariana Fedele stepped into a castle and shivered. More precisely, it was a *manor*, but to her small form, the lonely, stony, pointy place may as well have been a castle. It looked down upon the tiny village of Alpenzell, where the roofs topped with snow mounded like soft, sweet cream. The village was a pocket of twinkling lights, lanterns in windows in the dark of winter. Mariana

153

watched from her own window as a boy and a girl—brother and sister—formed snow into spheres in their mittened hands and proceeded to pelt each other, their laughter flying too.

On the windowsill, she kept a portrait of her brother. He was older, much older than she. But she could imagine it—the way his dark eyes would crinkle beneath his smile if she were to blast him with a ball of snow. He was more like a father to her than a brother, but he spoiled her every chance he could.

She traced the imagined scene in fog upon her window, her finger freezing and she not minding it. A wonder to her, that the droplets in fog upon the pane might have once been the waters she had left behind in Venice. And so, as she drew, she imagined a little piece of home had come to visit her there and given her a canvas upon which to work.

It was something she could do way up here at the top of the world—to draw what she saw, whether in window fog or scattered sand or bound in paper and ink. What it mattered, she was not sure. If she drew the manor, she had not been the one to build it. If she depicted the forest, she had nothing to do with growing it. What, she wondered, could be the good of being a—well, simply an observer? But it was within her, and so draw she did.

That night, after she had finished her scene on the window and it had fogged over once more while all the world slept, she tiptoed outside to catch the swirling snowflakes. Those ancient Genesis waters, dancing a feather-light, crystal-hewn spiral. By the light of the moon, delicate flakes melted into her skin, becoming water once again. She stooped, gathered them up into a snowball, marveling at the curve of solid water against her palm, the way it filled the hollowness. And then, stepping to the side of the hill, where if mountains, trees, distance, and darkness allowed, she would see the Adriatic Sea . . . she vaulted that sphere into the night sky. It curved up and then down, down, down, tumbling with a satisfying thump.

She smiled. The water would melt. It would run down, someday. Course through crannies and through the Alpen Dolomites, down to her sea.

Someday. Someday, she would be there again too. With her own brother. And not just for the one summer he had brought her back to Venice. One day, he would bring her home for good. He would look upon her and love her.

He loved her now, she knew, by keeping her here—for a better upbringing than he could provide on his own in Venezia. Here, she had a distant aunt and uncle, an honored place in the House of Rothford. A life capped in spires and turrets and dreams, always dreams . . . of some place this mountain wind tumbled down again to the canals. Her home.

Her brother came to see her every Christmas. Together with their aunt and uncle, they ate a fine and festive meal of many dishes, but the only one she remembered all the year through was the pandoro. A tall, golden-brown cake of their beautiful lagoon homeland—but this, they drizzled with the finest Swiss chocolate. A delicacy from her father's people topped with a delicacy from her mother's. She did not remember their parents, and she always stole a glance at her brother as he ate it. His mouth turned up in a nostalgic smile. Eyebrows drawn down into something somber. Regret?

Each Christmas, she unwrapped a parcel from him, knowing already what it would hold: paper and pencils. For her drawing and writing, which her brother realized kept her company while he was away.

But her most prized joy was the week after Christmas. Massimo would stay, and for that week, it was as if she were the only person in his world. They rode together, read together, explored the trees together. She drew in her new sketchbook. He loaned her his paintbrushes and brought color to her world. She always urged him to paint more, but he jested that all the great works had already been made, and what had he to offer? Beneath the lightness in his tone, a shadow underscored his question, as if he truly wondered what he—his very person—could possibly offer.

Everything, she thought. He was a good brother. How many men who were twenty years their sister's senior would do half as much as he did for her? He once brought a doctor all the way from

Verona just to see her when he received word from their aunt that she was not faring well. When she had protested the need, he'd given her arm a gentle squeeze and said, "Of course it is needful, Mariana. You were born for great things."

He was distant for much of her life, but when he was present, he doted.

Often, he scribbled things in a book. Often, he stayed up with the stars, tallying ledgers. Often, he disappeared in the evening to "attend to business." He never would tell her what nature that business was, but sometimes the business came to him instead—a man on horseback, sometimes two or three. They spoke late into the night, and on those nights he retired with measured, serious steps down the long corridor.

But in the morning, he always greeted her with his broad smile, as if nothing had transpired. He even—secretly, lest they distress the world—taught her to fence. She, a woman—fencing! But he was intent that she should know one or two things with the sword. Always with a countenance light, he taught her to parry and plunge, dodge and advance.

"Keep your distance, Mariana," he would say. Or "Never turn your back. And—as a matter of honor—never attack a man at the back. Unless it is a matter of your own life, of course."

She jested with him about his destiny as a great poet like Homer or Shakespeare. *Never attack a man at the back.* And he laughed, duly. But she remembered the phrase well, ensconced in the wisdom and warmth of his voice.

At the end of their fencing matches, he would behold her in solemn gravity, a twinkle in his dark eyes, and make her promise not to tell. "You'll scare off the suitors," he said.

One year, he had her portrait commissioned while visiting and took it away with him to show such suitors. It was a very strange thing to watch him ride away into the mountains on his fine black horse, with a likeness of her in his pocket. All to be shown to strangers, who would determine her future without ever speaking a word with her.

"Take me with you," she whispered, this time her breath fogging the windowpane and no scene drawn in its wake. "Take the real me." Not just the portrait. Not just a likeness as a bartering token in whatever future he, as her guardian, must arrange for her. And one day, the finest of days when the sun hit the snow and burst it into diamonds, he did just that. Back into a carriage she went. Grown, now, retracing the path of her little girl self, back down to the rippling sea. . . .

20

DANIEL

I awoke to the sound of voices on the lagoon. They seemed distant and yet familiar—fishermen, jovial tones about the morning's catches, mention of the Rialto market.

Something stuck to my face, and as I raised my head, I had a groggy realization: I had fallen asleep, pen in hand, with my sorry cheek pressed to freshly scrawled ink.

There was no looking glass in the room, but a glance at the aged and half-closed window confirmed I bore Massimo's continued tale. Tattooed, as it were, by my own hand, upon my own self— this account of a man atoning. And his sister, though I couldn't figure yet how it all connected.

I scrubbed in vain at the ink. Groaned, and sloshed water from the pitcher into the wash basin and scrubbed with increasing intensity, as recollections of the translation flooded in.

Venice was a great mingling of man and myth, and I couldn't yet perceive where on that scale this story of a secret society, a baby in a basket, a plague, a damsel on a mountaintop, a young man scorned, and a merry band of artisans fit. And what of this Unremembered Doge and his progeny? It all certainly seemed more fairy tale than fact, but then again, this was the floating city. It was impossible to say what secrets it kept.

Every now and again, an illustration that seemed more symbolic than specific made an appearance, and it struck me that someone had taken great care to carve the wood blocks that had made these depictions.

An inkblot stared at me from the page, where I'd frozen midstroke as I'd written of a golden Venetian cake drizzled in Swiss chocolate. A delicacy served only one place in the world, or so I had been told: Goodman's Fine Italian Treats. And that wasn't the only detail that had the book feeling uncomfortably personal. Wrestling with worth, striving for a place—it was all a little too close.

One thing I knew. Somewhere in the dark of the night before, as the oil lamp flickered over my words and made them seem oddly alive, as I glanced back over the installments I'd completed, the slightest hope crept in.

For if a merry band of artisans could see their way to raising the basket baby in every single one of their trades and homes, surely I could find a way to get an eight-thousand-pound bell through a maze of streets and to a man of questionable sanity.

Or if the man in the window was determined to be clever with words about bells that were impossible to bring or to ring . . . then perhaps I would answer him in kind.

Back at the courtyard of the Doge's Palace, I discovered my new friend the brick-stacker working away again—this time with a jaunty whistle. Perhaps this would bode well for my plan.

"*Scusi*, signore." I slipped into Italian. "You're the Keeper of the Bells?" I hoped the moniker might honor the man who had shrewd dark eyes, a prodigious moustache, and hands that darted to and fro between the bricks at his work, with the fervor of a fish pursuing shadows.

"Keeper of the Bells, Stacker of the Bricks, Scraper of the Gifts the Pigeons Leave Behind," he said, never stopping his work. "That is I."

I bent, gripped a brick in each hand from their position on a loose pile, and began to stack.

The man stood back, crossed his arms over his chest, and watched.

"Like so?" I continued. It felt good to feel the pull of my back, to have something solid in my hands, to see progress.

"No." He moved the last brick a centimeter to the left in its row. "Like *so*."

He watched me warily as we worked in tandem thus, odd partners in the cataloguing of fallen masonry. But I couldn't ask a favor without having earned it. I wouldn't.

"So?"

I lifted my head and pulled in a breath. "La Marangona," I began. "She is . . . out of service."

He drew his head back as if I'd said the most preposterous thing possible. "Marangona." He curved the word like a song. "Out of service, he asks. Foreigners. Have the fish ceased to swim the lagoon? Has man ceased breathing? Has the sun refused to rise?"

"Well . . . no."

"La Marangona is *always* in service." He stomped toward the lady in question. "Just because she has no tower does not mean she is not in service."

I shifted my weight, my better judgment disallowing me from speaking the logical inquiries that echoed where the bell was silent.

The man's face, in a pinch of passion, seemed to register me as a person, and a pitiable one. Impoverished of what was so abundantly clear to him. His voice became less indignant, but no less filled with conviction.

"Does time march on?"

Like pencil marks upon paper. "Yes."

"And so, she waits. Waiting is her service, now."

But service was toiling. Doing. Striving. . . . Wasn't it?

"You do not see," the man said, with something like pity in his voice. "Come." He led the way to the bell, stuffed his hand in his pockets, and pondered for a moment before speaking.

"In her song, she marks our days. In her silence, she holds our days. A . . . promise," he said, the right side of his moustache twitching as the corner of his mouth pulled up. And, in the same gesture, seemed to pull him up out of this posture of contemplation. "So!" His voice returned to a roil. "Do not tell me she is out of service!"

"I understand," I said. "And—" I tried not to think of how insane this would sound, or about how it was possibly the only chance to meet the demands of the man at the flat. There was no way to couch this in terms that would help it make sense. "May I borrow it?"

He beheld me, still as a statue for a good many seconds, and then burst out with laughter that resounded up and out of the courtyard. Probably shaking ancient windowpanes along the way.

"He wants to take the bell!" He wheezed the words in between laughs. "Do you plan to put it in your pocket, sir?" He pointed at the gargantuan bell and then at me, laughing so hard he bent to brace at his knees. "Thank you for the joke."

My mind whirred, trying to find an alternative. "I know I can't borrow the whole bell," I said. "I was just hoping for—the ringer."

Increased laughter. I didn't blame him. The ringer itself was the size of a man.

"Well, may I—may I borrow you, then?"

The laughing stopped. "What?"

"You're . . . the Keeper of the Bells. All I need is just an afternoon with the ringer. You wouldn't need to let it out of your sight, if you came. A man nearby would like to see it, and . . ." As I went on to explain the circumstances, I saw a thousand protests line up on his face.

"Wait." I pushed my hands out in front of me to halt his protest. If I was going to convince him to do something preposterous, I was going to need to use his own words. Make him see the beauty in it. "You said she is in service. Holding the days of Venice. Yes?"

No answer. Narrower eyes. What would a visionary say? Someone who could talk to people and make them feel the heart of something? What would that person say to a man who was passionate about this bell and his city? What would Mr. Wharton or Vittoria Bellini say?

"Imagine it," I started. Gulped. *Pretend to be a visionary.* "The very bell who has presided over Venice, sending workers home, summoning the sun, marking days to rejoice and mourn . . . But never, not ever, mingling among the souls she has tended for all of these centuries. And then, after all of that, to survive a fall that no one can account for . . . What if that fall could be turned into the opportunity of a lifetime for her?"

The slightest tilt of his chin. Brows drawn down. He was listening.

"What if, for the first time since she was cast—cast upon molten fires—she, in her silence, was allowed to be taken to the very streets she's kept vigil over? To experience the light and shadows, the stones and wonders, up close? For this ringer—her very voice!—to be carried through the alleyways that only her echoes have traversed before." I took a breath, spreading my shoulders like a visionary, I imagined, would. "We could be the ones to do that for her." My conclusion lacked a certain spark, but it was all I had.

He wasn't impressed either. "You . . . realize it is just a bell, signore."

I swallowed. Wanted to concur with everything in me, but I was too far in to retreat now. "Is anything ever . . . 'just a bell?'" I used a knowing tone but had no idea what I actually meant.

For a moment, his face was grave and contemplative. He took a step forward. Leaned in until he was so close I could see brick dust upon his nose. Looked at me at an angle and, lifting a furled fist, knocked thrice upon on my head.

"Ah," he said and nodded conclusively. Like a doctor with his diagnosis. "Empty."

Air was expunged out of me, and hope too.

"Like the Marangona will soon be. Get the cart, Signor Bell-Brain."

And just like that, air and hope surged back into me. "You mean—"

"You will owe me," he said, already ducking beneath the bell and taking a tool out of his belt to free the ringer.

I halted. That might be a problem.

"Yes. Good," I said, closing my eyes and thinking fast. Feeling the press of the brick stacks around. Did I imagine it, or did they lean in to scrutinize me? "I . . . can pay in labor. Every morning, for the next two weeks," I said, wheeling the cart to the bell. "I'll help with the bricks."

"Make it one week," the man said, emerging from within the bell. "I don't know if I can stand too much of this . . ." He waved his hand up and down at me, searching for a word. "This . . . talking that you do."

I breathed easy. "That makes two of us," I mumbled. Best to leave the visionary-speak to Mr. Wharton.

How does one move a bronze ringer the size of a man through a city of water? With the help of a bell-keeper with connections, a ferry driven by a merry Jacopo, a cart, several ropes, a strained shoulder that would make a week of brick-hauling a little more intense, seven obliging passersby, one dented wooden post after a near catastrophe, and a tagalong dog who joined up somewhere near Santa Croce.

We arrived by some miracle back at the flat where, once again, the lion's mouth looked ready to devour. I pulled the chain, the curtain fluttered, and the same voice sounded. "I am not here."

The Keeper of the Bells raised his eyebrows. "He is crazy too, eh? No wonder you are friends," he leaned in and whispered.

I stepped forward, as if this was all a matter of course.

"Signore?" I asked. "I've done as you requested."

The man appeared at the window and began to tug it closed.

The bell-keeper pulled a small hammer from his belt, waited until the man above was situated where he could see, and struck the ringer one single time.

He gripped the cart handles as the bright and melancholy brassy note faded. "There," he said. "He has gotten his ring. I will see you in the morning, yes?"

But the window above was creaking open now, instead of closed. I couldn't see the man well, for the way the light bounced from an opposing window set him in a shadow. But his posture—the way it froze and moved slowly away from the window, wordless, said plenty.

That he had thought me a problem solved. That he had constructed a riddle that he had believed unsolvable.

And that—as the slowly creaking door before us now proclaimed—he had been wrong.

The man emerged, his movements slow but steady in a way that belied his age. Up close, I could see the man's deeply mapped face, hair that tumbled from his head in meandering rivers of white, joining with the length of his beard. And though he wore his years plainly for all to see, though he was likely near unto a hundred years old, it was something more, something deeper about him that washed the campo with a sense of the ancient. Of things known and kept so close, the secrets had become a very part of him.

"It cannot be." His gaze only briefly stopped at me as it traveled to the bronze ringer, there in the middle of the campo.

The bell-keeper drew himself up to his full height, making to show off the artifact with some great proclamation. But the older man's presence seemed to work its spell even on him. He stepped back as the older man approached and uttered not a word.

"Marangona," he said. He reached out a hand and laid it upon the bronze like it was treasure. A lost friend restored. Closed his eyes and seemed to freeze time with the gesture. The moment suspended around all of us until he opened his eyes again.

His expression cleared, as if he'd emerged from another realm— one of memory and shadow. His eyes settled on me and seemed to penetrate straight to my soul as he spoke three small words.

"Who . . . are . . . you?"

21

"The Book of Waters, you say." Across the room, the man stirred his coffee. It was a small flat, not much larger than my cell had been. And yet where my walls had been stark and stained, my only companion a growing collection of brightly covered books and my scrap of paper, this man's walls were shelves.

Floor to ceiling, a veritable trove of treasures and story. It was a strange place and had the sense of being a hidden thing discovered. Molding and a half-covered fresco seemed to declare it had once been a part of a residence much grander—a residence that had been parceled into smaller flats as the needs of Venice had changed.

He pulled in a sip of his coffee, watching me the whole time. I did likewise and jolted at the extreme heat of the liquid. When we both set down our coffee cups in their saucers, I nearly sputtered when I saw that his was empty. From that one single, long swig.

"How did you do that?" I said, reclaiming composure.

The man looked at the cup and shrugged. "Good coffee needs no delay," he said. "I learned long ago that when you have something good in hand, it is folly to delay without reason."

He fell silent, and I studied the objects on the shelf behind him. A map. An hourglass fading from clear glass at its center to Murano blue at its expanding ends, hinged upon a metal frame. A row of small, colorfully clad volumes of books, lined up so cheerfully that they seemed like a row of grandchildren, adorning the home of their stoic grandfather.

The man wasn't *grumpy*, exactly. Despite my first impression of him, being here in his small world seemed to grow him. He seemed a little serious, a bit mysterious . . . perhaps somewhat mad.

"I do not have the book you seek."

Make that maddening, I amended my last thought.

And I was eighteen again, at a dead-end in a San Francisco alley with policemen giving chase. *Assess the situation. Evade the obvious. Find an escape.* The fail-safe trifecta to get out of any predicament. Until it had failed, permanently. Still, it was one tool from that time that I could make use of with a clear conscience.

Assess the situation. I'd have to tread with care. This man was my only lead, my only hope of obtaining what I needed and closing the door at last on the scourge that was my own past while securing my mother's future.

I cleared my throat.

Assess. I scanned the room, looking for tools to help. Another old trick of the trade. My eyes landed on the hourglass, and he didn't miss it. Reaching behind him so that his chair creaked, he spun the hourglass once on its axis.

The sand within began to trickle down in a whisper, a singular shimmer to it. Almost red in color. He fixed his stare on me and his message was clear. *Your moments are numbered.*

Evade the obvious. I couldn't come right out and ask him where it was.

"You know about the book, then?" I asked, a thousand other questions burning. Questions about atoning and chocolate-drizzled cakes. Questions having nothing to do with the story's whereabouts and everything to do with the story.

The man's fingers tapped in a light and quick pattern on the arm of his chair. "Know about it . . ." he mumbled, transported to another place far away. One that left a sheen over his eyes. "Yes."

Find an escape. The final point in my fail-safe trifecta would not work here. I needed the opposite. *Find a way to stay.* It felt foreign, and hard, and good.

"Do you . . . know where the original is?"

He gave an ironic laugh. "You have a copy of it, you say?" He

leaned forward. "I wonder how. Only a small number were made
. . . and they were never meant to leave the homes to which they
were given."

I pulled it out and handed it to him. Hesitating a moment, he
took it. Wrapped both hands around it as if he meant to never let
it go. "The man who will be deserving of the original," he said at
last, "has all he needs to find it, right here."

Everything in me dropped a few inches, hope making its escape.
The red shimmering sand dwindled from the hourglass's top half,
mounting in the bottom like the dread growing in my stomach.

"What is your name, sir?" the man asked.

"Daniel," I said. "Daniel Goodman."

He leaned forward, and I awaited whichever of the dreaded
questions came next: *What is your background? Where do you
come from? What brings you here? What are your plans?*

"What is it that you desire, Daniel Goodman?" He seemed to
perceive my unease. And more—he leaned forward, as if he recognized it, knew it well.

My desire? To fix a hole in a San Francisco roof. And a hole in
the heart of the one who resided there.

"I . . . am on a mission of sorts." I sighed, leaning my elbows
onto my knees and closing my eyes. There was no way around this
but through it. "I am not—have not been—the man I should be."
I felt his study of me. "I wish to make that right. The book . . . it
will help me do that."

I lifted my head. His features drew down. "I cannot fathom
how the book came to be in your possession," he said. "But one
thing I know . . . If it has any chance of giving a man hope, then
it will accomplish what it was written for."

I swallowed. We were in a strange and unfamiliar place, this
man and I—a place without pretense, where questions that hovered were simply asked.

It was odd. And wonderful.

"Did you write it?"

At this, he closed his eyes. Flickers of memory and emotion
traversing his face. He raised a weathered hand to his forehead,

light from the window glinting dully from a ring that looked like it had lived many lives, some of them harrowing.

"A great many people wrote it," he said. "A great many people lived it."

A thrill shot through me. "It's true, then. I wasn't sure, it seemed so like a story—"

His eyes flew open, their dark depths wide. "You've read it."

"Part of it," I said. "I've been tasked with translating it, and the work is slow." I shook my head. "So—it's true?"

"Keep reading. You will see."

"And if I do, I'll find the original?"

"That, I cannot say. Only you can."

Now it was my fingers that tapped in excitement, cataloguing all that I could of the man's world. Perhaps there was a clue somewhere here. I let my gaze stop at the map.

"You will not find what you seek with that map," the man said. "You have everything you need on those covers if you are the person to receive this story. You will see," he repeated and stood slowly, signaling that our meeting was at a close. His English was very good. Not even "broken" English, as some would say. More of just a jaunty kilter with the occasional replaced word.

I left the flat with more questions than answers, with the man's reluctant permission that if I must, I could come back.

THE BOOK OF WATERS

The Tempest

There is a realm in which unseen things duel. A current of air tumbles down the frigid granite of an alpine mountain. Another dances north from the warmer south, gusting with the golden glow of the Sahara.

And then, in a star-crossed rendezvous, the winds collide. Shattering air around them to a shivering state, where currents become exiles, gusting over waters, stirring chaos upon the surface of the sea.

The water moans, awaking its depths. The waves reach and swell, giants rising from cerulean slumber until there, in the fragments of air and ghost-winds of the Alps and mirages of the Sahara and the frantic search of the water for where to go, what to do—a storm is born.

The annals of La Serenissima tell us of such things. Attesting that not so very long ago—only four hundred years—a storm had "broken indeed the shores in several places, entered the towns of Lido Maggiore, Tre Porti, Malamocco, Chiozza, et cetera."

Broken indeed the shores.

Sebastien Trovato knew such a storm. The shores broke along the island, to be sure. And deeper, farther, until all he had known—every truth, every question—was left without asylum. No seawall to hold back the swell and the only thing for it was to set out upon those waters and ask the question that had long pursued him: *Who am I?*

He had grown past boyhood, past the brink of adulthood, and into a man who found himself caring now for the ones who had cared for him. He had lived a quiet life. Quiet, but good. And in that time, he ceased migrating with each season and migrated according to need.

A week here with Pietro, to help craft an ornate chandelier for one of the grand palazzos. A month or more with Valentina as her bones creaked more with age and her lacemaking slowed and she admitted, at last, her undying love for the man who drove her batty: Giuseppe.

Sebastien still accompanied that man on his fishing expeditions, especially when it was cold and managing the lines was tedious work for Giuseppe's own aging hands. Sebastien laid all his training as a gondolier to rest as the man retired from that profession, rarely venturing into the city but for market deliveries.

He would spend days with Dante, when needed, but Dante's print shop was rather slow of customers of late. Something to do with the increasing population of occupying soldiers and the rising whispers of plots to "do something about it." Tensions rising, and there were few who entrusted their plans as far as ink and press. They relied more on secret meetings, paid arrangements, clandestine plans.

But mostly Sebastien dwelled on the simple isle with Elena, who had been more mother to him than many a man was blessed to have, and he found great pleasure in tending the earth there. She often jested, always in fondness, about his way with the plants. . . .

"No wonder you are drawn to the trees, Sebastien. Like calls unto like, you know." She smiled at him, poking fun at his very tall form.

He attempted his best withering look at her comment. She laughed and winked but warmed the comment in her usual way. "Not just that you are tall, my love. And tall you should be, for you are one of the giants of character in all this world."

This, he did not deserve. "I'm just a gardener," he said, and meant it. He was no philosopher, no priest, no king. He spent the days with soil caked under fingernails and face smudged in dirt.

"The trees . . . They live to shelter. To reach for light, and with it, give life and rest to those who would stop in their shade. Gardening is the work of life."

"You're suggesting I cast a shadow with my presence?" He tried to lighten the conversation, for the gravity of what she was saying settled upon him like a blanket. But even in its goodness, it held a weight with it.

What if the things she said were true? He had seen his share of trees fall, in this place where gusts tangled like ageless foes. What if he failed to give shelter or solace? What if he fell instead?

He was getting too old for ponderings like this. Too much life lived to still hear echoes of the old question in the bell of the Marangona.

And so, he determined to live on as he always had. Setting his hand to whatever lay in front of him and giving his all to it. It was a simple life and a good life.

"What mischief will the statues get up to this night?" Elena sat beside the small hearth one night as those winds howled in a rising ruckus. She flashed a smile, though her dark eyes held concern. The way the rain drove at the windowpanes, foreboding wound through Sebastien too.

She spoke of the old legend of Venice's statues of saints coming to life amid a tempest, masquerading as ordinary men, beseeching a boat ride of an unsuspecting gondolier to the Lido and there, upon the waves, doing battle against otherworldly fiends who had conspired in a graveyard to destroy La Serenissima. Only when victory was at hand did they reveal themselves in the legend to be Saints Mark, George, and Theodore, who returned to their stone-clad forms that very evening. In the fairy tale, only the ring of Saint Mark, left behind in the possession of the stunned boatman, offered proof of what had transpired.

Sebastien had been out on the water enough times with Giuseppe to know the signs of the storms, how to watch the moon to see if it bore a ring around it, and if it did, to prepare for the worst. He also knew that even the most seasoned boatman knew only one thing for certain: The sea does not tell all her secrets. She may turn in an instant from a small breeze to a ravenous storm. She may deliver calm waves when all had prepared for the worst.

Tonight, she was in a fury.

"Perhaps the sea has come for the ring of St. Mark," Sebastien said, attempting to lighten the atmosphere. "I never did understand how the ring was to have been proof." Changing the subject sometimes eased the strain from Mother Elena's shoulders. Though strong, they carried much. "Could not the gondolier have had a ring made or stolen the one it was supposed to have been?"

"It was kept under care of three keys," Elena said, raising her brows. "Bejeweled just so, in a way no boatman could ever afford. How, if he told a falsehood, had he procured such a precious stone, offered it to the Doge with his story as proof, only for the noblemen to discover upon hearing his account that the ring they kept so secure was missing indeed? And returned, happily."

Wary doubt and joy in the story mingled in Sebastien's voice. "Did that truly happen?"

This was their game. She would tell a tale of this island-city who loved their legends as much as food and drink. Sebastien would ask in dubious voice, *"Did that truly happen?"*

"Who can say?" Always Elena's reply, twinkle in her eye. It had been a long time since they'd had such an exchange—the growing rarity having something to do, he thought, with the way he towered over her now, nearly twice as old as she had been when he was a baby.

A crack lashed at the window, so loud Elena flinched and Sebastien felt it to his core.

"The storm grows," she said. "Should we bring the hens in?" It was so like her, to think of even the smallest creature out in this. The most nurturing spirit this world had known. She rose to go, laying aside the skein of wool she knit with.

"Let me," Sebastien said, and beat her to the door. She had protected him from many a storm in his life. Locking up a few hens was the least he could do.

Outside, the rain stung, more like glass than water. Pelting at an angle, to which he raised his collar against his neck, and made for the henhouse. He wrestled the door open against the wind, narrowing his eyes as though doing so could slice through darkness and help him see.

"*Una*," Sebastien began the usual count. "*Do, tre, quat*—" but no. There was no *quatro*.

Two whites, a yellow, and a grey . . . and it was the grey who was missing. Elena's favorite, for the way her feathers were rimmed in black. "*Like a little storm cloud,*" she said, naming it Tuona. Well, she was earning her name tonight, little Thunder—escaping into a storm. She would be destroyed if he did not find her.

He secured the door, found the slip between net and frame where she'd escaped, and ran for the house. He would do little good out here without a light.

Close to the glow of the house, he nearly collided with Elena, who was rushing out with a glowing lantern in each hand. She read the concern on his face. "Tuona?"

He nodded, reaching for a lantern. "I'll find her," he said. "You shouldn't be out in this. I can—"

She shook her head, holding on to her own light still. "Is it any good to argue with me?"

She was right. As much as he wished her inside to safety and warmth, she would never go. "I'll take the outer shores, then. If you will check the glade."

They were yelling over the wind by this time. Bending to spear the gusts with his body, Sebastien made for the beach and began the route he knew so well from boyhood. He had traversed the marshy cattail forest, which now only rose to his knees. He slogged through the inlet, waters rising fast. This would bring *acqua alta* to be sure. Not so catastrophic for them here as it was in the city, but still—a hen would not fare well. And Elena . . . though she was strong, he worried for her. She had borne much in this life, and she had deserved much in this life—much more than she had been given. If he could do this small thing for her . . .

As he approached the salt creek, he began to lose heart. He was nearly around the small island, with no sign of the hen. Perhaps she had found high ground or shelter. They would know in the morning. The urge to get Elena to safety was now overtaking the concern for Tuona. Sebastien turned in the direction of the house, but something tugged him back. It would only take a few minutes longer to press on and check the ruins. If it promised Elena peace, and that soggy little hen a little respite, what would two minutes cost him? He was already soaked.

It was decided. Sebastien made for the ruins. Through the cattail forest, around the towering cypress, through the glade—and then he halted.

For there, by the light of his dwindling lantern, lying upon the soggy and rising ground, was not a hen . . . but a woman.

Sprawled facedown, white skirts streaked with mud and floating eerily around her. Ophelia, incarnate. Escaped, somehow, from the small volumes of William Shakespeare Sebastien had printed with Dante, where her ghostly form had been caught in the ink-upon-block prints. But she had stepped from the pages and here she was before him, precious seconds wasting into the roar of the growing storm.

The moments blurred as instinct took over. He tore through the bracken, not registering the bare branches slapping back as if to prevent him from reaching her. He scooped her up, climbing and willing himself not to stumble on this slippery ground as he lay her upon the table at the center of the ruins' stone seats. He bent over her and prayed as he had never prayed before. He could not and would never hear a thing over the wind howling through the trees like so many banshees. He laid his hand upon her shoulder, desperate for any sign of movement or life.

Nothing.

He moved his hand to her neck and did the same, bending over her, taking her face in both of his hands.

Nothing.

And just as he laid that head back down, just as he stroked the stray hairs from a face that he now saw was so beautiful that his own breathing near stopped—he felt it. A tiny flutter, there at the side of her neck, beneath her jaw.

A heartbeat.

"*Dio,*" he prayed. He knew not what to add to the plea. *Warmth.*

She needed warmth. Scooping her up with care, he held her against himself and traversed the marshy isle blindly, cutting through the black night and branches headfirst, if the lashes upon his face and arms were to be believed later.

He arrived at the small farmyard and its glow of hope through the window, the sight of Elena running to him, Tuona tucked beneath her arms.

"Sebastien?" So much bursting from that question. She rushed over and laid her own shawl over the woman in his arms.

"Inside," she said above the pelting rain. "Quickly."

Elena led the way to her own room, where she pulled back the covers on her bed. He laid her there beside the fire and recalled the time as a child that a neighbor on Burano had fallen through the ice when the canal had frozen in winter. How the boy's father had brought him nearer to the inferno fire of their glass shop and how they had removed his wet clothing.

He hastily threw the last two dry logs on their hearth fire, and when he turned, Elena drew near, a kettle of hot water in her hands.

"I will see to her clothing," she said. "I will need jars to fill with hot water, to warm her beneath blankets."

"Of course," he said. Knowing Elena to be the force of efficiency and purpose that she was, he knew she would call out if she needed him—but sensed what was most needed now was for him to stay away. He flushed at his own buffoonery. He had rarely been so close to a woman near to his own age, let alone one so beautiful—or one on the brink of death.

That last thought sent him piling wood into the garden barrow faster and scooping up every last spare jar in the storeroom, plus the two jars of brightly colored Murano glass that Pietro had given him. He pumped water into a pot and hung it upon the kitchen spit, willing it to boil.

Elena ushered him in upon his knock and exclaimed, "You'll have her thinking she has awakened in the tropics, with so many jars warming her!" She managed a smile, but Sebastien did not miss the way her eyes remained fixed on the girl with grave concern.

The clock on the mantel ticked ever louder. The rustle of the hen who had dried happily and was fluffing her feathers buoyed the room with a nonsensical hope. If they could find a hen of so little brain out in this . . . and if she could fare as well as a countess, thoroughly warm, feathered, dry . . . surely this woman would claim such a fate too. She must.

"What can I do?" he said, feeling his muscles strain to be in motion.

"Wait," Elena said, her voice soft. She sat on the spindly wooden chair in the corner and patted the empty one beside her. Stiffly, he lowered himself onto the chair's edge.

"I could go for more wood—"

"You've brought enough to fuel ten houses," she said, offering him an indulgent smile.

"Eleven would be better," he muttered.

"Just wait."

He did, feet bouncing silently, bones begging each second to do something. Sitting idly by while watching the rise and fall of the girl's body as she found breath was like ignoring a repeated cry for help.

He stood and looked longingly at the door.

"You know," Elena said, taking his hand in hers. When had hers become so small in his? He had always found safety in the wrap of her hand around his. Now his fingers dwarfed hers—and the burning to do something for her, too, grew stronger. "Eleven *is* a very good number," she said. "Perhaps we do need more wood."

He gave her hand a grateful squeeze. "I'll return soon."

When he did, he was dripping afresh and bore enough wood in his arms to construct a pyramid of logs to dry for burning. Elena was in the kitchen, and he was alone with the girl.

She was so still beneath her blankets. Her face and hands, peeking from one of Elena's nightgowns, were so pale, cold dread overtook him. Perhaps she had—but no. As he drew close and picked up her hand, he felt warmth. Life.

For the first time, he studied her slowly. The details of her face. Her hair, as it dried, lost its wet darkness and glinted golden, even in its tangles. Dark lashes lay upon fair cheeks, and everything about her seemed delicate. The lines of her lips, the slender curve of her face. But beneath this dance of feather-light beauty, there seemed a force that was anything but delicate. Perhaps the set of her jaw, perhaps the very fact of her presence here in such a storm . . . Whatever it was, it shrouded her in strength and mystery.

Even the details of her clothing, hung by the fire to dry, were ethereal. The dress's embroidered designs almost invisible, white-upon-white. But their filigree had caught silt amidst its swirls and curves. He did not know much about women's clothing, but these seemed very fine.

Elena rustled behind him with a bowl of steaming broth. His stomach rumbled to life, the brute. Betrayer of hunger, traitor to chivalry.

"There is a bowl on the table for you," Elena said. "She may eat or she may not . . . I will try the spoon to see if she'll swallow, even as she sleeps."

He hesitated, the strings of this woman and her veil of questions holding him fast. Elena laid a hand upon his shoulder. "A lady would not wish a gentleman to see her eat if it is to run down her face, which it may do." She said this as much for the girl's propriety as for his stomach's sake, proved as she ushered him toward a bowl waiting on the kitchen table.

When the storm had reached far into the night and he lay in his own small chamber on the other side of the home, listening to the wind, his thoughts slowed enough for the first time to think on the events. He remembered, watching the scene in his memory as if reading a story in a book.

A story that he hoped, rather than knew, had just begun.

23

DANIEL

T he next afternoon, I emerged from the Biblioteca Marciana, the library that Vittoria had recommended I visit. My hands ached from the morning's brickwork but ached even more to get back to translation. And maybe even—sketching? My head swam in dates and figures from the library until they were all a cloud, but one shone so clear and bright, something inside came alive.

The storm in the book was so real, so vivid that I was sure—or rather, I fiercely hoped—it had made its way into a record somewhere. But in this land where people had set fact to paper over the centuries, enough to fill hundreds of private, public, and government collections—none had made mention of storms except for those of particularly catastrophic note.

I'd learned there had been several of that variety, and a few had stood out, especially for their winsome wording, even in the face of catastrophe.

From the 1200s: *"the water flooded the streets higher than a man."*

From the 1600s, the very one the writer had quoted in the Book of Waters: *". . . broken indeed the shores . . ."*

And one from June 1846, which I had read and promptly copied down, word for word: *"The outer islands were ravaged, one swept asunder, and for a time, a daughter of Venice was presumed lost to the waves."*

I should have exulted in the victory of finding a date. Being the discoverer of the first fact that surely validated the book as true made me feel somehow a part of it and made the story feel less fantastical.

But the woman, the daughter of Venice . . . Her fate shadowed me with each step. What had become of her?

I thought of another daughter of Venice, dark-haired and dark-eyed. The Garbin, that gust-infused girl who blew life into the empty corners inside of me. Vittoria would know where to look next.

When I arrived at the bookshop's campo, all was eerily still. Not even a ruffle of feathers. The turquoise door was locked. I turned to go but stopped at the sound of a whistled melody coming from around the corner. Following the sound, I ducked to pass through a tunnel between the bookshop and its neighbor and found myself on the canal side of the building. *Rio*-side, I corrected. This was one of the smaller canals, with no embankment to walk upon, the buildings stopping abruptly at and disappearing into the water.

Moored there in the mingling shadows of the buildings was a gondola—one unlike any other I'd seen. It was black, like the others, but in place of the open seat, a small black cabin perched with curtains of royal blue velvet. The whistling stopped as a figure inside emerged.

"Daniel Goodman!" Vittoria swiped a stray dark curl from her eyes with the back of her hand. "Will you always appear when I'm setting about the high calling of book delivery?"

I studied the boat and noticed that inside the windows of the little cabin, shelves had been mounted. A few on each wall, with the glint of gold spine-lettering snatching light and twinkling it back at me as if they truly did hold all the enchantment in the world.

"What is this?" I asked.

She planted her fists on her hips and looked at me as if I'd lost my senses. "It is a gondola, signore. Perhaps you've heard of them? Vessels of timeless travel in our most serene city? I can sing you a tune if you like. The Americans are always asking the gondoliers for a song. But I advise you, as your friend, that if you value your ears, you would do much better to let me whistle instead." She trilled a whistle and curtsied, awaiting her applause.

I smiled, and she looked pleased. This sensation of a smile—it was foreign, strange to my face—but seemed to be summoned to life around Vittoria. "But this one is different," I said. "You've made it into a . . . bookshop?"

"Of sorts," she said. "I read once of a peddler wagon in the mountains of your country. Bringing wares and tales and some-times even travelers to the people there. The same on the mainland here in Italy." She clapped a hand over her mouth and looked up at the open balcony window. "Pray my aunt didn't hear me say that."

"Mainland?"

Vittoria shook her head and leaned close, whispering, "*Italy.*" She drew back, nodding gravely. "We haven't long belonged to Italy. It's the only motherland *I* have known, but it was only just before I was born that we became part of Italy. There are some"—she pointed up toward a window wherein the aforementioned aunt presumably resided—"who believe the whole thing is a joke. Something to do with a bungled vote when we gave over control to Napoleon long before."

I tried to keep up, but she spoke so fast, and my history wasn't up to snuff. "Who was French."

"Yes, and so were we, for a time, and then Austrian, and then French, and then Austrian and finally—" she rolled her hand in the air as if readying to perform a magic trick—"Italian! But not for some. And always, no matter what else, Venetian. Anyway, they have the peddler wagons in other parts of the country, but here? No horses, no bicycles, no autocars. So?" She gestured at the boat, pride beaming.

"A gondola peddler wagon . . . for books?"

"The Book Boat!" She pulled out a painted tile and hung it

from hooks over the cabin's entrance. It indeed read *The Book Boat* and seemed to smile at me as it swung on its hooks from the *felze*, the little cabin.

"I wish my mother could see this." And my smile grew. Again— when was the last time I had smiled at the thought of her?

Vittoria's face brightened. "She likes books?"

I laughed. "That would be an understatement."

"Well, you must tell her! Bring her next time!"

There was so much of a future in those two commands that I dared not even imagine . . . but something akin to hope kindled inside.

Here was a dark vessel stocked with goods, about to leave . . . and *deliver* them to people. The last time I'd been in a dark vessel—a wagon stocked with goods, about to leave—the goods had been plundered, and by my own hand. Perhaps it was the stark contrast of this boat's story and mine, but I felt anchored to it.

"Could you . . ." I tried to act nonchalant. Hands in pockets, shoulder shrugged, foot in a shuffle. " . . . use some help?"

"Of course you're going to help," she said. Her words were tempered by a smile, a shared joke. "I need to know the latest on the Book of Waters, after all. And I could use an extra oar man. My arms, they are sore from some brute colliding with me at the train station the other day."

Her eyes laughed when I looked up in concern. "I jest, Daniel Goodman. I am fine. But I would very much welcome your help."

She gestured me on board and I obeyed, taking in all the details. The black paint, chipping but shined with care. The head of a winged lion, carved into wooden scrollwork along a seatback. The lion holding a book inscribed with Latin, of which I could make out a few words: *Peace to you.* A small likeness in brass sitting atop the entrance to the cabin, in the shape of a child holding a book skyward, as if it might fly off into the clouds. The blankets tucked beneath the lone chair.

"In case someone wishes to sit and read a while," she said, watching my study.

"And this?" I knocked on a wooden box beside it.

"See for yourself," she said, and lifted the lid. Inside, the same blue fabric as the cabin's curtains lined the box, and a glass coffeepot sat in a brace of scrolling metal that elevated the pot above a base below meant for a candle. But there was no candle.

My head tipped. "Is that a . . . brick?"

Vittoria crouched and lifted the glass pot from its place. "Not just any brick."

I looked closer. It was incomplete. Jagged and broken, marked with the white patina of age.

She whispered, "From the campanile." She watched me expectantly. Satisfied, apparently, by whatever surprise registered on my face. "What? You think you are the only one who can take something from the great fall and do something good with it?"

"You heard about the ringer?"

She laughed, smile dimpling. "Not just heard *about* it. I heard it! And yes, heard all about it, as all of Venice did. You are becoming notorious here already."

Perfect. I thought my days in the headlines and gossip were long gone. I much preferred disappearing.

"Don't look so somber, signore," she said. "It is all right. We gave one of the fallen bricks a proper burial at sea. As you saw, we are preserving all of the ones that may be used to rebuild. And this small bit? Well, it's been saved from a fate of being forgotten. Used instead to warm the hands of whoever may sit in this seat to consider their future reading material. I warm it in the oven, and it keeps the whole chamber warm. Coffee too! Would you like some?"

I shook my head in wonder. "Who . . . *are* you?"

"I am Vittoria." She shrugged, her hair bouncing in loose curls worn down. "You know that."

I did. And she was entirely disarming and a good bit enchanting. This woman made the world seem somehow a friend and our own budding friendship somehow much older than a handful of days and mishaps.

"I mean—what are you? Bookseller, gondolier, liberator of bricks and coffee . . . Is there anything you can't do?"

"I cannot wait any longer to hear what you learned from the man in the flat," she said, taking up the long oar and launching us onto the canal.

I hadn't expected the chance to experience the quintessential gondola ride. It was smooth and swift, and there were frequent moments when I was thoroughly convinced Vittoria meant to smash into the buildings at the tight corners of these narrower alleys, but she was a skilled and able gondolier. I felt rather useless, perched there in the seat, and she must have sensed that.

"It isn't a real gondola," she explained. "Well, it is, but not one of the official fleet. It's an older one my father and I brought back to life together. Would you like to try?"

I was at the stern in two strides, wrapping my hands around the offered oar and my mind around her instructions to row only on the right, to not worry for the way it seemed always to tilt to the right, to beware the bridges due to my height, and finally, to not look so serious.

We rowed on as I filled her in on the man in the flat, the sound of water swishing around the oar and the far-off song of another gondolier echoing down the canals.

Vittoria sank her chin into her hand, processing what I'd told her.

"What will you do next?" she asked.

I told her of the storm, the date I'd found. "I'll keep translating," I said, "and hope for another clue. If you have any ideas, I'd welcome them."

She nodded, thoughtful. I watched a series of expressions cross her face, as if her thoughts, even in silence, could not be silent.

"What?" she asked. "You look as though you wish to laugh."

"I'd . . . just give anything to hear your thoughts." I laughed.

"You? Signor Reserved and Reticent? I am trying to be like you!"

At this, I did laugh. "Trust me," I said. "I'm not someone to emulate."

"I beg to differ. The words, they are buried deep inside of you. You are always a mystery. One has to work to invite your words up. Build a staircase with questions, that they might climb out.

I . . . am like a floodgate that has lost its gate. A flood of words! It's terrible."

"It's wonderful," I countered.

"It's maddening."

"It's refreshing."

"People here do not like floods, Daniel Goodman."

"I do."

"Ah—" She stared, mouth slightly open. Speechless, in earnest, and cheeks coloring. I shrugged, rather enjoying this, and rowed on. "Your thoughts are most welcome, Vittoria. Whenever you wish to share them." And there it was again, my mouth pulling up into a one-sided smile.

Green moss ran the length of the canals, showing the places the water had previously reached, and I wondered how many people these waters had carried to their destinies. How many conversations had taken place upon them, how many dastardly deeds and regattas, victories and defeats, futures determined and hopes buoyed, all upon these waters?

"Where are we going, exactly?" I asked, at length.

Vittoria, welcoming the change in topic, brightened. "Today, to Santa Croce," she said. "There is a man there who welcomes the floating *libreria*. He doesn't have much and shows great gratitude when someone takes note of him."

She asked more about the Book of Waters, and I filled her in on the two boys, the sister, the woman in the tempest, and the date from the library that morning.

"And your hands?" she asked. "Did all that translating bite you?"

I looked at my hands, which were scraped and marked from my work with the Keeper of the Bells that morning. I explained my deal with him.

"See, Daniel? Not here a week and already you have steady work in the very heart of our very great city."

"One of its hearts."

"Just so. Who can do such a thing?"

We tied the gondola to a red-and-white striped pole outside of a mansion of brick—they called a grand house a *palazzo* here.

Scrolled iron formed a door directly between the canal and the structure—the *porta d'acqua*. A limestone arch adorned it from above, with the keystone displaying the carved face of a smiling woman. Vittoria pointed at it. "We'll use the water entrance," she said. "He'll be expecting us."

Just as she'd said, a bespectacled man with a cane came down the steps into an indoor alcove of sorts, where water sloshed at times over the top step and into the entrance. He made no mind of it, and with a jaunt to his step and the help of his cane, stepped aboard the gondola with amphibian-like agility.

The two slipped into the music of the Venetian dialect, Vittoria eagerly showing him to the cabin's contents, pulling a volume down, making way for him to pull a few down as well, and seating him in the "Tome Throne," as she called the chair near the coffee chest. She poured him a steaming cup, set it atop the box, and backed away with palpable delight. She looked upon the scene with pride and joy, like a mother looks upon a babe.

"This is why we come, Daniel. Look," she whispered. The man's countenance lit as he sat, rocking in the waves upon the water, ferried away to another time and place through the book on his lap.

But I was puzzled about something. "You said he didn't have much?" Old habits arose, noting the gleam of his watch, the intricate carving of his cane, and the reach of his palazzo.

She understood and dropped her voice more, limiting our conversation to English. "He cannot venture into the world, so we bring the world to him," she said. "He was once a banker who traveled the world for his business. Now . . . well, Venezia is beautiful, and it is home. But it is not an easy city to grow old in. Steps and bridges, slippery *fondamente* . . . There are many who are homebound. And it is they who made this place our home, when I was a wee thing. Is it not something I can do now, to honor that?

"Small flats or large palazzos, the impoverishment of company does not know the bounds of neighborhoods. In material ways, yes. I have known times of hunger, I know it very well. But . . ." She looked up, her dark curls tumbling down her back. "Perhaps it was the times of hunger that helped me see there are many forms of suffering. It can be a difficult thing, to be always alone. A small thing we can do, to simply knock on the door, yes? There are those who say a book is only ink and paper." She shook her head. "They have not seen a countenance lift when a gift is offered from one heart to another. They have not seen . . . *that*." She lifted her chin toward the man, who was chuckling at something and wiping an eye.

When the man had chosen two volumes—"until next time," he had said—I helped him back up the steps to the water entrance, into the alcove, and to the inner door, looking on him with new eyes. A whole lifetime, an entire universe, inside this solitary person.

The man adjusted his spectacles and looked at me. "She is a bright gem, Vittoria. No?"

"Yes," I said, watching the very girl unwind the rope from its mooring post. "She is."

The man leaned in, perched above me on the step up to his door. "Bright gems deserve careful guarding," he said. "If you take my meaning."

"I do, sir."

"I mean that you had better treat her well."

"Yes, sir."

"I mean very well."

"I will, sir." My face was growing hot.

"Good. *Ciao*." It was a new word to me since I'd arrived. I'd been told it meant *your servant*. But the man looking at me now, with a formidable brow raised, infused it with more of a fatherly threat.

"Ciao," I said, and meant it.

We made five more stops that day—to a convent, a campo crowded with shoeless children, a school, and two more private residences, one of them an even more impressive palazzo than the first.

During the rounds, Vittoria coached me in the art of "suggesting" books, which was not suggesting at all. "Don't suggest.

Don't ask permission. Lay out the options you feel might be a good fit and invite them in. Venice is a living story, and her people are eager to enter into each page for themselves. This will serve you well, Daniel, as you speak with people about your book too. Let them lead."

This I attempted with the last "customer." I wasn't sure what to call them, for I quickly became aware that these were not paying customers, but that Vittoria operated her Book Boat more as lending library. A young boy stood on the outskirts of a cluster of children, turning a ball in his hands and looking more than a little uncertain. He cast a longing look over his shoulder at a solitary place shadowed in wisteria, as if he thought perhaps he belonged over there and not here among the books and people.

I made a perusal of the books in the cabin and, as the other children flocked inside, tucked two under my arm and went to the boy, kneeling on one knee. It was an attempt to make myself less tall, less intimidating to the boy, but it was the boat that accomplished that when it lurched briefly in the wake of a passing rowboat and nearly toppled me over. My arm braced against the gondola's hull, but the damage—or magic?—was already done, for the boy's previously worried mouth curved up into a smile around a stifled laugh.

That laughter twisted into me and pulled a laugh from me, too, as I righted myself, pushed unruly hair from my face and held the books out to the boy. I remembered myself at this age—so like this boy. I never possessed the charisma of Emilio or the quick ways of the other children in the neighborhood. In a place known for boisterous dinners and outspoken thoughts, I'd been the one to watch and wonder from the edges.

"Buongiorno," I said, and for the first time the boy's dark eyes met mine.

"Hello," the boy said back, biting his lip.

"I nearly met a very wet end there, didn't I?"

The boy grinned and nodded.

"What's your name?" I tipped my head a little to the side, offering mine to help pave the way for him. "I'm Daniel."

He bit his lip again and gripped the ball tighter as if unsure what to do with himself. "Matteo."

"Matteo," I repeated. "What a good name. *Gift from God*, it means. Did you know that?"

His eyes grew round as he looked at me, disbelieving. "How do you know?"

I shrugged a shoulder. "Names. I studied them once, when I had a book of them and a lot of time to read."

"What does your name mean, signore?"

I gripped the books with both hands and drummed my fingers on them, making a show of searching the archives of my mind. "It means . . . *man who falls over in boats*. Yes, I think that's it."

This earned a laugh, and then he eyed the books in my hands shyly.

"Would you like to look at these?"

The grin disappeared as he pressed his lips together and shook his head. "They're for the others," he said quietly.

"Oh?"

He nodded.

I waded through possible next words and imagined myself again at that age. "These ones jumped off the shelf and into my hands when they saw you."

Again, the stifled laugh. "Books don't jump."

"No?" I gave the books a little toss. They somersaulted in the air between us, and I caught them again and held them out. "What was that, then?"

He laughed, the shadow of uncertainty falling away.

I opened the first book, *Le Avventure di Pinocchio*. "This one is about a puppet made of wood who comes to life. He is very naughty." I flipped through the pages and paused on one where Pinocchio's creator is being led to jail because of a lie Pinocchio told. I gulped. I had not recalled that part. An old familiar twisting in my stomach began and suddenly, in the illustration, I felt not Pinocchio watching on, but myself.

"But—" I hauled a breath through the thickness in my throat. "He works very hard to become good and to become not just a puppet but a real boy." I clapped the covers shut a little too suddenly, and the boy flinched.

Hastily, nearly dropping poor old Pinocchio in the canal between the boat and the fondamenta, I opened the other cover. Smaller, thinner, just the right size to fit in the boy's hands in perfect proportion. It was deep purple and gilded upon the spine with the words *Le Piccole Storie: The Book of Masks.*

"And here is a truer story," I said, clearing my throat and trying to forget how true *Pinocchio* suddenly felt to me. This one told the story of *carnivale*, with masks illustrated in wood-block prints and scenes of the costumed revelers. The illustrations were so detailed, so intricate in their scrolling flourishes and the way the faces of the people seemed to come to life. There was something familiar about it, but with all of the frescoes, mosaics, Tintorettos, Canalettos, and Titians that adorned the many walls of Venice, it was nearly impossible for me to remember which art belonged to whom. Not without seeing it with my own eyes, right before me.

The boy leaned in, reaching out his hands and taking the books. As he continued to flip the pages, he came to a scene of what appeared to be a table, set with a feast and seven seats. But the people seated around it were set apart from those in the rest of the book in a striking way: They did not wear costumes. There were six of them, dressed in shabby finery. One empty seat, and at the last seat, the head of the table, a young boy.

It struck me like a punch to the gut. I knew these people.

24

re you certain?"

Back at the bookshop, Vittoria's jacket fell from her shoulders in a whoosh of eagerness. With her hands she book-ended a row of colorful-spined books, transferring them to a round table by the rio-side window.

I followed, grabbing her green jacket as I passed.

"Look at me." She beheld the jacket like a wayward child. "Perhaps the stationmaster is correct—I am nothing but a Garbin after all. Leaving things in my wake!" She reached for the coat, and I drew it back.

"The Garbin brings a great many good things, I hear."

"Your sources are questionable." She took the jacket with a smile, draping it over a wingback chair. "So. Here are the histories. Shall we see if the illustrations are indeed a match?"

I reached to take the Book of Waters from my jacket pocket but then stopped, protective of the new hope that might be dashed.

"It is just a book," Vittoria whispered. Her dimpled smile gentling the moment.

"Is anything ever . . . just a book?" I tried the same question I had asked the Keeper of Bells and was met with a similar smirk.

"You know stories in Venice travel very quickly," she said. "I know you said the very thing to the bell-keeper."

I could feel my face turn two shades redder.

"But there is something about you, Daniel Goodman, that makes me think perhaps you are right. That a book, or a bell, or anything, might be wrapped in a thousand invisible threads, lives entwined without us even realizing." She narrowed her eyes. "You have a sort of—how do they say it—second sight? About things."

My dry laugh broke through the irony she'd unwittingly uttered. She stepped back, and I didn't blame her.

"I don't mean it in the mystical sense," she said. "Not that you see the future—but that you look at a bell, and you do not only see a cold and metal object. You think of the people over hundreds of years who have heard it, what it marked for them, how their lives were lived and changed in the shadows of a belltower, how the song tied them all together, across years. You don't look at a book and see only paper and ink. You seem to—to somehow *feel* it. The heart who wrote it, the lives in the pictures taking on heartbeats so that you can look at the faces of the people in one book and recognize in them the souls from another." She held up the purple book to prove her point. "This is a rare thing. So, please do not be so derisive with your laugh. If not second sight, perhaps it is—echoing sight."

Now it was downright uncanny. "Echoing sight." I repeated, shaking my head.

"Do not be angry! I only mean—"

"I'm not angry," I said. "Not at all. It's just—" The words pled for belief in the depth of her sincerity. How was it that she, without knowing anything of my past, my condition . . .

"It's just that—second sight, as you put it." I shook my head. "I have nothing like that at all. Precisely the opposite, actually."

"I'm afraid I do not understand."

I hadn't meant to speak of this. This was my burden, not hers. To begin to explain would mean to tell all. That wasn't what we were here for.

I set the Book of Waters on the table and reached to open it. But Vittoria laid her hand upon mine, the book gently closing again.

"What is it, *Daniele*?" She summoned the Italian form of my name, and her voice was gentle, inviting. Her presence warm.

I pressed my eyes closed to darkness. Opened them and saw her, waiting.

I had done this so many times—before the judge, jailer, overseer, telling them all that they needed to know to sentence me, house me, employ me. Disclosing. Stacking myself up into a list of facts and dates, deeds and repentances.

But never with just a—friend. Someone wishing to know not a detached criminal record in cold, hard facts, but inviting the story—the person.

Which I did not know how to give.

No job or sentence hung in the balance here. Just . . . Vittoria. Looking at me, seeing me. And in that, everything hung in the balance.

It would be so easy to close that door.

She squeezed my hand gently.

I pulled in a breath, and something rusty-hinged opened inside me, fearful of the light.

"Echoing sight," I said. "It's only that—well, that's exactly how things are. And I've never had words to explain that before. I . . . had an accident, many years ago." My chest pounded. Alluding to that night, seeing the way it registered in Vittoria, who didn't miss a thing—I knew we would be discussing the details of that accident. If not now, soon.

I continued. "I hit my head on the street. Hard."

Compassion mingled with concern pressed upon her forehead.

"When I awoke, something had changed. A lot of things. One of them was I could no longer picture things when I closed my eyes."

"You cannot . . . imagine?"

I shook my head, confirming her summation. "Not in the typical sense, no."

"But you are so imaginative!"

I laughed, knowing better. "If only that were so. I used to be able to build an entire scene in my mind. To reach for it with my hand, pull it out of this invisible place, and set it down on paper with ink or a pencil."

"But you . . . are here to sketch, so certainly you . . ." She trailed off.

"No," I said. "Not anymore. I can study object or building and make a likeness of it, but it's so different." Putting words to it felt like a sort of grief. "I deserve it. I was entrusted with an ability, and I chose to use it in ways that were . . . hurtful." I'd never before dared to articulate the depths of this. "God gives and God takes away. And I can't say that I blame Him."

"You perceive it to be a punishment?"

"What else? I deserved it."

She blew her cheeks out. "That is a very good question. Perhaps it was, perhaps it was not, but I think there is more to the story."

I wasn't ready to subject her to that. "Perhaps another day I'll tell more, but—"

"I meant more to the story of what this is for," she said. "This—blankness? Darkness? What is it that you see?"

"Both. When I close my eyes and try to imagine a scene—even something I've seen before—I see only a black canvas. Like the painted swath over the Unremembered One's portrait. Nothing, where once there was a whole life."

She thought, nodding, receiving. "Paul was once blind, you know."

"Paul? Was he one of the men we met today?"

She laughed. "The Apostle Paul. You've heard of him?"

The irony . . . He'd near written my ticket to Venice, in that sketch of the Cathedral of Santi Pietro e Paolo. I nodded.

"He was struck blind. Some think as punishment, for the things he had done. In his time of blindness, he was brought very low. A man who rested mightily upon his own stature, suddenly subject to being led by the hands of others. To know their reaching touch, their help. To see, in his darkness, the truth of the One he had persecuted. To be given a vision, even in his blindness!—and to be changed, again, by the touch of another."

I knew the story well. And appreciated that Vittoria desired to give hope. But . . .

"I am not Paul," I said. "And as for visions . . . I have only darkness."

"And yet . . ." Vittoria tapped the blue book. "You have keenness of sight that I have never seen the likes of. The smallest details take on the greatest meaning. Was it always so?"

"I don't know." I searched my memory. Had I always been so? I was so busy reveling in the way imagined things came to life in my hand . . . Had I ever paid close mind to the actual world before me? Until it was all I could see?

She flipped her hand down like she was shooing a fly. "Well, time enough to think on that, yes?"

Relief traversed my bones. How did she do that? Beckon me to plunge with her to the depths and then roll out the sunny shallows for me to climb back out before I was irretrievably lost?

And so we opened a twin copy of the purple-cloth covered *Piccole Storie* to the illustration of the feast. I opened the rough-cut pages of the Book of Waters, too, until I found the entry on the history of the guild.

Our heads nearly touched as we examined the scene before us, nearly identical to the one in the children's book. A rudimentary table of stone, surrounded by seven seats. Only in this depiction, the seats were unoccupied.

"Look at the details," Vittoria said, pointing at what was mirrored in both images: scrollwork filling the empty space between scene and frame.

"And here," I said, tapping a structure I hadn't noticed before, small in the far distance of the scene. "Is that the campanile?" I remembered the cold hammered-brass of La Marangona's ringer against my palm, the way it had made the man in the flat open a closed-up world. I could almost hear its full ring, in the time before the tower fell, echoing across the waters as Sebastien Trovato lay upon a stone table.

Vittoria stroked the page with her thumb as if she was touching the very moment

"It is," she said. "Which would make this . . . somewhere out in the lagoon."

With the pages arching in her hand like a bird ready to take flight, the end pages peeked through.

"And this," I said, flipping quickly to the end pages in the bigger book. Both books, adorned in colorful marbled paper.

"Many Venetian books are finished in this way, with the marbled end papers," Vittoria said. "But you are right. The patterns, even the colors used, look very alike indeed."

"Who did you say these books come from?" I turned to the front pages and found no publisher's name.

"Not a who," Vittoria said. "But a *where*. I have never seen who produces them. A courier comes, or we retrieve them ourselves at a small press. Little more than a room in an old palazzo."

Excitement welled within me. It was absurd, really, that these people were beginning to feel like friends, that I worried for the fate of the woman and felt uneasily familiar with the man Massimo.

"Will you show me?"

She turned to go right then, gleam in her eye, but stopped herself. "My aunt," she said. "When she wakes, she will be needing me."

"Tomorrow, then," I said, and her face broke into a smile to light the sky.

Tomorrow, we would go, and perhaps there would be a clue. Or better still—did presses keep originals in their archives? All could be answered.

"Your aunt," I said. "Is she . . . all right?"

Vittoria's joy seemed to flicker then. "She is a wonderful woman. Keeper of this shop for forty years. But, like many in our city, she fell upon difficult times. When the people can barely afford food, they rarely buy books. And when they rarely buy books, she also can barely afford food. So? She sold the piano nobile of this building—the main floor, on an upper level—and moved into a smaller apartment up there." She gestured at the inward balcony where the spiral staircase led. Balustrades marked the length of the room, and more bookcases adorned the walls beyond, interspersed with windows. Robert Browning ruffled his feathers from the iron-scrolled balcony.

"She is unable to walk, now. She would grieve it—and I believe she does, sometimes—but she can see the lagoon from her window and writes letters all the day long to people throughout the city. People who were once customers and became friends over time."

"She sounds remarkable," I said.

"She is. I asked her once what made her so full of life. I have seen many shut-ins, with the Book Boat. Not half of them live with joy, as she does. Do you know what she said?"

My spine prickled, feeling shame at my own way of having lived in the confines of a cell. "What did she say?"

"She said—'Vittoria, life is still life! I may be confined to these four walls, but do I not have breath to breathe? Do I not hear the bells and the birds, just as I would if I were walking the streets? I have a very full life. I just move less.'" She concluded her impression, and if it was to be believed, I could tell where Vittoria came by her spark and passion.

"Her word is law. When she moved into the apartment—it was mine before, you see, and—" Vittoria stumbled over her words for the first time. "She did not want to displace me. I assured her I could make a very comfortable place to sleep somewhere else and she said, 'All those books! Imagine how they would haunt your dreams. It is not right!' She lost that argument, and I am here to attest that stories do not haunt dreams. Though one can always hope, for I wouldn't mind learning more about that stone table in my dreams tonight."

Her words tumbled out faster and faster, as if to cover over something.

"Do you mean to say that you . . . sleep here?"

Silence.

"Among the books?"

A shrug.

"But where?"

No answer, but she darted a look to the corner beneath the spiraling stairs, where a lidded wooden crate stood. Presumably holding her blankets and pillow.

She saw it happen, the understanding as it sank in. Drummed her fingers on the table until she threw up her hands. "Yes, yes," she admitted. "So I sleep among the stories. So what? I defy you to tell me of a more wonderful place to rest one's head. Just think of it: Gulliver and his Lilliputians! Mr. Andersen and his fairy tales! These are the places my dreams may dwell. What do the unfortunate possessors of beds get? Fluff and feathers? Poor fools."

She clamped a hand over her mouth as she realized I was likely afflicted with a bed.

"I'm so sorry. Why do I speak before I think?"

I laughed. "It's better than thinking so much you barely speak."

"Trust me, Daniel Goodman. Yours is a better way to live, I am sure of it."

"I . . . rather enjoy you. The way you are." Now it was my turn to wish my words back. "It's refreshing. To know what someone is thinking, to not have to wonder."

Her eyes rounded. "Well. You are very kind. And I enjoy your way of speaking; it leaves something of a mystery. You're like a . . . kind question, Daniel. You wait, and you listen, and it gives others a chance to feel waited for and listened to. That is a very large thing in a world that grows faster and louder every day."

Echoing sight, kind question . . . What would she call me next?

She continued, "And truly. About being confined to feathers and bedrooms in one's dreams, I don't mean to offend. I do challenge you, though, to imagine—" She caught herself, recalling my blank canvas. "To *wonder* what might happen if you found yourself without the confines of a bedroom."

A creaking iron gate sounded in my mind.

"What?" she said, biting her lip in uncharacteristic timidity.

I shook my head, unable to answer. I'd thought this part of the conversation might wait at least a little longer.

"What is it?" she insisted with a laugh. "You, too, think me a fanciful fool. Well, it's a magnificent place to sleep, though it must be nonsense to you, with your fine suit."

"I . . . have been without a bedroom, now that you mention it."

"Oh?" She looked me up and down. "Was it when you had to travel in your personal railcar? Or perhaps you were forced to sacrifice your bedroom for the halls of a suite?" She smiled, tromping up the stairs and motioning me to follow.

She flung open the glass double doors, and we stepped out onto the outer terrace, Robert Browning swooping to follow and settling where the railing met the bricks, beside another owl. Smaller, white feathered with yellow eyes, looking unamused by my existence.

"There are two of them?"

"Of course! Meet Elizabeth."

I laughed. "Elizabeth Barrett Browning?"

"Don't be ridiculous. She is Elizabeth *Barn-owl* Browning."

She rotated her head to behold Vittoria with undying devotion.

"You were saying? About the railcar."

This was it. Two words, and we would cross a threshold we could never uncross.

"In prison."

Her hand froze midstroke upon the owl's feathered chest.

I watched the word—*prison*—knock upon her understanding. She turned, tilting her head to me in silent question. She flicked a gaze toward the doors, her shoulders easing when she confirmed they remained open.

And then she found her unflappable manner again. "Oh?"

As if I had merely just confessed to stopping at the fish market today.

"It was theft."

She turned the word this way and that in silence, then crossed her arms.

Did you do it? Is it true? Were you falsely accused? I braced for the inevitable questions, whose hopes I would have to duly crush, leaving destruction once again in my path. Would I never stop hurting the people who had ventured close to this beating, unruly thing in my chest? It drummed wildly, now, as I awaited her question.

When it came, it was small. "Why?"

"What?" That was not the question I'd expected. All my ready answers shattered.

"Why did you steal?"

"I—I'm sorry. Most people want to know whether I did it or not."

"You just told me you did. I trust you."

"Maybe you shouldn't," I said.

"Then tell me why."

I pressed my eyes closed, and in a fleeting instant, remembered the Daniel who was more boy than man, stars in his eyes, getting it in his misguided head that he could be the hero his mother deserved.

Instead, he'd been the greatest sorrow of her life.

I told Vittoria as much. Of my father, out upon the island of Alcatraz as a military offender, kept from us by prison until his eventual death. Of my mother, up late working—baking, darning, anything to make ends meet. Of the grand houses on Nob Hill, where the people left for balls and dinners, bejeweled and oblivious that a limber kid stole from the rich and, like Robin Hood, believed himself justified. He'd scale fences, open windows, target jewels that were least likely to be missed and most likely to fetch a tidy sum. Of the stairstep at home with the loose board, where I kept that cache.

"We all make mistakes," Vittoria began, that flicker of hope in her eyes. She saw my questioning look. This was more than a mistake. "Many make bad choices in their youth."

"It . . . gets worse." I went on to tell of my older cousin, who discovered my escapades and brought me into his loop. I'd jumped books—straight out of Robin Hood and straight into the Artful Dodger and Oliver Twist, aiming for bigger houses, larger spoils.

"But you've stopped, yes?"

"Yes. Long ago. But . . . it gets worse."

She didn't mean to, I was sure of it, but she drew back. Ever so slightly.

I told of the day I arrived home to see an officer lead my mother away in handcuffs, for all to see. The cache had been discovered by a customer, and then she was brought in to be questioned. The best soul in this world. Who fed the hungry and never missed a Sunday service. Whose face always lit just to see me . . . And who hadn't seen me again since that night.

"I watched from the shadows," I said, voice dredged in shame.

"Coward." The word seethed at my old self. "I'd give anything to go back. Stand up, step into the light, confess. And I tried to. I went by the dark of night to the station but found everything locked up, my mother held in a cell inside as a suspect. I sat on the steps. I—didn't want her to be alone. And determined to wait until morning."

Vittoria's eyes brightened. I held up my hand. "But . . . I didn't stay." How many times had I tried to untangle my garbled, misguided thoughts that night? And it always came back to the fact that *I'd* been the one at the helm. Doing the guiding—or misguiding. I couldn't just pin it on youth or zeal or a misguided sense of justice or even a wayward cousin.

Wrong as it was, it had been my choice to make. To go for the Big One, as my cousin Emilio called it. He'd had me study the place, draw up the plans. But why should they get the spoils of my hard work? Why, when I was the one who'd spotted the ivy-covered fire escape ladder? If I was going to confess—I was going to be locked up. And if I was going to be locked up, I'd get one more job in if it meant it would replace the spoils that had been hidden in that bottom step . . . and provide for my mother in the way my father never had.

"But it was a cold night," I said. "When fog freezes on ivy, it's slippery."

I remembered the bone-chilling cold, the sinking dread that pleaded with me to come down, go back, not do it—and then the choice to climb higher. One of the rungs was missing, as if it, too, conspired with the forces to make me go back. I reached, furled each finger tight around the higher rung as I lifted my foot and, in that moment—with all of me hanging from one icy, ivy-covered rung—I slipped.

Knowing that if I fell, it could be the end. Blindly in the tangle of metal, plant, and man, I took hold of a lower rung and held fast to it.

Inside—I remembered it as cold dread—a light had come on. A head poked out of a window. I tried to hold still, but my foot slipped against the slick stone wall. Someone shouted.

And then . . . I'd run. Dropped myself to the ground as soon as I could and tore into the night as someone emerged from the house, rounding its corner, coming fast.

The memory flooded around the dam of that dark canvas, reaching long, sinewy arms, clutching me right back into that night. The scene came in the form of sound. Feeling. Every muscle tensing until I could feel how the tendons had flexed in my legs, urgency coursing through them, carrying me blindly. Pulse hammering erratic over the sound of feet upon the ground. The frantic pound-pound-pound and then a slick patch of ice, black as the night, spotted too late. The twisting, ripping of those tendons as I collapsed. Ground rushing up, I rushing down. Thinking only—*I'm finished.*

My head hit with a sickening crack.

The ground, the dark that followed . . . it swallowed me up far more than the four walls that I awakened to.

I finished the account, hearing the sound of a clock ticking somewhere inside, the flutter of an open book's pages as a breeze swept inside past us. Chatter somewhere down the canal, as if life really was sunny and I hadn't just laid every shadow out before the best person in this city.

But there it was. Every stupid bit of it. Bitterness filled my mouth and did not allow me to look at Vittoria.

This—the shame, always before me—was my chosen lot. "It was my fault," I said. "Mine alone. And I can't—" Heat choked inside as I thought of all those jars, all those doorsteps, all those hours I'd toiled to make recompense. "I can never undo it."

The silence was long. I blew out my cheeks. Swiped at my face, wishing I could disappear into the canal below and be hidden.

The soft rustling of Vittoria's skirt gentled the sharp edges of the moment as she turned to face me. In her silence, she beckoned my gaze, but I couldn't lift my chin.

"And . . ." she started. "Your mother?"

I gulped, nodded a single time. "She was released, right away. I confessed to all of it."

"I meant . . . has she forgiven you?"

Forgiven? "I don't know," I said, and my voice caught. This, too, was my fault. "She . . . wrote to me. When I was locked away. Sent those old histories." I lifted a hand half-heartedly. "One at a time, with letters. But I never—I just—I wanted to wait to see her. Until I could come back as the son she deserves. Until I had paid back everyone I had wronged, in full."

"But your prison sentence is fulfilled," Vittoria said.

I confirmed.

"And they require this restitution too?"

"No. But I have to make it right. I want to be able to go to her with every hole I've dug filled. Every tear I've ripped mended."

"Daniel," she said, her voice so tender. "She is your mother. How she must long for you! Do you not think she would take you while your holes are not yet filled? She does not want perfection. She wants *you*. From how you speak of her, I am certain of it. To meet you where you are and to help you fill the holes and mend the tears."

I shook my head. "You didn't see the look on her face the night they took her away." The ache in my throat closed in. "It was . . . *anguish*."

Her hand rose, her thumb brushing my jaw, then falling to her side. "I have seen that look, Daniel. You wear it now. But if she is the woman you describe . . . this woman of faith, then I think she must know the ancient truth . . . of a man who came to heal the sick, not to boast in the perfect." She leaned forward as if to impart one of Venice's infamous secrets. "I am an expert in myth and story. And there is no myth greater than that of perfection."

Her words chipped away, until a crack began, beginning a vast and foundational crumble—the likes of which I witnessed at every corner of this "decaying city." On Venice, it seemed beautiful. As if song seeped from those cracks.

On me . . .

It was not song, but fear. All my mistakes.

A place Vittoria did not deserve to be dragged any deeper.

"You mentioned my private railcar," I said, an attempt to lighten the moment. "How did you know?"

She paused, not so quick to release the moment. But with a knowing glance that told me we were not finished with this conversation, she indulged it. "Was it on the trip to Venice?"

"Long before that."

"And did you have red velvet curtains drawn with golden cords and all the opulent glory of the Orient Express? I peeked into one of the cars once. Do not tell the stationmaster."

"Mine . . . was abandoned on a beach. Or a wasteland, if you want to be precise." I told her of the abandoned railcars in a land that had once been only fit for the dead.

"You lived in one?"

I nodded.

"So you found your refuge in a wasteland that nobody else wanted."

My flat smile affirmed her conjecture.

"I think you should see something," she said, leading me back inside. Instead of going down the spiral staircase, she opened a paneled door that revealed a second stair, this one simpler. It took us up a flight, then another, until we arrived at a small landing, where a trapdoor hovered above us, a ladder fixed to the wall.

She motioned me upward, then followed. I unlatched the door with the distinct impression I was unlocking a portal to the very clouds.

I nearly laughed when I was met instead by the sound of cooing pigeons and the smell of the fish market, wafting upward. It was no celestial refuge, but the look on Vittoria's face said that there was something special about this place. A sea of red-tiled rooftops rose and fell in stationary waves, leading to the lagoon and the sea beyond.

"You know of Venice," Vittoria said. "Of how all of this is built on what some would say is a wasteland? Fit only for the dead?"

I recalled the Book of Waters and its account of refugees fleeing, building impossible homes upon stilts, and the islands themselves composed of stilts. "It's amazing," I said.

"You are not so far from home after all, Daniel." She slipped her fingers into mine, as if lacing them there would stitch this truth to me. "Your Sand Rubbish—"

"Sand Waste," I said, smiling.

"The Great Sand Waste," she said slowly as she tried on the words, "and my Swamp City. These places that others considered lost and unwanted else . . ."

She gestured over the city, where evening breeze billowed through humble clotheslines and regal flags alike. Where travelers the world over came to behold treasures of art, music, architecture and—perhaps above all—hope. For I was beginning to see that the longer one spent in this city, the less it was a place forgotten by time, but kept with care, a living testament to perseverance and redemption.

"Perhaps the desolate places are not so desolate after all, no?"

In the distance, the golden statue of Fortune atop the Punta della Dogana twisted in the wind, an ornate weathervane that stopped with arms outstretched toward us.

"See what they have become," she said. "Murano, where molten fires create shimmering glass. Burano, so bright with all its color-ful buildings and spinning lace so fine there are legends about it. Torcello, with its mosaics and a fabled throne. And on it goes. All from a wasteland."

Her eyes met mine in a weighty pause. "See, Daniel Goodman? Such marvels. So good." These last two words she spoke like a benediction, letting her hand alight beneath my elbow in a brief touch.

It tore deep into the one vault I had secured rather than broken into. With two words and the smallest touch, she cracked it open until it hurt to breathe.

It had been a long time since someone looked at me with what I saw written on the gentle lines of her smile: hope.

And I could not let her be broken by it, as another had.

I cleared my throat. Withdrew and watched something shutter on Vittoria's expression. I hated myself for it but better to disap-point her with one small step back upon a rooftop than do further harm by drawing near.

Vittoria, true to her windblown self, would not let me escape so easily. "Why do you do that?"

"Do . . . what?"

"This." She waved a hand up and down at me. "You . . . disappear yourself. Just when you have shared something true—you go and hide away again. You were not meant to disappear."

"I just . . . don't want to make trouble."

"Hmmm," she said, thoughtful. "My zio has a saying. 'Do not trouble the waters,' he says, telling me to take care when rowing near other boats, so that I do not disrupt their voyage. But you, Daniele . . . could it be that you were meant to trouble the waters?"

"I've caused enough trouble."

"But perhaps to trouble the waters is only to move them. Today, when you knelt before that boy and a wave toppled you, you did more than you know. That boy has never spoken, not once, in all the times I have seen him. I see him go home to dark windows. I see him walk alone. Today—you knelt. You allowed yourself to be there, to be seen—to not disappear. You troubled the waters . . . and you brought life to a lifeless place. What book did you first show him?"

"We were looking at *Pinocchio*," I said.

"Ah." She nodded, knowingly. "Well. Do not disappear, Daniel. You were made for this time."

I turned my eyes back out over the lagoon, where the light grew purple as dark whispered in. And pretended she had only been discussing islands and waters and not offering me a lifeline.

"Tell me about that island," I said, pointing. It was the same one I'd inquired after on the train—the "doomed" island.

Vittoria's eyebrows rose, a twinkle of mischief rejuvenating her. "Malodetto. There are as many stories about that one as there are families in Venice! Some say it is a place of haunts, some say any who land there will stir up the old plague, for they say some quarantined there long ago to spare their families. Others say it is a place where all wits vanish, for it became an asylum for the insane for a time. Some think it is all a lie, meant to keep visitors away."

"And what do you say?"

Vittoria narrowed her eyes, leaning out over the rail as if Malodetto called to her. "I know only two things to be true of that island."

I joined her at the railing. "Two?"

"Sì. One, that nobody truly knows what secrets that island keeps . . ."

"And the second?"

Her mischief faded, face growing serious, determined. "That I will find out for myself one day."

THE BOOK OF WATERS
The Island

Two days. Two days the young woman lay unconscious beside their fire. Sometimes with Elena at her side, sometimes Sebastien. Though he held a book in his hand, it was she who held his attention.

She was unlike the other Visitors they'd had. Those who came to learn to work the land, that they might provide their own food in their lives of exile. They stayed a short time, in this very room, but always departed still shrouded in a cloak of mystery and unknown future.

This Visitor . . . was different. She did not seem a Visitor at all, in fact. In need of refuge like the others, yes—but also, as if she fit here, somehow.

He began to know her breathing, when it was softly regular, when it paused long enough to summon him to the edge of his seat, releasing his own captive breath only once she returned to a steady rhythm.

He began to know the way the light played across her face at different times of the day. Why did she not wake?

Somewhere near the end of the second day, when she had become more familiar to him than his own humble reflection, he could no longer think of her as just "her" . . .

Outside, a breeze danced through the leaves of an olive tree, and she stirred. She often did this, as if the sound called to her.

He thought of the wind that had stirred up the storm the night she'd come. It had come from the north and acted just as its namesake suggested: *La Tramontana.* "From the mountains," and with just as much beauty and strength.

The name fit the night, but it did not fit her. *Tramontana.* He whispered it, and it fell flat into the air. He could not call her so.

He thought of the grasses he had found her among. A small glade—*radura.* This, too, he whispered, and though the setting it conjured befit her, the word somehow did not. He shook his head.

Finally, he thought of the seas that had churned the lagoon that night and lifted her, somehow, upon the shores of this island. *Mari*—"seas." He whispered the word and the breeze outside stirred again. This time, the woman stirred too. Taking in a deep breath, turning her head to face him, eyes closed. He sat up tall in the chair, its wooden legs creaking in response. Silence, and then he offered again, this time in a low voice, "Mari. Is that you?"

The breeze tapped a tentative branch against the age-obscured glass of the window, and her lashes fluttered open.

He froze. What was he to do? What did one say to a woman who had washed up on shore, seemingly out of nowhere, and turned the world upside down? What did one say to a woman at all? His presence there would frighten the wits out of her.

So he stayed very still, as quiet as he could, and willed himself invisible.

She blinked, filtering the growing light. Seeing, then puzzling over the unfamiliar scene before her.

She turned her head toward the window—away from Sebastien. At length, she raised herself onto her elbow and stretched to see better. She made a picture herself, there with her hair brushed into a long plait—Elena's doing—and the green-blue of the lagoon sparkling beyond, as if to welcome her back to the world.

He shifted to steal away, fetch Elena. Hers would be a better face to greet her than his scruffy, awkward one. But as he stood, the chair creaked.

He winced. She turned, sitting up straight and pulling the blanket tight around her at the sight of him.

They both stared, unspeaking, eyes locked.

"*Benvegnù*," he said lamely. Not a welcome to rival that of the lagoon with all its dazzle and shine. But he did not wish to speak loudly, to frighten her.

She turned her head almost imperceptibly, assessing him and the situation at hand.

"Where . . ." she began, brows furrowing. "Where am I?"

Her words, in a voice quiet from disuse, were spoken in an accent he did not know. Very much like his own and yet with a lift to it, the sense of a far-off land.

"You are on *Isola di Giardino.*"

The confusion on her face grew. It was the look of one who had never heard of such before. Perhaps she knew of it by the name Elena had begun to tell the Austrian soldiers, along with tales that would frighten them away. Malodetto, the island had become known among them.

"Malodetto?" he said quickly. "I assure you, they are only stories—it is why they don't patrol our beaches and haven't turned our old abbey into an arsenal like the others." Still, no trace of recognition. "You . . . are on a small island in the lagoon of Venezia."

"Venezia," she whispered, her gaze dropping for the first time.

"Sì. You have been with us for three nights now."

"Us?"

As if summoned by the word, Elena entered the room, bearing a tray of hot food.

"Ah! You are awake!" Her pleasant face broke into an unbridled smile. "How marvelous. I am Elena," she said, "and this is Sebastien. And you, my dear, are hungry."

"I—I am?" The concept of hunger appeared to seem as logical to her as the concept of waking up in this strange place.

"Certainly. Come, eat!"

Sebastien watched a procession play out across her expressions. Wariness, confusion, uncertainty with a glance at the tray of food, then the two that puzzled him: a look at the lagoon that bespoke fear . . . followed fleetingly by an inexplicable flutter of peace, as her shoulders dropped and her eyes returned, softly this time, to the tray of food.

"Grazie," she said. Her accent was foreign, but her words came out a woven mixture of Italian and the Venetian dialect.

She beheld the assortment on the tray warily and picked up a strawberry. She brought it to her lips and chewed a bite slowly, closing her eyes and savoring it as if the entire world had melted away. Swallowing, she startled herself into a realization that there was no longer food in her mouth, which she quickly remedied with great speed and astonishing quantity.

Sebastien watched, awestruck by so many things before him. Elena seemed to find the whole scene amusing, particularly his own present state.

He excused himself, returning to his work outdoors to give the women time and to force fresh air into his addled brain. What was wrong with him? Was she a siren, that she could make an inextricable tangle of his limbs and thoughts? It was as if no one had ever seen a hungry woman before. He had been combing the island since the storm, looking for any sign that might explain her. Her presence here, her identity—anything. But all to no effect. He had found only bits of driftwood, seaweed that at last was beginning to dry and relinquish its grip of stench upon their small banks. And he had made the sad discovery that in the excitement the night of the storm, he had never returned to pull their own boat in, leaving it to be battered upon a jetty. The damage was not catastrophic, but it was enough that it would need several days of work before it would be seaworthy.

In the hens' dwelling yard, Sebastien raked the ground clear, scattered garden scraps, deposited fresh grasses into the boxes that he had built, and then turned to secure the gate. He began his ritual count of the feathered creatures, only half paying attention.

"Una," he began. "Do, tre, quat—" but no. There was no quatro. He did not even need to examine them to know that there would be two whites and a yellow, but no grey.

"Tuona," he breathed. This time, he went straight to the most recent haunt: the stand of cypresses beneath which Elena had found her in the storm.

There, happy as could be, was the grey hen.

Sitting in a boat he had never seen before.

He stepped softly, as if to avoid waking the vessel. As he drew near, though, he saw that even if it were possible for a boat to awake, there would be no danger of that here. It was shattered at the bow, split at the stern, and bore no hints as to the lady's identity. It was a sandolo, like so many of the flat-bottomed boats made for the lagoon. Very much like the gondolas, but simpler, lighter. Which made it the choice of many ladies, but also made it rock much more than a gondola. Certainly not something to be caught in a storm with—though, truth be told, no boat would have fared better in a storm of that strength. It was a miracle it was here at all, and even more so that its rower had survived.

He realized he did not know how to think of her—a girl, a lady? Perhaps twenty or thirty, likely somewhere in between. He was not accustomed to deciphering these things. She had the fresh beauty of a girl grown, but it had not escaped his noticed that she had the height and figure of a woman. He had not lingered on that, for it was not for him to notice. She was perhaps part of one of the patrician families, with her embroidered linen and skin untouched by the Adriatic sun. There were not many in Venice, any longer, who could afford such finery. Such a woman would be destined to marry a man of rank and destiny. Not to keep company with an island farmer.

Stooping, he gathered three wooden shards from the wreckage and closed his grip around them. He remembered the flash of fear that had visited the girl's face. It had an edge to it, something broken that had made him wish to gather the pieces up.

Holding these pieces close now, he tucked Tuona under his other arm and returned, securing the hen once more in her yard.

He approached the house with care, entering only when he heard Elena telling the story of the day Sebastien had ascended the ruins as a boy and proclaimed himself king of the lagoon. Elena laughed, and when he entered, she turned to face him. Though her countenance was bright, he saw that it was for the girl's benefit. She was concerned, he saw in her eyes.

"Are you telling tales about me, Elena?" he spoke steadily, quietly as he chided, following her lead. He, too, held concern—but it would not serve the girl well to heap it upon her.

"Are they tales if they are true?" She loved to answer questions in a question.

He took the chance to present his news in a lighthearted way. "If they are, I have a true tale for you," he said. "For both of you."

"Good!" Elena rose, gesturing to her seat. "I fear Mariana has tired of me hovering." *Mariana.* Was it her name, truly? Or had Elena built upon the one he had tried to speak, the one that seemed to have summoned the girl awake?

"I'm not tired of you at all, I—" The girl lifted herself to sit straighter upon the bed.

"Hush," Elena said gently. "I jest, but I do know that I hover and fuss. But only with such a one as you. This one, however . . ." She looked sideways at Sebastien and shook her head. "So independent I must tie him down to get him to eat sometimes." She offered a wink, and he felt the heat rising in his face. With that little gift, she left.

The quiet in the room hung with a tension that did not fit squarely in the walls. Sebastien wasn't certain how to find his way around its odd shape, to speak to this Mariana.

So, he began with only her name. "Mariana," he said, feeling the roll and tumble of it into the world like a waterfall. "That is your name?"

She gave a nod so small he nearly missed it, as if she were not certain.

"And you are Sebastien," she said. She studied him as she spoke it, measuring whether this "Sebastien" was one she could trust.

"Yes," he said. "And despite what Elena would have you believe, I eat most willingly at her table. I only . . . lose track of the day sometimes. When I am late, she likes to say such things. But she means it in good humor."

Mariana looked puzzled. "Elena," she said. "She is your mother?"

It seemed a simple question. It would have been a simple question, to most people. For Sebastien, it dug into the question that knocked ceaselessly at his mind of late.

"Yes," he said, drawing the word out. Then pressed his brows together. "That is—no."

Mariana looked as perplexed as he felt.

"I have many parents," Sebastien said finally. As if that would satisfy the question rather than introducing ten more.

"And I have none," she replied quickly.

Now Sebastien was the one puzzled. He tipped his head, each of their statements giving way to a thousand mysteries swimming between them. And through their watery form, he saw a glimmer of something he had never known: one like him.

"Where do you go that you lose track of time enough to miss cooking like this?" She lifted her empty plate and, for the first time, also lifted the corners of her mouth. A smile.

"I'll show you, if you like," he said. "When you're feeling better. But for now, I've brought you something."

He pulled his chair closer, into that sea of invisible questions, and felt them slip over him, bringing him into her world. He held out his hand, displaying the large and jagged splinters of boat.

Sebastien did not speak. Only watched her as the tentative smile faded quickly into immediate recognition. She swallowed, then looked at him.

"And . . . what is it?" she asked, spinning lightness into her voice that couldn't hide the shadow hovering.

"Your boat, I presume."

"I have no boat," she said.

Sebastien's eyes grew wide, inviting her to explain. She did not.

"That is true," he said at last. "If this boat was once yours, it is no longer. You're stranded, I'm afraid."

Sebastien had feared such news would be too much sorrow. But when her shoulders dropped, it was in relief.

"But I can fix it," he said.

She tensed. What her soul would not speak, her body betrayed.

"Surely a thing like that would take a very long time?" she asked. Tentatively. Hopefully.

He weighed the matter, calculating. "It would be land-bound for this week, at least. And possibly the next. My own boat has been damaged, too, but it can be fixed more swiftly than yours. If we begin there, then I can take you wherever you need to go. Return you to your . . . home?" he asked it as a question, inviting her to fill in the empty places of the story.

Her forehead creased, but she offered no answer.

Sebastien continued. "I can visit Giuseppe—he's a boatman, you see—and get what is needed to fix yours. Elena and I can return it to you as soon as it is ready. Wherever you like," he offered.

The silence rolled heavier as she let it linger, no longer meeting his gaze.

"I have no boat," she murmured again, closing her eyes. The weight upon her looked so heavy—whether grief or fear or something else entirely. It summoned a fight within Sebastien, but if she would not speak of herself, there was little he could do.

Outside, a bird trilled, and the sound of it seemed to rouse her once more.

"You will show me?" she said at last.

"The boat?"

"The place you go that makes you so often late."

A beginning, at least.

Elena came back in, her timing much too perfect. "Of course he will show you. The sunshine will be the best medicine for you, and the air is very fine today. Sebastien, away with you, and our Mariana will be out very soon. You wait, yes?"

Our Mariana. It sounded . . . right.

"Sebastien?"

"Yes," he said, shaking himself from thought and into action.

Mariana opened her eyes, and the beginnings of a question etched her face. But when she spoke, it seemed to vanish back into her. "Thank you," she said at last, and smiled.

26

DANIEL

I couldn't sleep that night. I worked at translating, and worked some more, but it was oddly the story that had caught the boy's attention in the campo that kept waking me. Pinocchio, the puppet, who wished to be real.

It was a fairy tale. The stuff of imagination. Written for children.

Not convicts.

So why did it rouse my old shackles from their silence and keep me from sleep?

Why did it seem to shine a light upon all the money I'd earned, restitution I'd made, jars I'd left upon porches? Why did it do this and seem to carve them into caricature, puppet-like, and clatter like a hollow-boned marionette? I had seen paintings in the Doge's Palace and the biblioteca where the artists placed shadows against light dramatically, causing the subject of the paintings to shine as in a spotlight, taking on an almost dimensional presence. *Chiaroscuro*, they called this method.

It would seem that Venice was intent on using this same technique on me. Illuminating things I would rather leave well buried.

I would go mad in this room if I stayed.

I threw open the window, hoping for a Garbin or a Tramontana

215

to blow in and throw a cold veil over these thoughts. Instead, I was met with the sight of the basilica's dome, its silver-grey tones muted in moonlight, the silhouette of Saint George standing proud in statue form atop. George, who was said to have saved a girl from a dragon.

He smote me. As if he knew all about me.

Throwing on my jacket, I opened the door and stepped out, something shuffling as my foot hit it.

It was a package, wrapped in brown paper and written in a scrolling hand—Vittoria's.

Don't forget the end of the story.

And then, below that, in firmer hand that I recognized from Jacopo's boat:

And don't forget your brickwork tomorrow! Jacopo will take you. Or else!

Opening the package, I beheld a well-loved volume of *Pinocchio* and laughed. Flipping through the pages, I saw snatches of the wooden puppet's journey—his attempts to become a real boy through striving to do well and the winding roads that diverted him from that hope for so long until, at last, he returned home, humbled and loved and ready to love well.

On the last page was the image of a boy, awaking in his bed to see the wooden puppet, lifeless in a chair.

He was a real boy—in fact, a new creation, entirely. It was not his striving bones that had become real.

My own bones felt stiff, lifeless within me. I clapped the book shut, placed it in my room, and made my way outside into the night. Here, all was quiet. This isle, though only just across the canal's expanse from the heart of Venice, felt a world away.

A haven graced, just now, with the trailing and melancholy chanting from within, the monks up for their nightly vigil and song. The sound drew me. I entered the doors of the white basilica and found myself standing upon a floor of deep red and beige parquet, leading the way in their diamond-points like arrows to an altar ahead.

Where the monks were, I wasn't certain. In the *chorum noc-*

turnis, perhaps. But their voices filled the heights, tugging me further inward. I sat upon a wooden pew, alone but for flickering candles, towering white columns, and the same domed roof I had seen from my window.

Craning my neck, I lifted my face skyward and took in the curve of that holy roof. Who was I, to sit beneath it? To sit in such close proximity to a holy place whose purpose I didn't entirely understand, this altar with its artwork of disciples and desert-wandering Israelites flanking it? There was a time when I'd believed art like this was something I had been born for. Something good and beautiful and worthy I could give to the world, to offer to my Maker.

But now . . .

I closed my eyes against the view of that pristine dome in all its white holiness.

Saw, in a flash, another dome. Opposite, in every way.

Instead of white: black.

Instead of sturdy: flimsy.

The patchwork attempt of a man to protect the mother he failed, by bundling a bouquet of umbrellas together.

Again, my shackles rang out.

Again, the monks' singing echoed.

What were they saying? It was what one of the monks had explained to me before—the *Lumen Hilare*, the Gladsome Light. The dips and rises, steady climbing of men's joined voices traversing invisible steps. It resounded with peace and reverence—and yet there was no trace of either of those things inside of me.

That "gladsome light," that chiaroscuro, seemed intent on summoning out all I had worked to bury.

Standing, feeling my collar tighten around my neck, I backed away down the aisle. Unable, somehow, to turn my back on the white dome and all that it covered—and unable, too, to stay within its presence.

Blindly I walked with purpose, as if I knew what I was about. Down corridors, beneath keystones, through a reaching doorway until I burst into the night, feeling something at my back. The light, the pursuing light, following me.

"What is it?" I asked through gritted teeth.

The old burning in my legs returned, the yearning to stretch them and run, run, run without stopping. But once again, I could not. This time confined not by walls, but by the holy limits of a holy isle, water bordering all around, me a blight upon it.

Those legs carried me into the cloister, courtyard bent on walling me in further. In the center of it, the wilds of hedges pruned into boxy lines. Even in its symmetry, the closest thing to a wilderness I'd seen since arriving here. I welcomed the dark. Plunged into it. Followed the path to the center of the courtyard . . . and fell to my knees.

Gladsome light? Pursuing, relentless, shadowing light—but there was nothing gladsome about this thing that pulled me down until I could smell the spice of the soil, feel the blades of grass upon my palm. In the distance, the singing continued.

"What?" I hissed into the earth. Bowed and ashamed, wishing to both hide from and deeply awake to the fact that I could no longer disappear.

"What is it you want from me?" I wanted to rail and ask of God, wanted to let all the questions loose. Why now? Why, when I was just weeks away from making enough of myself to rectify my wrongdoings? To make things right for the woman who bore me—to rise up and see Daniel Goodman become an actual *good man*? Why this reckless pursuit, this thwarting of the scales that were so close to being balanced, at last?

This shapeless force that pursued me here, it was either my past . . . or someone who knew entirely about it.

Lifting my face, I winced, swallowed back the hot rush gathering behind my eyes.

Deeper.

The word made no sense. But as a catalogue flipped through my consciousness of all the domes, all the art, all the saints and statues, and gilded everything that surrounded me on every side and made plain my own lack of shine, that was the word that stamped, like an imprint, on my heart.

Go deeper.

But where? There was nothing deeper. Venice had few subterranean levels. What few basements or crypts there were, all flooded. How could I go deeper?

I picked myself up off the ground. I would not sleep this night and could not fathom what "deeper" meant, or how I was losing my sanity so swiftly in this place.

As I oriented myself to try and find my way back to my room, a soft light came from within one of the doors. It summoned me with its quiet glow, and I heeded the call, passing through one doorway and then another, up a staircase and into a room that reached in every direction. Climbing heights, domed and cross-pointed in its simple white. Length of the floor reaching, unfurling like a carpet until it collided starkly against a massive white wall that seemed to bleed emptiness into the room. As if it had been built solely for the purpose of something—and that purpose was entirely gone now.

Blank canvas.

"Welcome," a voice said, and I noticed for the first time the monk, seated at a simple table that seemed out of place here. He worked at something with his hands, moving pieces around, arranging and rearranging.

I muttered a thank-you, feeling myself to be an imposter, and looked at the gapingly empty room. "What is this place?"

"*Reficere*," the man relished his Latin, continuing his work as he explained. "To remake, to restore. *Refectory*."

"The—dining hall?"

"Once upon a time, yes. Though built as much to house a work of art as a host of hungry men."

I studied his work, recognizing the pieces of a mosaic in progress. Watching him turn a piece meticulously, search for another whose broken lines seemed made to match.

"Is it difficult art?"

"Difficult?" The man considered. "Mosaic . . . it is the art of empty spaces. Broken things, harvested as treasure and pieced together into something entirely . . . different. Old, but new. Broken, but whole."

I gulped, and he looked up for the first time.

"Perhaps you know this art?"

I did not answer. Reached for a question to fill the silence. "And this is the art this place was built for?"

He laughed. "No," he said. "Napoleon took it upon himself to take that particular work with him." He gestured at the achingly white wall. "This space was filled entirely," he said. "The scene of the great wedding feast, water turned to wine. It was too large to carry. So did they leave it here?"

The answer was heavy in the air.

"They sliced it. Piece by piece, carried it away to Paris where they stitched it back together with needle and thread. Piercing it with holes to make it whole."

I felt the words piercing me too. "It . . . seems a shame," I offered lamely. "For this space to just sit, empty."

The man raised his brows in musing, continuing his work. He tipped his head to the left, then the right. "Forsi forse. Empty places . . . are not always lost places."

The question clawed up my throat, determined to get out. An empty place lived inside me. And it seemed entirely, irretrievably lost. "H-how so?" I tried to sound nonchalant. But he looked up. Saw what I knew to be desperation in my eyes.

"Think of them," he said. "The tomb, empty upon the third day. The cross, empty. Even the seams between these *tesserae*." He gestured at the mosaic pieces. "Why are they empty?"

I shook my head.

He leaned in. "Life," he said, and even in a whisper, the word echoed. "They make way for new life."

"What—" I forced the words out, the question feeling entirely too tied to myself. As if I had been stitched to that sliced-up painting so far away. "What will become of this place?"

His silence was troubling. "Who can say?" he said at last. "It has been a refuge for exiles—Medici included. It has been a place of prayers. For a great many years now, there have been only few of us here, allowed to stay and keep this place in some small way, and to watch on as so much of the monastery has been transformed from a home for our brotherhood to a garrison for the brotherhood of soldiers. From a place that housed beauty and prayer to walls around weapons when our books and treasures were stripped away. One can only hope . . ." He trailed off, dark brows furrowed, hands moving pieces of clay pots and bits of glass into the form of a radiating sunrise over a mountain. "So I come, in the dark, to piece together things of hope from things of destruction." The scrape of mosaic-upon-table passed a few moments.

I watched his hands move, my fingers aching, for the first time in many years, to move pieces—and make something. Perhaps I could no longer create something from nothing . . . but watching this man, his work of transformation, restoration, stirred something nameless deep within.

"*Pictor Imaginarius,*" he said, gesturing at me.

I was no Latin scholar, but knew enough to roughly translate that neither of those words applied to me. I could not imagine.

"Would you like to try? You seem to have the eye of an artist, a designer of images. Pictor Imaginarius."

As if he had reached into my own past, harvested the broken bits, rearranged things, and offered them back to me.

And all I had to do was open my hands and accept.

But all I knew was the blank canvas.

Stammering an excuse and a thanks, I exited in a daze, feeling my own edges frayed like the canvas of that sliced painting. The edges of those broken pieces, moved by a master's hand, until they uncannily matched together.

27

THE BOOK OF WATERS
A Friend

In all his life, for all the richness of family he had been blessed with, there was one thing Sebastien had not known.

The gift of a friend.

Someone who was not tied to him by family but put up with him anyway. And more than put up with him, somehow . . . understood him.

In the days that followed, Sebastien became guide to Mariana. Venturing only to the henhouse the first day and making for her a place in the sun nearby where she could watch the feathered friends and be cheered.

The next day, strengthened by that sun, they ventured farther. First to the old stone arch that welcomed visitors over the seawall and onto the island, where she sat with bare feet dipped into the waters and smiled.

Then, on to the cattail forest. Where he asked after her story, how she had ended up in a boat in the lagoon, alone. She looked sheepish.

"I was never supposed to venture so far," she said, and spoke of a favorite teacup she had rescued from the rubbish bin as a child. It was chipped and discarded but depicted a ship upon a wild sea. "I used to wonder where that ship was going." There was a long pause. "My future is . . . There is not much in the way of wondering." This, said somberly, but with determination. "And so I determined that I should at least venture out in a boat once, before all is said and done. I owed it to that little girl who used to live so far from the sea.

"And so I convinced my . . . my guardian that I could row the Grand Canal, perhaps also the Giudecca, and return safely. He has instructed me in many things over the years, and after much convincing"—she laughed— "much, much convincing, he allowed it. He was away when I departed, or he never would have agreed to let me go with the sky looking as it did. But I . . . rather welcomed it.

"So much so that I lost track, the lagoon pulling me farther and farther. It was foolish and yet—I wouldn't go back. And then I couldn't go back, for the storm pulled me farther than I ever intended." The fear she must have experienced etched in her expression, until she looked around at the emerald sea of cattails. "And then it brought me here," she said, her voice much brighter.

Mariana changed the course of conversation, coaxing from Sebastien accounts of his youth hiding among these rushes as if they were a fortress. "Hiding among the rushes," she said, laughing. "Like Moses."

At which he fell silent, not knowing how to tell her he quite literally had been found in a basket upon the waters.

She did not miss the odd shape of his silence and asked after it. Putting his story into his own words for the first time, Sebastien watched his tale meet first with puzzlement, and then with growing wonder.

"Giuseppe says I missed my fate by a mere six meters," he said, finishing the tale.

"Do you wonder what would have happened? If you had drifted to the orphanage instead?"

"Sometimes," he said, and grew serious. "But if I wonder that, I have to wonder about all of the other possibilities too. What if I had never been placed in the basket? What if the basket had not kept out water? What if a wind had carried me the other direction, out into the lagoon and out to sea?" He shook his head. "The wondering . . . If I let it, it could swallow me up, and then where would I be? Still here, but blind to all I've been given. No . . . It's not a 'what if' that visits me."

"What is it, then? I can see a question at your back. It follows you like a shadow."

He couldn't articulate it. The three words that followed at his heels felt like a part of him. He was ashamed that it still afflicted him—and perhaps more than that, didn't know what he would be without that question, so much a companion had it become. *Who am I?*

Right now, he was here, with what seemed to be a friend.

In the days that followed, it was Mariana who became guide to Sebastien. Asking questions that channeled into the depths. Receiving, with her kind smile, whatever it was he had to say. Offering opposing views sometimes, agreeing views at others, and making the world an altogether fascinating place.

Friendship, he began to see, was something of a miracle. Built in the smallest of stitches, like Valentina's lace. Each stitch a word, a look, the offering of a hand to help on unsteady ground. Small and almost imperceptible, these stitches, but all together . . . they wove a garment that wrapped a heart. Made one feel less alone and suddenly, somehow, visible.

As Mariana gained strength, they ventured farther from home on their expeditions, that cloak of friendship growing stronger by the day. . . .

Mariana was unsteady on her feet at first. She was clad in a simple frock of green that Elena had produced from a trunk and offered with curious care, as if the garment itself—even in all its island simplicity—was a treasure. It was the color of emeralds, and in it, Mariana seemed part of the island as she and Sebastien approached the ruins all covered in vines. Her long hair hung in gentle golden waves, all the way to her waist, and when she turned to peer over her shoulder, her sapphire blue eyes met Sebastien's in a question.

"Signor Sebastien," she said tentatively.

He would have laughed at the foreign and formal use of *signor*. It had never been used with his name—for he was a shadow in Venice. There to serve, and not be seen, by those who would be called signor.

But the phrase of respect tumbled off her tongue without a second thought, and the thoughtful pause that followed was so full of question, Sebastien would not intrude with a correction.

"How . . . or rather, why . . . is this place so hidden? I had thought this island abandoned, you see. I didn't know any buildings survived here. The vines and shrubs do not reveal that there is such . . ." She ran her hands along the door of the old abbey, lowering her voice in hushed reverence. "Treasure."

Her question sparked another in return. "You thought of our island?" It surprised Sebastien, for theirs was an obscure isle in the lagoon—not large or brimming with industry and inhabitants, such as Murano or Burano or even the Lido.

Mariana paused, as if deciding how to answer that, how much to say. "I am a student of Venice," she said carefully. At the name of the city, she cast a furtive glance in its direction to the south. She furrowed her brow and shifted to face Sebastien entirely. "From my balcony, and with my telescope, there is very little that I cannot see. Islands, churches, bridges, boats . . ." Her smile creased with a fondness that ran captivatingly deep. Her love for this place, quiet, strong, abiding, was palpable. "I even know which gondoliers prefer which routes through the canals. In fact . . . I know it isn't likely, but have you any brothers who ply the oar by trade?"

When Sebastien didn't answer, she shook her head. "No, of course not," she said. "It was silly of me to ask." But then, with an examining sideways look at him, she asked, "Or a cousin, perhaps. Or very young uncle?"

"I have no such uncle or brother or cousin," Sebastien said.

She looked wary, disbelieving. She began to walk slowly around the circle of stone seats. Steps slow, pausing to lay a hand on each of them. Sebastien's footsteps followed, keeping the table always directly in between them so that he could see her, and she, him. She paused at the lone remaining wall, peering through its circular window.

"Not even him?" She pointed, and he joined her. Through the tangle of ivy growing over the outside of the wall, a fishing boat passed far from the shore, its solitary occupant studying the island.

It was strange. They rarely had anyone come so close or take such interest in their humble world. Sebastien narrowed his eyes, for there was something familiar about the way the man stood, though he could not make out his features. Foreboding trekked up his spine, and he could feel Mariana's careful study of him.

"Not even him." Sebastien shook off the odd sense for her benefit. "Probably just someone out to see Torcello." The man drifted off, his gaze lingering too long for comfort in their direction, then disappearing around the bend.

"There is a gondolier who I sometimes see from my terrace. I've seen him only a few times, but the way you stand—and the way he stands—" She shook her head. "You're very alike. Your faces too. I've never seen the boatman near enough to say with certainty, but—you're sure you haven't a twin?"

"I have no twin," he said. "Or rather—I suppose it is possible, given the circumstances of my birth, but in all my years in and around La Serenissima, I've had the very good fortune to never encounter my own replica."

His quip earned a smile that reached Mariana's eyes, but it was quickly followed by a look of disappointment and puzzlement. He could no longer withhold her answer in good conscience, when it was his to give.

"Unless, of course, you count the reflection I discover in those dark canals whenever I am about my own work as a gondolier."

Her attention snapped to him, eyes alive with surprise and scolding. "*You*, a gondolier? But . . . Venice is there"—she pointed to the south—"and you are here."

"Right you are," he said, reaching for the best way to satisfy her quite valid queries about this discrepancy, without opening the carefully sealed place where he kept his own unanswered questions. "I . . . have been very fortunate to grow up under the tutelage of some of Venice's most accomplished artisans—and a gondolier, which he would proclaim is an art form too. He apprenticed me as a child and gave me my own *Arte del Gondoliere*." He named the school that trained in history, landmarks, rowing in the style of *Voga alla Veneta*.

"The artisans are a dying breed, some say."

"Sadly, there aren't so many as there once were. But I can attest that though I am but an understudy to many of them, there is talent and craftsmanship enough to last far, far into the future, and it draws its strength and tradition by reaching far, far into the past.

The hundreds of bridges in Venice, they are not the only bridges here. That's what Elena has always said. The artisans are living bridges, and so much more."

"But what you say makes no sense," Mariana said. "These trades and arts, are they not passed down within families? Does not a man dedicate his life to the one art which shall be his? Are there not scuole in which to study, and guilds to which loyalty is owed, and standards, codes, oaths . . ." The mystery of it all teetered on the pause before her final question. "How is that you belong to so many?"

"Simple," Sebastien said, though the answer was anything but simple. "Each of them *is* my family." He went on, explaining his seasonal migrations among the isles and canals, the trades and arts. "They are the ones who took me in when I was a child. It is unorthodox, a guild that crosses trades and encompasses so many." He gestured at the empty stone seats they continued to slowly circle. "But that is what makes them . . . remarkable. One of many things."

She studied him, nodding her understanding. "It is remarkable indeed," she said. "To belong to so many." There was the wonder in her voice of a heart trapped on the outside, looking in upon a warm scene.

"And you?" he asked. "Who belongs to you?"

The sky was turning, painting a living tapestry as the day spent its last for them.

She hesitated, the pause heavy. To not have a quick answer to that question . . . Sebastien leaned in, tending to her answer before it came.

"My brother, I suppose, though he is not the sort of man to belong to anybody." She told him of her upbringing by an aunt and uncle in the alpine mountains to the north, of her brother's visits. "When he brought me home, I hoped we would be a family. But . . . it seems not meant to be."

There was no bitterness in her tone, only a wistful reckoning with a chasm between hope and reality. Sebastien waited.

"He has other plans for me." This, murmured, and followed

immediately by a quick inhale as if to fill herself with courage. "But . . . he *is* a good man," she said, and he couldn't escape the impression that she was trying to convince herself. "We are just . . . very different. And I don't fault him. He is a good deal older than I, and never asked to be tasked with a sister to be responsible for. He carries much on his shoulders."

Her countenance shuttered in the pale light of night, and the conversation laid itself to rest, the silence a safe place for the aching emotions between them.

Her slow revolution around the ring of seats had come to a close, and they met in the middle, at the table. They sat upon it side by side, beneath the very stars Galileo had watched from the bell tower that now tolled across the lagoon.

Dong . . . And there was Sebastien's old question: *Who am I?*

Pause . . . And there was Mariana's silent, palpable hope, tossed into a chasm and learning to swim.

Dong . . . *Who am I?*

Pause . . . Hope, aching hope.

And in the dark, in this world unto itself, his hand reached out . . . and found a home in hers.

THE BOOK OF WATERS

The Man Who Would Be King

Massimo Fedele, the boy who would not be king, was no longer a boy.

No longer ruled by the whims and machinations of his elders, no longer a pawn in their game to be knocked aside.

In fact, he was no piece on the board at all. He was a master in the game of chess. The man planning the moves.

He would sit alone, for hours on end, studying a board. All in pursuit of the perfect move now, which would set up the perfect move ten hours, ten days, ten weeks later.

He was a patient man.

But patience and strategy can only do so much in a world beset with variables such as the movements of armies, the changing of governments, the betrayal of allies . . . and the disappearance of one's sister.

The queen upon the board—who wielded the most power, though she did not know.

She needed him. Venice needed him. Venice needed her. And she—who had she in the world but him?

Had she been lost to the storm, truly? The thought slammed a hidden part of him into a dark room, one not visited since the death of his parents. Grieved and sickened. Driven to his knees.

Had he failed at this too?

THE BOOK OF WATERS

Found

For two whole weeks, Mariana belonged to the Isola di Giardino. She seemed as though she had always belonged. Tending garden beside Elena, fishing from the shore with Sebastien, shrieking at the flapping of a fish and surprising him with tears that sprang to her eyes at the sight of the struggling creature. Her hands in his, they freed the mackerel and set it free to swim again, its silvery form flashing a reflection of light like a beacon of thanks.

She, too, whispered thanks, hers directed toward Sebastien. "It was just . . . too soon. Poor creature."

One night, he found her staring at the basket that occupied a low shelf of a stucco bookcase set into the wall of the house. The same that had once carried him . . . and by the look upon her face, this was a fact she recognized well.

The next morning, he watched her converse quietly with Elena, her humble manner seeming to request some sort of tender permission before she lifted the basket with care, cradling it in her arms and disappearing out the door. When he returned that evening after his work repairing the boats, it was to a house smelling of fresh bread, two women with flour-streaked faces, a crock of freshly churned butter on the table, and beside it, the basket. No longer empty, but filled with a bouquet of colorful flowers.

Two faces watched on, to see whether the sight was a wounding force or something else, and two smiles spread when they watched his reaction. Even the small scroll of paper that had been tucked into his blankets as a baby was rolled with care, a blade of tall grass ribboned around it and tied in a living bow. She hadn't even read it, he found, so he showed her the scrawled line later that evening by the light of the fire: "He is called Sebastien. He was well-beloved. Please give him a good life."

This was Mariana. She brought life, she brought beauty, she filled the lost places with both.

The same, when his boat was mended. Elena, glint in her eye, requested that Sebastien deliver some of their fresh bread loaves to their friends, insisting that "There is always time for bread." Tension dropped away from Mariana at the suggestion, and she welcomed the chance to stay for one more day.

And so, he brought her on rounds to Pietro's glass shop, where Pietro's grandchildren gravitated toward her like bees to a flower and told her of the scarlet glass orb their great-great-great-grandfather once made for one of the doges, to top his scepter. Mariana dropped her jaw in exaggerated wonder, and the children soared at the honor of having been the cause of such a feat. "You are like Mama," one of Pietro's twin grandsons said. "She likes that story too. Will you be a mama someday, *signorina*?"

Mariana's cheeks tinged pink at the comment and all the more when her eyes met Sebastien's as they both searched for a place to land amid such a question. She appeared not to know what to say, and a flicker of sadness skittered over her. "I would love nothing more in all this world," she said simply, then brightened her countenance and watched, hands clasped and thoroughly entranced, as Pietro made for her a small glass horse in less than a minute, the liquid glass gleaming, morphing from blob into being with each careful motion.

She turned the cooled object in her hands like treasure and carried it with her. Pietro, moved by her childlike entrancement with the fires that had created such a thing, moved like a dervish, gathering up stray candles and bundling them for her. He lit one, placing it in a lantern. "There," he said. "Now you will always have the fires of Murano to warm you!"

She carried the lantern with pride, on to the home of Valentina at their next stop. With Mariana clad again in her white linen, Valentina caught her by the wrist and exclaimed, recognizing her own work in the draping lace cuffs of Mariana's sleeves.

"You . . . made this?" The younger woman's eyes were bright with awe.

"Yes, but I never imagined I would see it upon its fine owner! To think, something from my humble hearth might find its way onto such a one as you." She cupped Mariana's cheek with the fondness and familiarity of a *nonna*.

Mariana clasped the older woman's hand right back and whispered to her of the places the works of her hands had been: a snow-capped village in the Alps, carriages and boats, a castle, a villa on the mainland. How they had given her a pattern to trace in her frosted windowpanes. How a masquerade, very soon, would see her handiwork.

Valentina's eyes shone with tears of gratitude.

"Come." The older woman clutched Mariana's hand with a conspiratorial look. "I will show you the work of the sun." She led the way to a small chest of drawers and pulled out a parcel of airy paper, unfolding it and withdrawing a work of lace so intricate, so light, it seemed spun by the fairy world.

Mariana breathed awe. "Oh, Valentina, this is . . ." She shook her head. "There are no words to do justice to the beauty of it." It was intricate, but not gaudy. Meticulous, but not stuffy. It was air and light, fluttering with every movement. "What do you call it?"

"I call it the Miracle Keeper. I only work at it for a few minutes each day—at sunrise and at sunset. For when I make a stitch, I am stitching that moment into lace, that the wearer of it may someday be gifted those moments. This . . . is a tapestry of every sunset and sunrise, for years now. It reminds me that if the sun comes up, the day has beautiful purpose. For God made it so. Yes? And if the sun goes down? All those colors, all of those clouds, different each and every day—the day is a work of art. For God made it so."

Mariana held the lace with all the care and reverence of one cradling the sunrise in her palms. "It might be the most beautiful, lovely, good thing I have ever beheld, Valentina. I hope you use it for something wonderful and so deserving someday. Perhaps a garment for yourself, yes?"

At this, Valentina laughed to the rafters. "We shall see, *cara mia*," she called her, and meant every bit of the endearment.

Giuseppe showed her the small field where he had taught Sebastien to fence as a lad. He tossed an obliging branch to Sebastien, and one to

Mariana, and proceeded to instruct her in the art of the parry, the retreat, the advance. She listened and nodded and took up her branch to meet his.

"Like this?" She parried with the skill of one who had honed her skills long before, smiling with gentle victory when she pinned Giuseppe.

"I think you've been bested at last, Giuseppe," Sebastien said and, for once, received no belligerent protest from the man. He bowed his respect, and as she walked ahead of the men, gaped silently at Sebastien, who waved him off, pleading with him silently to stop. Giuseppe dropped his jaw even deeper.

Dante would delight in a delivery of bread, and Sebastien could picture how well-matched a conversation between him and Mariana would be. Quiet and pensive, billowing with thought as they assuredly spoke of philosophy and stars, the meaning of time . . . the two were so alike. But Dante's home was in Venice, and Mariana was so dearly clinging to this last day away from the city. Perhaps another time . . .

The thought of their time coming to a close was the only unwelcome presence that day. This unspoken but very present knowledge that Mariana's departure was imminent. Sebastien could almost feel the mechanical shift of clock hands in St. Mark's Square, keeping time louder and louder. That this treasure of Mariana—she was missed, surely, by her other home.

The day had faded deep into the night as he helped Mariana back into the boat for the short trip back to Isola di Giardino.

Sebastien slowed as their boat neared the old and empty water altar. He told her of the times he had traversed the sunken island, told how the emptiness of the altar had made him wonder, as a child.

Mariana looked to the lantern Pietro had given her. Without speaking, she steadily traversed the boat and stood, reaching to open the cracked door of the small-roofed structure. To a foreign eye, it might appear as a large birdhouse upon a stilt. With care, Mariana placed her lantern within.

"There," Mariana said. "Perhaps it will shine for some soul, lost out in a storm like I was. To show them the way home."

If there was anything—any small thing at all within his reach to grant her—he would do it without hesitation. He turned the boat, and they were soon stepping upon shores of moonlight-spangled sand.

"This is the place," she breathed. He listened, having learned that when given room, she rewarded with answers most magical, in her own time.

She spoke of the marriage to the sea—that procession of times past, led each year by the Doge. The lagoon brimmed with boats to witness as he tossed a golden ring into the sea, proclaiming, "I wed thee, sea, as a sign of true and everlasting devotion. . . ." Mariana was wistful, jubilant in the telling, but in her voice also lingered something lost.

In return, Sebastien told of his trips to comb this very beach for a ring when he had learned of the old tradition as a boy. Wishing for a chance to see what would never again be seen, now that the doges were no more. The sea would have long ago buried any of the old rings in her floor, eaten it away with salt, until nothing was left.

"Something round . . . and luminous," Mariana said. "This is what you sought?"

"Yes," he said. "Just some bit of that old promise."

"Perhaps if you shifted your perspective?" She looked up, countenance bright, and silver light poured over her from the moon above. She closed her eyes as if to keep that moment, always. "Do you see it, Sebastien? There is your promise. There in the sky."

With great difficulty, he pulled his stare from her and fixed it on the moon above.

"How do you do that?" he asked.

She looked at him, awaiting an explanation.

"I search my whole life for something, and you give it to me in an entirely different form, far richer and better than I could have imagined. I was looking for a ring . . . and you gave me the moon."

"I didn't do that," she said. "It was there all along."

They returned home. The morning dawned, feeling like the sea was about to devour more than a ring. For it was time to return Mariana to Venice. . . .

There was something foreign in the air as they approached Venice to the rhythmic splash-drag of Sebastien's paddling. In all his "seasonal migrations like a bird," as Mariana had said, Sebastien had never experienced the city at length in this season. The hot, thick months had always belonged to the islands, where breezes from the Adriatic brought relief.

It was this oddly foreign feeling, coupled with the silence coming from Mariana, that made every splash of oar into the lagoon hum in a foreboding lilt.

The bells of Santa Maria della Salute unfurled like a herald unrolling a velvet carpet for a royal upon her approach, and Mariana looked every part the royal. Though her white frock was simple, the way she sat beholding the city—back straight, head high, chin tilted up—had a regal air to it. Or perhaps a defiant air. She had no need of a crown, for the sun coronated her golden hair.

And yet, for all her regality, all her mustering of strength or defiance, the color drained from her face.

"Mariana?" Sebastien asked.

When she met his gaze, the distant look in her eyes flickered briefly to something warmer, more at ease.

"Are you all right?"

For a long time, she did not answer.

He waited, giving her time as she turned it inside her like one of Pietro's masterpieces.

"Show me," she said at length.

Sebastien waited, thinking perhaps there was more to come, but she inclined her head, eyes wide, hopeful.

"Show you what?" He asked. Splash-drag. Splash-drag. The oar propelled them closer, until the Giardini della Biennale stood tall with its impossible island trees to greet them as they glided past its green gardens.

"Show me your Venice," she said, plucking a spindly twig from where it had fallen from a tree overhanging into the canal. "I thought I knew this place. Massimo and I explored the canals and rios, the campos and calli when I was younger, but now that I have seen your home, Sebastien—your *homes*—I am beginning to understand my little corner of this world is only a very small piece."

She ran the branchy twig through the waters like a master weaver through threads intimately known. "There is magic in this place, Sebastien. You can only see so much of it from above. If there was a way for that girl in her mountain chamber to know the way light dances here, the way life is held in the mortar of these bricks and floats from the windows . . . These days spent on your islands, with your family—they've awakened something in me. Caused me to know this place with a heartbeat, and not just a map's key. It's a world I'm going back to, I know . . . but first—" She paused, looking pale. Releasing the twig with a twirl and watching it float away, summoning strength as if this would be the most costly request of her life. "Will you show me your Venice?"

His Venice. It seemed presumptuous to think of any piece of this place, so steeped in tradition and majesty, being his.

And yet . . . the chance to add just one more stitch to this fabric of friendship . . .

"Are you certain? It will be dark soon, and—" He didn't know how to speak the rest into fitting words. A young woman would never be seen alone with a young man, most especially after dark.

She read his hesitancy, understanding as was her way.

"I'm certain," she said. She pulled her cloak a little higher over her head, the effect shadowing her eyes so that only the delicate lines of her jaw gave any hint at her identity. "You forget," she said. "Venice is such a place of secrets. . . . Any who wish to hide do so in a felze. No one will pay mind to a woman in a boat with no cabin to hide in, with an honorable boatman at the helm."

He held the oar still, the lapping water speaking his uncertainty.

"Please, Sebastien," she said. A troubled glance over her shoulder at the palazzos lining the Grand Canal. "Once I return, I . . ."
She faced him, her hood shifting enough to reveal troubled eyes. Her unspoken words hung like a mist—the same thought that cloaked him.

Once she returned, it would be to another world.

One in which he would never see her again.

He plunged the oar into the water with fresh determination, angling the sandolo into a side canal.

"Very well," he said, his voice echoing oddly in the narrowness of the space between buildings surrounding them. "I will show you all of the places where Venice holds your promise."

"Holds my promise?" She tipped her head.

"The one you gave me last night." Sebastien looked up at the sky and waited for her to catch the vision.

"The moon." She smiled. Ease overtook her and she began to morph, once again, into herself. She laughed softly. The yellows and corals of twilight in Venice were just beginning to brush across the sky. "But it will be hours before the moon is high."

"Well, then. We will use our imaginations. So many come to hear the operas or dance in the ballrooms or marvel at the buildings, and yet they miss something entirely. This place—these stones of the buildings, the colonnades and bridges, the arches and arcades—they were built, I am certain, to hold . . . the moon." Sebastien spoke the phrase with lightness.

Her eyes sparked with delight, though her brows drew down into a silent question. "You'll show me," she said, confirming his promise.

"Yes," he said simply, a smile overtaking him.

"I like that about you, Sebastien," Mariana said, studying him. "I have known a great many . . . people. Or met them, if not known them," she said, choosing her words with care. "Many of them take any question—any pause in conversation—as a chance to ring out with a thousand words and prove themselves an expert, as if their words could lay steps upon which to ascend a throne. You . . . say what you mean, and you say it simply."

Sebastien shrugged, shifting under this insight. "I am a simple person."

"But that's just it," Mariana replied. "You're anything but simple. You are . . ." She trailed off, studying him once again.

Her unfinished sentence threaded its way into the keeping place of that old anthem question. *Who am I?*

Of course she couldn't answer. Even he could not.

"Here," he said, happy for the chance to relieve her of the unanswerable thing. "We'll start with this bridge." They passed beneath its brick form, Sebastien ducking. His tall form wasn't always a natural fit for the bridges, but so long as he kept a wary eye, he would keep from making a fool of himself.

Once through, he slowed the vessel and pointed. She turned

around, beholding what was just one of hundreds of bridges stitching the platform-islands of Venice together in their aquatic seams. Nondescript among its more ornately arched and iron-scrolled neighbors, it rose humbly and descended. It had only a winged herald sculpted in stone to adorn it, one of its wings having long ago plunged into the waters or been plucked away by a presuming visitor.

"Which bridge is this?" she asked, turning her study upon it as if it were one of the great sculptures of Michelangelo.

"It is . . ." He searched and found no name. All of the great bridges of Venice told stories—the Bridge of Fists, where feuding clans would fight until the victor knocked his opponent into the waters. The Bridge of Sighs, where prisoners headed to their cells would expel a wistful sigh at their last look at La Serenissima. And this—a nameless bridge on an obscure rio, with a one-winged herald offering quirky welcome.

Mariana made a picture, beholding it. Her hood sliding toward the back of her head, a warm breeze lifting strands of hair from her face into rays of setting sun.

"The Bridge of the Sun," Sebastien said.

She turned, facing him skeptically. "Oh?"

"Yes."

"And you brought me to this Bridge of the Sun . . . to see the moon?"

His stories were crossing.

"Ye-es," he said again, drawing the word out to give himself time to connect the two. "The sun lays down a golden road, to pave the way for the moon."

"Which won't rise for hours."

He hesitated. "Well, if you must know, this bridge has no name. It just seemed . . . fitting, to give you a bridge named for the sun."

"Oh?" That question of hers again. From another, it might sound condescending, or haughty. From her—only inviting.

He cleared his throat. "If you wait until the moon rises—there is a point it reaches in the sky when its light spills down the length of this canal, all the way through and beneath the bridge. And . . . what is the moon's light but an echo of the sun?"

Her face lit. "I like that," she said simply. "The Bridge of the Sun it shall be, Sebastien Trovato. Where will you take me next, in this Venice of yours?"

And so began their stolen waltz through this land of enchantment. Past the walled garden of Palazzo Giuliano, where two oleander trees as old as time grew in storybook fashion from barrels upon the roof. Here, he told her, the moon continued her journey as she ascended, pausing briefly to be flanked by the silhouette branches like guards making way. She closed her eyes to his words, imagining.

They stopped at a mask shop near St. Mark's Square. When they entered, she slowed, seeming uncomfortable in the presence of a thousand feathered façades for faces.

"It's an odd shop," she said, "isn't it? With no carnivale now for so many years, and yet there are those who will still don masks. Playthings for those on Tour, I suppose. But the masks . . . they seem to be always hiding something, don't you think?" She shuddered.

His hand alighted on her back briefly, and her shoulders eased in response.

"Perhaps," Sebastien said. "I don't care for them much either." She smiled but seemed glad to leave the shop and continue on.

He pointed out the statue of Fortuna atop a building, where the figure's outstretched arm caught the breeze and turned like a weather vane aimed at the sky, aimed at nothing, but where the moon would soon be.

Onward to a campo through a maze of calli, pausing at a street so narrow one would have to turn sideways to traverse it. He led the way, clearing a few stray webs.

"There"—Sebastien pointed—"the entire moon fits where no man could hope to. At least no man in his right mind." And in the campo at the center of the maze where a fountain sang, he knelt, beckoning her. "At just the right time of night, you will see the moon held between stone and water. Just beneath this arch."

He lifted her hand to catch the splash of water. By now, her hood had long since given up its place, setting her hair free to flow down her back.

Up the spiraling stairs of La Scala Contarini del Bovolo, enclosed in arched windows and their spinning vistas, stopping to point through the ones that would, given time, play host to the moon.

He showed her a cracked garden wall, where a broken chink gave way to spidery cracks in all directions, and the moon allowed herself to be framed for any who would pause to behold it masquerading as the sun, with the help of all those radiating cracks for rays.

Again, Mariana's upturned face with eyes closed and imaginings dancing, now illuminated in the dark by flickering lanterns upon a wall.

The beating in Sebastien's chest seemed to stop too. Her eyes opened, meeting his gaze. The lantern light sent the blue of her eyes deeper than the waters, and her lips turned up into a gentle smile.

In another life—one where his arms were unschooled by the work of the waves, the turning of glass, the stoking of hearth fires, the chasing of hens, and the levering of inked presses—in a life where he knew the insides of the palazzos and not just the delivery doors, he would have taken her in those arms. Pulled her close and held her. Always. If she would have him.

In another life.

But his was the life of a question mark and a swamp. And—it was a good life.

"It's remarkable," she said. "All of these lost places."

"Lost?" The word felt cold, for it lurked in the shadows, the phantom always at his heels.

"They've all lost something," she said, pressing her palm gently to the cracked wall. "And yet you have found a way for them to hold treasure. The moon itself. Many people would only see emptiness, Sebastien. You have seen . . . a miracle."

Her words rattled inside, knocking that word——*trovato*—

loose from its cage. *Found.* "I—I don't know that I would call the moon a miracle," he said.

"It shines with a light to cast away our shadows but has no light of its own. How is that not a miracle?"

He had no answer.

"Where to now?" She looked alive. He should ferry her safely to her home, he knew. He was taking far more of her time than he had a right to. But the pull to stretch this stolen moment with her was strong.

"One more stop," he said. He glanced at the sky. If they made haste, they could arrive in time.

The city was theirs. All was still on the Grand Canal but for a few quiet gondoliers, and soon they were moored, passing by foot through the twin pillars that stood sentinel at Piazza San Marco. It was another world at midnight. No pigeons flocking, ruffling, pecking. No travelers who had all come by daylight to see the basilica, the palace, *the* campo of Venice. No swarm of bells from all over the city to drown out La Marangona.

His bell. His story. At midnight, this bell took her stage over a slumbering Venice to sing a haunting, tolling lullaby. Striking twelve—six on the side of today, six on the side of tomorrow, as tomorrow arose to become the new today.

And in the fleeting pause in between, back on the island he used to whisper, *Who . . . am . . . I?* One word ringing with each toll, the question repeating.

Mariana's slippered feet tapped against damp pavement as they approached the tower. The basilica watched on with her ramparts and adornments. The entire moment was wrapped in hush, and the distant plash of water upon seawalls.

Mariana, sensing that hush too, whispered, "What is it?" Her eyes sparked with the anticipation of a child, darting all around the square.

"Listen," Sebastien said, invitation raspy in his voice.

And the tolling began. Sounding from above, struck by a bell-keeper in a tower once built to keep watch, now kept to mark time. Steel upon cast bronze and a whole universe echoed in the sound that seemed at once a lament and a hallelujah. Again and again, until the sixth time.

Mariana's hand slipped into his, and for the first time, he was not alone in his question. Seven tolls, eight, and on . . . Until the twelfth had run, and the pair stood, statue-like. They seemed to belong there, frozen in time and holding minutes between them in their clasped hands.

Again, Mariana asked, "What is it?" This time, her eyes locked onto Sebastien's.

How to answer? How to put into words that the question he had asked every night, for as long as he could remember, had flickered this time with something new? He didn't have a ready name for it. Something higher than hope, stiller than peace.

A promise.

They continued on, chasing the moon now that it was well and truly risen. Wind flapping laundry lines with pomp, snatches of laughter from late-night diners or those leaving the Fenice, singing an off-key rendition of whatever performance they'd attended. Stray bits of violin and cello, reaching down dark canals and wrapping them in concerto.

Mariana and Sebastien, hand in hand, stretching the night as far as they could until finally, murmured so quietly he almost didn't hear it, Mariana said, "We must go."

Three small words, and yet they ripped from Sebastien the warmth of the earlier sun.

They were soon back upon the Grand Canal, passing many a water entrance where he had delivered fish. And nearing one, the place of his very first solo delivery when he had been a boy. He had been buzzing with the energy of independence, his first time out on Giuseppe's boat unchaperoned, entrusted with an entire delivery for one of *the* families. A family that went back as far as the city did.

Sebastien laughed, recalling it now.

Mariana asked what the cause of his laugh was, delighted at the sound.

"Just something foolish from my youth," he said.

She waited. He told. Of how, oblivious to the etiquette of the situation, he'd approached the grand entrance. Fixed his shirt, tucking it in until his suspendered pants were too high on his belly, so eager to look proper for his first delivery. He had knocked upon the door with a basketful of shellfish. When the *majordomo* had opened the door and young Sebastien held his offering out with practiced pride, the man said only, "I believe . . . you'll be wanting the *other* entrance. Sir."

He said it so properly, Mariana laughed and Sebastien joined her. "I can't account for what I was thinking. I was naïve about a great many workings of this city. I still am, I suppose." He shook his head, pulling into a boyish grin again. "The young master of the house was none too pleased, I can tell you."

Her cheeks dimpled as she listened on.

"He sent the majordomo away, upbraided me until the whole of San Marco *and* San Polo must have heard," he said, recalling the way the Rialto Bridge separated the two sestieres, and the palazzo towered in grand presence, watching with unblinking windows and a gape-arched mouth in the form of a boathouse at the water level. "Called me a—how did he put it . . ." Sebastien closed his eyes and recited. "A 'good-for-nothing swamp rat,' and recommended I take my wares to—well, elsewhere," he said, warming at the recollection of the man's harsh recommendations.

Here, her smile became stiff, unnatural. Dimples disappearing.

"I'm sorry," Sebastien said. "I should never have alluded to—I mean, I need not have—"

"He called you a 'good-for-nothing swamp rat'?" Her face flushed red in the moonlight.

Sebastien dipped his chin, feeling some of the old shame return.

"Those precise words?" She awaited his confirmation.

It had been a lifetime ago, but he remembered it well. "Yes," Sebastien said finally. "But in his defense, I did trail fish stench to a doorway more elaborate than the Salute."

"And . . . I suppose it was this house," she said, half-heartedly lifting a hand toward the palazzo at left as they approached.

He looked upon the building, where pale yellow tones dappled umber in the night. Its windows' Byzantine forms resembled four-leafed flowers punched from the building and filled in with glass bordered in white.

He narrowed his eyes at the grand entrance, where angels in plaster greeted visitors . . . including one high-trousered young fishmonger, a long time ago.

"Well—yes, this is the one," he said. "I remember those windows, but—it's strange. What I remember most of all is a sound. I turned to go, and there was a soft thud behind me. I looked, thinking a bird might have collided with the door. But instead, I saw . . . petals, of some sort. Red ones, filling the air, drifting down around me and clinging to the wet dock. It was so strange, and yet somehow those petals, falling from wherever they had come from, seemed to wrap up the bitter taste the encounter had left and cover it over with this sweet, ridiculous sight."

"Flowers falling," Mariana muttered.

"I know it sounds odd. Ludicrous, even. And yet—stranger things have flown into the sky, here. Rings, from the Doge, for one. If he can wed the sea with the toss of a ring, perhaps it isn't so farfetched to think that petals from nowhere could erase the sting of my mistake that day." He laughed, recalling. "They even slipped beneath the cracks of the planks in the dock. I remember stooping to see where they went and thought they'd found a much nicer place floating below the dock than my place there above it. Safe and quiet and hidden."

Mariana stood, the boat rocking slightly beneath the movement so uncharacteristically sudden. "I'm sorry."

She looked pained, and he wondered again at the depth of her compassion. Sebastien shook his head, eager to dispel her worry. "It was so long ago. And I should have known which door to go to."

Her face looked pale as her eyes darted between the palazzo and him. "That door," she said in a murmur. One lined in a far-off hope that this time he would not say yes. She pulled her cloak's hood back up around her like a cave to retreat into and dipped her head toward the peaked gothic arch and the heavy planked door that filled it.

"Yes, that's the one," Sebastien said, stilling his oar and fixing his eyes on her. Her pale throat dipped around a worried swallow, eyes wide and form stiff as a statue. The boat rocked as a ripple traversed beneath them, and she looked ready to topple.

Quickly, his hand went out to steady her. "Mariana?"

Those seeing eyes, searching him, fixed upon him as if to never let go.

Sebastien could feel it, the way he, too, froze, an invisible rope anchoring them to each other. A thought marched out upon the rope, a line of unseen letters until they perched there upon the rope, between Mariana and Sebastien, proclaiming what they both knew.

You will not see each other again.

Proclaiming, too, what the pounding in his chest wished to shout.

You will not be the same. Not ever.

And he knew it to be true. The breath went out of him as they drifted, his eyes unwilling to tear themselves from her. Never had the connection between them been stronger—and never had the distance between them been so great.

For here stood Sebastien Trovato. Fishmonger. Gondolier. Man of the islands.

And there, rising above her, was her home.

The damp air around them grew darker. All around, water, lapping. Above, a throat clearing. And then a hush . . . and a distinct smell of warmth and ash descended upon them in a serpentine cloud.

He looked up and saw the figure of a man exiting the palazzo onto a small balcony. The molten glow of orange embers flared and darkened in rhythm—a cigar.

Mariana, too, lifted her face to behold the sight. She saw him. He saw her. She waited, uncertain, as if to ascertain the man's reaction before speaking.

"*Sorellina?*" The man gripped the railing, cigar in hand, and leaned over, happy disbelief in his voice.

Little sister.

"Sì," Mariana said. And the single, diminutive word from her solitary, diminutive form split the night.

The man disappeared in an instant, and in his absence, Mariana turned to Sebastien.

"This . . . is my home," she said.

The words—he knew what they meant, but they just lingered there at the door of his mind, asking in all their logic to be let in, and yet something inside could not comprehend.

"This is your home?" he repeated dumbly. This answer to the question he had so long wondered about Mariana—it only birthed an army of new questions.

In the growing dark, the grand door opened, groaning as if it recognized the fishmonger of old and had been dreading his return all this time.

Footsteps on the dock, squashing the phantom flower petals and grinding their memory into the soles of black boots. The glowing cigar—and the man who came with it—drew near, with three servants on his heels. It happened so quickly, Mariana helped out of the boat by one of them.

And then she was gone, ushered inside with a sorrowful look over her shoulder.

DANIEL

a'Fedele?" Jacopo skewed his face to show that the notion was nothing short of insane. "You do not want to go there, Daniel. Unless you wish to earn your name, for it is indeed a lion's den. Or was, long ago."

"I do. Wish to go there, that is," I said, pressing the sketchbook tight against my side. I could almost feel the heavy door close behind Mariana, almost hear the lap of the canal around Sebastien, left out on the dock. I had stayed up most of the night translating and losing myself in their story, evading the words that had found me beneath the moon the night before.

Go deeper.

The vaporetto rose up over a wave that attempted to topple me as it had yesterday. Did these waters have some system of initiation, some vendetta against imposters like me? I planted my feet firmly, determined to pass any such rites of passage. "You are meeting the Garbin there?"

"Not until later," I said.

Jacopo grinned wide. "Ah."

"Ah, what?"

"Ah, you must be careful. She will blow you away! Yes?"

Yes. I didn't speak it. But I knew it. Something in me was irrevocably spun about by the wind that was Vittoria Bellini. I tried

247

to change the subject. "I'm only going to Ca'Fedele to sketch it," I said.

"There are more impressive places to sketch," Jacopo said. "Ca'Fedele, it has been empty for years now. Bought by an owner from abroad. They come sometimes, but most times it just sits, Wasting away, empty."

The word *empty* hit me when I thought of the soul who once filled it. Though I did not know her, Mariana was, even now, a quiet light, burning. If her home had been sold . . . I hated to think what that might indicate as to where Mariana might be today.

"Even when the owners are in residence, they do not welcome visitors."

"I'll keep my distance."

"Ha! You? I do not know if you realize this, but you are not a man who keeps his distance."

"I have no idea what you mean." Keeping my distance was what I did best. Disappearing, as Vittoria had said.

"You glue yourself to things, Daniel! You have been here only days and already you have lugged a bell across the city—"

"Just a ringer," I corrected.

"Mangled your own flesh with the city's fallen bricks—"

"Just a few scrapes." I held up my free hand to prove it.

"Buried yourself in so many books you are very likely on the verge of becoming one yourself. There are many who come and stay for months—years!—and never get so close."

I was unmoved. He sighed in exaggerated exasperation. "Show me your art."

"It isn't ready," I said.

"You have nothing in that book?" He pointed with a thick finger.

My silence betrayed me.

"Show Jacopo!" He thrust out a hand, keeping one firmly gripped upon the helm.

I set my chin and braced myself, watching for any flicker of emotion upon his face. But held no hope of seeing any. How could I, when I'd felt nothing as I'd sketched them? I'd produced rudimentary drawings of nearly all of the buildings Mr. Wharton required and yet felt as if I hadn't even touched any of them. They were productions, not creations. I felt it in my bones. Anyone who looked upon them would too.

He drew his forehead up and his mouth down. "Hmmm," he said in an approving voice. Too approving. It felt . . . manufactured. "That is very good, *Daniele.*" He let his eyes linger on a perfectly engineered likeness of the Salute. Every angle correct, every adornment identical to what the architect had designed centuries before.

Something flickered in me at that thought. That even in a dry-bones drawing like this, something had hopped through centuries and onto my page. I'd touched another man's work, his genius.

Jacopo shifted his look to me, raising a brow. "It is very precise," he said. "Like the plans of an architect!" He infused a hopeful spin over the words. He turned the page. There was the rendition of the same church, the one I'd closed my eyes and attempted to draw without looking. It had come out more like the scribble of a child than anything else, and my face burned.

"Ah! This one. This has . . . feeling. Do you know the story of the Salute? How desperate the people were, back then? They thought the world was ending. So many lost to the plague, so many empty beds, empty homes. Empty future until they feared the losses would never end but overtake and defeat them altogether. And out of that . . . came *this.* Their cathedral, built in desperate plea. This"—Jacopo thwacked the page with the back of his hand triumphantly—"has it! Feeling. Shadow and light. Desperation! Hope!"

"Perhaps . . . but no form. If you hadn't seen that just after the other one, you wouldn't have known what it was a depiction of."

"So turn in your building plans, if you prefer. They are just fine." He handed the book back to me, and I nodded, defeated.

"That's just it," I said. "I wasn't hired to produce building plans. I was hired to create original art that would move people to experience the spirit of Venice from afar."

Jacopo thought for a moment. "'Do not be downcast, O your

soul!'" He raised his face to the sun, reciting a psalm—or what sounded like one.

"Do you mean 'O *my* soul'?"

"My soul is very happy in this moment. I mean *your* soul. Do you know that psalm? 'Why are you cast down, O my soul? Why so disturbed within me?' You are not without hope, Daniel Goodman. This is a good start. You are meant to move people? Be moved!"

"The truth is—" The truth stacked up inside, colliding. I pushed it out. "I can't draw like I once could."

"So?"

The abrupt word rattled through me.

"So . . . I used to be able to create art."

"And are you the same person you used to be?"

"No." *Thanks be to God.*

"Then draw like you can now. Do something new."

The next question hitched in me, plowing recklessly to the surface. "What if I can't?"

And with it, all the other questions: *What if I am the same person I was? What if everything good in me died along with everything bad? What if at that fork in the road long ago, I forfeited this entire life?*

"Then learn a different way!" Jacopo said. "Perhaps what you had was lost. I do not know. Mourn it if it is." Once again, his directness took me off guard. "But allow yourself to think—perhaps there is another way, and perhaps it is a way you would never have discovered! Do you know that the man who drew the plans for the Salute was trying something new? Only twenty-six years old, and he proposed 'a new invention.' That with what 'little talent God had bestowed upon him,' he thought to build the church in the shape of a crown. A round church! It was unheard of back then. Can you think of it? Venice without the Salute? No one would recognize it today! It is how people know they have arrived!" Jacopo paused his impassioned speech and squeezed my shoulder.

"Twenty-six?" If someone my own age could do *that* . . .

"Sì. You can do this, Daniele. A new way? What a thing to discover! . . . And maybe pick a different place than that one." He pointed, and there it was. Ca'Fedele. Just as it had been described in the Book of Waters. My pulse picked up strangely, half-expecting to see young Sebastien standing amid a fall of flower petals, or Mariana, looking over her shoulder as she was ushered inside by her brother.

It wasn't on my list of places to sketch. But it called to me as nothing had in a long time. Jacopo waved grandly as he departed.

I set myself down across the Rialto Bridge, listening to the murmur of pigeons and the steps as people climbed the bridge. The cry of gulls as they took flight somewhere nearby drew my eyes upward to the skyline.

And there was that palazzo. I didn't know what would transpire beneath that roof, in the pages I had not yet translated. But looking across the canal, something in me pulled. And pulled and pulled, summoning with all its might to see what wasn't there.

Mariana. Sebastien. An uncertain future. Hope.

But those hopes, pull as they might, were not strong enough to summon vision within me where there was none.

So, I closed my eyes, forcing myself to meet that darkness head-on. Trying to break through it, but to do as Jacopo suggested. *Try another way.*

I breathed in the city. The smell of coffee, the air tinged with salt, varnish, paint—perhaps from a nearby *squéro*. I thought of the baby in the basket, of the older boy who strived and strived, only to be deemed *not enough*. I thought of the snow that swirled upon mountaintops, of the tide that rushed up beneath Mariana in a storm, of Mariana and Sebastien on the Lido. Of waters from the beginning of time, witness to every moment. Of the chase of the moon—the home they had found in each other.

Their parting.

My pencil hit the paper. Downward strokes that pulled from heights of hope to depths of desolation. I opened my eyes, caught a glimpse of the dock. Drew it plank for plank and remembered the flower petals. Scanned the scene before me and latched upon the sight of small green leaves clinging to an olive tree branch.

Watched a few of them shiver in the breeze, watched one of them twirl to the ground. Captured it, eyes to leaf, pencil to paper. Replicated it, feeling in its spiral the twist of the fates of Massimo and Mariana and Sebastien.

I kept on this way, piecing bits of the scene before me into a patchwork image of the story that would not let me go. It transcribed itself onto the paper in shifting shadows, in crevices and cracks I saw as I waited and watched the building as a living thing, the way it responded to the light in silent conversation as the minutes—or hours?—blurred. The paper became a workshop—a place to try out pieces, move them about, like I once did in my mind. Building upon that scratched-out foundation of feeling that had come from the story.

I lost track of time entirely. Flew, pencil in hand, upon the page until I saw that story. There, from my own hand. My own . . . imagination.

My breath caught.

My hope—*hope? Could it be?*—surged. Disbelief escaped in a laugh.

This was not a grand work of art. This would not be hung on any wall or displayed in any Great Hall at the Venice of America.

But it was a miracle, right there on paper. A thing once lost—found.

Trovato.

As if my hand had a mind of its own, it searched my satchel for another thing long lost. I pulled out the hinged case, creaked it open, and held my old blown-glass dip pen. The one I had not used in so long, for so many reasons.

It was made as art, for art. It was made for ink—and I worked only in pencil, that the lines on page could be blotted up, rubbed out, moved as needed, without my mind as a middleman for envisioning.

But with this house taking shape from this place of story and gut, feeling and study, shifting light and changing shadow . . . it almost felt—*alive* on the page before me. Ready, perhaps, for the permanency and wild, precise scratch of ink.

I studied the house across the canal. There was something strange about it. Something in the details that didn't quite seem right, that made it seem busy somehow, or extraordinarily ornate, though it held no more of the arcades and arches than its counterparts up and down the Grand Canal. I just couldn't put my finger on what it was—

"Daniel Goodman!" I looked up to see Vittoria approaching.

She pulled behind her what appeared to be a wooden child's wagon, filled with aged books with places marked throughout with bright white paper.

"Hello," I said, standing. Pulling myself from the stupor that had overtaken me and clamping the pen case closed, stuffing it back in the satchel. "What is it you've brought with you this time?"

"This time? You ask as if I always have something." Her face was so open and curious, it delighted me that she didn't realize that every time I'd encountered her, she carried adventure with her in some form.

"Books in a crate, coffee in a box on a boat, inventory in a wheelbarrow—you transport universes and deliver hope, Vittoria."

By the way she settled her shoulders back and her smile dimpled deeply, this notion pleased her.

"Says the man who moved an impossibly large bell," she said.

"Just the ringer." It was becoming my trademark, apparently.

"The very heart of it! Venice is alive with talk of you, Daniel." A snippet from the past, a recollection of a city alive with talk of me—and she caught it, not missing a thing. She squeezed my hand. "In a very good way," she said. "The only thing you have stolen here is their hearts."

"Then they haven't met me yet," I said, trying to jest away the strangeness of all of this.

"Just wait until they do" was her only reply. She peered with interest at the sketch in my hand. "This is very good!" Instinctively I closed the book. Heat flushed my face.

"You are disappearing yourself again, Daniel. Come, let me see it."

I did, and something flopped about inside me as I watched her peruse my work.

"You say you cannot create art, Daniel, but this? You have brought it to life!"

"I can't," I said. "Not like I used to."

"Well, perhaps what was needed back then was the way you used to, and perhaps what is needed now is what you did here. Does not God have as much purpose for the Daniel of now as he did for the Daniel of before?"

Her words stacked upon the foundation of Jacopo's earlier.

"I don't know," I said and received the papers back from her, tucking them gladly away.

"At the squéro, the gondola builder uses different tools for different jobs when he creates the gondolas. Perhaps you are becoming a new tool for a new work. God is not bound by the way things used to be, Daniel. There is great hope in that." She squeezed my hand gently. "It is very natural, and even good—honoring, cherishing—to mourn something lost. This dark canvas of your mind? And yet, the creator of waters from nothing, can He not also make a way where we ourselves see no way?" She pointed at my satchel. "What you have there, Daniel . . . it is good."

The thought billowed between us, sail in the wind. And then, flitting with ease between topics of the eternal realm into topics of the day, she remembered her wagon load. "These are from my uncle," she said. "For the printer. Remember his book-restoring station? He sometimes marks pages that need to be reprinted. Smudged ink, torn paper—anything that obscures text. He hunts down what it should say, transcribes it by hand, and sends it on to the printer, who prefers to see the entire book so that he can match paper size. We are going to the printer still today, yes?"

"Yes! What time is it?" I looked around for some clue. I was learning to tell time by the city and to hold it loosely like those who dwelled here. It seemed to me that they all entrusted the blue clock tower in St. Mark's Square, with its golden numerals and stars, with their time. They didn't walk around with their clocks strapped to their wrists or chained to their pockets, and I began to wonder—why was it that we subjected ourselves to chains?

"Are you ready?" Her wide smile lifted.

"Ready."

We took a brisk walk of twenty minutes or so, passing through iron gates, hopping over a puddle, crossing over a small bridge with no railings.

"Where are we?" I asked. It felt strangely familiar, but I hadn't passed that way before.

"Nearly there," she said. "The calli pass more quickly than you think. Long ago when they laid the streets, they made many of them look longer than they are by laying the bricks longways. A trick of the eye, you see! So you fly over them much faster than you think you will."

I knew the tactic well, from use in sketching. "Perspective," I said.

"It is everywhere, here. Even in the windows—large ones on the bottom levels of buildings, smaller ones on top floors, to make it seem as if they are far away, disappearing into the sky when really they are just a stone's toss into the air! Not to mention, more windows means lighter buildings. The more levels there are, the more windows, the better business is on Murano for the glass factories, and the better off our mud-and-stick foundations are underneath. . . ."

"Glass being lighter than stone," I offered.

She nodded. "It is all art and science."

The building before us, however, made liberal use of brick, with white-trimmed windows. Vittoria did not knock or ring a bell but made free to open the door and traverse a corridor that looked very nice, if a little neglected. A few stray leaves twirled in a dance over the black-and-white checked floors. Furniture draped in cloth gave the place an abandoned feel.

"Are you sure we're in the right spot?"

"Oh, nobody lives on this floor. Whoever owns it never seems to visit. We're just going to a room upstairs."

Splitting the load of antique books between the two of us, we climbed a staircase bedecked in scrolling ironwork and stopped at the third door down.

"This is as far as I've ever come," she said. "Usually the books I come for are set outside this door in a crate."

There was no crate in sight, and no person either. Only a small brass sign mounted beside the door. Etched in wood-block style with filigree surrounding the initials *D. C.* No sign of whether this was a printer or not—and perhaps with good reason. If printers had often been the handlers of sensitive pamphlets during times of unrest, it made sense not to make their center of operations conspicuous.

We looked at each other in question, and I knocked.

No answer. I tried the knob. Perhaps the proprietor was in but hadn't heard us. The door creaked open to reveal a room strangely stark and simple in an otherwise ornate building. Plain white walls, floors of Venetian marble in shades of white, too, and in the middle, a wooden printing press.

We both entered tentatively. On the wall to the left stood a large wooden chest with drawers of varying sizes. On the wall to the right was a small bookcase, containing bolts of fabric in bright colors, jars of paint, gilding tools, thread, needles, and two rows of the *Piccole Storie* looking ready for adventure.

Smells of fresh paper and rich ink filled the place, mellowed with the tinge of old wood.

But no person.

"Should we come back?" I asked.

Vittoria hesitated. I saw the way she looked at the drawers. I knew that look well—not on her, but on myself. It was that of a mind scheming, planning a riffle through a place it did not have admission to go.

"Let's come back," I said.

"I'll just leave a note," she replied. "And then we'll go. It seems the right thing to do."

I tensed. I'd stayed as far as I could, for so long, from anything remotely resembling a break-in. We hadn't broken in, necessarily— only entered an unlocked place of business, but still . . . I was eager to leave.

"All right," I said and crossed to the window opposite the door while she searched for a pen. A shelf held several wood-block carvings, all cleaned but bearing marks of ink from past usage. It was a curious style—with clean and angular lines as with most wood-block prints—but the backgrounds of these were sanded down slightly, so that when inked, they would give the impression of an image blurred. Bringing the primary subject into sharp relief. Like the chiaroscuro style I had seen in paintings. Curious, for it to be applied in this manner.

Down in the campo below, an orange cat lounged. A girl dashed by, clattering a stick against the cracks in the stucco on the building. And a woman wheeled a wooden cart past, spilling with green plants.

I blinked. Had I leapt back in time? It was the same woman who had sold me a pot of ivy only days before while I awaited my chance to speak to the man in the flat.

I rotated, trying to orient myself, and peered down and to the right. If I was where I thought I was . . .

Yes. There, I could see the top of a lion's head protruding from the wall and knew that it housed the would-be doorbell. Which meant . . .

"Vittoria," I whispered.

"Hmmm?" She tapped a golden pen against her dark curls as if searching for just the right turn of phrase.

"I know this place!" We must have entered from the reverse side of the building this time—and in doing so, afforded ourselves a glimpse of a house that had once been much grander.

But there was something not fitting, something more I couldn't put my finger on. It wasn't just the man or the lady with the plant cart.

The feeling trailed me all the way back down the stairs and into the wide corridor. The cat had found its way inside, and it let out a mew that echoed amid the reaching columns of the old place. Sounding almost like a baby, in its small noise.

Baby. A distinct twist of knowing deep inside. Standing on the landing, I peered down as if I could see it unfolding before me: the wide-shouldered form of Giuseppe, carrying a basket down an old corridor with draped furniture, until he entered a—

I let my footsteps turn in that direction, let them follow this ghost from the story and enter the door where there was—yes!—a kitchen.

I couldn't be certain. Surely there were many houses in Venice that might fit the description, but I couldn't evade the conviction that I was standing in the very place where this story began. The very place where, once upon a time, a guild had gathered around a sleeping babe and changed forever the course of his life.

THE BOOK OF WATERS

The Man Who Returned

It came to pass that a certain tradesman delivered the daughter of a certain patrician family to her palazzo, following her fated disappearance into a tempest.

Upon her return, when she had been presumed lost forever, the woman's elder brother, Massimo Fedele, was overcome with gratitude and lavished his thanks upon the unsuspecting boatman. Ordered that a bag of lira be given to the boatman, that he dine in their kitchens, that he warm himself by their fire before venturing back out into the night.

To his credit or to his shame, only a fleeting cringe beset Massimo Fedele's jaw when his sister suggested that in addition to lira, polenta, and a stint beside the fire, the boatman be given a room to stay until morning. They had plenty of empty rooms, she reasoned, and further flattered the brother that she knew he would never send the man who had saved her life out into the cold, so late in the night.

He acquiesced, showing the boatman to a room in the attic and arriving again at that door before the sun was up to escort the boatman out and on his way. Never imagining that this was not the first time he had seen this particular man out onto the waters . . . though the first time had been by basket, and the time after that beneath the shower of flower petals.

Never imagining that the boatman never slept a wink but had lain awake, going rounds with a fact he could not accept: Somewhere, beneath this roof, Mariana dwelled. The closest he would ever be to her, again, in this life. That each moment henceforth would take him farther from her, and farther, until he broke. Until she was swallowed up by the eroding he had seen begin in her the moment she crossed the threshold of this home.

And he was to leave her here?

He could no more do that than breathe underwater.

And so, in the dead of night while the House of the Faithful slumbered, Sebastien Trovato traversed halls until he found the kitchen, until he found a certain chipped cup that was wrapped in the age-old scene of a ship upon the sea and tucked a slip of paper into it. He placed it upon a tray that was readied for service in the morning and prayed it would stay there . . . and be found.

"In the dark, look to the lost island." The simplest phrase.

That day, Mariana was swept into a swirl of fussing and fiasco: a visit from the doctor to ensure she was well after "all she had endured." A visit from the tailor, the cobbler, the family lawyer. All the people she had left behind and forgotten about, for a sweet and perfect moment in time. And through this new tempest, she carried treasure: a scrap of paper, found in a chipped teacup.

And she carried it with her that night to the rooftop. Looked to the lost island of the north . . . and saw there the smallest glow.

Murano fires burning for her, in a lantern in a tilting house upon a pole. Sebastien.

Here, she brought her bundle of candles. Lit them all, placed a mirror behind, and hoped they glowed bright enough for him to see too.

And she knew. Though they had parted . . . they would never part. Not truly.

In the meantime, Sebastien did more than set a lantern to glowing each night. He delivered goods more often to the city, listened more intently, learning, and planning.

What did he learn? Massimo Fedele, larger than life, was a grand actor upon the grand stage of his city. He held the pearl of the Adriatic in the palm of his hand, befriending Venetian, Austrian, Frenchman, and Italian alike.

And yet, for all his affable ways, he was in a predicament. Massimo Fedele was a man about town without a way around town. He had lost another boatman, as was his way. For all his garrulity and amicability with the Austrians and French and Venetians and Italians, he did not extend that generosity of character to those of the serving class.

In point of fact, he had angered a great many boatmen until it had become almost a hobby of his, and a matter subject to wagers by his friends—How long will the man Lazarro last as boatman? How long, Ludovico? Or this newest one, Beppe?

Three months, two months, one week, respectively.

Making the way for the nameless boatman who had delivered his sister safely home to approach the doors—the water entrance, and not the grand entrance, he knew very well—to offer his own services.

And now the upper rooms, those servants' quarters of Ca'Fedele, jingled in new wagers. How long would the swamp rat of a man, who arrived not even in a proper gondola, last as the boatman for the Greatest Faithful?

One week, two months, three months . . . And still, Sebastien remained.

Sebastien stared at the ceiling, watching for the first sign of light. He had learned it well, the way the cracks traversing the embossed ceiling's lines appeared as night began to fade. The lines summoned him to rise, to prepare the master's boat. The cracks of the house were many, plaster chipping, paint flaking, in all places but the rooms where Massimo entertained. In these, all was shine and impressive restoration. Sebastien had become accustomed, as much as a man could, to Massimo Fedele's whims. The man sometimes slept until noon, sometimes arose before the sun. Sometimes attended a *conversazioni* at Palazzo Albrizzi, where the resident *contessa* played hostess to lively conversation among artists and writers. And sometimes he attended pursuits of a less intellectual sort inside the casino. Sometimes hosted dinners himself, sometimes retiring early, beneath some cloud that regularly overtook his countenance.

Massimo was mercurial—one moment fire and the next one ice. Sebastien was learning to watch the tap of the man's finger upon his knee as he sat in the gondola's seat. If it beat fast, like the skittering of a crab over the embankment, he was firing away at some scheme, his mind churning, turning, planning. The energy of the whole city seeming to run through his veins. But when it slowed, it was not to the pace of a man at rest. It was to the steady pace of torment, an eerie darkness cloaking him in a way that sent a prickling up Sebastien's spine.

Such was life as the boatman for one of the few remaining grand families of Venice. Sebastien watched, always, for a glimpse of Mariana and grew to understand that she did not venture out into the city. Venice was brought to her—or rather, anything she needed from Venice. He understood, now, the wide-eyed wonder she displayed when he had taken her through the canals and calli. She was a foreigner in her own birthplace.

He learned which rooms were hers and slipped letters underneath her door at night. And he learned to love the sound of paper sliding over the aged, rough wood of his own attic floor when she was able to write to him too.

When he had not seen her face to face, not after three weeks, he began instead to discern in a different way. The sounds of this palazzo told stories.

Every Monday, the fishmonger would come—to the kitchens, of course, not repeating the same entry mistake of the foolhardy boy of yesteryear. A barrister came bearing a serious face and even more serious attaché stuffed with ledgers and files, and he met with Massimo for hours, ensconced inside the map room. It was a curiosity, the room in its circular form, bedecked with maps of Venice and the lagoon and Adriatic, in its many antiquities. Massimo dwelled there often, whether alone or with the barrister. One got the feeling he was consulting with the maps as with a council, deliberating plans and decisions, spooling the future of the lagoon into a coil deep inside himself.

Every Wednesday, a gentleman was escorted to the floor where Mariana's apartments were kept, to a sitting room. If the balcony doors stood ajar, Sebastien could sometimes make out the sounds from within, if he moved out of the boathouse and moored the gondola to a pole. There, he would shine the brass boat fastenings and polish the gondola's wood and listen to a great absence of conversation, pages turning, or the accidental clink of tea ware. And once, the slow notes of a pianoforte, weaving a song of somber beauty. When that gentleman left, another gentleman was brought up, and Sebastien began to wonder if suitors were being paraded before her, perhaps to give her some choice in her matrimonial future.

Every Tuesday and Thursday, Massimo attended the salons of art and culture that sprang up in drawing rooms of some of the other grand palazzos. Or he gathered with other sons of the Old Venice at a private room at the casino, where they entered with grave faces, spent hours solving the problems of the world, and emerged into the nearing dawn with faces either graver still or decidedly buoyant—and in varying states of intoxication.

Sebastien had learned well the scale of Massimo's sobriety. Like the ancient three Greek Fates he had learned of in the books of myths, Massimo took on facets of past, present, or future, depending on how often amber fluids had refilled his goblet that night.

There were nights he abstained, maintaining an upper hand over his connections, fully utilizing his polish, flattery, and cunning to achieve his own ends. These times, he held tight the future, and one could almost hear the precision of his mind's turns and clicks, shifting pieces into place in the game of strategy he was always about. Like Lachesis, the first of the Greek Fates—always measuring, always with an eye toward the future. Only his measurements, when he spoke of signatures needed on a petition, of seats filled in an auditorium, of magazines needing to be filled, became more like counting. As weeks wore on, the counting became calculating—with an urgency of one nearing the end of an equation and the scales still being too far unbalanced.

There were nights when he imbibed enough to lay that trifecta of persuasive powers—polish, flattery, cunning—to rest and make of himself a straight talker. These nights, a ruthless side of him emerged. He seemed to bear blades on his very being, and like Atropos, the second of the Fates, his role was to cut. Atropos cut the threads, and Massimo—well, Sebastien would not wish to be present to find out how far or who the man would cut, when challenged in such a state. He seemed a man haunted. Anchored in the past.

"Tell me the name of the Doge of 1648," Massimo demanded of Sebastien.

Sebastien drew his oar and drew his brows down, shaking his head.

"You see? A man may strive and achieve, and still he is forgotten."

"You . . . wish to be remembered?" Sebastien ventured. "It is a very natural desire, I think."

The man was silent.

"You wish to make a place for your name." Sebastien tried again to engage the man.

"Place . . . name . . . Only one of those two things matters." He swigged something. "And despite what you imagine yourself to know, I have very little regard for my name." Massimo spat over the edge of the gondola. "I care nothing for being remembered."

They passed a statue of Saint Theodore, the martyr.

"Now there is a man who knew the value of a life," Massimo said. "A life is meant to be given, is it not?"

"A life may be given in many ways, Signore. Perhaps most of all, by living."

This, he did not respond to.

And then there were nights when he tipped the scales and joined the ranks of the intoxicated, waxing eloquent about his one love, the lady Venezia. Sadly, these were the only nights Sebastien caught a glimpse of what he had come to call Genuine Massimo. The core of the very man. Like the last of the Fates—Clotho, the present, whose job was to spin the threads of life.

It was sad, Sebastien thought, that this side of Massimo only emerged under such influence. It seemed the truest part. The meeting of past and future, right there in the present. Where the agenda-laced words were set aside, and he spoke man to man. Almost as if Sebastien were . . . a friend.

On rare occasion, this spinner of life-threads became so real that the three Fates split away to reveal something deeper, something that chilled Sebastien to the bone: a man held captive by his own ceaseless striving. Less like the Fates and more like Arachne, transformed into a spider. Massimo, the prisoner, in these rarest moments, proved himself prisoner to his own schemes.

The man was brilliant, tipping the scales into the land of genius. The sort of genius who succumbed, in those aged myths, to madness or ruin—but never before also causing the madness or ruin of others.

But whatever he had become on these nights—Lachesis, Atropos, Clotho, or Arachne—every Friday, Massimo sprang to life early, a new man, and took himself away to Terra Firma to oversee the family's country estate, where they grew their vegetables and farmed their animals. Many of the noble families kept country estates on the mainland. Most of them customarily retired to them for various extended holidays from the city—and that was where Massimo Fedele differed. He never felt the need to retire away from Venice. *"It is in my blood,"* he often said. *"Venice . . . is La Famiglia Fedele. La Famiglia Fedele . . . is Venice. You cannot extract one from the other."*

The man ate, drank, and lived for the place with a fervor that was either inspiring or troubling. Sebastien could not decide which. In any case, Massimo insisted upon these country days that Sebastien "grant himself a holiday" and do as he wished. These were the lagoon days, the suppers back at Elena's table or Valentina's hearth, at Dante's printing press or turning the glass for Pietro. This being shrimp season, he would often end the evening patrolling the waters with Giuseppe.

After these expeditions, Sebastien returned to the palazzo bolstered of soul and full of heart—and sorely wishing he could find a way to bring Mariana. Everything felt incomplete without her. But he filled his letters with news of the lagoon and messages from the guild, who loved her dearly. He purposed to give her that life, on paper, for as long as he could. Her letters in return always took on a distinctly hope-filled tone, and she filled them with lists of things to ask: *How is Valentina's Miracle Keeper lace coming? Will you take this biscuit to Pietro's dog, and these candies to his grandchildren? Tell Giuseppe his shrimp tastes of freedom. Will you give this to Elena, with all of my love?* This, in reference to a painted vignette of the farm cottage, with Tuona pecking in the farmyard. She had captured every bit of the warmth of that place with her paintbrush.

And so, Sebastien's weekly trips to the isles fueled them both with life, while Massimo's weekly trips to Terra Firma saw him return in an increasingly agitated state.

There was little chance for Sebastien to be in the palazzo unless to snatch stolen windows of sleep at the whim of Massimo's maneuverings. And there was no call whatsoever, it seemed, for Mariana to leave the confines of the palazzo. With this realization came a growing grief—for the loss of seeing her, surely, but also for something more: the vanishing of the woman who had been so free, so alive, so curious and full of wonder during her short time in the lagoon. Feet unshod and hair flying free behind her, she had been like a water sprite, swift and alive.

In this frame of her world, he began to understand that her expedition in the tempest had not been a fanciful whim of an impulsive girl. It had been, perhaps, the only window into a full life that she would ever have. A moment where she could taste and see and feel and *live* her world entirely.

Sadness began to grow in Sebastien, at this realization. It grew form, and the form grew structure, and the structure grew muscle and mind until it was Anger, with a will of its own.

At who? At Massimo? At the world, society, the life she had been born into? At the life *he* had been born into, that he could not save her from it? Who had done this to her?

Was it God himself?

He did not like to let Anger venture to that question. He tried to restrain it, lash it to the realm of impossibility—but there it beat still, subterranean, unspoken. Sending ripples up through the very foundations of this world.

Until one night, at last, he saw her.

Massimo had left a meeting of the minds in the company of a poet and a playwright, two men bent on showing him something at the Accademia. Without need of his own boat, he bade Sebastien retire to Ca'Fedele.

When Sebastien approached, there was the house, its yellow façade mellow in moonlight and lights glowing bright from within. All as usual. But then—a movement, on the far side of the palazzo upon its roof. Just a wisp of white fabric. It was all he could make out, but it was enough.

He secured the boat with careful speed and silence around this moment's fragility. A feeling that if he treaded too recklessly, too fast, too loud, the figure on the rooftop would vanish.

He climbed the stairs to the attic and beyond, finding a narrow door he had not seen before. It was open. He passed through, feeling winter's approach on the breeze as his eyes adjusted to the darkness and he took in his surroundings—two lemon trees, potted and spry, flanking a row of chairs overturned to protect them from wind and wear in their disuse. And beyond, in the shadows, she stood. Flaxen hair in ripples down her back, the wind lifting its ends as she looked out over a rooftop sea.

"Mariana?" Sebastien offered her name as one might knock upon a door, wishing to know if their presence was welcome.

She turned, and the look upon her face undid him. She wasn't startled. She wasn't scared. She was in a state of longing. Eyes wide, shoulders rising and falling slightly but quickly, as if she dared not believe his presence beside her.

"I—" She swallowed, stretching to see around him. He turned, ensuring nobody was there. He wished to close the door, if that was her concern, but knew it would do her a disservice, if he were to be found here alone with her in a setting that locked others away.

He left it open, instead moving himself closer to her, but angled so that she had a clear view to the door.

"I hoped you'd come," she said, her posture beginning to ease a little.

"Are you all right?" He moved closer, and she inched back. He froze, anchoring himself, not wishing to be the cause of any discomfort for her.

Her eyes shifted to one side, then another, mouth pursed.

Who was this?

She seemed unable to answer that question, and turned, gripping the railing and looking out over the canal. "It's falling, you know," she said, voice somber.

He drew up next to her, his arm brushing hers. At this, her shoulders eased a little.

"Our home." She anticipated this question. "Bits of it crumble away and fall. Angelo has been using them to shore up the end of the dock." She named the manservant who seemed always the one people turned to in this place, but whom Sebastien had yet to meet. "He's doing it now," Mariana said. "See?"

He followed her gaze and, for the first time, saw the oft-mentioned Angelo. For a man who seemed legendary in the house, he appeared entirely ordinary. Perhaps a bit taller than the average man, and his features were obscured by the shadow cast over his face by his hat. He knelt, placing oddly angled bits of brick just so, strengthening the dock.

She turned her focus to Sebastien. "Are—are you well?" she asked, still not letting her eyes meet his entirely.

"Am I well?" he repeated, shaking his head. "Mariana, it's you I'm concerned for."

A small sniff, and she grew rigid. Like the Mariana freshly awakened after the tempest, refusing to give answer as he held out the shards of her boat in question.

"Please," Sebastien said, almost in a whisper. "Tell me. Whatever it is, you shouldn't have to carry it alone."

A long pause. She gripped the white railing tighter and shivered, though the sharp wind had settled down. He removed his jacket and placed it on her shoulders. She closed her eyes, settling into it like an embrace before looking his way furtively.

"Have you been to a masquerade, Sebastien?"

It was an odd question. Asked in an odd way, with thin cheeriness. He weighed his one-word answer to see if it could stretch into anything that might help thaw the ice gripping her. "Masquerade . . ." He feigned befuddlement. "A gathering in which lively characters collectively celebrate?"

He waited, his silence inviting. She turned, finally beholding him, a flicker of a smile betraying that she was fully aware he was up to something.

"Yes, that is correct," she said.

"I've been at such a gathering."

Now, he had her full attention. She tipped her head in question.

"Giuseppe, Pietro, Dante, Elena, Valentina . . . Gatherings don't get much livelier than that," he said. "But no masks."

And then, a miracle: She laughed. Silvery like the moonlight, cheeks dimpling. "This is true," she said. "Never have I encountered a livelier crew." She grew quiet again, contemplative. "I miss them."

He took a slow breath in and gripped the railing next to her, glad for this glimpse of her heart shining through. She was still there, the Mariana he knew.

"Yes," he said. "I do too."

"You can go to them." Her eyes glassy, she pasted on a smile for his benefit. "I am so grateful you've been here, Sebastien. You can never know how—" She halted. "It has meant the world. More than the world. That you have been near, that you have—" Her voice wavered, and she stopped. "But it would be selfish of me to keep you here, away from them." Her brows pinched together. "Massimo, he could have had a hundred other boatmen. But . . . your guild?" She shook her head. "There is only one Sebastien."

He didn't know what to say. He loved her for the way she thought of them—but couldn't imagine tearing himself away, leaving her like this. Where she was the island.

She tried to cheer the silence. "I know we haven't seen each other very often . . ."

A noise escaped him, something between a scoff and a laugh. He gave her an amused look. "'Very often'?"

To which she laughed again, becoming more and more her old self. "Well, I have seen you, Sebastien, even if you haven't seen me."

"You have?"

"I see the way you ready the boat each morning, in case my

brother has one of his early days. I see the way you pass the time when he does not, by reading."

Now he grew warm, knowing he shouldn't have taken the book without permission. "I just—I found the book in the drawer in my bedstand and thought it wouldn't be missed, and—"

"You and your apologies, Sebastien." She shook her head. "Who do you think put it there?"

He hadn't thought anyone had. It looked like it had been forgotten there long ago, but . . . How like her, to be thinking of him. To see him in his idle hours, to know how idleness brought him only madness. And to tuck something into his world to help him, even if he never knew it was her.

He pictured her there, standing in her glistening gown in the stark simplicity of his room. Taking in his startling lack of possessions, not even a book to keep him company. Seeing only the bed, the chair, the—

Oh.

There was the carving.

There, upon the chair, was his block of wood. Always awaiting him when he searched for something to set his hand and heart to. Kept from the wreckage of her boat, carved with their moments. Had she seen it? When whispers of his island home visited him with longing at night, he took to carving, setting the seven seats into wood. She, seated in one, he in another. Setting his soul at ease that somewhere across the lagoon, the stone table waited, and La Marangona tumbled over waters, and all was well.

He had never imagined anyone else might see the carving.

He could picture Mariana, slipping the book into his drawer, noticing—as was her way—the block. Refraining from picking it up, as was also her way. So perhaps she had not seen his bumbling attempt at depicting the moments they had shared, the moments he had seen her become a person so alive, so different from the way she lived here.

"Why did you come here, Sebastien?" she asked. "The basket that carried you in these canals—it delivered you to such a good life."

A sound from within arrested their movements, both of them looking to the door. But nobody appeared, and upon Sebastien's investigation, only a curtain inside swayed in the night breeze. As if Mariana's question had taken on life, stepped out upon the roof with them.

He returned to her and to her question. *Why did you come here?* Her eyes pleaded, as if the fate of the world teetered upon his coming words.

You, he wanted to say.

But would it be too much?

So, he lifted his hand instead. Suspended it in the space between them for a fragment of time, feeling her warmth radiating. And then, when she did not pull away, when her eyes only grew rounder, a swallow traversing her throat—he gentled it upon her cheek. Cupping her jaw. Feeling his chest surge as she leaned, ever-so-slightly, into his hand, closed long lashes over a coming tear, and reached up to place her hand upon his.

She had her answer.

How long they stood this way, Sebastien did not know. But when she lifted her cheek and looked at him, she kept his hand grasped in hers and laced their fingers to weave them together. Raised them tentatively to the press of her lips, the thrumming in his chest louder, and louder.

In this land of tapestries and ropes and lace, there were no threads more intricately twined than their hearts. As if for all of time, they had been stitching and weaving toward each other until here—now—they met. Joined. Chosen, in an eternal breath, this tender stronghold, a knot pulled fast, to last forever.

His other hand lifted, catching a strand of her hair as the wind tousled it. Her shoulders rose and fell; she looked upon him with all the light of all those stars they had watched—bundled up, cinched tight, and resting on *him.* Mirroring his own longing until he raked his fingers gently up into her hair. Pulled in by her, right along with that starlight—and met her lips. Slow, and strong. His breath hitched as she leaned in, sank deep into this place of belonging, peace, longing.

It was a depth he had never known. Her warmth, this fitting together, this place of no questions, no masks, nothing but home-coming and heart. Arms encircling her, he savored the feel of her—*her*—in his embrace. Mariana, who marked life with color and joy spinning from her very being, leaving every place she touched with hope.

And in this moment, she, this bringer of beauty and light who could have chosen anyone, anywhere—had chosen him. And in this moment, too . . . she was safe. If this thing that they shared did anything, he hoped it was to ensure that she knew, beyond even a shadow of a doubt, that he belonged, irrevocably, to her.

Pulling away slowly, she shivered—a different sort of shiver, this time. Peering up at him with a smile both timid and entirely at ease.

He drank in the sight of her. The presence of her. Reaching for words and finding none that would do justice to this pounding from the chambers of his bones, the fullness of his lungs, his heart.

A flicker of a smile, and then she spoke. "So," she said. The smallest of words. She pulled in a breath. "You've never attended a true masquerade," she said, bringing him back to the moment.

"No," he said, laughing low. Running his thumb over the back of her hand. "Not I."

"No," she echoed. "It wouldn't be like you to don a mask. You hide nothing."

She grew serious again. A flicker of sorrow over her brow. "There will be a masquerade," she said.

Sebastien nodded. This, he knew well. He had been tasked with delivering many requests, obtaining many materials, all in crates and scrolls, for the event seven nights hence. Artisans had been brought in to restore faded paintings, chipped walls, crooked bal-ustrades, sparing no expense to make the piano nobile stun and entrance, as in the days of old. All while the obscure corners of the house were forgotten, left to continue in their state of graceful, long-stretching decay.

"The people will be . . . masked," she said cautiously.

"At a masquerade?" he said, half-hoping but little expecting for her to jab him with her elbow as she had at his sarcastic comments

272

among the isles. He raised his eyebrows to ensure she knew he jested. She offered a smile, but no easy retaliation.

"What I mean is . . . That is to say . . ." She seemed tongue-tied suddenly. "Many will come," she said at last. "And if a loyal member of this household—if a book-loving boatman, for example—wished to don a mask, there would be none who would stop him."

As her meaning sank in, shock surely registered upon his countenance. Shock, and even more—hope. Not for a ball, not for a costume—these, he could well do without. But for the chance to be at Mariana's side once more, even if only for a moment, without the need for shadows and rooftops.

Her own face mirrored his joy but quickly flickered into something else. "Sebastien, you should know . . . It will be a very difficult night, in some ways." She seemed to wrestle with what to say, choosing finally to leave it at that. "I should never have—" she pulled her hand from his and he caught it, grateful when her grip eased again.

A difficult night. All the more reason to come. Whatever it was that Mariana was facing, he would give anything, do anything, to be there with her. Beside her. To help her, however he might.

"I'll be there," he said.

An answer that both pleased her and tormented her, by the look upon her face. What afflicted her? She was so conflicted.

"Mariana—" he began.

"Mariana?" This, at the same time he spoke, came from somewhere within the palazzo, in the sing-song voice of her companion, Francesca.

"I must go," she said, the blush fading from her cheeks. She opened her mouth to say more, and Francesca called again.

Before he could answer, before he could assure her that he would be there—at a masquerade, or anywhere else she ever had need of him—she was gone.

The masquerade was soon in the air like the very mist over the canals. The Night of the Seasons, it was to be called, and the magic of it cut through the coming chill of winter and through the pallor brought by the growing number of Austrian soldiers occupying the city. Sebastien overheard it at the fish market—two mongers bickering over who would provide the most sardines for the event. A ring of women laundering clothing in a campo, one of them proclaiming it to the heights as "an event to rival the old days of carnivale! My sister cooks in the kitchen at Ca'Fedele and tells me they have foods for each of the four seasons. . . ."

And Pietro had been commissioned, at Mariana's recommendation, to craft a chandelier portraying a tree in glass with four branches: one in the full leaf of summer, one in spring blossom, one in barren winter, and one in golden-hued fall.

Other conversations were overheard too. Men, in heated conversations as to the future of their city. "We must tie ourselves to the Austrians. The only hope for power is with them," some said. "Never!" others replied. "Venice as we once knew her will return—and stronger." This, always attached somehow to the name of Massimo Fedele. And murmurs of another rebel by the name of Daniel Manin, who had plans for the arsenals. Long plans, plans that had the power to stay and to grow.

These were the conversations that Massimo listened to intently. "We will show them, Sebastien," Massimo had confided in him in the gondola. "Austria . . . They may send their soldiers. But they will not stop us from living. *That* is what this masquerade is."

"A . . . rebellion?"

"Yes. A civilized rebellion. No, more than that—a declaration!"

Sebastien admired the man's undaunted tenacity but couldn't help noticing the dark shadows beneath the man's eyes. They grew deeper, darker by the day.

"If I may, my lord," Sebastien began, using the customary address.

"Of course, of course, anything, my friend."

It was a strange and overly familiar response, but it landed as the bridge Sebastien needed. "Thank you," he began. "It's only—is there nothing I can do on your behalf? Something that might allow you more respite?" *More respite* should more aptly have been called *less madness*.

"You come from the outer isles?" Massimo asked with the air of one who already knew.

Sebastien nodded, wary.

"Born and raised there, yes?"

Sebastien held his silence, uneasy at the darkness lingering over the man's words. "It was a good place to grow up," he said simply.

"And you came to work in the House of Fedele because . . ." Something dark slithered in his tone.

I am devoted to your sister. I love her. I do not like the way she is caged here. The truth pounded and came out in measured words. "It is where I am meant to be."

Massimo stared hard.

"Take care," he said, his tone smoldering. "'Meant to be' . . . Those are the sort of words that have seen men labeled usurper. Traitor. Pretender to the throne. And worse."

These were the mutterings of someone shadowed by paranoia, whether with good reason or not.

"I only mean to do good," Sebastien said, dipping his oar and pulling it, gulls crying above as if to affirm this statement.

The dark countenance shifted lightning fast to a friendly tone as he leaned forward in his seat. "You hail from the isles. Do you know the man Pietro?"

"Yes," Sebastien said.

"The glassblower, I mean to say."

"Yes," he said again. He declined to say how well he knew him. Why, he could not say, except that a sense of distinct protection arose in him, telling him to stand between Massimo and Pietro.

"And you will be going to the isles today, no? This being Friday."

At his affirmation, Massimo instructed him to visit the glassblower, to pay him well—at which he equipped Sebastien with lira aplenty—and to ferry the commissioned chandelier back to the palazzo with great expediency and care.

Sebastien knew Massimo made it a point to know everything about everyone but felt not a little unnerved at his awareness of Sebastien's connection to Pietro. Who else, among his family, had the man been gathering information about—and to what purposes?

275

It was a strange sensation, rowing across the turquoise expanse with a pocket full of money, rather than rowing across the turquoise expanse in order to earn enough coin to stay alive another day. What would it be like, Sebastien wondered, to live always in such a way? Being a giver of coin?

He did not like to entertain the notion too much. There was little good that could come of it. So, he took himself to Murano, just as Massimo had said. Procured the chandelier, helped Pietro package it, wrapping each branch and leaf of the piece in muslin, then cushioning it inside its crate with dried moss.

"Watertight." Pietro patted the metal box with pride and detailed how his sons had been the ones to invent a rubber-lined metal vessel for the keeping of their glasswares in transit to their many waterborne destinations.

Sebastien gave due marvel to the innovation, ensuring he had sealed it correctly. But when he turned to go, a silhouetted line of figures stood at the door of the storehouse. There was no question of who they were. If their distinct figures had not given it away— from Giuseppe's jovial portly form to Valentina's wiry strength— their chattering removed all doubt.

"What is this?" Sebastien asked, stomach flopping like a fish. Not wishing the question to sound off-putting, he rephrased it. "*Qual buon vento ti porta?*" Better to inquire what good fortune had summoned them.

"We are here to help" came Elena's voice as she stepped forward, her elegant silhouette becoming full human form as light spilled upon her. There was a secret delight on her expression. His stomach fish-flopped again. All of them, together? In life, he encountered this group in many different combinations: various pairs of them here, and on the rare occasion, three of them all in the same place at once. But never—but for their monthly meetings in the city, which they assured him he need not attend—never all of them, together.

"Help with . . . the crate? I don't wish to trouble anyone," he said.

Elena laid a hand on his arm, her touch soft and kind. "We are here to help *you*, *caro*."

"It's very kind of you," he said, confusion burrowing outward and chiseling his brows downward. "But as I said . . ." He lifted the box, keenly aware of the fragility within.

Elena smiled. "How I adore you, Sebastien. A genius about so many things, and about others . . ." She shrugged, indicating he was something of a lost cause.

He set the crate down. Clearly he wouldn't be permitted to leave until they'd accomplished their end.

"Giuseppe says you're going to a masquerade." Elena stepped back, folding her arms in front of her and looking him over like one of her garden vegetables when discerning its level of ripeness.

"Well . . . I . . . ." Burning. Sebastien's face was hotter than Pietro's fires.

"And what will you wear?"

"I thought—that is—well, I only have my normal clothes, besides the boatman's uniform. So, I thought to go in them, with a simple mask."

"The *bauta*. Yes, very good. But as for your everyday clothes . . ." Elena tsked, shaking her head.

Valentina rushed forward, her spry form springing into action like a tiny whirlwind. "It will never do, *Sebastiano*, never do." She picked up one of his arms and began to measure it.

"But I shouldn't stand out," he said. "If I wear working clothes, I won't draw attention, and it would be so much better—"

"Sebastien, my darling." Elena lifted the lid of a box he hadn't noticed before, revealing the form of a bauta, black and simple, enough to just cover his face. Pietro, Dante, and Giuseppe seemed to have accomplished a most convenient disappearance and not bothered to take Sebastien with them to whatever safety they had found. Traitors.

Elena continued, "You are looking at it backward. You wish to blend in, so you don the clothing of a . . . a sea urchin! A rock!" She picked up his sleeve with two fingers, as if it were indeed a foul thing of the depths and dropped it. "This is what you would wear to blend in to *your* world. Our world. It isn't your fault, of course. You've never known the essence of carnivale. How to explain to one who has never seen?"

A shuffling at the window sounded. It was Dante shuffling back inside, hands in his trouser pockets, like one refusing to be complicit in a crime. He heaved a deep breath. "Simple," he said. "First, envision every adult, with all the concern for right-doing that an infant would have. Then, give them a mask, so that any shred of remaining decency attached to an ancestral sense of propriety is now entirely vanished. And finally, douse the city in temptation, revelry, and a swath of spies intent on reporting misdeeds, even if the doers of those deeds are masked."

Sebastien gulped, looking at the mask in his hand warily.

"Dante!" Elena scolded. She pointed at the chair, indicating it might behoove the man to allow the chair to bear his fiery wrath a while. With a spark in his eye directed at Elena, he strode to the window, hooking the chair aside with his foot and standing to face the canal outside.

"Such a cynic. Pay him no mind," Elena said, though fondness warmed her words. She squared Sebastien's shoulders and gave them a gentle squeeze as she assessed his ensemble with the eye of an artist. "Even Dante knows there is enchantment afoot at carnivale." She winked at the statuesque man, and the gesture seemed to melt away some of the marble from his façade as he shrugged one shoulder in reluctant agreement.

"Carnivale is . . . well, yes, it had come to be many of the things Dante said. But!" She strode across the room to Dante's window and stood beside him with a hand upon the heavy red curtain. "It is also"—she gave a mighty tug, bringing the curtain clattering from its rod, and holding it up victoriously as dust mites spun in a twist of golden light—"*magic*. Isn't that so, Dante?"

He studied her, and the faintest flicker of a smile pulled at one corner of his mouth—the closest she would get to a resounding yes from the stoic Dante Cavallini. She squeezed the man's shoulder much in the same manner she had Sebastien's, and this time, he did smile—fleetingly. Then he seemed to recall there were others in the room, cleared his throat, and returned his gaze to the age-clouding glass.

There was indeed magic at work in this room, Sebastien thought. But her name was not carnivale. It was Elena.

And now the magic was near swirling from her as she summoned the others back inside, whispering something to Giuseppe, then Pietro, neither of whom spoke, but both of whom left the room again at a clipping pace. Pietro with his dog trailing behind with a happy-wagging thump against every possible surface, and Giuseppe with much more spring in his step than he ever displayed when "on his land legs," as he liked to say.

"Where are they . . . ?" Sebastien said in foreboding curiosity.

"They will return before the masquerade," Elena said. "For now? Follow me." She pulled her worn measuring tape from her apron pocket. "We have work to do."

"Work to do," as it turned out, included Elena taking measurements, shaking her head, and muttering wonderings about when in the world her boy turned into a man—to which Sebastien only laughed. Then, she shooed him out the door, off to do a chore.

Acquiescing, he pulled logs from the barge and took ax to them with far more vengeance than was needed, hoping the pounding inside his chest might leave some of itself behind in the act. He had thought he was coming here to procure a chandelier, deliver greetings, and leave.

The energy buzzing about Elena, and the mysterious disappearance of Giusseppe and Pietro, bespoke a different tale. A tale that waited, in the form of those very faces, when he returned with an armload of wood.

"Silence!" Giuseppe proclaimed in his booming voice, and a chipped plate rattled from its place upon the wall. His voice would have been formidable, absent of the warmth he exuded, gentle giant that he was. "The *Serenissimo Principe* has entered these walls."

Sebastien began stacking the wood, eyeing the gathering with narrowed gaze. "I know nothing of entering walls. And am decidedly not a 'most serene prince.'"

"Ah!" Giuseppe waved away his literal qualms. "You know what I mean, *Sua Serenita*."

His Serenity? "What are you about? Am I to dress as a slumbering man? The American Rip Van Winkle, perhaps?"

"He doesn't know the Doge's names," Pietro muttered out the side of his mouth.

"And why should he?" Elena asked, infusing warmth into her voice. "There are as many titles as there were doges! But if we must pick one, I would call him—*Protosebastos*. Like the ancient doges. It nearly has his name in it!"

"What does all of this mean?" Sebastien laughed as he placed the last piece of wood beside the fire, clasped his hands in front of him, and faced the gathering.

"Show him, Papa!" This, from Pietro's twin grandsons, clamoring and pointing at the long parcel the glassblower held with care.

"Very well, very well," the older man said. "But do take care with it."

Sebastien received the parcel, unfolding layers of muslin from around it, over and over, until a gleam emerged.

From the folds, he pulled what appeared to be a scepter made entirely of glass, twisted with color.

Sebastien held it in awe, this fused piece that joined two elements into one. It was the very technique he had always wished to master and always managed to shatter: *incalmo*. The conviction that the treasure would surely slip from his hands and shatter into a thousand pieces overtook him.

"A world within a world," Pietro said proudly.

"Like Venice," Sebastien recalled.

"Like you." Pietro leaned in and began to point out the unique markings of the work, as he always did in the workshop. "See how the glass interlaces here and crosses the rivulet there and how the gold sparks just so in the light—"

"The time, Pietro!" Giuseppe interrupted.

"Yes, yes, of course." And then quieter, leaning in, to just Sebastien. "Later," he said, tapping the scepter gently. "I will tell you later."

Elena approached, carrying a carefully folded garment of some sort. Deep crimson, familiar and yet foreign. Valentina walked alongside, stitching something.

Elena whispered something to Valentina.

"But the hem, it isn't fit yet for—"

"It is perfect, Valentina. Your work shines, as it always does." Elena reached a hand around to pat Valentina's as she pulled a thread and resigned herself to knotting it.

"It is not perfect enough," she said. "Not for our Sebastien."

By now, Sebastien's eyes were round with apprehension. He hardly dared ask, eyeing that garment with suspicion. "What . . . is it?" he mustered, at last.

"Your cloak, of course."

Dante muttered something from his place at the window where he leaned, hands in pockets and amusement sparking.

"Do you speak to the window," he said dryly. "It appears a little . . . cold without its winter layers."

He tipped his head behind him and the bareness of the wall shouted accusatorily in its cold silence. Sebastien's mouth opened to utter a wary realization.

"A curtain . . . ?"

"A *cloak*," Valentina exclaimed, and Elena flung the garment, clinging by corners to let it flutter with dramatic effect as they pinned it around his shoulders. A cloud of dust flew up, setting everyone to coughing.

"It is—" *cough*—"perfect—" *cough-cough*—"No?" said Valentina, beaming through the dissipating cloud.

Elena held the ends out, clapping the garment to clean it with unfazed efficiency. "Indeed," she said, her smile radiant.

Through the settling veil of dust, Giuseppe thrust a hat. Gold and red, quite worn. "Dante's great-great-grandfather caught it at the marriage to the sea when the wind plucked it off the Doge's head. And now? It is yours!" He inclined his head, as if to impart a great secret. "Every family in Venice likes to tell how many doges they have given. We like to tell of how many doge's hats have chosen *us*!"

Sebastien smiled. "How many?"

"One!" Giuseppe looked incredulous. "How many did you think? And now, it is yours." Giuseppe clapped him on the back. "Tonight, you are a king!"

"Mamma mia, Giuseppe, a doge is not a king. A doge is not a king!" Valentina pinched her fingers in the air for emphasis.

Giuseppe grinned and nodded at Valentina, swinging an arm around Sebastien and walking him to the boat. "You will be the first doge in the history of the great republic to row his own gondola. A doge who rows his own boat is a king in my book. Boats are freedom! Go with God, Sebastien. It will be a night to remember."

THE BOOK OF WATERS

The Unmasking

For the first time in decades, the people of Venice stepped out into the night in a flurry of costumes. Napoleon had taken carnivale, but with whispers of injustice on the rise, this occasion proclaimed loudly: We Shall Celebrate Despite You.

Oars stirred rios flowing from every direction to one single point, like arteries to a heart. Arriving at the beating center of the night: Ca'Fedele. Inside, they gathered inside the piano nobile. . . .

The house awoke from a long slumber that night, floors and steps groaning and creaking in welcome as people swarmed. Costumes rustled in a symphony of silken whispers, their hush buoying music as a quartet played strains of the city's own beloved Vivaldi. Laughter spilled from conversations. Wafting in waltzes invisible to them all, there above their heads, between the people and the cherubs and saints painted above.

These were foreign sounds, here in this city where many had sworn themselves to lives of defiant somberness in protest of their current Austrian occupation. But here, for one night, a sliver of the days of old carnivale resurrected.

The room flowed with anticipation. For what, nobody knew. But in the gilded and embossed invitations, the lush extravagance oozing from every detail, this homage to a tradition in the form of rebellion—all could sense it.

Massimo Fedele was up to something.

This sense of anticipation flexed its reach until Sebastien was certain the air must be pushing right out of the windows, slipping onto the balcony and tumbling over the waters below.

He wished he could follow. He was a spectacle, he now saw. For not only were there at least three other Doges in red costume— but their costumes dripped in gold trimmings and lavish wealth.

His . . . had been a curtain.

He turned to go, wincing at his own foolhardy notion that he might see Mariana. Now that he was here, he realized he had no place here.

Nowhere among the revelers was a firebird, the costume that had been designed for Mariana. As boatman, it had been his task to ferry masks and fabrics to and from Ca'Fedele, deliver them to Francesca and await her verdicts, and return those which "would never do, not for our firebird, not for a momentous night such as this."

But after all of that, there was no sign of the firebird. No glimpse of anyone who might be a masked Mariana. And without her . . . why was he here?

And yet . . . for her, he would wait. Always.

Caught between everything else pulling him away, telling him to leave, and the determination to stay as long as it took, whatever the cost, he froze. For there, entering the room, was a sight that took his breath.

He did not know the correct words for fabrics and things that shined. But the woman before him was adorned in flowing blues of every hue, from the turquoise of the lagoon in the morning to its deep-hued royal blue beneath clouds. Greys here and there, and sky blue, too, all of them falling in waves around her that seemed woven of liquid and air, their twists mimicking currents and their pools upon the floor.

Her mask scrolled in silvery-blue upturned peaks and curls, glinting beneath Pietro's chandelier. Her hair, worn long in curls, fell over her shoulders in silvery-golden waves, simple and pure.

Deep blue eyes took in the room with trepidation. And despite her ethereal beauty, despite the way she held herself in quiet poise and unassuming grace, it was something else that assured him of her identity. Two things, in truth.

First, the way she, upon assessing the slow-churning currents of the room and people before her, did not lift her chin in haughty expectation of a reception. Quite the opposite. She quietly took herself to the outskirts of the room, to a small alcove that on a normal day was occupied by a stately chess table left to gather dust in its shadows.

And second, the way she seemed to sense him. She turned slowly, searching for the source of whatever was drawing her awareness, and found him. Locked eyes with him.

Behind her mask, her eyes narrowed in careful study, then grew round with growing realization. A swallow traversed her delicate neck, and she leaned to whisper to Francesca, her constant companion, who seemed none too pleased at whatever it was she'd said.

Francesca gestured insistently at the dance floor. Mariana, with gentle resolve, shook her head and spoke again, to which Francesca left her side and threaded her way into the throng.

And then Mariana waited.

All thoughts of escape from this place dropped to the ground, rolling out before him, a walkway leading straight to her.

Vivaldi's summer symphony struck up, and Sebastien treaded upon those notes, through costumed revelers, until she stood before him, inches and a universe away, all at once. No mask could hide her identity. This woman whom he'd watched over, prayed over, long before they'd ever spoken a word. He reached for the words of their first conversation now.

"Mariana," he said, feeling the roll and tumble of it, this time into his very soul. "That is your name?"

The question he'd first asked her, in what seemed like another lifetime. Back then, she had nodded the smallest affirmation. This time, though, a cloud passed over her as she dropped her gaze. As if the speaking of her identity brought torment.

"I'm sorry," he said, voice scraping over his regret. The entire draw of masked balls such as these was the anonymity, the thrill of moving among question marks, across classes. And he had just trampled upon that. "I shouldn't have—"

"And you are Sebastien," she said, her voice a quiet melody.

Her first words on the island too. But this time, instead of searching to ascertain whether he could be trusted, her voice carried relief, and belonging, and trust, and regret, and—was it fear? But why?

He lashed his hands to his sides with stubborn resolve. They ached to take that downturned face in them, to lift her countenance, to help her.

A look around noted a few curious stares at their restrained stance. It was entirely out of place, among couples spinning and energy resounding.

And so, he lifted a hand, palm upturned in the small space between them. "May I request the honor of a dance?"

Only a moment did she hesitate—and then she took that hand.

Symphonic notes unfurled in their strange triplets of ascent. Mysterious and compelling, a story soon to give way to quick and vivacious frolics of violin, tempered then with tentative tiptoes of soul-shaped strains into flights of fancy.

It was their story, and upon these notes they moved dreamlike, the world falling away, guarded in the happy oblivion of those around who were entirely consumed in their own costumed fancies.

At length, when the violin languished in quieter interlude, Sebastien spoke, his words constructing, brick by brick, a cloister around them in their own refuge.

"You look—" He halted at the pallid failure of the word to accomplish what she deserved. "You *are* . . ." He shook his head slowly, searching. What could complete that sentiment and do justice to what she—her very presence—affected within him?

She was stunning. Beautiful, certainly. Singular, without question. But each of these, as they lined up for audition, fell flat. She was not the completion of a description. She was the entire thought, the very life and action and heart of what any spoken sentiment would be, though any was doomed to pale.

The freedom and music that she was, beckoned him to stop toiling. Stop searching, and instead to linger, root into the deeper realms, where answers waited rather than eluded, brought peace rather than torment. "You arrest me, Mariana." And something about her freed him too.

She blushed at his words. "I've missed you," she said simply.

"And I, you," he said. There was a cruel and beautiful irony, living beneath the same roof as this woman who was closer than his own heartbeat to him. And yet, in many ways, farther than ever before, their worlds cleaved in stark separation. He, in the attic, in the boathouse. She, in her balcony, in her ballroom.

Their souls twined, always.

"You are beautiful," he said. Wishing he could say it better, like Dante could, with all his poets of old.

She shook her head in a manner so humble it only added to her beauty. "I am just . . . the sea. My costume, I mean."

A picture blinked across his mind of him clambering to the top of his crumbled castle to look out beyond the Lido to the sparkling sea beyond.

"Of course you are," he said in a quiet that she seemed to lean into with her whole presence. Upon the sea she had come to him. Upon the sea she had returned. It was . . . a part of her.

The steady delight in the tenor of his words seemed to settle peace upon her, if only for a moment. A sensation he relished, the way her arms relaxed, as if she had come home. A thing he wished to give to her always. And yet, just as quickly, it twisted into something else when her steps slowed in their dance, out of time with the music.

"I am the sea," she said, curving the words upward in unfinished form. Whatever the coming conclusion to her phrase, it seemed to require resolve for her to say it. "And you are the Doge."

The way she lifted her eyes asked him to hear more than what she was saying.

"It was Giuseppe's idea," he said, embarrassed at the presumption of his own costume. "You know how he is. And then the others took up with the idea, and before I knew it . . ." He shrugged a shoulder, resigning himself to the present reality.

Mariana's mouth lifted into her smile. "I can picture it," she said, assessing his costume, guessing who contributed which elements, all with cunning accuracy. "And the cape," she said. "It looks strangely . . . familiar." The glint in her eye behind her mask told the rest of the story—she knew just the workshop window from whence it came. The laughter they shared shattered away whatever unseen tension she was battling.

"Sebastien," she said his name as if it were a gift and a plea for him to understand what she was about to repeat. "We are the sea . . . and the Doge."

Their movements, turning to the storied, shadowed strains, slowed until her words—and their unspoken meaning—rooted into him with a shock that knotted his breath.

Between the sea and the Doge, there was only one timeless, everlasting connection.

They stilled so long they might have been one of the statues carved into marble, held for all of time. But despite the briefest thrill that theirs could be a story stitched together . . . there were surfaces harder than marble. Hard enough to crack it, crumble it, vanish it all to dust. Surfaces such as truth.

He was a child of the murky lagoon, born upon dark canal waters themselves. And she, a daughter of Venice's remnant of glory. By rule, she would not marry down. Tradition, and a brother bent on tradition, ensured this.

The sea and the Doge were wed indeed . . . but the dogeship had died, long ago.

There was no future for them.

Even still, Sebastien held her hands, laced his fingers into hers at their sides, aching, bursting to say, like the Doge, *"I wed thee."*

In a room with listening ears and watchful eyes, in a world where no lasting connection was possible for a swamp rat and a daughter of Venice, in a life where he was born with a name and no more, upon canals and destined for a life of rich and full obscurity, hers was the only pledge to him she would ever be permitted to make.

She had broached his deepest longing in the only way it could ever have even a small hope of becoming reality—by coming from her. In her quiet resolve, she had laid steps for him to climb, to ask a question he could not—or should not, by all logic and rules of society—be permitted to ask.

And then, that stillness of time broke, the bells of all the towers in Venice seemed to peal their proclamations in his chest, clanging to answer her, to chase off this uncertainty he saw clambering over her.

"Mariana." His voice pitched low, in a tumble of sincerity, disbelief . . . hope. Could he claim her, ask her, invite her? Away from this place, which seemed to choke the very life from her. Into a life of simplicity and scarcity—but into a life where he had seen with his own eyes, she thrived.

If he had it within his reach to give her a life of freedom, then this was, perhaps, what he was born for. He would be the Doge to her sea, if she would let him.

Happiness seemed almost a blasphemy of a word to use in the face of what surged through his veins. It was so very, very much more.

"If you can find it within you to—"

The quartet struck up a few bright notes heralding a proclamation, commanding every eye in the room.

A masked man presided there in black jacket, black shirtsleeves, black vest.

"Friends!" he began. "The House of Fedele wishes you well on this auspicious evening."

A murmur sounded of reciprocating well-wishes and glass-clinking.

"It is our deepest desire this evening to honor you, our guests. Like you, the House of Fedele arises to honor the rich heritage of La Serenissima, the traditions our forefathers have given us. I salute your masks, my friends!" He raised his glass, a sparkling beverage sloshing within.

A resounding "*Salute!*" echoed back to him.

"Like you," Massimo began again, "the House of Fedele is steadfast in devotion to our city in summer"—he gestured to the quadrant of the room bedecked in emerald and blue—"in autumn"—a gesture to the golden-hued quadrant—"in winter"—the blues and whites—"and in spring." He gave a final sweep of his arm toward the pinks and violets. Strings of leaves and flowers hung like descending forests, imported from far and wide, woven into a floating garden for the occasion.

"La Serenissima, too, has seen her seasons. The new life of spring, in her humble beginnings. The glory of summer, in her years when she grew from a small seed to a flourishing power of commerce, tradition, and honor." A pause, and the crowd replied in expected applause.

"There was an autumn. A great and glowing crowning season as she approached what some thought would be her end. Our parents, and theirs before them, saw Venice at the height of her beauty and reign."

Massimo grew somber in his posture and tone. "We honor them, this night." A long pause, as if mourning a death.

"And then a winter," he said. With great emotion, he offered his grief. "When those who had nothing to do with our city presumed to make her their own. When the Great Council made a farce of a vote," he said, voice thick, trembling with restrained passion.

Now, a tremor of unease through the room. This was a matter of delicacy, even among those gathered, some of whom embraced their newfound "liberation from the ways of old," as they viewed Napoleon's taking of the city. Some of whom railed against the ravaging of the city by his troops. Others who felt some of both. And still more who felt betrayal by all parties, who watched Venice reduced, in the eyes of their occupiers, to a prize in a card game, traded off between entities as if they were not living, breathing people with true lives, real families, real businesses . . . and real love for their homeland.

With these undercurrents churning about one another, the topic was not an easy one. Particularly in mixed company at an event that had been touted as an evening of amusement—something sorely needed, in this time of somber occupation by Austria.

"You have been cast under this spell of winter, my esteemed friends," Massimo Fedele said.

He seemed to relish the unease he had set upon his unsuspecting audience. He waited, drawing it out until their discomfort peaked and primed them, made them yearn for a single word. A word that, at last, he offered like a gift upon a golden platter.

"But . . ."

The word dropped upon the crowd and released a collective exhale. Ushering palpable relief before he had even finished his thought. "Can you feel it, my friends? *New* life creeping in? Buds preparing to burst forth in bloom? Spring is upon us once more. And like the Venetians of old, those stalwart souls who built a kingdom from a swamp . . ." This last word he spat, and Sebastien flinched. Did he imagine it, or did Massimo's gaze settle on him?

Slowly, Massimo removed his own mask, as if to say, *You can trust me.* "We shall rise and build this kingdom again. My friends, in tribute to this season of new life, it is my greatest joy, and deepest honor, to announce at last a union that marks the beginning of a new era: the betrothal of Signor Andreas Endrizze to my sister, Mariana Fedele."

Sebastien's throat closed in. Pain burning but barely registering. He turned to look at Mariana beside him . . . but she was gone.

THE BOOK OF WATERS

Words among Shadows

The room parted like the Red Sea as a man entered from the east doors. Silver of hair, he, too, was clad in black, his bauta painted in black and red alternating diamonds, and he approached the platform where stood Massimo. A shirt of scarlet beneath his black overcoat crept up his neck in a cloying way, giving the effect of a man ready to be choked by his own collar. He looked uncomfortable. Hot. And his face turned red as moments ticked by with no sign of Mariana.

Massimo stood with eyes affixed to the east entrance. The doors were opened by two footmen . . . but nothing happened. The crowd, in response to these cues, parted just as they had for the man . . . but nothing happened.

Francesca hurried out into the passageway, absent for some minutes as growing unease churned within the crowd, an unseen guest intent on sparking rumors, piquing the latent secret-keeping, secret-unearthing ways of Old Venice.

At last, a soft swish sounded, and there she was. Mariana, all in blue, defying her brother with every step she took toward him.

By the look on Massimo's face, he was none too pleased with

her costume choice, a departure from his plans. His intent had been a vignette proclaiming the joining of two ancient families, each of them clad in red and gold, just as the golden lion upon the scarlet flag had presided for centuries over the republic. Colors of power and fire.

And here she was, dressed in blue. A fall of water dousing a flame.

She looked at no one. First, she fixed her gaze upon the checkered floor as she moved, silent as the night, to the stage that awaited her. Then, she stopped. Swallowed. Found Sebastien's gaze.

He reached up, removing his mask. Nothing would stand between them—not now. He attempted to read her, shaping his stricken face to say instead, *I see you. You are not alone.* All the while, his heart thrashed against his chest wall, railing against this foreign notion of Mariana with this man. The man Sebastien recognized as the Wednesday visitor, who weekly sat in silence for hours with Mariana.

Lifting her chin, tearing her gaze from him, she pressed on, one step at a time. With each one, he wanted to draw her back, step back time, meet her in the alcove of fifteen minutes earlier and say, "*Yes. The Doge and the Sea. Wed, they shall always, always be.*"

But he was too late.

He watched her lean in and whisper something to Massimo—watched her brother's jaw set like a cage around simmering anger, watched him shake his head. Cut his gaze to the man as if to redirect Mariana from whatever she had said to the man beside her. They almost made the perfect semblance of a holy union, if her brother had been a priest. He, facing the crowd, they, facing each other. He, joining their hands, lifting the twined fingers in triumph.

What followed was a blur. The two of them, dancing an impossible waltz—he, fire. She, water. Through an odd veil of what felt like a very bad dream, he watched them. Saw her mouth, fixed at first into an unmoving line, work very hard to say something. To summon, with all her strength, a smile.

There she was. Mariana, who could not bear to be the cause of another person's discomfort—though it cost her everything.

The man, whose once-dark hair was generously peppered in white, did not seem to know what to say in return. He was very occupied, it seemed, with watching the people who watched him. Where Mariana shriveled to be in the limelight, he relished it enough for the both of them. Offering nods and smiles to them all and not a word to the woman he held in his arms.

Massimo, meanwhile, took himself from the scene, vanishing into the hall with purpose driving his every step.

Follow. The word descended upon Sebastien with urgency and conviction.

Through the odd and otherworldly veil, the dance continued as Sebastien withdrew, music muddling in his ears. The room spun, the press of people suffocating. He was loathe to leave Mariana but did not trust the determined drive of Massimo's stride.

Looking both ways down the hallway, he spotted a shadow cast eerie and large as Massimo turned a corner. Sebastien followed at a distance, his pulse driving him to catch up as his mind warned him to keep quiet, to watch and learn.

The chase ensued silently around turn after turn until the steps faded, then fell silent. Sebastien's stomach sank. He had lost him.

Somewhere deeper into the labyrinth, the open and close of a heavy door sounded. Sebastien followed, finding his way into a wing of the house he did not know.

Here the ceilings were lower, trimmed in a wood of a deeper hue than the rest of the house. Doors carved in time-weathered vines stood guard up and down the corridor. The framed artwork hung gallery-like, depicting scenes very different from those of the ancient myths that were portrayed in the piano nobile of Ca'Fedele.

Even the air here felt different. Less . . . frenzied.

It was strange, so different that it felt as if he were in another home entirely.

Two palaces in one. The phrase blew in from the past, tumbling from his boyhood, in Valentina's amused tones as she worked at her lace and told him stories of the old families. What had she said, all those years ago? The story of a palazzo growing up beside another, building over the top of its roof.

"Ca'Fedele," she had said. *"Though you will never set foot inside, my boy."*

And here he was. Standing at what seemed the interlocking of the two homes, opened unto each other somewhere in time. Had the Famiglia Fedele purchased, perhaps, the other home?

The history was a muddle, and so was the house. But he could not shake the distinct impression that he had entered another place entirely, here in this new wing.

Sebastien scanned the bottoms of the doors, looking for any light slipping out, any semblance of life—but found none.

Footsteps sounded behind him. Acting upon instinct, he gripped the handle of the door on his left and ducked inside. If he'd been thinking, he would have stepped into the character of his costume. Drawn his shoulders wide, lifted his head, and acted every inch the Doge.

But he was a peasant imposter at a ball, on the run, and had acted every bit of it.

The room was dark, the only light a slip of blue moon from the opposite wall, which arched with windows high and numerous. As the footsteps receded, his eyes adjusted before he crossed the room and took in the scene outside. Though he knew the layout of the palazzo fairly well, there was still much he had not discovered, for sheer fact of being so often absent.

Outside, he could see a garden, clambering with ivy over brick walls. A pathway meandering through two trees that grew tall, some of the only of their age in this vast city. He studied them, the way their leaves shimmered in a breeze, and thought of their roots casting down, gripping ancient piles made of their ancestors. A forest standing upon a forest.

And wasn't Venice such? Wasn't life just such an anomaly? If not for the people who had come before them, the idiosyncratic creases and folds left by an era unfolding like a garment pressed by time and circumstance . . . would not his life have been entirely different?

The thought gripped him until an answer fell silent inside him. He would wish for no other life.

For all the questions, all the mysteries, all the maddening ambiguity of his own life—he could not imagine it without Pietro's universe of shimmering glass, or Valentina's hearth fire, or the mellowed wooden clack as ideas inked into words in Dante's universe, or Giuseppe's midnight shrimping expeditions, or Elena's warm and welcoming home.

. . . or Mariana, treasure to his very soul.

He would not, for all the answers in the world, wish these things away.

Who am I? The old question scrambled around in the dark, as if looking for the rest of itself. Incomplete. Who was he? It could have been anyone, in that basket. How had he been the one to be taken in, raised up . . . loved?

Who am I . . . to be loved?

Across the garden, he could see that he had landed in a wing extending to the back of the property, affording him a view straight through those two trees and into the glowing ballroom on the piano nobile where the throng of people continued to swirl.

And him. Standing still, watching it all go by.

At length, he withdrew from his portal into their world. His eyes had adjusted much better to the darkness, and he could make out a sitting room with pale walls—perhaps blue, like the sky. A vineyard scene painted across the far wall, where a marbled fireplace held court to stuffed chairs and settees, a sofa, and a population of tables tucked about like slumbering creatures.

The floor spread out in the diamond pattern typical of the rest of the house, but here, the squares were goliath. A single square might play foundation to a pair of chairs upon it, and a chess table between. The startling breadth of each square was warranted, for inside, each boasted a circle of stunning blue stone, its center composed of alternating shapes and hues of blue. *"From lapis to cerulean and every blue in between,"* he could imagine Pietro remark, always with the eye of an artist. In the corners untouched by the circles, adornments in meticulous mosaic scrolled, their forms identical but their pieces unique. Even the floor was a work of art.

And yet, the ceiling was oddly vacant. Palest blue, an occasional streak of white, a break from Venetian tradition. It seemed a stark contrast, at first, but then Sebastien considered what would happen when the sun came through the reaching windows. The light would shine upon the swimming dimensions of blue stone, the reflective bits of mosaic, and cast a kaleidoscope of light, always moving, shifting with the day, upon that ceiling.

There was something more about the room that felt . . . off-kilter, somehow. He couldn't place it, looking around. Certainly, it held an air of general neglect, and none of the glitter and pomp of the ballroom, but it was more than that.

Stepping toward the fireplace, he ran his hand along the smooth marble surface.

A book sat upon the mantel, and he picked it up, searching in vain for a title. There was none. The cover was mellowed and soft, but absent of dust and neglect. And yet the mantel it sat upon had a thin layer of dust upon it, which he had never seen a speck of in the rest of the palazzo.

Taking in the entirety of the room, he knew: this place was to someone else what his ruins were to him. A refuge of one's own in this chaotic world.

As for the person it belonged to, he could picture her—there, on the faded red chair, legs tucked up beneath her just as she had done in the field on Burano, when she had seemed free and natural and so very alive.

He stood in her sanctuary now and felt at once an intruder, and yet he also felt a deep and growing sense of protectiveness to guard this, her one sliver of solace.

The notion instructed him to leave.

But footsteps sounded, approaching in haste.

In three strides, he reached his only hope of disappearing: a curtain, velvet and heavy, floor to ceiling. A pair of them flanked the mantel he had just stood beside. He made haste to hide. The door groaned with the echoes of the ages, closing swiftly.

Sebastien held his breath, listening for some hint of who it was, and met with only silence.

Slowly, as if even a breath would bring the curtain down and the house along with it, he shifted toward the outer edge, leaning to see.

At the door stood a figure all in blue, hands pressed to the door as slim shoulders rose and fell, her own breath slowing as she eased in backward steps into this sanctuary-room.

Mariana.

He moved to go to her, but in that instant, she turned, and the look upon her face was one he had never seen before. It anchored him there, watching as something swept her features. Torment, easing into realization as her brows furrowed. A small shake of the head, as if she were playing something over in her memory. Fingertips rose to her mouth, touching on the beginning of a smile and then the lightest laugh, clamped over with that same hand.

Her eyes danced with the feeling that flowed from her so poignantly it crossed the room, wrapped Sebastien's ankles, wended up into his soul until he felt it too.

Freedom.

And just as he moved to go to her, the door handle gave a brackish rattle, admitting Massimo with all the force of a breached dam. "Mariana." His voice cut like a cleaver. Silence billowed. Sebastien's curtain, too, swayed. He flinched, willing it to stop.

"You know I love you above all else in this world," Massimo said at last. His words measured, spun with the shine of honey. Too much of it.

"It's why you sent me away?" Mariana spoke, her words quiet but courageous. What had it taken her to speak this question?

"You weren't 'sent away,' Mariana. You were gifted a chance to grow up among a true family, to receive education and opportunity—"

"*You* were my family, Massimo."

Silence.

Mariana continued. "Remember when we were young? The time that it rained for days, and the house was in a flurry because of the flooding—everyone was moving vases, chairs, art, up and away from the floor—and in the flurry, you forgot about me."

"I would never forget you."

"I tried to help move things, but everyone kept saying, 'No, milady. Let me do that for you, milady.' It was the first time I thought that if being 'milady' meant doing nothing, I didn't want to be 'milady.'"

"We all have such thoughts. We all wonder, sometimes, what it would be like to live a different life. But the fact is, you were born to this—and with good reason, Mariana. Did you hear how the people hushed when they saw you tonight? Even if you did pull that trick of switching costumes."

Mariana waited, in her patient way, then continued as if Massimo hadn't interrupted with his interlude.

"That rainstorm . . . was the day I found this room. All the furniture was shrouded, the air was thick with dust, but it was a quiet place in all that madness. I began to move things around, and I remember how the rain seemed to sing me along as I did. I opened the window to hear it, to let its fresh air in, and I felt—so alive."

Massimo was strangely silent, at that.

Mariana continued, "I felt so guilty for loving the rain that was causing such havoc. But for the first time, this place felt like *home*."

"And so it is," Massimo said. "Every room, every door, every step, stick, and brick. It is your dowry, after all."

Sebastien's chest thundered now.

Her one home would be hers . . . if she wed, as he intended.

"What?" Her voice was small.

"The palazzo," he said. "Did I not tell you? Your husband-to-be knows and has all manner of plans for it. Imagine the extravaganzas, even grander than tonight. You'll not be in want of a home, Mariana. Is that what this is about? I must say, your disappearance for so long did not reflect well on the House of Fedele. But was I not the soul of understanding? You had your little adventure out on the lagoon. And now it is time to rise to your purpose."

Silence.

Silence from the girl whose very presence was waves lapping, leaves rustling, all the mighty whispers that breathed hope into creation.

"It was not a little adventure, Massimo."

He laughed indulgently, as one does with a child. "Very well. Your grand adventure, then."

Mariana spoke at length. "Our home . . . will be his?"

"Yes. Your husband's."

"And this is why he has taken me as a bride?"

Massimo's voice was tender, protective. "No. The House of Fedele . . . certainly you have a dowry, as is befitting the daughter of a patrician. But I have made a study of these things. Your husband has agreed to provide a certain sum—"

"He is—purchasing me?"

"Not a price, sister. You are not for sale. Never. No, no—it is a *bride token*, as a show for the treasure that you are. The *honor* of aligning himself with our family. No one could ever purchase you—you are priceless. The very best in all the world. But for a man of his stature to do this—why, it is more respect paid us than even Penelope's suitors paid Icarus the Spartan king! This, for us. The unremembered. Do not forget our heritage. This, sister, is the very making of all our forefathers strove to make right. *You* . . . are it. We have done it. Made right the sins of the Unremembered One. And with these funds, the revolution has a way forward and—well. No need to trouble yourself about all of that. Just know that it will bode well for you and your children and your children's children . . ."

"You say that as if you know there will be children. But, Massimo—"

"Not to worry, Mariana."

Sebastien bit his tongue. The man cared for his sister, clearly, but had gotten it so inextricably tangled in these maneuverings, he had given her no choice.

If he could give her that choice . . .

Mariana spoke. "And you . . . Will you stay here too?"

"I have other plans."

"I see."

"Plans that have been crafted with care, for your own good and the good of Venezia. I'm not at liberty to say yet what they are—"

"But they will take you away."

A pause, and then, "Yes."

And then footsteps. Resigned, slippered steps, followed by assured steps doling out confidence in staccato beats. The opening of the door, the closing, the resuming of voices as they moved down the corridor.

Exhaling, Sebastien rested his forehead on the wall.

It was true, what Mariana had said about his life, growing up. Migrating. She understood the movements of birds, their search for a home, even more than he. And now, this last vestige of a home was to be given to a near-stranger, as his settlement for marrying her.

He could hear it now, how Massimo would protest this loudly— *It's all for her! She will keep her home, she will have a continued place in society—these are all the things I, as her guardian, must secure for her. It is my duty as her brother. Do you see?*

He did see. For all his professions and even actions of love, Massimo continued to bruise his sister's heart. Words like *tasked, secured, plans crafted* . . . as if she were a commodity and not a soul.

Perhaps it was not his fault, entirely. His family had risen to power through trade, and so he used the language of business.

And yet . . . Her silence echoed, her pain with it. It drove him to wordless prayer, that this God who created her might see her even now. Might not abandon her in this, the moment her fate teetered upon.

He opened his eyes, head still braced against the wall where the mantel met the framework of the adjacent white stucco.

And found himself staring into a chasm.

Minuscule in width, and certainly not remarkable in a house where cracks were commonplace. But this one was different. It did not web but reached, top to bottom, straight as could possibly be. Emerging from his cloistered place, he investigated the curtain's twin, and found another crack. Top to bottom, rigid.

Standing back, he examined the fireplace.

Marbled and innocent. Logs poised for igniting, a bed of cinders beneath. A painting of an island framed above it.

He had not seen it before, the painting. The growing moon spilled in from outside, illuminating a scene where aqua waters broke in waves upon a seawall. An arched entrance. In the distance, a stand of trees, sap-green in their young and spindly form.

He knew that wall. He knew that arch. He knew those trees, though they had aged by decades since the time of this painting.

It was his home.

All at once, recollections came to him like a still-life, painted and fleeting: Mariana standing, awestruck, at the sight of the arch. Dipping her feet, unshod, over the seawall and letting her toes skim across those waters.

She had known his island all along.

The facts lined up like lines in a story, awaiting his understanding.

Stepping close to the fireplace, he noted again the strange beauty of this floor's pattern. One of the blue circles extended from the fireplace, the wall bisecting its arc perfectly. The arc of the blue, lined in black.

He stooped to look closer. The line . . . was not a line. It was a cut. Deliberate and meticulous.

This . . . was a moving floor.

34

THE BOOK OF WATERS

The Spinning Room

Sebastien pressed against the mantel.

Nothing.

He moved to the side, standing to the right of the mantel, and pushed again.

Nothing.

The same to the left, up high, down low.

Nothing, nothing, *nothing*. He thought of Elena's tales, her fables and legends of Venice. A fireplace in the round, set to rotate and guard some secret, would not be outside the realm of possibility. In fact, it was just fantastical enough to make it entirely plausible in this enchanted city.

He examined it, attempting this corbel, that book, another tile. Prodding, pulling, pushing this and that in hopes of setting the mantel and hearth into motion.

Perhaps he was imagining it all. Perhaps he was tired, perhaps he was at the end of himself, his purpose and role at Ca'Fedele disintegrating before his eyes.

Who was he, after all, to be here?

He laughed dryly. Who was he, after all, to presume he had discovered something of this house its own residents apparently knew nothing of—or perhaps knew a great deal of and took pains to hide.

He looked again at the painting, the scene pulling at strings deep inside him. It was flanked on each side by candlesticks mounted in scrolling iron to the wall. Narrowing his eyes, quieting his bounding hopes lest this, too, be in vain . . . he reached up to the one on the left. Gripping the protruding curve of the candleholder with firm but gentle motion, he tilted it toward the painting.

Something clicked. But nothing moved.

Moving to the opposite candlestick, he repeated the motion, but found it would not tilt, not at the same angle. Holding his breath, he attempted tilting it the other way, pointing toward the painting, opposite its counterpart.

Click.

And slowly, with stops and starts . . . the platform began to turn, groaning with whatever pulleys were hidden to make such a thing possible. It made a quarter of a turn and stopped, leaving the fireplace perpendicular to its original position and leaving whatever it hid exposed.

He could not see in, the darkness inside seemed so complete that it seeped into the original chamber like a cloud of ink.

Without warning, the door behind him opened and closed quickly. He whirled.

Relief washed over him at the sight of Mariana, carrying a lantern.

"H-hello," he said, and wished for all the world he'd had a better word to offer, in the wake of all that had transpired.

She froze. If there had been any question as to whether she'd known about the fireplace's secret, her wide eyes and open mouth quickly answered. She rushed across the room, picking up her whispering gauzy skirts. And then, shifting her gaze to him, her expression grew grave. "Sebastien? What is this?"

He explained what had happened, her face flushing as she understood he had witnessed her conversation with Massimo.

She inhaled deeply. "Well, then," she said. "There's only one thing to do, wouldn't you say?"

Picking up a candle from the mantel and lighting it from her lantern, she handed it to him, and they entered together.

One tentative step at a time, discovering steps downward. Each of them extended their candles about the room until they faced each other.

"What is this place?" Mariana said, nearly in a whisper.

A sea of white-sheeted furniture gathered in odd shapes around him. The room itself was not so much a *room*, as four walls hidden somewhere beneath layers of paint, gilded millwork, and plaster formed into ornate frames and frescoes. It was in such stark contrast to the airy surroundings of the room to their back. The effect here, in contrast, was almost suffocating, summoning walls close and ceilings lower until the room felt rather like a trap, or perhaps a dungeon, with its lack of windows.

Paintings sprawled over the walls without a care, a mingling of scripture and artistic imagination, depicting tales of old. Baby Moses, floating among the reeds. The fishermen-apostles out upon a stormy sea. Sebastien drew closer. Would they be the work of Tintoretto, perhaps? And hidden away here, in the shuttered room of lost things . . . Sorrow cloaked him.

Inexplicable, for he knew there were rooms like this scattered throughout Venice. Many noble families had boarded up rooms to hide treasures of canvas and marble, writings and more, upon Napoleon's invasion. And Napoleon had not been the first foe of this city. Yes, this sort of treasure was surely not uncommon.

But something about the frescoes *was.*

Sebastien listened, straining to hear and gauge the placement of sounds: the orchestra from the piano nobile. The earnest and serious voices of men, from the opposite wing across the garden. Both distant, both a world away.

Mariana, too, heard the voices, casting a look over her shoulder and hovering her hand in front of her candle as if to hide it.

"You opened this with the candlesticks?" she asked, studying the oddly tilted scrolls of iron above the hearth.

"Yes."

And before he could register what she planned, what the

implications were, how she took her very life—or reputation, at least—in her hands in doing so, she righted the sconces upon the wall and stepped back as the fireplace groaned its acquiescence. It turned until it was flush with the wall.

And they were alone. Sealed away in a hidden, hushed chamber.

Twin sconces to those outside assured that they could trigger the release from within, but by the hushed wonder between them, there was no thought of retreat just now.

All the noise and uncertainty of the outside world rolled away until the only music present was that of time and mystery.

Wordlessly, with some unspoken understanding twining between them, they began to unveil the odd shapes of cloaked furniture. The sheets flung up in the air, unveiling a child's desk, the desk of a grown man, a bed in the corner. Marble statues of Socrates, Plato, and Aristotle looked on from behind the larger desk, as if they had frozen in time and only awaited the call of their pupil to awaken and teach.

The far wall was shelves upon deep-hued shelves wall to wall and floor to ceiling, packed with books. A ceiling that, upon closer examination, was verifiably and truly short. As he unveiled the last bit of furniture—a chair in deep green—he looked up from his task to see the sheet settle in white ripples, Mariana moving about the room, lighting candles one by one. Bringing light with her own small candle until a mellow glow filled the chamber.

What was this place?

The question ricocheted in Sebastien's chest as he laid a hand upon the small, empty desk. What child's hands had rested upon this same surface? Where were they now? Was it the mercurial Massimo? Not Mariana, whose education had been finished in an alpine hamlet. He turned to her, swimming with questions about this night. But the only one that broke the surface was "Are you all right?"

She dropped her head, lantern light flickering over her.

"I will not marry him," she said, answering all of the other unspoken questions.

He caught her words with his heart, caught her chin with his hand, met her gaze with his. "And—if another man dared to ask for this hand?" He picked up that hand and waited.

She lifted her gaze, eyes welling.

"There is more that you should know, Sebastien."

She trembled, and his hands moved to her shoulders. "We should go," he said. "You're cold—"

"No, please," she said. A flicker of a smile. She took in the room's curiosities. "Whose room do you suppose this is? Or—was, rather?" She swiped away a cobweb that strung itself between a rocking horse and a bedpost, where an old map upon the wall displayed an ancient view of the lagoon. She studied it, seeming unready to speak the things she alluded to.

He would wait.

"Whoever it is—or was—I do not envy him this room. More like a cell, really."

"Sebastien?" Mariana stood at a wall, stooped to examine a sequence of frescoes framed in wrought gold. He joined her and leaned in.

He was no art scholar, but he had seen this style before—with the subject illuminated so starkly against dark background. Chiaroscuro, Dante had once told him as they turned the pages of an art book, once long ago. The eerie mood of it seeped from the walls, curling around them in tendrils. Darkening all but the pictures before them. They were small, for frescoes. Most in Venice took up all, or most, of any space given, making of the house a canvas. These smaller ones, each the size of a book, fit the odd scale of the room. Lined up side by side, showing a sequence. A story.

A rustling sounded behind him, and he looked to see Mariana pulling paper scraps from the rubbish bin. Laying them straight upon the table, gentling her palm over them to ease their creases.

And then she froze.

"What is it?"

She lifted one of the scraps, holding it with such care. Her eyes pooled with tears.

"Mariana?"

She opened her mouth to speak, but no sound emerged. Instead, she extended her arm toward him, offering him the paper.

He took it. In the dim light, he saw that only a few words spanned the scrap. Angling himself until they caught illumination, he read them.

Please take care of my son.

Scratched out.

I, Margherita Mendeli, do implore—

Scratched out.

He is called Sebastien. He was well-beloved. Please

An ink blot obscured the line, and the writer had left off there to try again, but Sebastien knew the rest by heart.

give him a good life.

The paper was torn below, where presumably Margherita had tried once more. Gripped this very paper with the very last of her strength . . .

For him.

He knew the lettering—he knew the wording. He would have given anything to know the writer. She had written her small scroll, which was tucked away on a shelf in Elena's cottage, even now.

Breath came thin and shallow, the room closing in until the ceiling seemed to loom even lower.

My—my mother?

Mariana's fingers laced into his, and she peered up at him. "This means . . ."

He shook his head. It meant everything, and yet—what *did* it mean?

Sebastien . . . Mendeli. Of this House of Mendeli. This—this very house?

He turned slowly, viewing the hidden room in new light. Recalling Massimo's derisive comments to his companions one night in the gondola, about the Mendelis, whose intended protégé-leader had "failed the cause of the Republic" upon his parents' death.

Cogs clicked into place, gears beginning to turn and make some foggy sense of it all. Sebastien and Mariana stood not just in a room of art hidden from Napoleon's plunderers, but in a room designed for the upbringing—and hiding—of a future revolutionary.

A future doge.

Him.

And here he stood, playing doge in a curtain from his true life. His real, true, and good life. The absurdity of it all—the shock—summoned a laugh from somewhere guttural.

"Sebastien?" Mariana's voice, kind, concerned.

"Who . . . am I?" The words out, dancing to distant Vivaldi in this room with answers, for the first time. And yet blooming, bursting, with more questions.

Numbly, he returned to the frescoes, this time searching them not as a detached mystery, but scouring them for clues to his own life. Muted tones of greens and greys. The basket upon the waters, where currents glimmered white against black night water, was like so many depictions he had seen of Moses. The style of these were such that faces were obscured, left to the imagination. Clear in color and form, inviting the viewer to impose their own familiarity upon the lack of details.

Perhaps it was this that made the pictures seem more real, somehow. Perhaps the details—the braided basket, the way some of its fibers had been painted as having come loose, a blanket peeking out like a secret—seemed to bespeak care for the one tucked inside. The scene pulled him closer.

He obeyed, moving on to the next fresco. Here, the fishermen-apostles, two of them, faced one another as waves, illuminated like the basket in the scene before, crashed with great froth against the side of their boat. The men seemed at odds with each other, but silhouetted as their forms were, it was difficult to make out which canonical scene this was meant to portray. Hadn't the apostles argued while Jesus slept amidst a storm? Was this it? Yet this scene, too, caught Sebastien's breath and an odd twist of his stomach warned him against viewing the next frescoes. But he continued, unable to stop.

The scene of an island, and Sebastien paged through the scriptures in his mind. Crete? Patmos? There was no shortage of islands in the Great Text, and yet this one resembled the far side of Venice's own Burano, that place of hushed threads and the making of lace and the humble riches of fish at day's end when fishermen returned.

Perhaps the artist had infused these views of the holy places with views from his own world. It would not have been the first time, and Sebastien stooped to discover who the artist had been.

But as he came close, eyes nearly to the wall, it was not an artist's name that arrested him. Indeed, there was no signature to be seen.

No, the thing that froze him was the sheen of the final fresco.

A scene of a man lifting a woman, enrobed in white, from the rushes of a stormy isle. Her hair hung long, dark with dampness, tangled.

And he was transported. For in this, he did not see a picture, but a memory.

Tentatively, as if any sudden movement would rend the entire palazzo and set it to quaking like his own foundations, he reached out a finger. Touched it, barely, to the scene. Pulled it away and drew back.

The paint was wet.

And the man in the painting . . . was him.

35

THE BOOK OF WATERS

The Essence of Gold

What is loyalty? The stuff of strength, of trust, of impenetrable walls and chosen belonging. What is it but gold itself?

But gold burns, as La Serenissima has seen. One man might enter a city with his navy. Might topple an indefatigable republic. Might ransack her gold and silver, melt it from creations cast long ago with care into shapeless ingots for nameless, faceless transport or transactions, transmuting into something empty of form and full of scheme. One man might, and Napoleon Bonaparte did. Whether for better or for worse, the people's opinions are forever divided.

The Libro d'Oro—the Book of Gold, this keeper of Venezia's noble names—he would burn ceremoniously. Seeing only pomp and the symbol of a flawed society, he saw nothing of the stories it kept. The hearts who beat behind those names.

These, burned, by the hand of a man growing in infamy. A man loyal, at every turn, to his purpose.

What is loyalty, then? Gold itself, or poison set to decay a soul, a republic, a world?

It depends entirely. Upon the holder of it, upon where their heart is set.

311

And therein lies the problem, for who can know the heart of man?

This humble volume may hold secrets, keep answers within its every page, but it cannot begin to know these things. In the room beneath Venezia, there are answers . . . But are answers truly answers if they only beget more questions?

DANIEL

Maddening. Without warning, the book shifted into philosophizing and a chapter too short to be a chapter—all when Sebastien was finally learning something. I clapped its cover shut, eyes bleary.

And yet there was much in these last passages that gave hope. Mention of letters between Sebastien and Mariana. Massimo's maneuverings and dealings. If these were true, would not there be some evidence, somewhere in this city that clung so tightly to its artifacts? But where?

Among all of the libraries, museums, private collections—only one corner of this city held answers.

So, I gathered up a humble pot. The patinaed pieces of the man's pot that had descended and shattered at my feet. I'd taken them, in the night hours, to the refectory and worked in silence with my monk friend, who told me that what I had was not a pile of refuse but a harvest of purpose. There in the hollows of the room that had once held a great piece of art, we worked with our broken pieces.

"Jars of clay," the man had said. "Treasures." He taught me the art of moving the pieces, tesserae, until my bones began to work in harmony with them. To watch the art build before me, gathered from around me, rather than pulled from within me. Until, like the sunrise the monk's mosaic depicted, something broke free inside, and I began to create. Affixing the pieces to a new pot. Filling it with soil and the ivy from our first ill-fated meeting.

The green sprig bent curiously now, bouncing with my steps, as if to ask where we were going. My feet wandered the city until they landed at the doorbell in the lion's mouth, where I reached up and tugged the cord.

Nobody appeared at the window.

"Signore?" I spoke, hopeful. Waiting. "Signore, prego."

A face appeared, expression unreadable. "Ah. Signor Bell. It is you."

"Signor *Train*, actually," I mumbled. He and Vittoria would get along smashingly.

"What's that?"

"Nothing," I said and rushed to add the rest before he disappeared again. "Might I trouble you for just a moment of your time, sir."

He looked ready to protest. "I told you that you have everything you need if you wish to learn that story."

"It's—it's about the letters."

He halted in his retreat.

"Letters," he said. Question, invitation, warning, I wasn't sure which.

"Mariana's letters?"

He hung his head a moment. Gripped the window's edge with both hands, and said at last, "Come."

I did. And found myself in a repeat of the time I'd been here before, clock ticking away as silent moments passed. This time, in a land not entirely foreign. For I knew I was near to the printing press, knew I was near to answers.

I held the pot out to him, wordlessly. Wordlessly, he hesitated, then took it. Thumb stroking over the tesserae, finger lifting a leaf of the ivy, as if it was an old friend.

I decided to cut right to the point, not knowing how long he would allow me to linger. Sensing that this was not a man who appreciated drawn out conversation that spoke of little.

"You are . . . Dante," I said, putting my guess into words before I could stop myself and watching for a reaction.

He appraised me, elbows to knees, hands pressed together in front of him. Spotted in places with ink.

"That may just be the best compliment I've ever been given," he said. "Not that I've received an abundance of those, or had reason to."

Something sank inside. "Not Dante, then."

A small shake of the head.

"But Dante is real," I countered. "They're all real?"

Another measured pause, and then he stood. "See for yourself," he said, crossing the small room to a painting I had not noticed before. It was like many of the oil paintings I'd seen of various Venetian moments, where the subjects were painted in candid fashion, unposed. The colors were vibrant in scarlet, azure, and emerald, with revelers milling about a room in full carnivale costume. Some in traditional black bauta, others in the long-beaked plague doctor mask, and yet more in various colorful masks adorned in jewels and paint, a menagerie of color.

There, in the upper left of the small canvas, was a woman in blues of every hue, bringing a sense of calm to her corner. Golden hair tumbling in waves. Many of the revelers turned to face her, and she, hand to mask, looked only toward one man. His back to the painter's perspective, red cape hanging, a man ready to spring into action and run with abandon toward her—but waiting. In the corner, a signature scribbled illegibly but for the *D* at the beginning.

"It's her," I said, shaking my head. "It seems so—"

"Surreal?" the man said, transfixed, though his eyes traversed the painting with great familiarity over its landscape. "*She* was surreal. And yet the realest thing I ever knew."

I turned to face him. If he was not Dante . . .

"You're him," I offered.

His silence, answer enough.

"I spent a long time trying to figure out who I was." He pulled in a breath and looked me straight in the eye, no longer a nameless man in a flat.

So many questions pounded to get out. But as I sorted through them and tried to discern which to ask, he beat me to it.

"Your book," he said. "May I?" I handed him my Book of Waters and watched him flip through it, pausing at a wood-block illustration of Mariana at the glassblower's workshop, surrounded by adoring children.

"Pietro's edition," he said. "I did wonder how you came to be in possession of this."

"It . . . is my mother's." I gave him the short answer. "It belonged to her father before her, and his father before him."

Something changed in the man, then, his gaze snapping to my face as if searching my features for something. And—in a flicker of light in his eyes—finding it.

"Yes," he said. "I can see that." He shook with a slow chuckle. "Pietro's little Mary," he said. "No?"

I stammered at the mention of my mother's grandfather. "Y-you know of my mother?"

He laughed, and it resounded with fondness and memories. "Indeed. She was always bringing me treats, even as a small thing. I knew her namesake well, too," he said, lifting his brows. "Very well."

My mother's namesake. He couldn't mean . . .

But his expression said that he very much meant just who I was thinking of.

I sputtered words as if they could summon me from my stupor. "I—meant to inquire about Mariana's letters," I said. "The book mentions that she and Sebastien—" My mind caught up with my tongue. "That you and she—" And my mind caught up with itself, now, face burning as I realized I was making reference to what were very likely his own love letters. Or what I presumed would be love letters.

I gulped. "More to the point, I thought perhaps they, or Massimo's ledgers—some other artifacts might still be about and might help in my understanding of things. That is . . . unless you wouldn't mind answering some questions."

A finger tapped his knee as he thought. "Mariana . . . I am sure you sense it from the tale. Magic surrounds her. And she had a very grand, if quiet, sense of adventure. There came a time when there were those who wished to silence, to forget—to make others forget—all that happened. And for a time, it became a war of wits. Me, hiding a story too dear to lose. Him, hiding things he did not wish discovered. Mariana, certain that it would be told someday and that it would mean something . . . to somebody."

He looked me full in the face, as if I were the fulfillment of a long-held hope, eyes crinkling at the corners. I had the urge to stand still and hide much of myself, my past.

"I might not be the best person." I hung my head, admitting what he could surely see.

His forehead lifted, a glimmer in his eye now. "Then perhaps you are just the right person," he said. He returned the book to my hands and patted it against my chest. "You'll find what you need. I won't rob you of that by telling too much now."

He led the way to the door, and my heart sank. But then, at the last minute, he turned with an air of distant hope. "But if— *when*—you find those letters . . . well, you've already brought me the impossible bell. A few pieces of paper should be no difficult task. You'll bring them when you find them?"

I nodded numbly.

"Signore," I said, pausing in the stairwell. "Why isn't the book finished?"

He lingered at his aged door, fingers running over wood made smooth with time and wind and wear.

"When it was written . . . I suppose I—all of us—needed the reminder that the story is not over yet." He lifted his head and looked to me. "A reminder perhaps you could use a dose of too?" And with that, he closed the door. I descended the stairs back out into the calli, hounded by the sense that I was even further entrenched in this living riddle than when I'd arrived.

"Great-grandson of Pietro," a voice said above me, and I turned to see a scrap of paper floating down in a spiral. "That should help."

I caught it, opened it, and read his shaky, loopy script.

Do not neglect the shadows.

The next morning, I worked the translation beneath a cypress tree at the back of the San Giorgio, vespers sounding within. Pages and pages I'd translated—and I yet the answers seemed, in some ways, further than ever.

What had Sebastien said to me at that first encounter?

"You have everything you need on those covers if you are the person to receive this story. You will see."

But I didn't see. Not anywhere in these covers.

So that could only mean I was not the person to receive this story.

But it gripped me. Holding, it seemed, answers not just to the people it spoke of, but to something within myself too.

I rubbed my eyes and set down my pen, thumbing through the pages. The cover was classic and fine, with letters gilded and adornments swirling about. Inside, the end papers were marbled in true Venetian fashion. *Carta marmorizzata,* they called it, and wasn't it the very epitome of Venice? To take the forgotten places—even the humble end papers of a book, which so many would just flip past—and create in them works of stunning art.

I traced the curves of the marbled pattern behind the front cover. Whoever had marbled it had chosen hue after hue of blue, turquoise, and green, as if the lagoon had skipped onto the page and nestled there, petrified to please the eye of the reader. The forms took on the *conchiglia* pattern, resembling the shell's coiling form.

I flipped past the soft pages, my eyes throbbing still, and landed at the back end page. The same blue pigments greeted me, and as I traced their form to let my mind wander, something pricked my awareness.

The curves of this marbling . . . were so strange. Where on its counterpart at the front of the book, they swooped and dipped in a pattern that repeated in the enticing charm of slight imperfection that showed its handmade nature, this one was different. Instead of repeated shell formations in the blue marbling, one of the "shells" appeared to unravel, descending the page in a curving meander, almost *S*-like as it hid itself among the marbling.

Tucking the book under my arm, I set to walking. My mind

always fared better when my feet were in motion. Back in my cell at prison, they called me the gravedigger. Said I was like to wear trenches in the ground with the way I walked that cell—and wear myself to an early death doing it. *"At least your grave'll be ready,"* the guard had said with a laugh. I'd kept on walking.

And I kept walking now, farther down San Giorgio, where a low-walled garden played host to the fishermen's children who chattered and jumped about.

I wondered what it would be like to be a man who returned home from hard work to a passel of young ones wrapping arms around his legs in eager welcome. It was a vision I'd long since given up, for who would want a criminal for a husband, let alone a father?

I sat on the wall's edge, warding off the old dark dread of those thoughts and working to find purpose.

"Oi, signore!" a young boy hollered, and just as he did, an odd wooden pin flew past my ear so close I could hear the roots of the tree it had come from bemoan its airborne state.

The pin climbed higher and higher and collided with the branches of an obliging tree, disrupting its flight and sparing the sun-sparked windows of the island.

"Oi, signore?" The boy's eyes pleaded, his meaning clear. I strode to the tree and reached for the pin, a part of a street game they had been playing involving the tossing and colliding, midair, of these wooden pins. It made sense that their games would vault up, and not out. Much as their buildings grew upward, where villas on the mainland sprawled outward. Out of her shortage of space, Venice made a practice of reaching for the sun.

My fingers brushed the pin, but I couldn't dislodge it. I hoisted myself up into the tree, planting a knee just high enough to vault my reach and grasp the pin. I lingered a moment there, taking it all in. There, across the Giudecca, was the Salute. And beyond that, the Grand Canal began its serpentine journey past St. Mark's Square, where I knew it would wind, *S*-like, past palazzos, beneath the Rialto Bridge, until finally it reached its end at the train station.

S-like.

I jolted. The branches shook in response.

"Signore?" The boy tilted his head of dark curls. "Are you all right? Are you going to fall out?" He looked ready to duck for cover.

"It's an *S*," I said under my breath. I jumped down, startling the boy twice over when I flipped the book open to the back end paper and pointed. "It's an *S!*"

He scrunched his face up and reached slowly for the wooden pin while pursing his lips, sheepish. As if keeping something from me.

"What is it?" I asked, unable to keep my grin back.

"The *S*, signore," he said. He pointed at the book I still held open. "It is not a very good one."

I flipped the book toward myself and examined it. "Why do you say that?"

"It is backward." He shrugged.

All the better.

"Thank you!" I said. "Grazie!" I clapped him gently on the back, tucked the book under my arm, and set out at a run.

"Don't run, signore!"

An hour later, I burst clumsily into the bookshop.

I nearly burst out upon arrival with *It's an S!*, but caught sight of Vittoria bundling a pile of books into brown paper for an elderly woman and I clamped my mouth shut.

As soon as the woman was gone, Vittoria tipped her head and said, "Let me fetch a bucket." She gave a decisive nod and made for a closeted panel of the oak walls.

"What for?" I asked.

"For when you explode," she said. "You look quite ready to, and I'll need to fetch water from the rio to douse the fire that will ensue and save the books. And you, I suppose."

I laughed, then held the book up, drumming my fingers on it. "Do you want to know?"

Her hesitation lasted all of two seconds before she broke into a conspiratorial grin and led me to a desk near the window overlooking the rio that was to be my salvation in the event of an explosion.

"Here," I said, showing her the front end papers, the repeated shell pattern.

"It's beautiful," she said. "I haven't seen one in quite such vivid color for a very long time." She was trying to be patient.

"And here." I flipped to the back, displaying the counterpart. "Notice anything?"

She took it up, holding it close. "A disruption to the pattern? But . . ." She shook her head, not understanding. I couldn't blame her. It had taken me climbing a tree to perceive it. I unfolded my worn map of Venice from my pocket and lay it on the desk, pointing to it and then to the marbled end paper. Waited. Watched.

She studied one, shifted her eyes to the other, narrowed her gaze, and repeated the process two or three times—and then that wide, overtaking smile broke across her being.

"La Serenissima," she said, wonder in her voice.

"You see it too! I'm not crazy, then."

"I said nothing of your sanity, Daniel Goodman. As to the paper . . . sì. It can only be Venezia," she said. "The Grand Canal—"

"—in its backward S," I completed her thought.

She tilted the book, allowing the paper to catch the light. "Some of the lines . . . Look. They shine."

I leaned in, noticing the metallic glint to a few of the curves and lines. I tapped a finger on one crossing the Grand Canal about halfway through its middle curve. "This would be . . . the Rialto, no?"

She laughed at my phrasing. "You are sounding more Venetian every day. Yes, that would be the Rialto Bridge. And here . . ." She turned the book until it caught another glint. "One of the palazzi just near it. Ca'Barbaro, perhaps? Or no—that looks more like Ca'Fedele." She shook her head. "It's difficult to say precisely." She clapped the book closed, and I flinched. "Shall we find out?"

I cleared my throat, hoping she meant what I thought she did. "Now?"

"Of course! Come, Daniele. The shop is due to close for *riposo*."

"But it's only"—I checked my pocket watch—"eleven o'clock." No one would be napping this early in the day.

"La Marangona is sleeping, remember? We can make of time what we wish of it."

We made our way by foot and *traghetto* this time, leaving the Book Boat behind and taking with us only one volume: the one that was beginning to write itself into my thoughts. On the way, I filled Vittoria in on the latest installments, an odd stillness filling the air around us beneath an ominous sky.

"The room beneath Venice?" she asked.

"That's what the book said."

"But Venice isn't on earth. How could there be a room beneath it?" She glanced slyly at me. "I have read your Mr. Poe, and I know his affinity for hidden rooms wherein to wall unsuspecting victims. We have more than our share of harrowing tales here, but I assure you, there are no rooms beneath Venice. It isn't possible! There is one crypt. One! And it is always flooded."

"Right." The water beneath us sang as the boat parted it. "The writer . . . He speaks in veiled ways at times."

Vittoria considered this. "A room beneath Venice," she said again.

I nodded. "And a palazzo disguised in a hidden map."

We disembarked across the Rialto from the palazzo and turned to face it. There it was, in all its nuance and stories. The two houses joined into one, the rooftop where two souls had joined forever. And now?

I had seen it when sketching, in that dizzying scribble of clutching for feeling, melding it with shape and form. The house felt so—alone. Solitary and empty, and it wasn't just the fact that when I looked up, I half-expected to see a young Sebastien beside Mariana, and saw instead only pigeons perched atop a row of small windows.

Just as before, something about the house's form sat oddly. Beautiful, but incongruous somehow. It turned inside, this feeling of the house asking to be studied, to be understood—for its secrets to be seen. As if it were an unfinished equation, its lines not entirely . . .

"Perspective." The word burst forth.

Vittoria's head tilted, questioning.

"What was it you said about the windows? The way they use taller windows on the lower levels and smaller at the top. To make it seem larger, yes?"

She nodded.

"And—the columns and adornments. Not just ornamental but designed to make the building lighter?"

"You are a very good listener, Daniel!" She said it with pride.

"But what does this have to do with—"

"This is one of the shorter palazzos," I said, gesturing around to demonstrate. I studied the house before us, its rippling reflection in the waters as boats sliced through it, scurrying home as the grey clouds billowed above. "And yet it has possibly the most windows and cutaway adornments of all. Almost as if . . ." I shook my head. "Is it possible there could be a sunken level? Even partially?"

"It wouldn't make the most sense, but you never know what secrets this city holds. There is only one way to find out," Vittoria said, and led the way.

We drew close and passed a weathered dock that slumped at one corner down into the water. The building itself, now that we were close, was imposing in its grandeur but slightly leaning, and in that, it seemed a friend, somehow.

We crossed the short walk that led to the ornate entrance. It was empty, according to Jacopo, but we knocked a lion's-head knocker and waited.

Vittoria, incorrigible Garbin that she was, gripped the handle and tried it.

"We can't just go in," I said. "Can we?"

"You are right," she said, shoulders slumping.

"Maybe the water entrance?" I suggested, recalling Sebastien's ill-fated mix-up between the two doors.

I had little hope of anyone answering our knock there, but we tried. Waited to no avail, turned to go—only to hear the slow creak of the door open behind us.

An elderly man in the garb of a majordomo appraised us, bored eyes barely managing to raise unimpressed eyebrows. "Yes?" Unceremonious and tired, as if he had fulfilled his quota for pomp-filled greetings decades ago. "To what do we owe this"—his eyes traveled our forms again, as if to confirm his suspicion that we were as exciting as the mollusks on the bottom of the lagoon—"pleasure."

Vittoria broke into cheerful chatter in Venetian, explaining that we had some interest in the house's history and "might we inquire within?"

"The family is not in country at present," he said. "Good-bye."

"Sir—signore—"

Desperate to save this chance to walk the paths of Massimo, Sebastien, and Mariana, I spoke before I had a plan. I recalled Vittoria's words from our book-delivering escapades. *"Don't suggest. Don't ask permission. Lay out the options . . . and invite them in."*

"I . . . wonder if we might procure your opinion on something . . . intriguing we've discovered. We've found what we believe to be a map, and—well, there is some question as to the identity of this building." I opened the book and pointed to the metallic-inked position of the palazzo.

A moment of staid perusal, and then something akin to a spark—or at least the puff of smoke that precedes a spark—lifted the man's countenance.

"There is no question," he said, spreading his shoulders in authority. "It is Ca'Fedele. Or *was*, rather. They plan to rename it, seeing as . . . well. Unfortunate legacy and all."

Vittoria gripped the man's hand in her excitement. He startled, noticing her for the first time as not a mollusk but a keeper of delight. The corner of his mouth pulled up, almost imperceptibly, for less than a moment.

"You believe we've found the right house, signore?" she asked, her warmth encompassing him with that sense of belonging she seemed to spin around everyone she met. I watched it work its magic—the most enchanting part being that it was not a ploy, not an act to gain access, but something so sincere in her that she didn't even realize the effect she had on people.

"We hoped it might be, but—we have questions about the history and wondered if we might look around. Family books, paintings . . . that sort of thing?" She trailed off, the hope dancing in her eyes undoing the man's aloofness to such a degree that he admitted us and led the way.

Everything was shrouded, layered in dust, smelling of damp musk, with the occasional evidence of bird or rodent. "Likely you'll only find anything of use in the map room," he said. "An office of sorts."

He warned us that there was not much to see, that the previous residents had purged nearly all personal belongings from the premises before the sale. He hesitated, a flicker of recollection crossing his face. "The ledgers that I was tasked with boxing up, when my employer procured this house . . . one of them listed someone who was keeper of certain documents. Someone by the name of . . . no, it was two names." He furrowed his brows. "Cristoforo and Michele. Perhaps you might try them next. Not much left to see here, I'm afraid."

He left us.

I studied the sparse contents of the richly carved desk: a set of weights and measures, piled upon one end of an uneven brass scale. Upon the desk, a layer of dust coated aged woodgrain, and in the corner, a stain settled into the worn varnish, as if someone had spilled dark paint or ink.

I turned to face Vittoria and found her gaze fixed up at the ceiling. Not an uncommon posture in Venice, I had found, where the walls and ceilings were canvasses—but something in her face made me follow suit.

The ceiling was entirely covered in an aged map of the entire lagoon. On the walls were framed many maps, from throughout Venice's history, showing the progression of cartography and the shifting topography of the lagoon and its isles over the years.

"The room beneath Venice," she said, holding a palm toward the ceiling.

I took in the circular place and its odd, low ceiling. It was a very strange sensation to have the map above me, the ceiling so low, and with my head nearly touching this upside-down world in all its ink and flecks of gold. She was right—we were, quite literally, below Venice.

I opened the book to the marbled map, and we began to survey the maps, looking for anything striking that might give us a clue.

We referenced and cross-referenced, noting the shifting positions and shapes and even names of some of the lagoon isles over time, even the melding of two islands into one when the rio between was filled to make more room on the cemetery isle. But nothing leapt out as something that might hold a clue.

I slumped against the wall, eyes settling on a painting that felt somewhat out of place here in this room of maps: a small, illuminated painting of the scene of Calvary. In it, one of the thieves hung his head in shame and the other turned his face toward that middle cross with something akin to desperate wonder on his expression.

It drew me, the painting. I was not drawn to religious scenes, had excluded myself from that world long ago. But something about this one . . .

Unbidden, my finger reached up and traced the image of the man's hand, there upon the cross. He was paying restitution for something he had done and yet his eyes were not on the device of atonement.

They were on the man beside him.

The distant echo of my shackles seemed hollow, so hollow, as it sounded in response.

"He is one of my favorites," Vittoria said, and I turned to face her.

"The painter?" I spoke past the thickness in my throat.

"The thief."

I shook my head, the expression of miraculous incredulity on the man's face opening up a hidden place inside me. "W-why?"

"I think, in many ways, he is all of us."

"You're no thief." I faced her. We were treading on shaky ground.

Ground that felt ready to give way beneath me at any moment and swallow me whole.

"Perhaps not in so many words. But we are none of us able to atone for our own wrongdoings. And yet do we not all ache to belong? To be new?"

It didn't make sense. But there was a deep shifting of something foundational happening inside of me, and I was rattled to the core.

"I can't say that I understand fully," I admitted.

"It is . . ." She pressed her eyes closed, and I wondered what she saw. Yearned to see it, too, as her lips pursed and her shoulders rose. "Venice," she blurted at last, eyes flying open.

I tried to follow her thought, hopping Vittoria-like and yet seeming to have leapt too far for me to follow.

"Venice?"

"She glitters, does she not? She is—*striking*, bejeweled with her gold and her frescoes and mosaics, and yet all of it is so simple at her very heart."

I waited, knowing more was coming.

"Underneath, Daniel. What is she built on? What, but wood. Simple and rough and ancient." Her shoulders rose and fell as she caught her breath. Gesturing lightly at the painting. "So it is with him, no? For all of His shining depictions around this city . . . for all of the gleaming places of worship . . . what is it all built on beneath these islands but wood? Simple. Rough. Ancient. This city breathes His story from her very roots. The pictures—they are filled with heart and soul and tradition. But what they stand upon—the truth of it all—dwells beneath us. So very much deeper."

The cross in the painting seemed so real, I could almost feel its splinters and dips, the rugged strength of it. *Deeper.*

There was that word again. I pressed my eyes closed, pondering. When I opened them, there was the map—and there, tucked out beyond Burano, nearly invisible in the way the gilded flecks shimmered about it like undercurrents, was something that looked out of place. I drew close, examining it. The same turquoise paint that had marbled a page of the book into a map outlined it—and it alone—here on this map.

A small island. Inconsequential, without even a name. It was not even on any of the other maps.

"Perhaps it was swept asunder," Vittoria said. "It has happened to many a marshy isle."

"But look." I held the marbled page open, and—there it was. With the turquoise hues waving around it in almost identical fashion to what was shown above. "Where would that be?"

She took the book and searched her memory. She glanced at me with brows raised, as if she had lit upon the answer and was waiting for me to catch up.

My knowledge of the lagoon was limited to my travel book, and to the woman on the train who had pointed out a few by name. *San Segundo . . . Isola Campalto . . . Malodetto.*

The doomed isle. The one she had quickly changed the subject from.

"This is Elena and Sebastien's island," I said, the pieces lining up. "Sebastien said the book would contain everything we needed. I see no other Book of Waters here . . . and if the house was sold, if Sebastien was intent on keeping the story out of certain hands, it wouldn't be here. But perhaps it is on the island?"

Vittoria nodded, grasping my hand and making to drag me out promptly.

But glancing back at the room, I was struck again by the sense of something not adding up. "The ceiling here . . . does it feel short, to you?"

A quick peek out into the hall we had entered from showed the ceiling was at the same level.

"The floor, then. We stepped up to come into this room. But this is the bottom level. Which means . . ."

"There is something underneath this room."

The realization came none too soon, for the majordomo was returning to usher us out just then.

"It has to be the hidden room behind the fireplace," I said.

"But the letters, the book—neither would be there, would they?" Vittoria said. "Not in Massimo's own house."

"I don't know," I said. "I don't know if he even knew—knows?

328

About the room." I paused, sheepish. "I confess, I would like to have seen it, all the same. Wouldn't you?"

"Daniel Goodman, look at you and your spark for the mysterious! We will return. There will be time! But now, if you are to complete your work, shall we go to the island?"

37

THE BOOK OF WATERS

Heart of Venice

A painting in a hidden room.

Was this . . . the answer to Sebastien Trovato's questions? If so, it was both a gift and a maddening force all at once, for it birthed new questions.

Whose was the hand who had painted this?

Whose was the hand who had set his basket afloat on the canal?

And above all . . . Why?

He had no answer. No basket, for it was back on the island. In fact, the only token he held of his own story was the grotesque coin that had been discovered with him, the one depicting a skeleton and words that had felt to him always a threat. As if some unseen foe was at hand, watching his every move, ready pounce at any misstep . . .

Remember your mortality.

The room became a pulsing presence in the days that followed. Seeming to whisper to Sebastien at night as he lay in his small bedroom. Seeming to pull Mariana, too, whom he found again in the room the next day, and the day after that.

But for all their searching, positing, figuring, none of the pieces would fit together in a tidy story.

Mariana did not mention what she had alluded to—that Sebastien had more to learn—and he did not press it. Something weighed upon her, and it wasn't any wonder. For she had refused her brother's chosen betrothed, and Massimo had made no secret of his displeasure. He had attempted to persuade, to guilt, to flatter her until he, too, began to walk like a ghost of a person about the palazzo.

Until one day . . . the pieces began to click together in the most disastrous of ways.

Sebastien came upon Mariana in the room of the simple blue ceiling—that antechamber to the secret room—and found her asleep. She lay upon a sofa before the fireplace, a book folded open upon her stomach. It was odd—the fireplace stood open, revealing the secret room. As if she had been investigating and forgotten to close it.

Mariana was as meticulous as she was thoughtful. Concern pulled him close and as he approached, he jostled a small table, knocking another book to the floor.

He winced, immediately apologizing—for there was no possibility of anybody sleeping through that.

But she did.

Deep concern tumbled through him. "Mariana?" he spoke softly, drawing near and crouching. Laying a hand upon her shoulder when she still did not respond. "Mariana." He moved his hand to her cheek and his chest pounded. It was so cold.

She breathed, but barely. He moved to scoop her up, carry her to safety, but where would that be? Another couch? A bed? What good would it do?

He burst into the corridor, hollering for help. Making for the boathouse to go for a doctor.

"What is it?" Massimo ran down the stairs, an urgent look on his face. It was not the expression of panicked ignorance. Sebastien's jaw clenched when he saw. It was the look of someone who already knew the answer. "Where is Mariana?" Bursting past Sebastien and into the room, he faltered when he saw the open fireplace.

Sebastien winced. Why had he not closed it? There had been

no thought to it—every thought was for Mariana. He watched for ire upon Massimo's face at seeing that his secret room had been discovered but saw instead complete befuddlement. Massimo . . . had not known of it? But there was not time for any of this now.

Sebastien pointed to where Mariana lay. "I'll go for the doctor," he said, shoulders heaving.

Massimo shook his head. "Angelo!" he bellowed.

Somewhere above, a voice responded with steadiness and hurried efficiency. "I'm going."

And that was when Sebastien knew—this was a well-rehearsed contingency.

Massimo knelt, listening to Mariana's breath, pulling her hair back from underneath her neck. Elevating her head.

"So soon," he murmured.

"What?" Sebastien asked, breathless. He had no right to inquire, in the eyes of Massimo, but his heart would not hear it. "What is it?" Desperation, growing.

Massimo shook his head, looking grave. Behind Sebastien, another man entered, and vague recognition struck. This was the man who came later in the day on Wednesdays to Mariana's apartments. Sebastien had presumed him another suitor, but here and now the man walked with the swift practice of a doctor, bag in hand, kneeling at Mariana's side.

"How long has she been like this?" the doctor asked.

Massimo looked to Sebastien, urgency in his eyes.

"I—found her like this minutes ago," Sebastien said.

The doctor listened to her heart through a funnel-shaped tool, and Sebastien tried to read his face. *Tell me.* He begged that face silently. *Tell me, please.*

But the medical man gave no indication, other than to say to Massimo, sorrow in his voice, "Not long now."

That could not mean what it appeared to. It couldn't.

Massimo closed his eyes, exhaling slowly through his nose. Nodding.

For the first time, Mariana stirred, and whispered something.

"The islands," she said.

"Delusions," Massimo said in answer to the doctor's questioning look.

Sebastien stepped forward. Realizing fully he had no right. Realizing fully that there would be none to stop him. "She speaks of the lagoon isles," he said quietly.

At this, a soft smile alighted on Mariana's lips.

The doctor drew his brow down, studying. "This is good," he said. "She may rally again. She has done so before. Stay, if you can, and tell her of these islands. I will check her again soon."

He left, and Massimo began to pace.

"Where is he going?" Sebastien asked, panic rising. "Shouldn't he stay? If something is wrong—"

"To his rooms, I expect. He is staying. He has been here for some time."

Which told a story all on its own.

"What is it?" Sebastien asked, the ache in his voice tearing it into a gruff tone. "Please."

Massimo fixed his eyes on his sister, somber. "Her heart." He said it distantly. "She . . . has always been afflicted. We knew it was growing worse, but have been hoping for more time. . . ." Massimo's voice cracked, fingers tunneling into his hair as he strode out of the room, leaving Sebastien with Mariana.

He knelt beside her, taking her hand in his. Weaving their fingers together.

All that time on the island, he had thought she'd been affected solely by the storm, recovering from whatever injuries and elements she had faced. But looking at her now, he knew they had been through this together before.

It sobered him. But it also sparked impossible hope in him. For he had seen what sun and air and friendship and adventure had done for her.

It could happen again.

It must.

38

THE BOOK OF WATERS
A Change in Plans

The chess player, that devoted brother and scheme leader, knew it as well as anyone: The queen was the most powerful player upon the board. She, upon whom everything rested—the future of the game, the resurrection of the republic, the happiness and comfort of any years that the queen herself had left.

But the chess player had not foreseen this. That in a scheme created to build a home for her heart . . . her heart would choose just then to fail. That in this same scheme, her intended—that wealthy giver of the bride token—would learn of her numbered days and conveniently withdraw any interest in being connected with the illustrious—and quickly crumbling—House of Fedele.

It grieved Massimo for a great many reasons . . . and for her too. Mariana was a jewel. Massimo had always known this, from the moment she was born. When he had been long since written off, labeled a failure by The Eleven, shuffled into shadows to watch as his parents grew older, buried three stillborn children, buried hopes along with them . . . and then held in their arms, at last, a baby.

Mariana. Everything good and right. Born unto loss, as her parents were taken in plague, like so many others.

And so it was Massimo's arms that held her. He, a young man by then. A man of ideals and vision, who pledged to her that things would be made right. The world would be better. He would see to it—and his heart ached with the longing for it.

And when he learned in her girlhood that the fates would take her too soon—how that longing beat unto bursting in his chest. How was this allowed? The injustice of the best soul in all the world beset with such a condition?

How he railed against it. How he paced the turrets of that alpine estate, how he wore trenches into the gardens of the family land on Terra Firma, where he dropped to his knees and rended the heavens with his grief, his questions . . . his pain.

But he could, and would, make the loss of her life mean something.

He took on the responsibility of his family's legacy, and of her upbringing, and of the knowledge that their coffers were well and truly empty, and that this—this moment—was the last chance Venice had of recovering any semblance of her former glory. . . .

He saw it.

His sister, the prized jewel.

His duty to secure for her a good marriage.

Her dowry, Ca' Fedele—a prize he would willingly forfeit, if it meant hope.

An aged husband, who would agree to a bride token and leave for her a greater inheritance still.

Family coffers, filled. Hope for the republic, restored. An uprising, with a foundation rich enough to stand upon and succeed.

If she must leave—his tragic, beautiful, beloved sister—if he could not control this wretchedness, he would control a revolution. And because of her, Venice would live on in restored glory, to honor her. He would lead Venezia back into independence. To give such a future to Mariana's own children, should she be blessed with them.

But now . . . it was all falling to pieces.

The baby of long ago, Sebastien, his would-be usurper in another life, was back. Grown and able. Discovering hidden rooms even Massimo had not known about, in the house that was—at least in part—Sebastien's. Neither Massimo nor Sebastien spoke of the fresh painting within the room— perhaps because they did not have answers, or perhaps because each suspected the other of being somehow responsible.

It seemed wise, then, to keep his enemy close, even if the man did not know himself to be enemy.

It seemed far more than wise now.

For perhaps there was a man who would marry Mariana. Perhaps he would discover that half of this house was rightfully his. Perhaps Massimo would be the hero to tell him so, to bless the union.

He saw how the man watched his sister. If any man would marry her now, it would be him. Perhaps he would not fill the Fedele coffers, but he would claim his own inheritance—the second half of their palazzo, the portion Mariana now dwelled in. And if some unfortunate fate were to befall Sebastien . . . why, the joined palazzos would be Massimo's. Ready to sell, if that's what it took to move forward from here.

And so, Massimo began to arrange moments for the two to be together. Asking Sebastien to be Mariana's reader as she rested. Her rower on the days she was strong enough to take in a gentle venture into the quieter rios, where the sun did her good.

When the pair of them approached him one evening, hand-in-hand, as Mariana held her chin high and Sebastien squared his shoulders protectively and told him of their plans to wed—they held their breath. And he let them, longer than he should have, before standing. Breaking his stoic face, at last, into a wide and benevolent smile and making himself the first to bless their union . . . and bless the return of the long-lost son of the House of Mendeli.

Mariana wished to be wed at the Lido, with the bounding sea before them. However, she was not strong enough for the voyage, and the doctor would not agree to it no matter how gently Sebastien promised to transport her.

And so, with the help of friends who loved Mariana well, they moved heaven and earth—or rather, lagoon and sea—to bring the Lido to her. The "marriage to the sea" procession of old, but in reverse.

Valentina, joints aching, orchestrated a warm soak for her hands for precisely twenty minutes and no more to prepare them for the work ahead. She pulled them out of their bowl, wiggled them into the air, and retrieved the Miracle Keeper, stitching an edging to the garment through the sunset and through the night, tying it up in its airy-thin paper with a spooling ribbon and tucking it beneath her arm.

"Your veil, cara mia," she said when she walked, shoulders hunched and eyes sparking with a shared secret, into the blue room of the palazzo.

"Valentina," Mariana breathed. "I could never—"

"Hush," Valentina clucked and set to fluttering the webbed masterpiece over Mariana's shining hair. "You are the sunrise itself, my darling. It was made for you! Even before I knew it, the Almighty did."

Elena arrived with a certain basket filled with flowers—bright ones for a bouquet, a crown of white oleander to rest atop the veil.

Mariana wore her embroidered white frock from her time upon the isle, declining the satins and silks that Francesca, frustrated to no end, paraded before her.

Giuseppe arrived at Ca'Fedele, pounding his thick fist on the grand entrance without ceremony and not caring a whit that "the likes of him" used the water entrance. "It's for the lady," he said, and strode into the house, brooking no further argument. Beneath his arm he carried a water-stained post, snapped from the lagoon and topped with a once-empty altar, her lantern resting inside.

Pietro, trailed by his jubilant children and grandchildren and jubilant dog and the dog's jubilant tail and his own sun-kissed wife, brought afresh the fires of Murano in another lantern, from which they lit every candle upon the rooftop.

And where, in all of this, was the groom? On the island that had captured his bride's heart. Corralling a certain rogue hen into a stick-built cage. She had led Sebastien to Mariana to begin with, after all. She must be there to witness their vows. It would delight Mariana, and he would cross the world a thousand times over to give her delight.

Dante, in keeping with his arrival at Sebastien's very first homecoming as a baby, was late. But when he came, he kept to the edges of the roof, making himself inconspicuous so as not to interrupt the procession. His reason for the tardiness sounded from below, where a solitary violinist played from the gondola. Vivaldi, just as the pair had first danced to.

This time, their dance looked different. Sebastien, descending the stairs, stooping to lift her from where she used all her strength to rise. He carried her in his arms, safe against his heart, step upon step to the moonlit sky, where he set her feet upon the rooftop garden.

In a whisper, the small gathering turned to behold her. Illuminated and radiant with joy. The music played on, but it was that joy bubbling up into a disbelieving laugh that filled the place with music.

"Is this truly happening?" she whispered.

Sebastien set her down tenderly and took her hand. Laced his fingers into hers and answered her low. "Forever. If you're certain you wish to join yourself to a fishmonger who uses the wrong door and never has quite the right words to say."

She laced her fingers tighter, her answer in her grip.

They crossed the roof of the house that had long ago joined their families, to once and forever join their hearts.

Past the proud Massimo, the handkerchief-clutching Valentina, the beaming Elena, the blubbering Giuseppe, and Pietro's passel of grinning beings, to the altar where they spoke their promises, wed beneath the watch of the promised moon.

They quietly forewent the traditional smashing of a glass vase that would predict, by its pieces, the number of happy years the couple would be blessed with. Instead, a vase, shaped by Pietro, was set upon a table, where each person deposited a flower within. Each of them knowing there would be no talk of future years . . . and each of them desiring to show the fullness of life they wished for the couple and the fullness of life the couple had given them.

By Mariana's request, the fare served was solitary and simple: the familiar golden-brown pandoro of Christmases past, lines of Swiss chocolate adorning it like small rivers wending from their Alpen homeland, along with sweet memories of snowball tosses and window drawings.

In all of the escapades and monumental events the red-tiled

rooftops had witnessed over the years—from Casanova and his famed escape to Galileo and his telescope—the union of Sebastien and Mariana Trovato seemed to rise above them all and hold the city spellbound.

Only Massimo Fedele left the ceremony as a troubled man, tormented by what lay ahead in the weeks and months to come.

THE BOOK OF WATERS

Born a Ghost

Sebastien Trovato.

Who was he?

Orphan son of a patrician family, according to Massimo. He couldn't believe it.

Born into a role that was extinguished before he took his first breath: Once and Future Doge. He was, all his life, a living ghost. A man dwelling in a role that he knew nothing of, and which did not exist.

Who was he?

Husband to Mariana Trovato. This, he knew. This, he loved . . .

Mariana did rally. Not entirely, and he was fully aware that it would only be a matter of time. But time was precisely what they had, whether one moment or one thousand, and he would cherish her for all of it.

It was strange, this living of a life he would have had.

He had stood in the great chamber of the Doge's Palace and tried to imagine what it must have been like there, the night of the abdication. What had it felt like to those who held Venice dear? He could almost feel the defeat. Grief, heavy in the air . . . He could see it floating to the ground to be trampled, along with the white papers and bits of dust and ash.

This was what he had been born into. Born out of.

So why, with these answers, did The Question still plague him? He quieted it whenever it came. Who was he? *I am husband to Mariana. Friend to Mariana.* She was what mattered, each and every numbered day.

They walked the palazzo together, sat in the sun on the terrace, spoke of the island together. What he wished, more than anything, was to get her away from here and back to the land of her heart. But she was not strong enough yet.

One day, they strolled through a part of the house Sebastien had never had cause to enter in his days as boatman. It was a gallery of sorts, a collection of paintings, artifacts, busts, statues. A knight's armor. This would be the place for Pietro's scepter—here on display in this museum-in-miniature. Not stored in his attic room, gathering dust. He would inquire about placing it here. Or—was this his home? Did he need to inquire at all?

In the center of the hall stood an extraordinary pillar, floor to ceiling. Sculpted upon the first half was the figure of a man in marble, his bearded face upturned and his arms raised. From them extended great lengths of marble in silken folds captured in stone, up and away until they reached the ceiling and swirled into constellations above.

A light swish sounded, and he felt her presence beside him.

"Atlas," he said. "I never did envy him, one man holding up the sky."

Mariana took his hand.

"I'd like to know his secrets," Sebastien said. "How can a man come beneath something so much larger than him and lift it for all who follow after?"

Beside Atlas, rising from the parquet floor, was another statue in white stone. This one of a man with flowing beard twisted into motion, face molded into something that landed between desperation and hope. His arms bare, sinew pronounced in strength, yet somehow, in his motionless state, giving the impression of shaking.

Defying an overwhelming weariness brought upon him by the gravitational force of the universe itself and the fate of a battle hinging upon him.

It could only be Moses, the moment when under ruthless siege of the Amalekites, he learned that while his hands were extended upward, the battle waged in favor of the Israelites, the people whose lives he had been chosen to lead, to save, to love.

For there beside him, just as in the account of Exodus, were Aaron and Hur, gripping his wrists, holding his hands high. They had moved a rock beneath him for rest and gripped him just when he thought he would fail.

Heat pricked Sebastien's eyes. He knew something of this story—what it was to be caught up by those around. To be held up as the world crumbled beneath you, and to be strengthened for the very thing you were made to do . . . all because of the hands of others. Elena. Dante. Pietro. Valentina. Giuseppe. They had gripped him, reared him, pulled him from waters, pulled him up from mire.

He was nothing without them. Would he now leave them? He could not. But would he then subject them to the rule of a man like Massimo? The pieces of the puzzle that was Massimo all pointed to a man bent on claiming Venice. Or reclaiming it, to his view.

Atlas to his left and Moses to his right, he faced one and then the other. One, the story he had always known . . . and one, the story he was fated for.

He felt Mariana's understanding—the rare kind that needed no explanation.

"I . . . don't know what my place is," he said, and could manage no more, his throat closing tight. She met his gaze with unspoken pain, the likes of which were only born of similar suffering. She stepped nearer to the sculpture of Atlas and let her eyes travel upward.

"I once saw a very different sculpture of Atlas in Rome," she said. "The sky looked as a boulder upon his shoulders, and he stooped in so much strain." She lightly brushed the man's face in the sculpture before her, and he could almost imagine the gesture of comfort meant for him. Her hand upon his face. "This one . . . it nearly feels as though the artist turned the tale upside down."

Sebastien blew out his cheeks. "I would like to meet that artist, then," he said. "Perhaps he might have some insight for me."

Mariana smiled, then pulled his hand gently, tugging him to come around to the front of this ethereal Atlas. "The story tells of a man condemned to hold up the sky," she said. "But does it not seem that the heavens are instead coming down? Reaching for him, drawing him up?"

He watched her study it, the hope in her eyes.

"How do you do it?" His words dissipated into the vague echo of the room.

"What?" She turned to face him, letting her hand remain in his.

"See the world that way? So much—hope. When you, of all people . . . have every reason not to."

Her chin dipped, cheeks rose-hued. "May I show you something, Sebastien?"

"Anything."

She led onward into the hall, where several busts stood atop pillars, with rounded arched windows as their backdrops, displaying an ever-changing canvas of the sky over the canal. They passed a likeness of Antonia Vivaldi, another of Marco Polo, several faces he did not know—and then a woman. Face demure, looking down and toward her shoulder, a small smile upon her face. What struck him most was the veil that draped over her head. Carved in marble and yet fluid, so fluid, as it fell in thinnest folds over her delicate features.

And then there was Mariana. Looking at the likeness as if greeting a friend.

"I first saw her many years ago," she said. "I was home from the mountains at last, and Massimo was determined I should 'learn Venice,' as he said. We saw the mosaics of Torcello. The great art of St. Mark's. All of the campo statues. And then we saw her. This sculpture, from the hands of a man called Corradini. Massimo kept going, talking and talking, his voice echoing, and I think he rather liked the sound of that echo. He didn't even realize I wasn't following him, just kept going, and here I was, with this lady." She laughed. "When he finally found me later, he moved mountains to acquire the statue. I insisted I did not need it, but he—well, he doted on me." A flicker crossed her expression, shadowed. "Massimo . . . has his faults. We all do. But whatever they may be, they cannot change his generosity. He has been a good brother."

Sebastien nodded, unsure whether she spoke to convince him or to convince herself.

She shook herself from the thought, focusing again on the statue. "She wears this veil of stone. Stone is heavy, I thought. And yet—see how thin it is? And she looks as if she holds a secret. A joy, though she is for all of time held behind a veil she cannot break through, she has found a way for it to become a part of her." Mariana drew in a shuddering breath. "I can't explain it, what that meant to me. I was . . . not well, and unhappy about many things. Why couldn't I do that, I wondered. Why should a woman of stone look happy, and I, with air to breathe and a heart beating inside, be the one living beneath the weight of stone? There are things in our lives we cannot change. But at that moment, I determined to let them be as a veil, like this woman. Something that perhaps might appear to bind me or separate me from the world—but through which I can see the world in a way others might not be able to."

"Seeing things such as Atlas being held up by the heavens rather than burdened by the weight of the universe," Sebastien said.

She laughed, the sound chiming through the chamber. "I suppose so," she said, and squeezed his hand. "And . . . like you." Serious again, her eyes were disarming in their earnest gaze, wide and true. "There is purpose here, Sebastien. I don't know what it is . . . but I do know that I can never begin to say how thankful I am that, of all the circumstances that brought you from the canal, from the basket, to the islands, to pull me from those waters, to be the man who you are, to be with me here and now . . . I am forever grateful."

Her words followed him through the day and into the night, where they tumbled into sleepless thoughts. *I am forever grateful.*

They met the old question that appeared for its nightly attack. *Who am I?* This, in his voice. *I am forever grateful.* This, in hers. And it began. The unfolding of a notion that the answer to his ceaseless question might lie somewhere more than where he came from. Mariana, whose family consisted of her brother—a man who would not be candid for all the world, who always schemed, who seemed to hold her as a pawn in his grand game. A beloved pawn, but a pawn nonetheless. Did not she, as much as he, deserve to ask that question—*Who am I?*

But she lent her voice to a statement so quiet and yet so full of decisive peace . . . Something in him opened up. Not in envy, but in yearning.

For the first time, the question did not shout, did not clamor like the bells of Saint Mark's, but whispered with an air of hope.

DANIEL

The vaporetto did not run to Malodetto. Vittoria and I could not find a fishing boat to take us either. Someone, somewhere in time, had taken great care to spin harrowing, haunted fables out into the world about the place—this "isle of doom"—and they had done their job in keeping visitors away.

But the entries in the Book of Waters had run out. There were no more clues, and so many maddeningly empty pages. What had happened to Sebastien and Mariana?

The book would not say. Perhaps the island would.

We rowed ourselves on the only vessel we had: the Book Boat. It would have been comical, the two of us digging oars to propel a floating library as fast as it could go, trying to keep our balance. But a sense of urgency and mystery cloaked us, as did the mist of the hovering storm.

It was very strange rowing through snatches of clouds that had descended to sit upon the surface of the water. The very waters that had once carried a baby in a basket, a woman in a storm.

The mist grew in rising tendrils as we passed the cemetery isle of San Michele, passed Murano, Burano, and onward out toward Torcello. Malodetto, overgrown and with an air of resident secrets, grew out of a rugged seawall. A brick-and-stucco arch, bits missing, marked the entrance to the island.

As if we ourselves unleashed it by approaching, the sky began to rain. Soft at first, but soon winds whipped, bent on keeping us away. We rowed harder, needing now to get to shore not just for pursuit of whatever was here, but for shelter too.

We scarcely spoke as we set foot upon the ground that had raised Sebastien and saved Mariana. Past the cottage, now roofless but still friendly with its two eye-like windows. I could almost hear the creak of that door open, welcoming Sebastien home, the smell of fresh bread wafting out.

We continued on until we discovered an overgrown thicket. Crouching down, we followed what looked to be the path of an animal—deer, perhaps?

We came to the other side of the thicket. "Perhaps it's the wrong island after all," I said, surveying the absence of ruins.

Vittoria's shoulders slumped, and she turned, skimming the vines and trees until her face lit. "Or perhaps it is the very right island,"

There, cloaked in a blanket of ivy, was the distinct form of a chair.

We searched until we found another . . . and another . . . and another, until seven chairs, true as life, marked the original gathering place of the Guild.

It was growing darker, the rain coming heavy. It only drove us on as we uncovered an altar covered in colorful mosaic, vestige of a long-ago abbey, before the Remnant had filled the vacant place with their meetings.

A small stream flowed past the wall, cattails growing on one side.

If I could only find what this book was trying to lead us to. The man in the flat did not have the original book—he'd said as much. And he'd said that my book held everything I needed to know. With the map in marbled paper leading us to this place, I felt it—the same old instinct that I'd relied on in so many San Francisco houses: the book was here, somewhere. It had to be.

The sky unleashed with new intensity. Vittoria shivered, teeth chattering, through a brilliant smile.

She would catch her death out here and grin her way through it.

"Please," I said, voice begging her to feel my urgency. The winds felt it, even if she did not, for they whipped around us like eels among coral, frantic and seeking. Rain pounded harder.

"Take shelter, Vittoria—in the cottage." My voice was low, so I bent low, my mouth near her ear, that she might hear me over the storm. So close I could feel her warmth—and the shift in her stance, warning me that she intended a battle. She was the Garbin, after all. What fear had she of wind?

Her fists clenched, a grip around invisible, invincible reserve. I turned, hoping she might stay here in safety but knowing she would not.

Her footsteps strode long, bounding to keep up.

"Please, Vittoria. It's not safe." My voice louder than I wished, to slice through the clamor of trees above us and churning sea beyond.

But she treaded on, determined. Attention fixed on the slick ground as she stumbled repeatedly, trying to find footing, limbs on the aged trees that threatened to snap as they waved us frantically away.

And here I was again. Everything hanging in the balance—and a faultless woman's fate too. All because of my own choices.

Go back! I wanted to urge her, to spare her—to wall her away from danger that my own pursuit had created. But the words caught in my throat as the night split, rolling away to another place of desperation. My cell, my mother's letters, tugging me toward her as if I were still a boy, and not two heads taller than her. Her words beckoning me homeward.

But I, in all my youth and zeal, could not see it. Could not see how a simple life, a good life, was enough for her. How all she wanted was me—*me*, wayward and broken as I was.

And I stared that love down in a San Francisco night where I clambered up a fire escape and fell to the ground, and never stopped falling. Knowing the shadows of this life were no place for her. I had gone too far. Taken too much. Steeped myself in lies until my very soul, surely, was lost.

Lightning flashed and summoned my attention to Vittoria. Her eyes searched mine. She did not go back. She stepped closer.

Stretched out her arm and waited. Reaching toward me. Flawed, broken, imperfect me.

"Daniel," she said, her dark lashes framing eyes that would not look away. Would not unsee me, as much as I wished to be unseen. "What—"

And then it happened. The eerie bounce, bounce, bounce of an old limb burned into a bounce—creak—bounce—crack—

"Vittoria!" I lunged, snatching her slight form out of harm's way as the branch descended with a sickening crash.

And she was in my arms. I pulled her close, bending myself over her to protect her as I ran for the nearest cover—a small corner of the abbey ruins that still held an outcropping of roof. With the vestige of an ancient building letting in rain only when it gusted, I set her down.

My hand reached for her face, where an angry red line slashed across her cheek.

Her face cold in my hand, I ran my thumb under the wound. Why had I brought her here? How had it come to this? Why couldn't I have watched where I was going that first day on the train platform? Let her pass, make her delivery, and gone our separate ways? Spared her this pain.

But I, blind as always to the people around me, crashed into her world and ushered her into this realm of secrets and story—she, who belonged on spiral staircases and glinting canals, among the company of owls and aunts and happy hearth fires.

Unthinking, I bent my head toward her until it touched hers. "I'm sorry," I said.

She stayed there, silent. So unlike her.

At last, with the quieting of the wind, she murmured, "What could you be sorry for, Daniel?"

Everything.

Except this one true, good thing . . . if I could find this book. My desire had changed along the way. Gone from a job for a California businessman, to a personal mission to restore something, rather than plunder something. To be a man who would pursue and deliver—and not hide among shadows and flee.

41

We built a small fire beside the stream, and as Vittoria hunted for dry wood, I searched for anything that might show us where to search. Not much held promise. The mosaic-covered altar in the abbey ruins appeared to open like a trunk, but it was locked, with no sign of a key. It did not budge as I tried to coax it with a stray nail.

I was driven by the memory of the word that had been pursuing me: *Deeper*. And all our answers seemed to lie on surfaces. Even the man in the flat had said it and looked me in the eye too—*Do not neglect the shadows*, he had written. They might just hold the key.

I was very familiar with shadows. Had lived my whole adult life in them. And had found no keys there.

Vittoria returned, arms full of sticks, exultant. "There was a pile just beyond the shallows of the stream."

"Thank you," I said. She was the true hero today.

I looked around. "'Do not neglect the . . .'" I looked at Vittoria. "What did you say?"

"Around the bend of the stream, there. The shallows."

"Shallows," I repeated her word. I scrambled to pull Sebastien's loopy-scripted note from my trouser pockets.

Do not neglect the shadows . . .

But the *d* did not join itself evenly as it should. A smaller loop, next to a larger loop—could it be two *l*s?

Shallows.

"Yes, where the stream is just a trickle, though it won't stay that way for long by the looks of things."

"Would you show me?"

She led through easing rain, and together we knelt. "I think there might be something here," I said, and began looking amid the silt and rocks. If a key had once been here, it would have been long buried by now.

Lightning flashed above, and Vittoria's eyes grew wide with the thrill. "At least we have light to work by," she said. It flashed again, this time illuminating something glinting not among the rocks, but higher—inside the crevice of a tree where a branch had broken away, long ago, and the trunk had healed around it.

A key, kept safe, hanging upon a nail.

Back at the ruins I stood in the place of homilies and secret meetings. Where mosaics encrusted an altar, depicting a leper approaching his Lord.

Unhealed. Imperfect. Approaching, to be healed.

Vittoria inserted the key into the altar, and with a creak, the lid opened.

In a damp and webbed place locked away from all the world was a lever.

I gripped its cold metal form, pulled it, and listened.

Nothing.

I turned it more, forcing it as far as possible—and then I heard it. A pained creak coming from the canal behind the ruins. Rushing around back to see, I caught the slight glint of the metal levee clinging to submerged pulleys that raised it from its prone position to that of a standing sentinel.

The song of the water began to slow, from a steady rush to a wandering trickle in the narrow canal.

The metal latches clicked into place with finality and triggered some internal clock that drove me to action. I jumped into the still-draining waters, my feet sinking into mud that sealed around my feet like shackles. Crouching, I plunged my arms into the muck and began to run my hands along the bottom, willing my fingers to see what my eyes could not.

Mud, sticks, rocks, twigs—and then something more. Something harder, unnaturally straight in its rectangle edges. I followed its perimeter, pulse thundering until—there. Yes. An aged lock, heavy and wet, holding fast to chains.

The water by now was gone, leaving only the slimy sludge to catch moonlight emerging from clouds. I tugged the key and its cord up from where it lay against my chest, over my head, and tried it.

The lock held its grip, a film of sand refusing the key its entry. The ticking clock inside of me grew louder as I climbed out of the slick embankment, scanning desperately in the dark for some vessel—a cup, a bucket, anything. I remembered the corner in the ruins that had seemed a kingdom of mud to a long-ago child and darted to retrieve that old bowl. Willing it to hold water, still.

Plunging it into the now-swelling canal on the full side of the levee, I returned to the lock and submerged it in this clean water, swishing this way and that, pulling it out, trying once more with the key.

The cogs inside seemed to bare their teeth inside their chambers, but I kept on. Leaning the key until—

Click.

Something registered. The metal loop securing it to the chain stayed put, but as I tugged, it reluctantly—centimeter by centimeter—gave way. Chains undone, lock flung aside, the trapdoor at the bottom of the canal obeyed my pull . . . and opened.

The door was the width of a man and no more. I strained to see inside but had no candle, no torch, no lantern to play herald.

Behind me, the swelling banks began to trickle down and around the levee. It mounded, embracing its obstacle, and it was only a matter of time before that slow trickle around its corners grew into a full overflow, spilling and filling again into this basin.

Whatever lay inside this chamber, the levee hadn't been built to expose it for long. In fact, it seemed intent on covering it back over—and quickly.

With time slipping past and water spilling in, I reached in blindly, up to my shoulder and as far as my arm would go—and touched only air.

I had to go in. All the way.

"Be careful," Vittoria said as I crouched down.

Breath-stealing compression of dark walls around me, resurrecting a memory of a confined place I had sworn never to land in again.

"No," I spoke aloud. As if the memory might heed my refusal and dissipate.

But it did not. The cavity in the ground before me yawned grave-like, ready to devour me.

So be it. My attempt at defiance stuck somewhere in the muck. I sat on the edge of the opening—and plunged in.

My feet hit the ground first—some sort of second earth, here beneath the filling waterway above me. My eyes protested, straining and failing to see.

In place of sight, my hands again sprang to action. The chamber was narrow—wide enough to extend my arms only halfway and meet the wall on both sides. But what manner of wall, I could not discern. Rough, and oddly undulating in its very uneven surface. As if someone had lined up trees, side by side, packed tight with gritty mortar both sharp and uneven.

Like the bars of a prison cell meant to keep a man in forever.

The darkness inside descended, pushing action aside and summoning a wave of sickness.

Petrified like the submerged trees in all their gnarled bark, something inside pushed back against the dark.

Move, it said.

I could not.

Water sloshed around my ankles, creeping over skin beneath my trousers like a creature on the prowl.

It meant to fill. It meant to take me under.

Move.

I could not.

The water rose, and I pressed my eyes tight, reaching for something. Anything. The thought of my mother at her glowing window, though I could not see it. She, pressing on though life had robbed her of all. A bouquet of open umbrellas, shielding her from above. Vittoria, and the thought of seeing her dark eyes spark with passion and delight. I heard her voice in the distance, urgent.

"Move," I commanded myself. And forced my hands to obey. The water rose quickly now. Eyes open, I could see silvery glints and dark lines enough to know that the walls about me, these prison bars that wished to clamp around me and remind me I was prisoner, traitor, thief, and fiend—they held no answers. No secret etchings or paintings. What had I imagined they would hold?

Yet still—the trapdoor, the hidden levee, the key—a person would not go to such lengths to hide nothing.

The only place left for anything to be was on the ground of this chamber.

Which no longer existed, not to sight. A growing sea covered over whatever it was.

I reached down and could not feel it, not with my ridiculous height.

There was nothing for it.

I pulled in a breath. Held it fast. And plunged, body and soul, into the dark depths.

Liquid ribboned and twisted as currents swam about me, bubbles protesting as I spun, groped in the confines, searching.

My lungs burned. Thoughts clouded. Seconds—minutes? an eternity?—ticked on, and I sprang from the bottom to break for a breath, only to find the last of the chamber filling, and fast. Barely enough to pull in a breath.

I went back down. My last chance, and I strained with everything in me to see. And then . . . it happened. A parting of the clouds in the night let the thinnest line of silver light transform into a swimming thing, lending a flickering underline to a dark object in the corner, the size of a book.

I dove. Spread my arms, the water swirling over my skin. Retrieved the heavy thing without a shred of clear thought—only the instinct of grabbing. But it held, caught by the root of something that had grown in and around it. My lungs burned, and I braced my legs against the wall, pushing until every muscle burned too

. . . and it broke free. Torn from what kept it with such force I could feel it to my toes.

Pulse throbbing in my ears like a drum, I launched myself from the muddy depths. Paddled fiercely with my free hand up and through the trapdoor and up even more until I broke, starving for breath, into the darkening night.

Vittoria clambered to help pull me out, and I hoisted the object to the bank and clung to the mossy blocks with what little strength remained in me. Folding my arms on the ledge and resting my head until I was certain I would not succumb to unconsciousness.

When my senses began to return and a shiver traversed my spine, I lifted myself, soggy clothes dripping onto the embankment, and pulled the retrieved object onto my lap.

I remembered vaguely thinking, underwater, that it had resembled a book. This proved only partly true—for upon it was etched *Libro d'Acqua*. The Book of Waters. But it was a metal box, shut tight and rusted over. With much coaxing and protest from the lid, it gave way to a final tug as I lifted it and saw, cradled with care within the rubber-lined interior, a perfect sphere. Made of glass in vibrant Murano patchwork, its base closed with a lid that screwed on tight, like a jar.

The cold air and my wet clothes collided into a serpentine shiver up my spine, and I nearly dropped it. Bundling it as carefully as possible, I tucked it under my drenched sleeve and together we made for the safety of the small cabin aboard the gondola.

With tempered strength and great care, we opened that lid. Vittoria reached inside, through the whispers of the past, the echoes of its story, the first person to touch these pages in a lifetime . . . and pulled out a simple blue volume. With the vestigial winds of the storm rocking us and knocking at the windows, we fluttered open the pages and saw penned in loopy script identical to the scrap Sebastien had tossed down to me, and with illustrations scratched out in pen and ink, the full and complete story.

42

THE BOOK OF WATERS

The Veil Lifts

It was meant to be Sebastien.

He was to take the boat out that day, venture to the islands, fish in the sea beyond with Giuseppe, bring Mariana back a bouquet of her wildflowers.

It was meant to be Sebastien for whom the hole was carved in the boat. Sealed with wax that would withstand long enough to carry him out across the water and crack against the deep sea's coldness.

It was meant to be Sebastien whose life ended that day.

For a new man had come upon the scene. Daniele Manin, charismatic and revolutionary, with plans involving arsenals and masses of uprising citizens.

But would he return Venice to her former glory? Was he born to be Doge?

Massimo Fedele thought not. And needed money to act soon. He had a palazzo to sell. A brother-in-law to dispense with, that it might set into motion the chain of events they had both been born for.

It was meant to be Sebastien that day. But Mariana . . .

Those two words, the hinge upon which Massimo's life swung.

She faded, though none wished to admit it. One night, while Massimo left for the casino and the meetings that consumed more of his time, his life, his soul . . . she woke her husband and asked to see the moon. Their promise.

It was high, the night was clear, and there was a journey she wished to revisit. To see the way Venice—this impossible place born of desperation—held treasure at every turn.

It was more than a whim. It was as if this small request was her anthem. The song of her life . . . a last journey.

And so, Sebastien played gondolier for his bride in the dark of the night. Where the water was colder than usual. Where there were no people to help when the wax cracked and the boat filled.

Venice slumbered, and the Heart of Venice—Mariana—sank. Nearly drowned, pulled to the quayside by Sebastien and carried home. Tended with care, for the scare had taken a toll on her warrior-heart.

"She must rest," the doctor said. "She must not become excited. The price will be her life this time."

Time . . . was almost out.

Sebastien seethed. He had discovered the hole, the wax. Had seen Massimo bent at work on the gondola earlier, after he had heard of Sebastien's plan to visit the isles. He had thought it strange. But when Mariana made her request, the last thing on his mind was her brother. He kicked himself for such stupidity now.

He entered the hall of figures in the deep of the night and waited, knowing Massimo's pathways well.

Two torches were lit on opposite ends of the hall, crisscrossing shadows. In between, white moonlight spilled in through the portico windows. Sebastien crossed to one of them, paused at the bust of the veiled woman. Recalled Mariana, the way the corner of her mouth turned up as she told him of this woman in stone. His chest ached at the thought of her.

If she learned what Massimo had done, it would crush her. It might even end her. He would see to it that that did not happen.

He placed a palm on the windows, opening one to hear the canal, the familiar split of waters as Massimo's boat drew near. Which Massimo would disembark? Which of the Greek Fates—Atropos, Lachesis, Clotho? Which iteration of man would Sebastien encounter, here in these shadows—the man sober, spinning webs for the future? True Massimo, that man pulled asunder by the influences of the glass, but who exposed his own humanity?

Or—and somehow, Sebastien knew it would be this—the man who had consumed a glass and no more, enough to remove all genteel polish and reveal the ruthless ruler.

Measured steps, each a brooding force, told it true. Atropos, the Fate who severed threads, propelled himself by heavy, even footsteps down the corridor. Fully possessed of his agility, ability, and strength. Dispossessed of any guise or gloss.

Massimo entered the hall of figures en route to his apartments. His steps slowed.

In the center of the room, where the shaft of moonlight stopped, he stopped too.

"Skulking with the statues," he said. Even his voice held shadow.

Sebastien stepped into view.

"Massimo," he said. He hadn't planned a speech, nor brought his evidence. He did not need to. This man had laid enough snares; it was only a matter of time before he stepped into one of his own.

"Sebastien," Massimo replied in equal gravity.

"How did you know I was here?"

"You're not such a secretive person as you think, Signor Trovato." He spat the last name.

"Secrets," Sebastien said, voice low. "You have your own fair share of those."

"Everybody does," he said, bitter. "We are Venice, after all."

"Everybody"—the words seethed from Sebastien—"does not plot to kill their sister."

Cold moonlight crossed Massimo's face. "I would never place my sister in any danger," he said, conviction so deep it seemed to depart from the man and become another being, one bent on convincing his own self that what he said was true. "Everything I do is for her. For *all* of Venice."

Sebastien closed the distance between them, paces measured but firm. Flames from the torches threw orange light and long shadows in medieval dance.

"You nearly ended her today."

Massimo lifted his chin. "She was never meant to be in danger." Even as he spoke the words, remorse passed over his face.

He had heard, then, what had happened. "Her days are numbered as it is."

As it is. Three words that shifted her somehow from the realm of soul to the realm of collateral. Hot tension shot through Sebastien's veins, shot his hand to gripping the man's forearm as if the action might halt him. Stop him in his spiraling madness.

The chin lifted higher until Massimo, matched in height to Sebastien, looked down upon him and spat.

Sebastien's grip tightened. His teeth too. "'Her days are *numbered*'? She . . . is not . . . a number." Words burning with restraint. With his free hand, Sebastien slowly wiped the spit from his eye and pressed his hand firmly against Massimo's jacket, wiping.

They stood still as the surrounding statues for one second . . . two . . . The atmosphere crystallizing into brittle walls that would shatter at the slightest move.

Three seconds . . . four . . .

Massimo lunged. Wrested his forearm from Sebastien and gripped him around the neck. Advancing until a marble pillar pressed cold at Sebastien's back. Hot pressure in his closing airways.

"Do not speak to me of my sister. Do not *speak* to me of honor. You do not know what it is to carry the future of an empire on your shoulders. *You* do not know the burn of a million futures, a million pasts, awaiting your next move."

Sebastien jerked, struggling to release himself from the man's grip. A cloud circled him—burning lungs. Spotting vision. The sick-sweet smell of the liquor on the man's breath.

"You are only"—he squeezed tight—"in the way. It's all you ever were. All you will ever be."

Sebastien jerked, jarring Massimo's grip enough to snatch breath and clench his fists.

But the man leaned in and growled contempt against Sebastien's ear. "I should have looked upon you for the very last time the night Angelo set you afloat on the canal. You should never have returned."

Sebastien stilled his struggle, and Massimo shoved him to the ground and released him.

"You seem . . . shocked," he said.

"Angelo," Sebastien said, rubbing his neck and restraining the fire in his veins. "What had he to do with—"

Massimo laughed, once. Loud. "Doesn't matter. You were leaving and that was all I needed to know." He shook his head. "I thought a baby couldn't be so horrible, so vile. Let him go live his life somewhere else. Let him go to the obscurity of the—"

"Orphanage," Sebastien finished.

"Is that what you think?" Massimo crossed to the knight's armor, setting a hand on the empty shell of a man as if he were a comrade in arms. Laughed again. "Perhaps you should go on thinking that," he said. "That you were rescued from that fate by a band of merry guildsmen," he said, infusing his voice with mockery. "That you weren't intended all along to be plucked from the waters by a fisherman who stank to the high heavens."

Sebastien could see the scene before him as if it were a play on stage: the basket, launched by unknown hands.

"Angelo," he muttered. A name that floated around this house like a spirit, for his ever-present accomplishments and always-absent body. The man who had been gone oftener and oftener since Sebastien had married Mariana.

That man had been the one to set him afloat?

Sebastien's mind clouded, trying to make sense of it. No . . . Giuseppe had saved him from the orphanage. It was the one true thing he knew of his origins.

"I saw it with my own eyes," Massimo uttered. "I followed Angelo that night. Your fate was tied to mine. If you disappeared . . . I might reclaim my purpose. Some things never change, it seems."

Arguments lined up in ranks in Sebastien's mind. But now was not the time for them.

"I thought you might drown, you see." Briefest flicker, torment, somewhere behind those torch-lit eyes.

"You didn't want that. You don't want that."

A cut of Massimo's eyes to the ground affirmed this. But he set his jaw against anything resembling compassion.

"What I want does not matter. I learned that long ago. To the canal you went. Angelo was on the same embankment as the orphanage. If he had intended you for it, for the wheel, he would have just walked twelve steps and made it so. You . . . were meant for the waters. For the stinking fisherman. And your *guild*," he said, the word venomous. "You were—you *are* —nothing but a foundling. Better off never born."

"You don't mean that." This was the man who had nearly gone bankrupt to vindicate his own family name. He was not without humanity.

Questions invaded like an army. Sebastien could not wrestle them now. For Massimo, his physical foe, turned upon him. He rose like a dragon, righteous in his cause, mighty in his power. And set his fire on Sebastien.

"I would never have harmed my sister," he said. And with that word—*sister*—the briefest flicker of True Massimo shone through. Soul broken, desperate. "She has enough woe. But you . . . she is in and out of consciousness so much, she would never have known."

Slowly, deliberately, he reached behind him. Gripped the handle of the knight's sword.

"Don't do this, Massimo. You're not thinking clearly."

True Massimo flickered away as the sinister version of the man emerged in full. Metal upon metal sliced the air as he unsheathed the sword. It glinted, cold and bright, as he turned and swung, the world slowing.

The Fates, they entered the chamber, invisible. Past, Present, Future—each of them spinning in succession, glimpses before his eyes.

The sword raising. The basket floating. Mariana, running barefoot and free somewhere good. Sword glinting. Stringed instruments ascending, reaching down dark canals, from the private concert to two unlikely lovers, transported here . . . to what would be Sebastien's execution.

For the sword, raised to the strain of a sustaining cello from that stolen memory, lowered. Sebastien lifted his eyes. Watched it come down. Slicing air, past, present, future, all of it—and saw, too, the hand of a baby. Reaching up from his lone place upon ancient waters.

Sebastien arose. Spun, dodging the sword as it came down and clattered onto the marbled floor.

They locked eyes. Two men—histories embodied in each other—perched on the precipice of this moment of truth. A rest in the music as the world held its breath . . . and Massimo lunged. Speared the sword at Sebastien's side. He dodged to the left, hand bracing against the cold wall.

Sebastien looked around for something—anything—with which to defend himself. He could run. He could hide. Massimo approached in his calculated way as Sebastien reached, quickly, for the only object that might stop the sword.

The Doge's orb-topped scepter. Tarnished, but strong.

Sebastien lunged. Pulled it from its stand, and spun just in time for it to collide, gold on steel, into the sword.

Massimo's eyes flew wide, fresh anger driving him, but this time Sebastien stood his ground. Advanced, fueled by the fire rising beyond the realm of thought and from blind passion.

The scepter was not made for this. But then, neither was Sebastien. And yet here they were, slashing, blocking, metallic clashes swimming in a blur. As Massimo parried, a cry arose from the arched entrance, and Sebastien turned to see Mariana.

"No, Massimo—!"

The slap of white-hot pain seared Sebastien as he tried to evade. The sword on his jaw, jagged in its journey to his mouth, withdrawing as dark liquid dropped to the white floor between them.

Time froze. If he advanced—gave way to the driving force inside that he *knew* would send Massimo flying through the windows, it would end this.

And with it, Mariana.

Her heart, so strong and yet so afflicted . . . how much more could it take?

If he did nothing, she would witness her husband killed.

If he rose to turn the tide of this battle, she would witness her brother killed.

It socked the air from him as he realized what this meant. *"The price will be her life,"* the doctor had said.

His face screamed in pain, but it was nothing to the inferno in his heart. His shoulders heaved. Massimo's did, too, as they stared each other down.

Massimo had not heard the doctor's warning. He did not know. His flame-lit eyes reflected torchlight and dared Sebastien to make a move. Something had pushed him, once and for all, over the threshold and beyond the reach of his measured restraint. A beast, unleashed. It had taken the man over, and the man did not seem to even register his sister's presence.

When Mariana's eyes fell on Sebastien's, they held the universe. Every night of island-wind listening, every morning of tall-grass-running.

"He is a soul," she whispered to her brother, desperate.

"He is a *scourge*." Massimo's reply.

"Mariana, please—" Sebastien said. She advanced, he saw from periphery, and he knew she would not stop. She would throw herself between them if that was what it took. She, who sat by fires and rescued mackerel and gathered bouquets, would not turn a blind eye.

A stab of hope—the only one left to save her—sent words from him. "Get Angelo," he said. The man who was never there. The man who would, he hoped, take some time to find. The man who had been there at Sebastien's beginning, though Sebastien knew him not, would be there at his end. It seemed fitting.

Mariana vanished from view, relief washing Sebastien in the same instant a fresh wave of fight did, the collision of the two opposing forces setting his muscles into buzzing intensity he had never known.

Massimo advanced, sword raised and descending. Sebastien ducked, spinning and blocking the blow with the scepter.

At his left, the figure of Atlas, holding up the heavens and looking anguished.

At his right, the figure of Moses, hands held up by the others, looking spent, poured out, but hopeful.

And in the middle, Sebastien. Arms raised like Moses and Atlas. Massimo's sword bearing down, locked, trembling, as the man's face grew grotesquely closer. Sweat glistening.

A dark, gathering force seemed to encompass Massimo. All the generations, the striving, the emptying pockets, the careful maneuverings, slithering from the ages and into him, into this moment. Lifting his arm . . . and plunging it at Sebastien.

The younger man dropped, searing pain at his shoulder, and rolled to evade. Predator and prey, Massimo pursued Sebastien as he, wounded, pulled himself to the edge of the room. To the open window where outside, waters stood mournful, ready to shroud him like a funeral garment.

Everything within Sebastien writhed to fight. He lifted the scepter, summoning every last strength . . . but his fingers faltered, and the scepter dropped, and the red-glassed orb, swirled with gold, shattered to a million pieces.

"You are nobody, Sebastien Trovato." Massimo stepped over him to stand behind his back. Placed his boot upon Sebastien's wounded shoulder where the crackle of leather met the holler of pain . . . and pushed.

43

THE BOOK OF WATERS

Sebastien

Sebastien's mind and body separated. Bones throbbing a dirge as he plunged into the dark canal. Mind pounding like one imprisoned. Beating to break the walls stacking up between him and life, walls closing in as water took him under in a muted twist of bubbles.

His lungs burned, mind registering and legs trying—but failing—to kick upward. All was heavy. All was dark.

It was madness. The canal was not so deep that it should be able to pull him under . . . but he was a fraction of a man, a splinter of consciousness. Above him, growing smaller as he sank, Massimo's silhouette haloed in torchlight, presiding over Sebastien's demise as he would preside over Venice. He stooped, picked up the scepter from its place on the ground, and planted it firm beside him.

Every bit the Doge.

In the currents, his sight obscured, Sebastien stopped thrashing. For the first time in his life, he ceased striving. Lungs tight, vision spotting, he turned his face upward and saw no sign of Massimo.

But something passed over. Oval and dark—like a basket.

Hallucinating. He was seeing things, here where he verged on death. Only rather than seeing from above, as some men professed to have done, he had sunk beneath these Genesis-waters, these waters of his own beginnings, and saw it play out above him. The shadow of a vessel, passing over, webbing light, threading through water. Hands releasing it with calculation, aiming it for a place across the canal. With precision and care, arms outstretched as if to guide it.

His life—his fabled, island-hopping, glassblowing, letter-setting, fire-stoking life—had not been an accident of six meters, after all.

Who am I? His heart beat the old familiar march. *Who am I? Who am I?*

He watched as the oval crossed diagonally and disappeared, lifted by unseen hands.

Found. A single slam of his slowing heart.

He was Sebastien Trovato. *"Found means someone was searching for you, running after you. You, the greatest treasure in all the world."* Elena's voice.

Found. His heart slowed further still.

He was the Last Doge of Venice, the One Who Would Never Be. A man born for the greatest purpose that the greatest empire could conceive of . . . only to grow up in a world where that purpose had vanished. He was a man outside of his time.

Found. One more heartbeat—and it might not beat again.

Son of the lagoon. Keeper of this city's greatest treasure—Mariana.

Darkness closed over his view, swallowing the crystal-webbed waters and taking with it his final conscious thought . . .

Live.

A last, impossible thrust of motion from the very depths of himself as his feet touched the bottom sent him arrowing toward the surface. Liquid molded to his body, displacing itself for him as the surface grew nearer, bluer, clearer until—

It broke. He gasped, desperate. Sputtered, taking in water, taking in air and thought and coughing in the tangled mix of it all. Back under and up again. Floundering to find consciousness.

The world clouded before him, wavering in and out of sharpness. Massimo was here somewhere.

But where? The place where he'd seen his silhouette through the veil of water was empty.

Sluggish thoughts crept into their places, making sense of this wet and woebegone world. Holding on to the stones along the quayside, he moved toward the dock of his youth, where once flower petals had rained down, where he well recalled climbing down iron rungs mounted to the canal wall to reach his boat. Just as he gripped that first rung and pulled himself up, a footfall sounded.

Sebastien swung himself to the side, pressing his body against the stone wall beneath the shelter of the dock.

The footsteps stopped. Sebastien tried to hold still, pushing away the shivering cold that traversed his skin and sank into his bones. His knees shook with it, and a foot slipped from the rung. His fist held tight its grip, barely keeping his leg from skimming the water again.

He needed time. Even a sliver of it to gather his wits, somehow find strength. His body screamed in pain.

Massimo stepped upon the dock. Took one step. Two. And a third, stopping directly above Sebastien.

His boot fell. A flash from the past—Sebastien, standing in that very place. Cast out from this place.

Massimo's other boot fell. A flash—Sebastien looking up at the palazzo. Wondering what it would be like to have just one home.

One last footfall. Five faces, flashing in front of him. A guild of hearts—his truest home.

Last strength coursed through Sebastien, who pulled himself back to the rung, up the next. And the next until, as Massimo faced away, Sebastien pulled himself dripping onto the quay.

He had nothing. No weapon. Less blood and strength by the second. He was not the first man to kneel here of late, though. This was the very place Angelo had been working, building up with fallen palazzo pieces.

Massimo turned slowly, doge's scepter still at his side. Stooped to watch as Sebastien struggled to his knees and then to his feet.

Sebastien gripped the quayside hard, the rough edge of crumbled palazzo-turned-pavement nearly puncturing his palm. He struggled to stand and water ran from his sleeves, down his fingers, splashing onto the ground. He gripped his side where he bled warm against the cold. Teeth chattering beyond his control, he stepped toward Massimo.

The man smirked. Shook his head in mock pity. And pulled something dark and pointed from his boot.

A dagger.

"You should have stayed in the canal where you belong," Massimo said, words low, seething. "Let it take you . . . once and for all. Swamp rat."

He advanced. Raised his dagger to stomach level . . . and thrust.

Quick to the side Sebastien stepped, evading the kill and releasing from his own hand the fallen piece of palazzo he had gripped—his only defense.

It met its mark with a solid sound that sickened Sebastien, but it afforded enough time for him to stumble back and let that perpetually crumbling palazzo catch him, brace him, as he watched the fall of an empire before him, in the form of a man.

For there, the Greatest Faithful, the self-christened last hope of Venice—Massimo Fedele fell to his knees, scepter dropping from his hand and rolling toward Sebastien.

A creeping dark river snaked from his leg, where his fallen dagger caught his fall, crippling him in his tracks.

He tried to stand, but fell again. Sebastien lunged but could not reach him as Massimo slipped into the canal, chin knocking the edge of the dock as he went, until a solid splash swallowed him whole.

"Sebastien?" Mariana's voice, from the hall of statues.

No. No, no . . . She could not see this.

Feet moving faster than thought could arrive in his mind, he lunged for the scepter and splayed himself out upon the surface of the dock, heedless of his body's protest.

"Come back," he said, staring into the black abyss.

Nothing. Only the shine of moonlight upon water, upon the trail of blood beside him.

"Come back. Please." Gritting teeth, the words climbed as if they, too, were desperate for air.

Nothing.

The creaking of a hinge as the door opened behind him and he knew, in the strong and quiet presence, who it was.

He whispered a final plea. "Come. Back."

He held his breath. A bubble breached the surface, and then another—and then the man himself.

Lightning fast, instinct surpassed thought, and all was a blur of water and man, limb and land as he extended the scepter. Gripped Massimo's hand around it to keep it from sliding as the brass slipped and protested beneath the clutch of wet hands. Sebastien pulled him, though his own lifeblood spilled the more, onto the dock.

Massimo sputtered, coughed, his leg hanging limp. There was a man crouching then, dressing the wound, binding his wrists, with equal parts care and conviction, throwing concerned looks Sebastien's way as if unsure which patient to treat first.

Sebastien's hearing blurred in and out, his vision too. Distinct glimpses of Mariana bending over him, stroking his face, taking his hand in hers. And then the man she had gone to fetch—Angelo—bent over him to begin his ministrations.

Something cool and steady against his face, his side. A low voice asking questions, words garbled in the sluggish echo of blood snaking through Sebastien's mind and ears.

". . . all right?" the voice asked. "Tell me where you are."

But that was not a voice of a stranger. It was familiar, so familiar.

The man's hand gripped his shoulder with the touch of a father as he began to speak old lines that covered him like a blanket. Words slipped in and out of his hearing, coming in snatches:

"Ancient waters, secrets keep . . . rios long . . . places deep. Hear them ring in kindest dreams . . . let them sing you off to sleep. . . ."

The voice of the man who had told him a thousand stories and taught him how to print them too. Why, then, did Mariana call him Angelo?

It was her face, so near now, asking one more question. "Do you know who you are?"

And the answer, crystal clear and sharp as glass, pierced the fog consuming him.

"I . . . am . . . found."

THE BOOK OF WATERS

Precium

On a somber summer day, the Greatest Faithful traversed the infamous Bridge of Sighs, shackled for high treason and intent for insubordination to the occupying forces. He lingered over his last look at his beloved city before being jostled onward, shut away in the prison cells of the very palace from whence he had meant to reign. Here he was to remain, the remainder of his days. But in Venice, in these times, nothing was certain.

This, he saw proved from his cell, where he watched a revolution unfold. The air was filled with word of it—from guards and voices from the canals. Daniele Manin, imprisoned just like Massimo Fedele, had his freedom forced in the throes of the uprising. Manin was victorious, it seemed—and Venice was in Venetian hands . . . for now.

"It will not last," said the chess player, always thinking ten steps ahead.

And it did not. Though Venice enjoyed a tenuous stint of independence, she was soon beset with troubles. An explosion of a magazine. A wave of cholera, ruthless in its timing. The bombardment of Venice by Austria from land and from sea. Dwindling food and rising unrest.

Daniele Manin, loathe to see his beloved Venice suffer, negotiated amnesty for all but him and a few others, who would be subject to exile.

"Others," it seemed, included The Greatest Faithful. A key opening his cell, only to imprison him away from his very purpose.

Before he departed the city for the last time, he awoke in his cell to five faces bent over his. He startled, bolting upright and flattening himself against the cold wall at his back as he took them in. Five souls he knew not, though he was intimately connected to, their roots twisting afar into history around seven seats and a stone table.

The ones his ancestor had left behind.

And now, like all that history had bound itself up into this moment, Angelo—Dante, it seemed his given name was—stepped forward, arm outstretched.

Massimo did not take the proffered hand. How could he?

So Dante closed the space between them. Elena handed him a basket, and Dante offered it to Massimo.

"Supplies," he said simply. "For the journey ahead."

Massimo pressed harder into the cold wall, shaking his head. "I have not earned this," he said. The broken battle cry pulsing silently in the cell. *I am nothing.*

In his time within this cage, he had counted bars. Weighed deeds. Calculated atonement. The current of the rising equation rising, wrapping tight around him, pulling him under.

"I can never pay the price of my past. Of my family."

Angelo dropped his gaze, considering. That soul of a poet, storing up words he could never write.

"The question is not the price of a man," he said. "That has already been paid. The question . . . is that of a man's worth. His value."

Massimo's jaw worked, gaze boring into the ground.

"Not quantum," Dante spoke in Massimo's currency of words. "But precium."

At the sound of the word of ransom and redemption, of value, Massimo's eyes pressed closed, a silent battle waging for the man's soul.

The guild retreated, revealing in their wake the presence of another.

One man, bearing two gifts.

The first, a coin. "I believe this is yours," the man said. He reached through the bars, meeting his brother-in-law's eyes and pleading silently. "You gave it to me as a warning when I was a child. To remember my mortality. I return it to you with one small change . . . And I bring you this." He handed him a flower. Oleander. White and true, the same blossom that had crowned his sister on her wedding day.

When the visitor left, Massimo turned the coin in his hand. Where once it had scrawled the ominous, angular words Memento Mori, the latter word had been rubbed away and etched with one word: *Vita*.

Life.

"Take me home?" Mariana's voice, music to Sebastien's ears, made this simple request. It was time, they both knew. Time to cease speaking of resting and protecting her days. Her days were too precious to be guarded now. They were so few, they opened their arms and begged to be filled.

And so, he rowed his bride across the lagoon. Lifted her from the boat, over the island threshold she had once traversed barefoot. The waves tiptoed up onto the bank, as if they, too, wished to help see her home.

The Guild had known she was coming. Valentina had adorned the bed with a blanket edged in finest lace. Pietro had lined her windowsill in bright glass vases to catch the light and make it dance for her. His grandchildren visited and nestled about her bed like birds in a nest, and she delighted in distributing to them her most cherished trinkets: a chipped cup depicting a storm-tossed ship, a pen she had used to write letters to a certain boatman, a mask edged in scrolling silvery-blue peaks and curls.

Their chatter and gentle bouncing energy as they soaked in her presence seemed to fill her heart in unseen places, as if she were imagining the future rolling out before each of them like a grand adventure. A future that would someday take their family lines off to distant shores where, even as the home fires burned strong in their Murano glass shop, new family businesses would open too: a Boston restaurant spicing the air with garlic, cheese, herbs, and music from the old country, swirling it even into dark wartime nights. And a San Francisco bakery spinning sugar and delight into Washington Square Park from a pie-slice building with a mural from the brush of a courageous young boy.

Elena was in and out all day, each day, with tender ministrations of tea and bread, song and smiles. Giuseppe, timid and unsure despite all his usual bluster and bravado, waved his large hand through the window with a sheepish grin, showing his empty fishing line—how he had set them all free in her honor.

Dante came the next day, bringing with him a blank volume, bound with care, its ends marbled with all the same hues of her dress from the night of the masquerade.

"Angelo." She smiled and took his hand. "It was you, wasn't it? The man in the boat passing the island when I was healing?"

The quiet dip of his head was answer enough. "I saw that you were in good hands," he said. "It was all I needed to know."

"Always looking out for us," she said, adoration in her eyes.

"From the moment you were both born," he said.

Sebastien's brow furrowed. "Do you mean from the moment Giuseppe found me?"

Dante smiled. "How do you think you came to be set adrift in the direction of a fishmonger and not an orphanage?"

Sebastien sputtered. "Massimo . . . told the truth? It—it wasn't an accident?"

"Life is no accident, Sebastien. Your mother's people once occupied one of the stone seats. She knew if there was a safe place for you to grow up in tumultuous times like yours have been, it was in the care of such as these." He looked with quiet fondness upon the beloved band of artisans.

"It was you all along," Sebastien said, and Mariana's eyes gleamed. This man with his ink-stained hands . . . was the hero of this tale. All of the guild were. "Thank you, Dante."

To Mariana, Dante turned and said, "You are a treasure, Mariana Trovato. Like Venice itself."

"Venice," she said, her deep love for the place resounding in her sigh. "Now, there is a story worth telling."

Sebastien would record that story for her in the days that followed. The ache of his soul in every stroke of the pen, for he knew how Mariana had longed to be a mother one day. And he heard how every bit of that love, the magic she would have spun for her own children, was given with abandon to the small histories she wished to place in the hands of children who were like she had once been. Who needed to know of the city that came from a swamp . . . a lost place that grew hope. She spoke the words, and he wrote them. She sketched the pictures, and he carved them into woodblocks, to be inked and printed someday.

At night, he took to recording their own tale. Beginning with the inscription—*For my bride*—and desiring that the tale would be kept close and safe by the members of the guild as long as they lived. And after that? Wherever the story landed, perhaps it might be a lifeline to some searching soul who wondered, like Sebastien, *Who am I?*

Wary of Massimo Fedele, whose future was yet to be determined, Sebastien planned to leave off the ending in all of the copies but one. The older man had proved he would go to great lengths to bury the shadows of his family. If he discovered this tale . . .

So, he would inscribe the ending by hand in only one. Build upon the island a vault, in the hands of the safest place he knew: the ancient waters. Keep the book dry in a glass vessel crafted with care by Pietro, for a soul who might one day discover this living story, when all was well and safe.

The days stretched mercifully, bending around conversations to be cherished, moments to hold hands, glimpses of sunsets and sunrises and clouds moving over them, come from the mountains to the north to bid their friend farewell.

One afternoon, Mariana stirred from a deep sleep, fluttered her eyes open and gazed at Sebastien.

"I remember you," she said. He leaned forward, concerned. Was she struggling to remember him? "I saw you from the terrace."

His concern grew, the word *delirium* twisting in his gut, for there was no terrace here.

"With your trousers pulled high . . . you had one green shoe and one brown, and the way you held that basket of fish made me think you might topple into the canal."

He laughed, fear fleeing as he recalled a vision of his youthful self knocking at the grand door of Ca'Fedele. "That canal was always waiting for its chance to gulp me down, wasn't it?"

She smiled, the gentle curves of her mouth soft. "Or baskets were always waiting to carry you to your destiny." She offered the quip and then grew serious. "What would have happened, Sebastien?"

He threaded his fingers through hers, willing away the ticking of time. "What would have happened?"

She closed her eyes, forehead flickering concern or concentration as she retrieved a memory. "I heard my brother call you names, and I stood up and plucked a geranium blossom from the window box and tried to toss it at him. But I was too late. He had closed the door, and you—I thought you might spit at it or curse him. But do you know what you did?"

He shook his head. All he recalled from that long-ago day was that he couldn't disappear quickly enough, make his delivery and vanish from the ill-fated naivety of his actions.

"I remember it," she said. "The sun was on you, and you turned to go, but paused. You stooped to pick up a ducat from the step. It was black and golden—I remember the way the coin glinted in the sun, there in your open palm. *Good*, I thought. *Good, take it.* You deserved it, and a thousand more, for the way he treated you. I wanted you to put it in your pocket and go and have a wonderful life. But then . . ."

A flash of memory, as he recalled the glint of a coin in his hand. He did remember it, just the shadow of an image.

"You turned again and knocked on the door once more and gave it to the majordomo, saying it belonged to the house. You were so good, even then." She met his eyes, her smile sad. "What would have happened if I had spoken with Massimo then and there? Tossed the geranium at his head quicker? Would I—would I have saved you, Sebastien? Saved your chance at a more just life?"

Sebastien felt every apprehension for how he would answer her question drop away. "Is that what is troubling you?"

A tear escaped the corner of her eye, speaking her answer without words. He lifted his hand, lifted the tear away.

"I would be very glad to have known you then," he said, weighing his words carefully. "But Mariana—" He shook his head, struggling to find words that would ease her burden and not wound her further. "I don't believe a flower would have changed Massimo's course," he said as gently as he could. Hoped the truth, though it was a hard one, might lift her burden of wondering.

"You haven't seen me throw," she said, quirking a brow.

He laughed, and it felt like hope. "Even with a legendary ability like yours." He smiled. "Massimo had been on his course for a very long time. His actions—they are not yours." His jaw worked as he struggled to find a kind angle for how he had treated her.

She seemed to sense the direction of his thoughts. "I was expendable," she said.

"Never."

"To him . . . I was just a bargaining chip. I have always been expendable."

Sebastien stood, placing his other hand around hers so that she was safe within his two hands, as if that might turn back time, place her in his care, set him in a place where he could defend and protect her sooner, so much sooner.

"You—" His voice was husky. The ache in his throat—it singed the words with gravity. "Are not expendable. You . . . are treasured."

"I have a confession," she said.

"You don't need to—"

"Will you deny a dying woman the rite of confession?" Mischief sparked from her, but her words were too true to respond to in the light way she intended it.

Sebastien held her hand tighter. "Say anything you like," he said at last.

"I am a thief," she said.

He shook his head. "You had nothing to do with what your brother did—"

"Look in my shoe," she said.

Picking up her boots from their place by the door, he shook them out until something small and round dropped into his waiting palm.

A coin of black and gold, gleaming up at him from the past—right here in the present. The ducat.

"I took it, that day. Snuck it from the house coffers where the majordomo put it. I . . . needed to be reminded of someone kind," she said. "In the years that followed, whenever things were difficult, I would go to my room, take out that coin, hold it in my hands, and close my eyes as I remembered the boy with the basket. I would whisper, 'There is someone good and kind in this world.' And I would pray to God in heaven to give that boy a good and very rich life. That he would defend that boy, where I had failed."

"I think your prayers were answered," Sebastien said.

She drew in a tired breath. "So, you see, I am a thief, Sebastien."

He would have laughed gently around her label if she hadn't looked so troubled. Instead, he brushed her cheek. "There is forgiveness for thieves," he said. "I know of one in particular who was promised paradise, even in his last breaths upon a cross. But—I would suspect he might have been guilty of stealing much more than a coin from his own house."

"You could have taken it but did not. I did not need to take it and did. I . . . am a thief. You have married a criminal." She smiled, shifted herself to face him, searching his eyes. "Forgive me?"

"You have nothing to be forgiven for, Mariana—but if you did, forgiveness would be yours."

She closed her eyes, her strength vanishing in the wake of her confessions. He laid down upon the bed beside her, pulling her to himself, resting a hand upon her warm shoulder and telling her in low, quiet tones of all the ways his life had been very rich—carrying her away in his rolling waves of words into a place enchanted and good. Speaking of the colorful menagerie of glass with Pietro and his plethora of children and grandchildren. In the printing press of Dante, where truth was told and courage was bold. In the quiet cottage of Valentina, where compassion and patience stitched through every movement of the needle. In the vast world of the lagoon and the secret-filled crevices of Venice, with Giuseppe. On the island—his home—with Elena.

"And with you," he said at last, feeling her breathing steady as she settled, unburdened, into a restful sleep. "Always, with you."

She slipped away that night, when the moon was high and framed by the island's trees, and La Marangona tolled out across midnight waters. As the morning dawned, it lifted with it a veil of mist. She took with her a story for the ages . . . and left behind a guild of hearts, changed forever.

Sebastien, grieved to his very soul, sold the palazzo of his forefathers, and of Massimo and Mariana's. With the funds, after a time, he paid the debts of a certain prisoner and saved the rest, vowing to be watchful for the rest of his life to use the eyes of Mariana and see what might be worthy of their small legacy—whom they might help, what good they could do.

He farmed the earth with Elena and farmed it on his own when her hands had given all they could to the soil in her older age. He set to work at Dante's printing press, tucked away in the upper floor of the man's own ancestral home, and turned out colorful volumes that would spill Mariana's warmth onto the world she had so illuminated.

He took to walking the length of the Lido whenever he could venture to that outermost isle of the lagoon. The place they had last visited together before their return to Venice and spoken of the Doge marrying the sea. Where he had confessed to searching all his life for one of those rings.

And where, as he sat with feet in the sand, he saw something impossible: the glint of gold.

He strode toward it, pulling from the sands that had come down, once upon a time, from the high mountains, all the way to the lagoon . . . a ring.

Slipping it on his finger, he set again to writing the tale he could still not believe. The tale he had been privileged to live. The tale that convicted him, with every page, that there was One who had written his story and brought him at last to the fullest answer of his age-old question.

Who am I?

Sebastien Trovato.

Loved.

By parents who had loved him and planned for him though he never knew them. By a ragtag band of artisans who raised him up in the good and worthy ways, his own cherished family. By his beloved, his Mariana, who washed ashore into his arms and, in so many ways, saved him. And by a God who flung the stars, hovered upon waters, and cradled his life with care from the basket to the islands and beyond.

He was found . . . and he was loved.

DANIEL

JUNE 1904

D aylight crept across the lagoon in pale light, the only trace of rain a memory from the distant night on Malodetto. *Isola di Giardino*, I corrected myself. A place not doomed, but filled with life, in so many forms.

The world awoke slowly, with gondolas gliding, fishermen calling, violin strains floating high as I rowed my passenger away from the city and into another world.

Sebastien lifted his weathered face to the breaking dawn, closing his eyes as he listened to the canal sing beneath his woven vessel. Not a basket, this time, but a humble raft. Built of aged piles pulled from an underwater chamber that no longer stood, upon an island that I hoped always would. Piles the likes of which upheld the floating city.

And now, they upheld the Last Doge of Venice—the one nobody would ever know of.

The boat was no bucentaur. It bore no royal crest nor gilded statues, and this obscure doge wore no royal robes of red.

But inside him beat the heart of a lion, of a servant-king. And in that, he did Venice proud.

What a different picture I must have made from the man who

had come downtrodden and defeated from far-off California, running into book-carrying strangers and tumbling across boats until I nearly fell. Now, months later, my shoulders stretched wide to drink in the air as I rowed upon a raft built by my brick-calloused, ink-splotched hands. Hands that worked in ways that did not steal and did not strive—but gave, and gave thanks.

Through the hush of labyrinthine canals into the flow of the Grand Canal and out, at last, into the lagoon, we went. I knew Sebastien Trovato's arms ached to hold the oar, to row these passageways himself that unrolled like corridors to his past. But he had to save his strength for what was to come.

The voyage took us first to the cemetery isle of San Michele— which, upon study of maps and the shifting names and shapes of the isles—I had discovered had been joined to the isle of San Cristoforo della Pace. San Michele and San Cristoforo: two names that—thanks to a prickly majordomo at Ca'Fedele—held great promise as keepers of letters. Not as the solicitors he had presumed, but as islands themselves. For Massimo Fedele, the sole remaining vestige of The Eleven, had sole control for a great many years over the empty grave and its headstone that read, ceremoniously, *L. S.*—and he had made a stop there before departing for his Alpen exile, never to see his Venice again.

A place that had once been used to distribute secret information . . . and which he later used to keep secret letters. Belongings of a beloved sister, things he could not bring himself to dispose of. Perhaps that bespoke hope for the man, perhaps not—but as Sebastien pulled a bundle of letters from the place that had hidden them away for decades, tied in simple twine, he pressed them to his chest . . . and returned to the raft with red-rimmed, grateful eyes.

We rowed on, past Murano, then Burano. Detouring to Elena's island, where the archway saluted as we passed, and then finally setting course for the Lido.

The raft stood still there, and as the sun tossed diamonds upon wave tops, I could almost hear the echoes of doges past: "We *wed thee, sea, as a sign of true and everlasting domination* . . ."

Sebastien pulled a ring from his finger.

Though I hung back, I could hear his hoarse whisper.

"I wed thee, still, Mariana, as a sign of true and everlasting devotion. . . ." They were the words of a man who, though gripping the purpose of each day, also yearned to be with his bride after too long apart. His life, the very picture of everlasting devotion. Weathered hands gripped the metal that had for so long refused to be dissolved by the sea. And slowly, as if it took all his strength, he opened his hand, palm to sky. The sun alighted and the ring took flight. Spinning, glinting, slipping into the waters that had brought a baby to a family, a woman to an island, a man to his destiny.

And now, they would keep the story safe, bury it in their depths. Take it, bit by bit, as years went by and metal eroded into glints among the sea-bottom sand.

And I would keep the story safe too. At Sebastien's bidding, I had inscribed my copy of the Book of Waters with its final installments and delivered it, along with my translation, to Mr. Wharton, who lit with excitement, rattling plans for encasements and displays, intent on sharing the magic of Venice with a new world at his seaside resort.

Sebastien took great joy in wrapping a bundle of books for Vittoria, by special request. The small volumes were crafted with care, as if someone who believed children were real people, with real souls, had made them, and now they were bound for a new land: America. Out of all the books at her behest, Vittoria had chosen these for a very particular purpose.

She wished to bring them across the ocean, to meet the woman who—though Vittoria did not know it yet—would one day become her mother-in-law. Bring a little of the woman's girlhood in Italy all the way to San Francisco. And more importantly, bring the woman's son and three brightly colored umbrellas. She knew what it was to have a roof in need of repair, too, and had a scheme to fortify my roof-dome with her own touches, coloring the roof of an unassuming building, just as she colored every place in the world that she touched.

There, on the rise that was Little Italy, I had watched a familiar vista from the street. Gripping the scene with every feeling it mustered—Hope. Loss. Regret. Redemption. Grief. Belonging . . . Home. I took out the Murano pen, dipped it in ink, and in a flurry of science, art, and observation, worked around the dark canvas and into this new place of etching sight, etching truth, all together.

I finished the drawing. And as my mother pulled that old chipped cup with the storm-tossed ship out from the cupboard by habit and held it in her hands, I knocked upon her door. I held an envelope of bank papers, all with happy contents, and when the door creaked open, I began my rehearsed speech, eyes fixed upon her.

"H-hello, Mother," I started. And like the cracks in Ca'Fedele, those words began webbing the wall of silence I had built between us. "I—I have good news. The bank has agreed to—that is, the loan they wished to—it's—it's all taken care of, and—" My rehearsed words betrayed me, scattering in this haphazard nonsense. I took a breath, determined to try again—to do better.

But she had reached out. Lifted my chin. Waited for me to meet her gaze, and when I did . . . I did not look into the face of disappointment. I looked into the face of purest, truest, deepest love. She blinked, eyes shining, and she pulled me into an embrace with the force of a thousand tempests.

As ancient waters descended from the sky that night in a steady trickle of rain, they rolled over a rooftop umbrella bouquet as mother and son were, at long last, reunited.

We returned to Venice—my mother, Vittoria, me, and a scruffy dog from the Great Sand Waste, bound for a bevy of new friends in a bookshop. Ballast was already devoted to Vittoria, and she to him, calling him 'Signor Ballast of the Book Boat,' making plans for traversing the canals with him along. And, inspired by a young woman long ago who took her boat beyond familiar shores, and in doing so, changed the world . . . Vittoria determined that someday we would take the Book Boat on a Grand Tour of its own, to deliver its wares on the Seine, the Thames, and beyond.

She was a wonder. With her easy smile and warmth, given from boundless stores, and always with a depth and directness. She pointed me, whenever the old shackles came rattling or the blank canvas loomed dark, to the story that Venice told, back and back and back. Every piece of art, every building, every adornment was nothing without the rugged, steadfast beams girding them with strength. Purpose. Pulse.

It was the city that had set me free, and hers was the heart that had captured mine.

When we arrived back upon the platform at Santa Lucia once more, the trains huffing steam all around and a Garbin blowing in from the south, I knelt as I had the day we had met. Only this time, instead of gathering books, I offered her something.

It was simple and small, a ring that she snatched up, holding it for all to see, and holding me too. Pulling me to my feet and spouting plans for our future, our bookshop, our book boat—and then remembering, when I looked at her with a quizzical, desperate plea, to say yes.

And so it went. We ran a very delightful bookshop, complete with spiral stairs and owls, a floating library, and a new addition— a counter serving Goodman's fine Italian treats, filling eager hands with cannoli and hearts with hope.

In the city of her girlhood, my mother found special meaning in visiting Mr. Sebastien Trovato, the man who had been like an uncle to her and her siblings, all of them clamoring at his knees as he told tales of adventure—some true, some legendary, and some they could never tell which.

Now she tended to him as if he had been her own aging father, whose dotage she had always regretted missing when she had immigrated long ago to America. She loved the way he spoke of her grandfather and her father and soaked in the role he offered her now—that of a second father, one long lost—and now found. Offering everything he had to her, taking her in as his very own.

As for me . . . Venice changed. It was not the same city of mere surface beauty I had once believed, for I had seen another side of it. I had seen the humble wood she stood upon, gripped it in my own sin-stained palms, and seen what humble wood could do in a tale of redemption. And I had never been the same.

And so, those legs that ached to run for all those years in my cell and in my self-inflicted strivings . . . they again took me out to the Lido, the longest stretch of earth around. I knelt in the sand, my face upturned as I choked out gratitude. For the chance to mend what I could and for the Man who had given all, to cover over all of it.

There was no sound from the echoes of my mind. No jangle of phantom shackles. And the legs that had yearned to run . . . they rose. Planted feet in the sand.

And ran . . .

. . . and ran . . .

. . . and ran.

AUTHOR'S NOTE

Dear Reader,

You're not the only one.

This thought engraved deep into my heart one day toward the end of the editing process for this book with such sudden and deep conviction. A conviction that I was not alone in what I had been facing, and that I was to finish this race as strong as I could for the other hearts and souls out there who are facing a "lost place."

You're not the only one. . . . Write this for them.

You see, this story began years before its publication with a flash of an imagined picture in my mind: a baby in a basket, floating like Moses upon the waters, but in a crumbling, ancient, magical city. Sebastien's story took shape, and Daniel's alongside. Somewhere in the plotting and planning of Daniel Goodman, I learned that there is a significant population of people who experience life without the ability to picture things. Who, as some of them describe it, "have no mind's eye." Some have experienced life this way for as long as they have been alive, and others have been ushered into this realm by means of something more sudden, such as a head injury. It's a condition that's been around for a very long time, but that has only been given a name (*aphantasia*) in recent years.

What would it be, I wondered, for someone to lose something that they held closely as part of who they were? For Daniel Goodman, an artist whose work interacted deeply with visual imagining,

387

to see only a blank canvas in his imagination? Could he learn to imagine without images?

A layered set of circumstances in the middle of writing *All the Lost Places* gave me a glimpse. It's difficult to describe, but as a result of some things I had gone through, writing felt like trying to see the story through a very long, very muddy tunnel. Gone was the ability to set pen to page, or to reach for a word and find it. Gone was the bone-deep sense of what was coming. Gone was my voice—I couldn't recognize my own words as mine.

Gone, in essence, was me. Or at least, I thought, a very big part of me.

And suddenly this idea of losing something that was part of what makes a person who they are was not a foreign thing at all. It isn't the first time I've lost the ability to write, but it was so deep and strange and lasting that I started to claw against a storm of questions.

Who am I? Who am I to bring words to this story? Who am I, except not enough?

The irony was almost laughable. Here I was, asking the same question that already haunted Sebastien. Fighting with the loss of what I once knew how to do like Daniel was—so much so that I decided for a time to not have Daniel face this condition, because in my own limited state, I couldn't figure out how to write him that way.

It felt like a strange form of grief. It felt disorienting, it felt unraveling, and it felt like landing in the wilderness.

But the wilderness is a place of new things too.

And more importantly—there's Someone else there, with a nail-pierced hand outstretched and waiting to take ours—in the wilderness.

It was here that this gentle yet strong whisper wrapped from every direction around my heart with old truths made new. *You are mine. Found. Beloved.* Not because of anything I could do or offer or couldn't do or offer, but because of God's profound, incredibly simple and incredibly complex, unconditional, totally unearnable, given-with-wild-abandon-and-deep-purpose love.

Bestowed lavishly—not like a tide that comes and goes, rises and recedes based on surroundings . . . but like a waterfall of those ancient waters . . . giving, and giving, and giving.

It was humbling. Unfamiliar and therefore terrifying. And then . . . Freeing. Exhilarating. So very comforting. To know that this—*this*—is the hand I get to take hold of as we step out on this dance floor called life. A dance floor way out here in the wilderness—oh, the hope in that! Nothing, in a Presence like that, is ever lost. That the lost places, in the company of this love, are places where the aches are cherished and held, and where the cracks are so gently transformed into places not of emptiness, but of richness.

Do you know the difference between a shattered vessel and a mosaic? It is only in the hands who hold the pieces—hands that can make something broken into something beautiful. Give shape to sharp edges and form to the found.

This story was a lost place. Splintered away at the hands of my own mind's limits—and then handed back to me by another set of hands, piece by piece, like a mosaic.

The wisdom of friends came like an embrace as I faced this, in suggesting that just as an artist selects just the right paintbrush for a painting, perhaps God was redeeming the loss I had experienced by crafting me into the instrument He needed for *this* story, for *this* time. And that before I was a writer, I was a child of God—beloved because of His extravagant love. Their words wrapped like life-giving magic around my aching, insufficient heart.

And then . . . that gentle, strong whisper around my heart said another thing: *You are not alone in this.* A soul-deep conviction that I was not the only one laboring in a void of loss. Trying to accomplish something with tools I no longer had, trying (and failing) to find and take hold of a former version of myself. Mourning what was, what might have been, what could be. Living in a lost place.

So many are facing life as they never imagined it would be. Whether due to circumstances, illness, the choices of others, duties never anticipated, or any number of causing factors, so many are dwelling in what may very understandably feel like a lost place. And in these places, there can be very real, very deep loss.

Dear and beloved friend, if you know a place such as this, my heart aches with you. I know that my own experience as described here has been so very small in the grand scheme of things. But if it gives me even a taste of understanding for where you are—for the future you hoped for that can no longer be—and if this story perhaps might reach arms around your own lost place and whisper an ancient tale of an Artist at work, gathering pieces with utmost care and impeccable intention, cherishing each shard, and imagining for it a new form . . . then I will be profoundly grateful.

Take heart for the shifting places. In the hands of our God, there is redemption at work. And in that, there is hope.

Trovato,
Amanda

ACKNOWLEDGMENTS

In many ways, a story is a composite of moments and influences that have arrested a writer's attention and said to them, "Pay attention—there is something of note here." To list just a few of this story's influences, I owe my thanks immeasurably to . . .

Mom, for reminding me of Dad's wisdom when he would say, *"You can't write the end of the story. Only God can do that."* Dante's adage—*"Courage keep and hope beget, the story is not finished yet"*—is hope sprung from both of you.

Raela Schoenherr and Wendy Lawton, for believing a story in Venice, set in an obscure time little explored in other Venetian stories, had something to offer.

Rochelle Gloege and Jennifer Veilleux, for their invaluable help in the editing process, and for being the voice and heart of God in reminding me who I was in the midst of my own "lost place." I'm deeply grateful. To Rochelle and Jen again, as well as Cheri Hanson, for lending their keen insight into this story. You are voyagers worthy of the Adriatic itself!

To the entire BHP fiction and art team. Have you considered forming a guild? You are as skilled and creative as all the artisans in La Serenissima's long and storied history, and I'm thankful every day to partner with you. To the marketing team for the beautiful title that lent so much meaning to the story, and to the art department for a cover that takes my breath away.

To cherished friends who helped me see this story and my humble role in it in a new light, framed through our God's never accidental ways, grounded deeply in His fathomless love. Lesley Gore, who asked of me something like Jacopo's and Vittoria's words about art and tools to Daniel—but in much nicer, much more "Captain Jim" ways. And Nicole Deese, who was a shining light as I pushed to meet deadlines and worked to get up to my elbows in this story time after time. Your messages were a bright spot of hope, and your friendship is too!

Kelli, who gave me my own Murano glass pen so many years ago. Thank you for fanning the flames of what felt like a far-off dream. I wonder if you'll ever know how many stories have been told and lived because of you, my dream-defending friend.

My Ben, who once told me the moon was a promise.

Samuel Johnson and Kelly Hellmuth, for their assistance with Latin translations.

Jenna Wirshing, who offered insights into Italian culture and language.

Karen Rhoades, what an incredible gift from God you were when you slid into a lunch seat at the same table as me at Fiction Readers Summit 2022. I had finished writing Daniel's tale and though I'd read personal accounts from several people who experience the world as Daniel does, I had been hoping and praying to be able to talk to someone personally who might be able to help me better understand it and to read some of Daniel's experiences to see if they paid respect to his journey and the journey of those who share his uniquely beautiful and purposeful way of experiencing the world "without a mind's eye." When you mentioned in passing that you didn't picture scenes as you read them, I hope I didn't jump out of my seat too much—and you took it in stride when after a few minutes and a few conversation turns, I leaned in and inquired more about this. Thank you for your giving heart, for the emails that followed, for looking over Daniel's pages and offering insight and encouragement. I'm grateful for you!

Likewise, to those who took the time to write messages or comments to me sharing your own experiences with losing part of your art, or what it would be like if you did lose such. Thank you for your honesty, the gift of your vulnerability, and the beauty you add to this world through who you are.

My kids, architects extraordinaire of "Mud City," inspiration for Sebastien's own childhood, his cattail forest and kingdom of mud. Mud City has been the highlight of our yard for years now, and I love that every day it's different, and that out of ancient waters and bits of earth tossed from world-traveling winds, you bake mudbricks in the light of a far-off star and build actual walls with them. I love that you make rivers and pools, waterfalls and grottos. I love your mud-caked, hard-working hands, and the grins you offer. I can't wait to see where you take this creativity in your own journeys. Keep digging, my loves! Look to the Creator of Venice for hope and inspiration—He is with you at every turn!

To my brother-in-law, Pierce, who introduced me to some extraordinary owls, and in doing so, planted the seed of Elizabeth Barn-Owl Browning and her companion, Robert, in this story.

In this book, several works of art are mentioned, or inspired various scenes. If you'd like to look them up to learn more about them, a few of them are as follows.

- *The Wedding Feast at Cana*, by Paolo Veronese, still resides in Paris in its restored form. However, in recent years, a full-sized replica of the larger-than-life painting was created and now adorns that wall that was built for it in the refectory at San Giorgio, where Daniel beheld its empty place.
- Antonio Corradini's *Puritas* (marble sculpture of a veiled woman), which touched Mariana in a deep way, is housed at Museo del Settecento Veneziano, Ca' Rezzonico, in Venice.
- Ivan Aivazovsky's *Venetian Lagoon by Night*, painted in 1842. This sunset scene of a woman being rowed to a curiously small structure, mounted upon a pile in the lagoon

(which I discovered to be a water altar), inspired Mariana's lantern inside the lost island's water altar.

There are many historical influences in the story as well. To name a few:

- Daniele Manin, a revolutionary in mid-nineteenth–century Venice, who inspired, partially, Massimo's fate, though their methods of revolting (or planned revolt) differed.

- Doge Marino Faliero, whose attempted coup d'etat in 1355 resulted in the dreaded fate of *damnatio memoriae*, the condemnation of memory, and whose black-paint shrouded portrait still hangs in Venice as testament to his erasure from history.

- *Ospedale*, children's homes or orphanages, and the infamous "wheel," where babies would be placed to ensure their warmth and safekeeping upon their arrival.

- The falling of the campanile in San Marco Square, the survival of La Marangona. While the bell is depicted as being stored in the courtyard during the tower's long reconstruction, some accounts list it as being moved inside the Palazzo Ducale itself.

- The bell at Glen Eyrie Castle, which I was overjoyed to get to ring, and when the tour guide told me I was moving the ringer and not the bell itself, the idea for Daniel's solution to Sebastien's wild-goose chase was born.

- Brother Clement, who, according to a *New York Times* obituary from March 20, 1944, "laid mosaics in a crypt in Italy from 1900 to 1914 at the monastery of Mount Cassino in Italy." The monastery had been recently bombed at the publication of the obituary, though Brother Clement had come to Minnesota in 1931. This brief glimpse into his life had me thinking of a man who would devote his life to the gathering and laying of broken pieces, the resonance of gospel therein. Whether that work was to last only decades before the bombing, or whether it had lived for centuries beyond—the work of his hands stirs me deeply, as does the achingly beautiful craft of mosaic.

- Ca'Fedele was inspired by the Palazzi Barbaro, a pair of adjoining Venetian palaces.
- Some of the words Daniel discovers about the history of storms—"broken indeed the shores," etc.—are actual accounts taken from the annals of Venice.
- The lore and legends of Venice are many and varied. The fable of the statues battling the fiends to save Venice was not invented for this novel but is a preexisting one.
- Malodetto's storied history of quarantine, asylum, and ruins are an amalgam of the real lagoon isles—some home to people, some to ruins, some lost long ago to the lagoon. They are fascinating!
- Abbot Kinney, who indeed turned a marshy stretch of beach into a canal-filled seaside resort town, Venice of America, which later became what we know today as Venice Beach, California.

And, finally, a note on this story's beginning and ending, and a final piece of gratitude. The writing of this story began and lasted, through most of its formation, with one question, as I worked to discover the history of the baby in the basket—"Who are you?" It was the same question Sebastien was asking of himself: *Who am I?*

Sebastien wasn't the first to ask this question. Neither are we. We know that as far back as King David, and very presumably far beyond that, people have been asking it. For David, it took this form: *"Who am I, that you are mindful of me?"* In the context of questions like this, I realized that Sebastien was only asking half of the question. Assuredly an important half, but I knew he would find peace, at last, in the second half of that question, once he learned to ask it.

We search. We beat with the question, sometimes, and we live in a world that has decided that perhaps there is no final resting place for it.

But there is peace, so much peace . . . and joy, meaning, purpose, fulfillment, in a truth that goes deeper still. *I am Yours.*

"Know thyself"? I understand why the phrase found itself etched in temples and tumbled through time as an unanswerable echo.

But . . . it is only a half-maxim.

Know thyself, reader, as a cherished creation of the Most High God, who crossed time and tribulation for you. Know thyself, friend, as His treasure.

So, to those who have asked the question, all the way back to the Oracle of Delphi, and to those who have written the hope-filled answer, whether in Psalms or in songs, I thank you. For the invitation for each of us to be known, be cherished, to be who we were created, with so much love and breathtaking purpose, to be.

And to the God who answers that question by wrapping us in His embrace, once and for all, in a place of unshakeable belonging: *thank you.*

Amanda Dykes is the winner of the prestigious 2020 Christy Award Book of the Year, a Booklist 2019 Top Ten Romance debut, and the winner of an INSPY award for her debut novel, *Whose Waves These Are*. She's also the author of *Set the Stars Alight* and three novellas. A former English teacher, Amanda is a drinker of tea, dweller of redemption, and spinner of hope-filled tales who spends most days chasing wonder and words with her family. Find her online at amandadykes.com.

Sign Up for Amanda's Newsletter

Subscribe to Amanda's newsletter for recipes, encouragement, and bonus material such as behind-the-scenes research and secret story connections between Amanda's novels at amandadykes.com.

More from Amanda Dykes

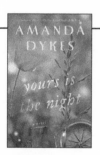

Mireilles finds her world rocked when the Great War comes crashing into the idyllic home she has always known, taking much from her. When Platoon Sergeant Matthew Petticrew discovers her in the Forest of Argonne, three things are clear: she is alone in the world, she cannot stay, and he and his two companions might be the only ones who can get her to safety.

Yours Is the Night

You May Also Like . . .

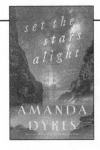

Reeling from the loss of her parents, Lucy Claremont discovers an artifact under the floorboards of their London flat, leading her to an old seaside estate. Aided by her childhood friend Dashel, a renowned forensic astronomer, she starts to unravel a history of heartbreak, sacrifice, and love begun 200 years prior—one that may offer the healing each of them seeks.

Set the Stars Alight by Amanda Dykes
amandadykes.com

When their father's death leaves them impoverished, the Summers sisters open their home to guests to provide for their ailing mother. But instead of the elderly invalids they expect, they find themselves hosting eligible gentlemen. Sarah must confront her growing attraction to a mysterious widower, and Viola learns to heal her deeply hidden scars.

The Sisters of Sea View by Julie Klassen
ON DEVONSHIRE SHORES #1
julieklassen.com

In 1942, a promise to her brother before he goes off to war puts Avis Montgomery in the unlikely position of head librarian and book club organizer in small-town Maine. The women of her club band together as the war comes dangerously close, but their friendships are tested by secrets, and they must decide whether depending on each other is worth the cost.

The Blackout Book Club by Amy Lynn Green
amygreenbooks.com

◊BETHANYHOUSE

More from Bethany House

After uncovering a diary that leads to a secret artifact, Lady Emily Scofield and Bram Sinclair must piece together the mystifying legends while dodging a team of archeologists. In a race against time, they must decide what makes a hero. Is it fighting valiantly to claim the treasure or sacrificing everything in the name of selfless love?

Worthy of Legend by Roseanna M. White
THE SECRETS OF THE ISLES #3
roseannamwhite.com

In 1910, rural healer Perliett Van Hilton is targeted by a superstitious killer and must rely on the local doctor and an intriguing newcomer for help. Over a century later, Molly Wasziak is pulled into a web of deception surrounding an old farmhouse. Will these women's voices be heard, or will time silence their truths forever?

The Premonition at Withers Farm by Jaime Jo Wright
jaimewrightbooks.com

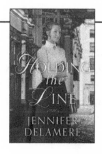

When widow Rose Finlay notices a young woman about to be led astray by a roguish aristocrat who could ruin both her and her family's reputation, bitter memories arise and she feels compelled to intervene. Rose and the young woman's uncle, John Milburn, join forces, putting everything they hold dear—including their growing attraction—in jeopardy.

Holding the Line by Jennifer Delamere
LOVE ALONG THE WIRES #3
jenniferdelamere.com

⬧BETHANYHOUSE

CPSIA information can be obtained
at www.ICGtesting.com
Printed in the USA
BVHW042239131222
654111BV00019B/33

9 780764 240829